DARKER JEWELS

Tor books by Chelsea Quinn Yarbro

DARKER JEWELS

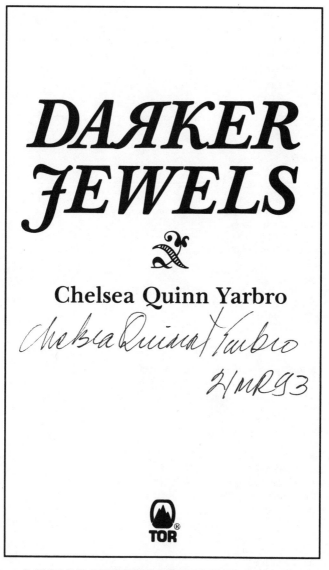

Chelsea Quinn Yarbro

Chelsea Quinn Yarbro

2/MR93

TOR®

A TOM DOHERTY ASSOCIATES BOOK
NEW YORK

DARKER JEWELS

Copyright © 1993 by Chelsea Quinn Yarbro

This book is printed on acid-free paper.

A Tor Book
Published by Tom Doherty Associates, Inc.
175 Fifth Avenue
New York, N.Y. 10010

Tor® is a registered trademark of Tom Doherty Associates, Inc.

Map by Chelsea Quinn Yarbro and Ellisa Mitchell

Library of Congress Cataloging-in-Publication Data

Yarbro, Chelsea Quinn
      Darker jewels / Chelsea Quinn Yarbro.
            p.   cm.
      "A Tom Doherty Associates book."
      ISBN 0-312-85296-7
      1. Soviet Union—History—Ivan IV, 1533–1584—Fiction.
      2. Vampires—Fiction.   I. Title.
      PS3575.A7D36   1993
      813'.54—dc20   92-44426
                                                                               CIP

First edition: March 1993

Printed in the United States of America

0 9 8 7 6 5 4 3 2 1

For
Lou Puopolo
who knows the Count
almost as well as I do.

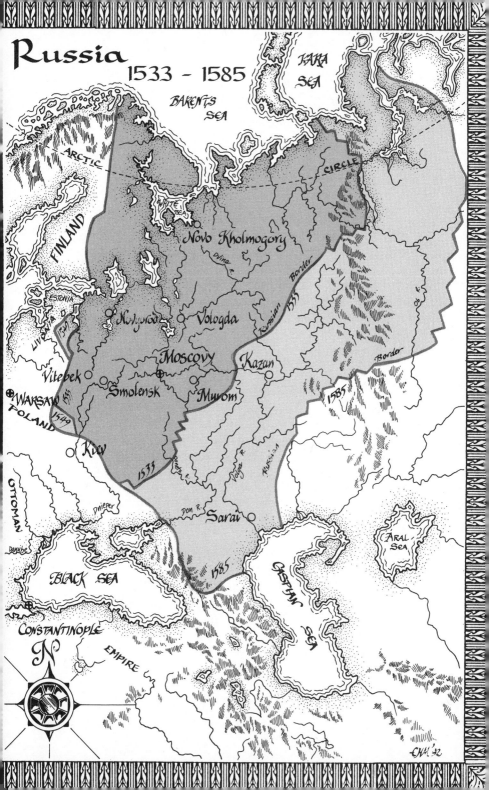

Author's Notes

Until the last three hundred years, for much of Europe Russia was a land more legendary than China, and more unknown than Africa: fewer Europeans went there, and of those who went, not many returned; those who did were not given the same enthusiastic reception as those who brought news of places more easily accessible and/or exploitable. While Europeans were aware that Russia existed—that it was a real place actually there—they knew little or nothing about the country itself or the peoples inhabiting it.

There were exceptions, of course. The Poles have an extensive history of rivalry with Russia, and the Swedes have occasionally gone to war with the vast and mysterious country. The Baltic States of Estonia and Livonia (modern north Latvia, and part of Estonia and Lithuania) spent the better part of eight hundred years in uneasy dealings with Russia, and the problems resulting from their conflicts continue to this day. The Mongols of the Golden Horde, the descendants of the soldiers of Jenghiz Khan, ruled Russia for more than three hundred years.

Through the Greek Orthodox Church eastern Europe and the Middle East maintained a degree of contact with Moscovy—the duchy that was the heart of Christian Russia—when western, Catholic Europe had generally turned its attention elsewhere. One of the few active conflicts between western Europe and Russia in the Middle Ages occurred because of religion: in 1237 a group of German knights of the Teutonic Order were sent to convert Russia to Catholicism. The Russian forces, under the young Novgorod prince Alexander Nevsky, met and defeated the German knights on Lake Peipus in April of 1242. For that act of heroism and faith, and for his later political acumen in dealing with the invading Mongols of the Golden Horde, Nevsky became a saint of the Orthodox Church.

But through the medieval centuries Russia's face was turned

eastward, toward Sarai, where the Golden Horde gathered to extend the empire of the Mongols and Tartars to the north and west, beyond the limits it had previously set. During that time, most of Europe had few dealings with Russia.

By the time of Grand Duke Ivan III, later Grand Prince Ivan III the Great, Czar of all the Russias (reigned 1462–1505), Russia had directed the greatest part of her energies to reclaiming lands from the Tartars of the Golden Horde. Because of the struggle in the east, there had been losses in the west to Sweden and Poland that blocked Russian access to the Baltic, a situation Ivan III's son Vasilli III tried to reverse but without significant success.

The energetic, ambitious, ruthless successor, Grand Prince Ivan IV the Awe-Inspiring, came to the throne after his father, Vasilli, in 1533. A capable, relentless, and intelligent man, Ivan was a complex and contradictory leader who suffered from an uncontrollable temper and an abiding sense of paranoia. With uncommon perseverance he and his Russian forces drove the Mongols back from central Russia and also succeeded in regaining, for a time, a Baltic port for Russia, which brought Russia back into the European view once more, and at a time when she was needed.

For Europe had troubles of its own; the Ottoman Empire was expanding, seizing territory in Greece and eastern Europe as part of a continuing expansion that was increasingly alarming to the rulers and Church in the west. There were attempts to make common cause with the Orthodox churches and Catholic Church against the Islamic Ottomans, but such alliances were generally short-lived and difficult, as much for reasons of what is now identified as culture shock as any conflict in military agenda. There were also very real, pragmatic problems resulting from the tremendous distances that had to be crossed, in a country famous for the severity of its climate.

One of the reasons that there is relatively little historical material available on Russia during the tempestuous years of 1100–1650 is the number of times major cities were besieged, sacked, and destroyed, ruining what few written records there were. And the amount of written records was small. In Russia at that time adult literacy has been estimated at five to nine percent of the population, the city of Novgorod having the highest rate, Murom the lowest of those where any estimates were possible. Unlike the tradition of the Catholic Church, Orthodox priests were usually illiterate, and records usually found in European churches do not often exist in Russian ones. Ironically, those who could read and write were generally competent in more than one language, the most usual combination being Russian and Greek or Latin. What little education was available was most often provided by priests to male children. Females were very rarely given any formal education.

As is usually the case in these stories, a great many of the characters are based on historical figures and, although presented fictionally, are as accurate portraits as the exigencies of plot will permit. In this book the following characters are actual historical figures: Istvan Bathory, Prince of Transylvania and King of Poland; Czareivich Ivan Ivanovich, the twenty-eight-year-old heir accidentally murdered by his father in 1581; Czar Ivan IV Grosny (the Awe-Inspiring or Terrible); Czareivich Feodor Ivanovich, Ivan's single surviving heir, possibly a victim of Down's syndrome; Father Antonio Possevino, Jesuit and Papal emissary to the Russian Court; Pope Gregory XIII the Great; Elizabeth Tudor, Queen of England; Father Edmund Campion; Richard Chancellor, the first English Ambassador to Russia; Sir Jerome Horsey, English Ambassador at the time of the novel; Nicholas Bower, who was a clerk or secretary for Sir Jerome; Prince Vasilli Andreivich Shuisky, although I have shifted his age by a decade; Ivan and Dmitri Shuisky, his brothers; the Nagoy family; the Kurbsky family; Nikita Romanovich Romanov; Boris Feodorovich Godunov, eventual regent to Czar Feodor Ivanovich, who was married to Boris's sister Irina; Marya Skuratova, Boris's wife; Erzebet (Elizabeth) Bathory, Istvan's cousin, known later as the Blood Countess.

Given that the story is set in Russia with characters who would be, in fact, speaking Russian, I have elected Russian usage for names of all Russian characters. Therefore, Vasilli instead of Basil; Feodor instead of Theodore; Ivan instead of John; Marya instead of Maria; Gavril instead of Gabriel; Feodossi instead of Theodosius. I have also included the use of the patronymic, that is, the middle name which means son-of: Ivan Ivanovich—John son-of-John; Anastasi Sergeivich—Anastasius son-of-Serge or Sergeant; Galina Alexandrevna—Helen daughter-of-Alexander. Upper-class Russians of the period rarely used the patronymic when dealing with the middle or lower classes.

A word about sixteenth-century Russian pronunciation—most, but not all, Russian words are accented on the next-to-last syllable, although there are exceptions, such as Feodor, pronounced FAY-oh-dor, Nikolai, NIK-oh-lie, or Anastasi, AH-nah-*stah*-zee. There are also names with double stresses, such as Boris, BOHR-EES; Ivan, EE-VAHN; Sergei, SEHR-GEYI. A few names are accented on the last syllable: Mikhail, Mik-hie-EEL; Gavril, Gahv-REEL. Male patronymics more closely follow the pronunciation of the father's name: Ivanovich is Ee-VAHN-o-vich, Andreivich is Ahn-DRAYI-vich, although Grigori, Gree-GOH-ree, becomes Gree-goh-REI-vich in the patronymic. Women's names are not as varied: Galina, Gah-LEE-nah; Xenya, ZEN-yah; Ludmilla, Lood-MEE-lah. Female patronymics more often follow the next-to-last-syllable rule: Evgeneivna is Yehv-gyen-YEAV-nah; Ivanovna is Ee-VAH-NOV-nah; Borisovna, Bohr-ee-SOHV-nah.

I have followed this with regard to other nationalities as well: Polish usage for Polish characters (with the exception of the honorific for the King, which at that time translated as Exalted-ness; I have used the more familiar but less accurate honorific of Majesty), Hungarian for Transylvanians, transliterated Greek for Greeks, English for English. As much as possible I have done the same for clothing, food, and weapons.

There are a few landmarks that will not be identified by con-temporary usage: Saint Basil's Cathedral (the one with the nine mismatched onion domes in bright-colored geometric patterns) on Red Square is the Cathedral of the Virgin of the Intercession and tomb of the Holy Fool Vasilli on the Beautiful/Red Market Square: in sixteenth-century Russian, the words "red" and "beau-tiful" were very similar and used interchangeably. The harbor fortress of Arkhangelsk on the White Sea had not yet been built; the first English ships arrived at the fur-trading-and-fishing port of Novo-Kholmogory. This was also a Russia before vodka. The potato had only recently arrived in Europe from the New World and was a rarity in most places. Within a decade of the time of this book, the Poles developed vodka and by 1596 were export-ing it to Russia.

Although the members of the embassy of Jesuits sent by Istvan Bathory of Poland are fictional, King Istvan did send several priests into Russia on diplomatic missions, not only in conjunc-tion with delegations from the pope, such as Father Possevino, but separately as well.

For their help in finding historical references and specific information, I would like to thank the incomparable Dave Nee (again), Joseph Lindstrom (for the first time), and Leighanne Barwell (also for the first time). Any errors in historicity are mine and not theirs. Thanks are also due tangentially to Maurine Dorris and the committee of the World Horror Convention, 1991, for their enthusiasm; to my manuscript readers for their comments and insights; to my agent Ellen Levine for her tenacity and encouragement; to my attorney Robin Dubner for her diligence on the Count's behalf; to my editor Beth Meacham who helped me sift through the various strata of Russian history; and to Tor Books for keeping the Count undead and well.

Berkeley

PART I

Ivan Grosny

Czar

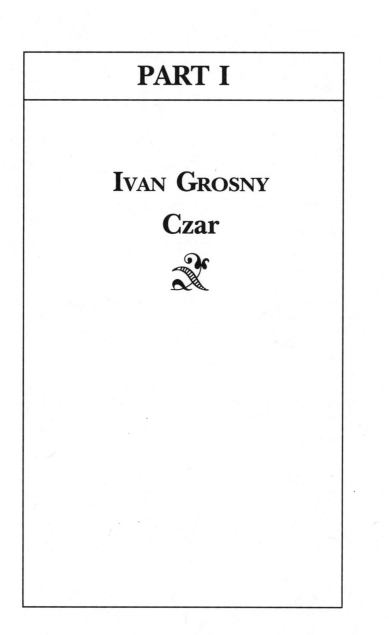

*T*ext of a letter from an unknown Russian nobleman written in Greek to Istvan Bathory, King of Poland, delivered 6 August 1582.

To the revered Transylvanian who rules in Poland, sincerest greetings from one in Moscovy who wishes you well and seeks your aid:

Since the death of the Czareivich Ivan Ivanovich, we have seen great changes in Czar Ivan, who is filled with guilt and endless remorse, for it was his hand that struck down his son: therefore he can seek absolution from none but God. He has declared that God alone can offer him redemption because God permitted His Son to die, and will have compassion on him for what he did in a moment of unreasoning fury.

He is a haunted man now, not like the farsighted leader he was when he drove the Tartars back and reclaimed our lands. He is filled with terrors and dreams that are as great as his vision was once. He has pleaded to be permitted to abdicate, but the Metropolitan has forbidden it because Feodor Ivanovich is so truly incapable of leading the country; he cares only for ringing bells. He has no interest in Rus or in his wife or in any other thing that would speak well of a Czar. Therefore it has been decided that Ivan must rule until God Himself ends his reign. No other course is possible if we are to keep from internal rebellion.

No matter how the court may appear, unrest grows within it hourly. Every passing day brings new alarms as the Czar wars

17

*with himself. Only his belief in portents and the power of jewels
has sustained him, and his obsession with jewels is boundless,
amounting almost to lust. He is always seeking more of them, of
higher quality, for he claims that it is through the jewels that he
will be shown redemption and forgiveness, as he has been assured of victory over his enemies in the past.*

*In that regard, let me tell you of a curious thing Czar Ivan
said the other day when he was displaying the jewels that con-
sole him:*

*"There is great power in diamonds. The most brilliant have
such strength that only the bravest man can dare to touch them,
so tremendous is their might. Those who have no courage would
be charred and blasted by the virtue of the stone. Those that are
smaller are not so dangerous to cowards, but in the hands of
one such would lose their shine, for their light comes from brav-
ery.*

*"Pearls are jewels for women, for they signify tears, and tears
are a woman's lot. They are light to show purity in joy and grief.*

*"But there are darker jewels, the ruby and emerald and ame-
thyst and sapphire, that can penetrate the passions and the
secrets of the heart. No living man can comprehend their depths.
They shine with the inward light of the soul."*

*Czar Ivan longs for such knowledge as the darker jewels
provide. He is lost in nightmares and frenzies. He moves about
the Kremlin as if he were dead already and haunting the palaces and cathedrals. If he continues in this manner much longer, I fear what will become of us all. The death of the Czarevich
was a tragic thing, but I am afraid that catastrophe will be ours
if no one can preserve the power of the Czar through his madness.*

*We who rule here would not be ungrateful to anyone who
would help us save the country from the ravages of the very man
who made it great again.*

*I send this to you in confidence. My life and the lives of my
family are in your hands; protect us, I beg of you. Say nothing
of how you have come by this information. On the Body of
Christ, I swear that I seek the preservation of Moscovy and
Russia. If you are determined to remain the enemy of Czar Ivan,
then burn this and forget what you have read. If you are willing
to lend us the assistance you offered once, then I pray that God*

will fill your heart with His forgiveness, and you will do what it is in your power to do to bring Ivan to himself once again. Or barring that, that you will remember Czar Ivan in your prayers; he longs for the healing of prayers and magic.

From one who is afraid for himself and for all Rus.

1

As he rubbed his face, Istvan Bathory tried to banish the fatigue that was consuming him; he had three more audiences to give before attending evening Mass. He concealed a sigh and smoothed his beard. What he longed for most was two hours to sleep; it was the one thing he could not grant himself. Not too many years ago he would have been pleased at so much activity, but that was before his successful start of the campaign against Russia. Now he felt the weight of hours more heavily even as time swept by more swiftly than ever. He attempted to sit more comfortably on the large carved chair his noble host had provided for him, but could discover no position that did not cause the scar of his year-old thigh wound to ache from knee to hip; it had bothered him less in the summer, but now that winter was near it took a toll on him. He was grateful for the fire that blazed in the hearth, for it provided some relief.

"Rakoczy is here," said the ambitious young Jesuit priest who served as his secretary as he returned from delivering Istvan's formal thanks to the nobleman whose estate they occupied. "He arrived an hour ago."

"Rakoczy," said Istvan, straightening up and ignoring the renewed pain it caused. "Already. He came quickly."

"Your summons said it was urgent. He acted promptly, which is fitting." The priest never smiled, but occasionally he showed an inner satisfaction; this was one such instant. "Hrabia, Prinz, or whatever he styles himself, you are King."

"Yes," agreed Istvan, his weathered eyes thoughtful. He

righted the coronet he wore. "But he has complied immediately, unlike some others—"

"The Turks are swarming over his homeland," the priest reminded Istvan. Though he was only twenty-six there was already a deep vertical line between his brows and it grew more pronounced. "He was driven out, in spite of long resistance. It has been the fate of many Transylvanians. He must be very pleased to have any notice at all."

Istvan regarded his secretary with sharp attention. "Father Mietek, I depend on men like him. Without them we could not do the Pope's bidding. There would not be men enough to advance on Russia. We would have no hope of gaining Russian help to stem the Ottoman tide. That the Turk overwhelmed Rakoczy's land is not to his discredit. There are many more who have surrendered, joining their enemies, and that is the disgrace, not heroic resistance." He rarely gave such a stern reprimand to the priest, out of respect for his calling and for fear of the power the Church could wield in these times.

"They say the Rakoczys have fought valorously," said Father Mietek as a kind of peace offering to Istvan. "The name has long been honored."

"Yes," said Istvan, establishing a truce between them.

Father Mietek indicated the massive, closed doors that led to the corridor beyond. "And Rakoczy is waiting."

"In the corridor?" asked Istvan, scandalized that a noble would be given such poor treatment.

"In the antechamber," said Father Mietek. "I left him there with two of your guards. To show respect."

"I hope he sees it that way," said Istvan dryly. "Better bring him here. Hrabia Saint-Germain ought not to be kept waiting like a simple tradesman, guards or no guards." He made an impatient gesture to Father Mietek. "Where is my aide? Where is my Captain, that I must send a priest to escort Rakoczy."

"They are at supper, Majesty," said Father Mietek. "Where you sent them."

Istvan nodded. "And the rest are preparing for the inspection tomorrow. Yes. Of course." He glanced around the room, reminding himself of the size of the building itself. "Has my host arranged for any of my company to stay at other estates, or are we all to remain here?" There was great risk in remaining all in the same place, knotted together. If his enemies should discover where he was, with all his officers and aides, it would be a simple matter for them to fall upon him, secure in the knowledge that there were no reinforcements nearby to come to rescue or avenge him.

"There is a town not far away. Most of the soldiers have been sent there for the night," said Father Mietek. "The inspection is the most important matter facing them. We don't know what supplies are left to us, or what repair we have for our weapons. You were the one who insisted that—"

Istvan held up his hand. "Yes, I'm aware of that," he said. "Well, I trust that Hrabia Saint-Germain will understand my situation here."

"I will explain it to him," said Father Mietek as he started toward the door.

"No," said Istvan. "If there are explanations to be made, I will make them myself. There is no reason for you to provide any."

The priest lowered his head in a show of humility. "If that is your wish, Majesty."

Istvan Bathory made a warning gesture. "Prudence, Father Mietek. I need this Hrabia to assist me; he is the only man I know of who can achieve what I require. It is important."

"I am here to serve you, Majesty," said Father Mietek as he left the chamber that had become Istvan's headquarters for his stay.

With Father Mietek gone, Istvan got to his feet and paced, letting his rolling stride take the worst cramps out of his leg. Tired as he was, he was restless as well. He wanted to pray but there were no more supplications left in him to address to God. Instead he recalled the letter that had been brought to him by a cloth merchant who had sworn it had been given to him by one of the military officers in Moscovy. That letter—assuming it was genuine—was the one promise of hope he had to gain influence with Czar Ivan. What he had read had prompted him to send word to Rakoczy, for he was known to be a powerful alchemist, one who had the wisdom to make jewels; he was also noted for his good sense, and therefore would not be easily trapped or compromised.

Father Mietek appeared in the doorway. "Hrabia Saint-Germain," he announced, reluctantly stepping aside for Ferenc Rakoczy.

"Majesty," said Rakoczy, his accent clipped and old-fashioned, while bowing in the Italian manner instead of going down on one knee, his sable hat in his right hand. From his black velvet mente to the silver-embroidered black silk dolman with ruby buttons beneath it, Ferenc Rakoczy, Hrabia Saint-Germain, was elegant. His black leggings were finest-quality wool and his heeled boots on his small feet had been made by a master. His dark, loose curls were cut short, and contrary to fashion, he was clean-shaven. He wore a single ring on his small hands, a dark signet ruby with the sign of the eclipse cut into it. Although he was of average height, he occupied the room in a way much larger men would envy. There was something arresting in his dark eyes, an expression that was at once enigmatic and compassionate. His composure was formidable; most men fidgeted when Istvan perused them; Rakoczy did not.

Little though he revealed it, Istvan was impressed. "You present an excellent appearance. And a prompt one," he said at last.

"Majesty is gracious," said Rakoczy.

"I'm nothing of the sort," said Istvan. "Father Mietek, I am certain you have duties elsewhere."

The young priest glared at the King, but he accepted his dismissal with what grace he could muster. "Of course."

"You have my permission to tend to them." Istvan waited until the door was firmly closed before he paced around Rakoczy. "I understand you've traveled."

"With what has become of my native land, it's been necessary," Rakoczy said calmly.

"Yes; unfortunate. But perhaps you will consider what I offer: I wish you to travel for me," Istvan informed him.

"From Bohemia to Poland, at least," said Rakoczy, not quite smiling. "As swiftly as you ordered, Majesty." He had covered the distance on horseback accompanied only by his manservant because the roads were too poor to trust a carriage, and there were too many brigands to tempt them with a show of property and wealth a larger escort would imply.

"And you may travel farther than that," Istvan said in a tone that would not permit an argument. "If you are the man I think you are?"

Nothing of his expression changed, but there was a quick jolt of fear that went through Rakoczy, as disturbing as it was senseless. For more than forty years he had concealed his true nature;

surely he had not been found out. He knew better than to demand that the King of Poland tell him what he meant. He steadied himself, and decided to risk disfavor. "What man is that, Majesty?"

"An astute one, at least, and one with a reputation for valor with a cool mind," said Istvan. "And perhaps something more."

This time the fear was stronger, but Rakoczy controlled it. "Whatever you believe me to possess, if it is truly mine to command, it is at your service."

Istvan laughed once, a harsh, ill-used sound. "Very pretty. Where did you learn courtesy? Certainly not in Transylvania. Or Poland."

Rakoczy shrugged. "Various places in my travels. Italy." Saying the word brought memories still less than a century old; they were painful. He banished the faces of Demetrice and Laurenzo, the burning paintings of Sandro Botticelli from his thoughts.

"Some trouble there, um?" Istvan asked, aware of the change in Rakoczy, a change that was gone even as Istvan remarked on it.

"There is often trouble in Italy, centuries and centuries of it," he answered smoothly.

The evasion was not lost on Istvan, but he ignored it. "Well, it is behind you. There are other tasks to concern you."

"Are there?" Rakoczy raised his fine dark brows.

"I think so," said Istvan, and reached into his sleeve to draw out the letter from the unknown Russian. "Read it." The command was also a test, and both men knew it.

Rakoczy went through the message quickly, frowning a little at the imprecise hand. "A . . . an interesting communication," he said carefully when he was through. "The writer has some understanding of Greek, but I suspect does not use it very often, not if this is an example of his comprehension. Is it authentic, do you think?"

"The very question I have been asking myself since I received it." Istvan clicked his tongue to express his doubts. "I have heard rumors, of course."

"Everyone hears rumors," said Rakoczy. "Even the peasants gossip about the Czar."

"And say that he dines with the devil and devours virgins, no doubt," said Istvan curtly. "Who can put stock in such tales?"

Rakoczy smiled fleetingly. "Indeed."

Istvan stopped moving and rubbed once at his leg. "But that letter—it troubles me. If it is true, it might mean, oh, a great many things. If the Czar is as distressed as the writer claims, there may well be disorder in Moscovy. Which may or may not serve my purpose."

"But you and Sweden have made peace with Moscovy," said Rakoczy. "Surely you are not planning to continue your campaign."

"We have made peace with Ivan, of a sort," said Istvan in some irritation. "But if he has fallen into madness, what peace will we have? And what chance is there of bringing Moscovy to join with us in stopping the Ottomans? Father Possevino has not yet been able to persuade Moscovy to unite with us, and if the Czar is in the state this writer claims—" He gestured to the letter as Rakoczy handed it back to him. "And why does he write to me? What is his reason?"

Rakoczy knew what was expected of him. He looked directly at Istvan. "Perhaps, if the Czar's mind is so filled with desire to expiate his . . . sin, he might be more willing to lend you his aid than he would have been at another time."

Istvan pretended the notion was new to him. "Yes. Yes. That is a possibility."

"Majesty," said Rakoczy, his face suddenly world-weary, "why not dispense with this game? What is it you want me to do? go to Moscovy to discover if what the letter-writer claimed is true?"

This was more direct than Istvan wanted to be, but he conceded the point to Rakoczy. "That is part of it, yes. I want you to go to Moscovy. I rely on you to get word to me about the actual state of mind of Czar Ivan, and of the state of his government. If there is to be rebellion or strife, I want to know of it."

"Why do you wish me to do this for you?" asked Rakoczy. "You have noblemen in Poland who would feel you had honored them with such a commission. Yet you send a messenger all the way into Bohemia to seek me out. Why is that, Majesty?"

Istvan nodded, acknowledging the question. "I have been told you are astute." He pulled at his lower lip. "All right, I will answer you: you are of ancient Translyvanian blood, as I am. Your family is older than mine, I have been told." He gestured to Rakoczy to remain silent; he went on bluntly, "And because of the Turks you are an exile."

"An exile," Rakoczy repeated, his tone ironic.

"And for that reason you well may be regarded with less suspicion by the Rus. They are wary of strangers, but an exile might not trouble them so much." He touched his blunt fingers together. "And there is a greater reason than those two, though they are sufficient to my purposes."

"And what reason is that, Majesty?" It was rare for a nobleman to insist on an explanation from Istvan, and rarer still for him to provide it.

Istvan decided that the question suited his purposes very well. "I have been told that you are an alchemist." He motioned to the closed door. "The priest isn't here. You may speak freely."

So that was it, thought Rakoczy, aware that were he in Istvan Bathory's position, he might well attempt the same ploy. "I have some measure of skill in the Great Art."

"A great measure of skill, or so I am informed," said Istvan. "It is said that you have the secret of jewels."

"And who claims that?" asked Rakoczy, once again feeling his apprehension increase.

"I have word here from His Holiness Pope Gregory stating that you provided him with four rubies and four diamonds upon the establishment of the Collegium Germanicum in Rome, jewels that you had made. That was eight years ago. Do you tell me now that His Holiness has lied to me?" Exhausted though he might be, Istvan was crafty and experienced in manipulation. "I requested information on several Transylvanian nobles who were displaced by the Turks. His Holiness most graciously provided me with as much as he could."

"I see." Rakoczy was staring into the fire, as if there might be secrets behind the flames. "Very well. I did provide the Pope with jewels." He paused thoughtfully. "I have . . . property in Rome. Occasionally I visit there."

"Was that why you gave the jewels to the Pope?" asked Istvan, becoming curious.

"No, not precisely," said Rakoczy. "Nor was it entirely to mark the establishment of the Collegium Germanicum." It had been the only means he could think of to turn the attention that had been paid to his alchemical skills away from the suggestion of diabolism, for many priests and bishops still preached that alchemy was devil's work. A gift to the Pope spared him their scrutiny.

Istvan decided to press the most important matter. "You gave the jewels to the Pope, though. Jewels you made?"

"I did." He turned his penetrating gaze on the King of Poland.

"And can you make more of them?" asked Istvan.

"If I have the proper equipment, and the correct materials," said Rakoczy. "Without them, the work cannot be done."

"I understand," said Istvan, and went on with dawning satisfaction. "But with proper materials you could present Ivan with jewels? On my behalf?"

"If I have the necessary equipment and the materials are fine enough, then it can be done." He felt a coldness within him that had little to do with the fading year or the setting sun.

Istvan clapped his hands decisively. "There are six Jesuits who are to leave for Moscovy as soon as the worst of the snows are gone in the spring. I want you to travel with them."

"To Moscovy," said Rakoczy.

"You will go as my emissary, one who is not a priest, who is noble and an exile. You will be able to tell for yourself the dangers posed by the Turks." He rubbed his leg again. "If the Czar is too crazed to listen, give him jewels and hope to persuade him that way, through their magic, since he believes in it."

Rakoczy watched Istvan closely. "Majesty, are you in pain?"

He shrugged, disliking to admit to any weakness. "Occasionally. I was grazed last year. There are times . . ." His voice changed, softening. "Yes. Today it hurts me."

"I have something that will help," said Rakoczy at once. "If you are willing to take it?"

Istvan shook his head. "No. As much as I may long for it, syrup of poppies may end the ache, but it stops thought as well."

Rakoczy studied Istvan a moment longer. "This will not rob you of your reason, nor make you sleep long hours. It has no lethargy in it." He gave Istvan a moment to consider it. "I carry such medicaments with me, as a precaution. You need not wait to use it. I can give you some before you eat tonight."

"An interesting offer," said Istvan, unable to hide his curiosity. "Is this another aspect of your alchemical skills?"

"Yes," said Rakoczy, thinking it was no more than the truth, for alchemy meant the Egyptian study, and he had learned to prepare that compound more than three thousand years ago in the Temple of Imhotep at Thebes.

"Most diverse, your skills," Istvan mused, then spoke more decisively. "Yes. Yes, I will avail myself of your offer." He regarded Rakoczy with increased respect. "I confess that what I heard of you at first made me suspect that there had been exaggerations about you. Now I begin to believe that if anything your abilities have been underestimated." He patted Rakoczy once on the shoulder, a familiarity that would have roused bitter jealousy in many courtiers, had they happened to see it.

Rakoczy had learned not to welcome such distinction; for what little favor such acts imparted, they reaped a greater share of hazard from those who coveted royal attention. "Majesty is most kind," he said very properly, relieved they were unobserved. "What talents I do possess, and in whatever measure, are at your disposal." His bow was perfect. "Even in Moscovy."

This made Istvan grin, and he decided to make the most of his opportunity. "According to what I have been told, in addition to your other talents, you are something of a musician and you speak several languages."

Rakoczy knew he had to tread carefully. "I can sing and play competently; as to the other, I have some knowledge of a few languages, yes."

Istvan nodded sagely. "English wouldn't be one of them, would it? They say that the English are in Moscovy, purchasing rope for their ships. If you could speak with them, you could be very useful to me, more than you are already."

"I can manage a few phrases," said Rakoczy, who spoke English and more than a dozen other languages fluently.

Something else struck Istvan and he rounded on Hrabia Saint-Germain. "And I'd almost forgot: you *do* speak Russian, don't you?"

Concealing a sigh, Rakoczy said in that language, "It will be an honor to serve you, Majesty."

Text of a letter from Atta Olivia Clemens, written in Latin, from London.

To my dearest and most provoking friend, Ragoczy Sanct'
Germain Franciscus, my heartfelt greetings;
So it's Moscovy, is it? Not content with facing Turks, you're
going to try the Russians? And do not excuse yourself with
claims that the king of Poland has ordered it. You know as well
as I that if it were not your wish to go, you would have discov-
ered any number of excellent reasons why it was not only im-
possible but inadvisable to send you there. I want to hear no
protestations that this was forced upon you. Although to give
you your due, you have not made any such protests.

But I am still annoyed with you, Sanct' Germain. You are
going to be farther away from me than ever, and that does not
please me. I confess I am vexed. It is all very well to say that the
Queen's Grace has commanded an embassy be sent to Mos-
covy—which is true enough—but to suggest that I use her Am-
bassador to be my messenger to you could prove to be dangerous
folly, and you are aware of it. You have not seen Elizabeth
Tudor, and you do not know her temper. Suffice it to say that she
has inherited her father's rages and added to them a will of steel.
I have seen her give vent to her anger once, and that was
enough to convince me I would do well to be prepared to return
to Rome on short notice.

You say in your letter that you do not believe you may return
to your native earth in any time soon. It saddens me to hear it,
for I know what it is to be far from Rome. Crates of earth are not
the same as the earth itself, and while it provides sustenance it
lacks the richness of home. You describe the precautions you are
making to ensure you have sufficient amounts of your native
earth while you are in Moscovy. I truly hope that they will suffice,
for it is a great distance from Moscovy to Transylvania or Dacia
or whatever those mountains are called. Do not remind me that
you are more experienced in these things than I am: I am well
aware of it, but that changes nothing. You are the one taking the
risk, and you are the one who will suffer if you prove wrong.

And that brings me to another matter. You make no mention
of when you are going to return. You indicate that Istvan Ba-
thory has not set a limit on your mission. Perhaps you would
care to guess? It may be that he wishes you to remain there until
his dream is realized and Poland has united with Russia. Have
you considered that? So suggest a year when I might expect you

to come to London or Rome; if that is too limiting, then a choice of two or three would do.

Incidentally, the Queen's Grace always refers to your Polish King as Stephen, not Istvan, although she does not change Czar Ivan to John. Elizabeth is a woman of strong mind and definite purpose, and does not welcome opposition, as Father Edmund Campion has found to his misfortune. She is also holding out against the change of calendar the Pope has declared. It would be rare for her to support anything the Pope approves, no matter how minor or sensible. So England and the Catholic countries of Europe will be misaligned by ten days. I predict there will be constant trouble until they are rectified.

Among those of the English embassy, there is a fellow you will wish to know. His name is Benedict Lovell, and I suppose you will find him a useful friend. As a student at Oxford, he was one of the scholars sent to study with the Russian Ambassador when Richard Chancellor brought him here, for he was skilled in Greek and knew enough German to read it passably, and therefore was ordered to learn Russian. While the people of London gaped and stared at the Ambassador, Benedict Lovell was learning his tongue, much to the disgust of his brother, who hankers to be a courtier and has neither the manner nor the money to do it properly. Benedict and I have had some dealings in the past, and for my sake he might well extend his goodwill to you. He does not know the secret of our blood—we were lovers only twice and it was not necessary to tell him. I will send word to him to make a point of speaking with you once you arrive in Moscovy. He is about thirty-four or -five, and was called from Oxford because of his knowledge of Russian to join the new embassy, at the request of the Ambassador, Sir Jerome Horsey. Do not chuckle too much, Sanct' Germain: the poor fellow cannot help his name. I hope the Russians will not find it as funny as the English do. I have met Sir Jerome twice but I have no measure of the man to offer. For that, consult Benedict Lovell.

I wish you a safe journey and the achievement of whatever you are seeking. And while you are gone, I will miss you as I would miss an arm or the warmth of a cloak in the rain. You are not to take risks, Sanct' Germain. I do not permit it. Not that I could stop you if you were determined.

Send me word when you can. And know that you can never

be so far away from me that my love will not find you, you infuriating man.

By my own hand and with my dearest affections,

Olivia
At Greengages, near Harrow,
11 November 1582, English calendar

2

Two years ago the house of Anastasi Sergeivich Shuisky had burned to the ground, so the one that stood in its place was not quite finished on the inside; woodworkers and painters strove to make it a fitting place for a Duke and his household to live.

"I wanted that room finished in time for Christmas; you knew that from the first," Anastasi told one of his cowering carpenters. "You told me it would be done by Christmas, and look at it." He flung his arm out toward the door of the offending room. "You cannot possibly do everything that is needed before Christmas."

"We will bring more men, Excellency. We will work night and day."

"And possibly burn the house down again," said Anastasi heavily. "No, that is not acceptable, not squads of workmen coming in and out." He got up and took a turn around the room, his head sunk onto his chest as he strove to control his temper. He wanted to shame the carpenters more than he wanted to punish them, at least for the time being.

The carpenter lowered his head, anticipating an order to be beaten. He dared not speak to Shuisky for that would make matters worse.

"That damned fire." He stopped moving and turned on the hapless carpenter. "I would have you beaten, but then you would claim you could not work, and that will not serve my purpose. You will not escape work. I tell you, therefore, that you—you—and your two assistants, none else, will work continually until you drop from it."

It was better than the carpenter had expected. He crossed himself and bobbed his head still lower. "We will do it. Yes, Excellency."

"I will have you observed all day and night. If you slack, you will be beaten and sent away if you are still alive." He glanced toward the room. "I will not accept inferior work, so do not do anything shoddy."

"No, Excellency," said the carpenter, his back already aching at the thought of the labor ahead of him.

"You will finish." It was more than an order; it was a statement of fact, incontrovertible.

"Yes, Excellency," said the carpenter, thinking that his reprieve was a bitter one, for if he failed, his two assistants—his nephews—would be subject to the same penalties he was. They and their families would become beggars if they failed to do as this Duke ordered them, assuming they were not killed.

Moscovy was subject to fires: a city of wooden buildings often covered in snow ran that risk as fires were constantly burning within them. The Moscovites had long since learned to make up the parts of a house in advance of building, so that the structures could be erected swiftly, sparing the occupants the dangers of exposure. Anastasi Shuisky's house was grander than most, as befitted his rank, but had been assembled in the same way that most of the other Moscovy houses had. There were fourteen rooms on two floors, with kitchens, a bakery and a bathhouse at the back of the property, the midden and latrines on the other side of a stone fence. As noble establishments went, it was fairly modest, but a man like Anastasi Sergeivich Shuisky came from an ancient and revered family, so had no need of extravagant display.

There were nine residents of the house, and three dozen servants to keep it running. It was not as large a household as many, for Anastasi kept his wife and children at his country estate where they would be in less danger away from the Court. Here in Moscovy his widowed cousin Galina Alexandrevna—ten years his senior—served as hostess for his guests and covered certain of his indulgences for fear of beggary. Her daughter, Xenya Evgeneivna Koshkina, was still unmarried at twenty-three and considered a disgrace to the family. She spent most of her time in charitable works, which suggested that she might one day become a nun, thus ending the stigma of her spinsterhood. There were two assistants, distant relatives, who had their wives with them; they were there on sufferance and knew it, and therefore were as compliant as Galina Alexandrevna. An elderly priest occupied two rooms and looked after the spiritual needs of the household; Father Illya was considered a learned man, which lent a certain importance to his position. The ninth resident was Piotr Grigoreivich Smolnikov, aged and blind now, but once a superb fighter for the Grand Duke, the father of the current Czar. He lived here on Shuisky's charity in recognition of his heroism and as a way to retain favor with the old soldiers who still controlled the army.

Anastasi Shuisky did not bother to look at his carpenter as the man bowed himself out of the Duke's presence. He sighed as he took his place at the long table where he had spread out several discouraging dispatches from Poland. There had been no new information for three months, and would be no more as long as winter held the north in its unrelenting grip. He had gleaned as much as he could from the reports, but he went over them again in the hope that there might be material he had overlooked. He was increasingly troubled about the embassy Istvan Bathory would be sending once spring came. Jesuits. That roused his suspicions, and he was a suspicious man; it was not at all what he had hoped for. Jesuits. He shook his head.

"Is something the matter? Have you had bad news?" It was his cousin Galina speaking. She had come into the room like a shadow, standing away from him, her widow's veils masking her features. Her deferential manner, intended to placate him, served only to aggravate.

"Nothing to concern you," said Anastasi, finding her presence an intrusion. She was tiresome but necessary, which encouraged him to treat her harshly.

"You looked angry," Galina observed, making no move to approach him. "I apologize if I have given offense."

"Not directly, no. But I have important work. I am not to be disturbed." He knew he was being brusque but made no apology for it. Cousin Galina was his dependent and as such she was required to take whatever he meted out to her.

She bowed to him, not quite as obsequiously as the carpenter had, but as self-deprecatingly. "I regret annoying you; I will be with Father Illya, for confession," she said, and started out of the room, her heavy fur slippers whispering on the bare floor.

"Yes. Get on with it." He made a gesture as if to wave away an annoying insect. Jesuits. They would not be trustworthy. Doubtless they would want to destroy the Orthodox Church. Jesuits went nowhere they did not intend to convert the people. It had been a mistake for Moscovy to attempt a reunion with Rome, as it had not so long ago. Now the Jesuits would use that to gain a foothold here. He picked up one of the dispatches, written in Greek, and went over it for the fifth time. He read carefully, examining each word thoughtfully, looking for hidden meanings or alternate translations of the phrases that might shed more light on what he was being told.

He had fretted himself through the papers for more than an hour when a visitor was announced: "There is a man seeking to speak with you," said the servant who guarded the doors.

"Who is he?" asked Anastasi, setting the dispatches and reports aside; his attention had been flagging for the last quarter hour and this interruption could be a welcome change from his anxiety.

"He is from Jerusalem," said the house guardian, meaning from the Orthodox Church, which had centered in that city since Constantinople had fallen to the powers of Islam. "He says to tell you his name is Stavros Nikodemios, a Hydriot."

"A Hydriot," said Anastasi with authority, as if he understood what that meant: he had never heard of the island of Hydra. He stood up. "Bring me a basin and a cloth."

The house guardian ducked his head and went about his task. Only when he had provided the Duke with these things did he return to the entry to escort the visitor to Anastasi.

"Welcome to my house, Hydriot," said Anastasi Shuisky, touching the hands of the foreigner between his own. "Let me offer hospitality to you." He turned to the basin and ritually washed his hands, drying them with care on the cloth his house guard had provided, as was proper protection when admitting foreigners to the house.

The Greek visitor nodded, unsurprised at this behavior. "Thank you for receiving me, Duke," he said in passable Russian. "It has been a very difficult journey. We nearly had to wait out the winter in Kursk. If our mission were not so urgent we would surely have done so." He held out a letter. "From Yuri Kostroma. It will tell you why I am here."

Anastasi took the letter and read it, his face deliberately blank. His cousin informed him that Nikodemios had very useful information from Jerusalem and the Patriarch. He implied that there could be support gained from the center of the Orthodox Church and suggested that at this time such an alliance would protect Holy Russia. He stated his own growing concerns about the state of the Czar's health. He urged Anastasi to hear Nikodemios out before making up his mind about what the man had to say. He closed with standard good wishes and a warning that he was afraid of what might happen with the Little Father so far gone in lunacy. "I gather you have had some discussion with my relative?"

"We have not concluded all our dealings, as some of what we do will be determined by you." Nikodemios said it like an experienced courtier.

"I should think so, if this letter is any indication," said Anastasi, pointing to his house guard and ordering him by gesture to bring a chair for his guest. "I am puzzled. What made you travel at this time of year? And why have you come here? Why do you visit me?"

"Necessity, Duke. You have read the letter. You must have some sense of my purpose here. There is need for immediate action." He sat down, looking directly at his host. "It is essential to be aware of—"

Anastasi cut him off. "Your necessity might not be mine. If you are here in the hope of enlisting my support for those who seek guidance from the Church in Jerusalem, you come in vain. Moscovy is the Third Rome after Constantinople was lost. My cousin and I have never agreed on this point. The Orthodox Church in Jerusalem has no right to impose its will on Moscovy. It is for the Orthodox Church in Russia to determine how the Church will respond to any trouble. At this time I will not support Jerusalem. There is too much at stake, things that Jerusalem cannot know and must not judge."

Stavros Nikodemios regarded him narrowly. "Am I to believe you are content to wait for God to decide? To leave matters as they are? Do you truly stand by the Czar? Even now?"

"Of course," said Anastasi, his expression darkening. "He is the might of the country. Even now." The last was especially pointed, directed at Nikodemios with strong intent. "Those who believe otherwise are traitors and fools."

"Fools and traitors," Nikodemios mused, his remarks addressed to the walls instead of Anastasi. "Why do you suppose that?"

"I am a Duke in Russia, and I am a Shuisky. We are loyal to the throne. Czar Ivan has pushed back the Tartars and reclaimed land that was stolen from us. He has brought us to glory. Everyone, boyar and oprichnik, knows that Czar Ivan has remade the world for us. I would be beneath contempt if I strove in any way to compromise what the Czar has done." He walked the length of the room, ignoring the sound of mallets in the unfinished chamber. "You come here to bring me information, and you begin by speaking against the Czar. That is idiotic. If you were not a foreigner, you would be knouted to death for such treason. You could be held accountable for every word you speak."

"But you will not speak against me," said Nikodemios. "You are too wary to risk losing what I might tell you, for you are ambitious. You want to protect your cousin Yuri as well as the rest of your family. It suits your purpose to claim you uphold the throne. And so you continue to declare for Czar Ivan, though you know he is lost."

"He is not lost." His voice had risen nearly to a shout and he gestured abruptly as if driving off an attacking animal. "His grief has consumed him. There is a burden of guilt from which he cannot free himself without greater expiation than he has made. He feels the weight of his sins very deeply, and that leads to melancholy. In time he will regain his composure."

"Regain his composure?" Nikodemios said. "How can you tell me that, when it is apparent to anyone that he is a lunatic." He, too, was growing angry.

"He is in the throes of grief. It has strained his mind." Anastasi Shuisky was most insistent. "Czar Ivan is a great man. Great men endure more than most of us, and what they suffer is greater for them than for most of us. He has had not only his family, but all Russia to care for. Therefore his grief is larger than yours or mine would be."

Nikodemios spat. "I have been a messenger for the Metropolitan for nine years, and I have seen the Czar change. Don't pretend that he is the same man he was three years ago. I know what he has become, and so do you. You puzzle me, refusing as you do to accept that the Czar is crazed. Especially since you have sent dispatches to Istvan Bathory."

This stopped him. "Never!" Anastasi was purple with rage and he made himself put distance between him and his guest. "What calumny is this?"

"You sent word to King Istvan of Poland. Last summer. It was carried by merchants." He said it with great satisfaction, smiling at Anastasi's wrath. "What was in that letter, I wonder? And why did you send it? What did you hope to achieve from it? Were you seeking an ally? They say that Poland wishes to unite with Russia so that the Ottomites may be driven back into Asia. Was that your purpose? To arrange such a—"

"It would be treason to suggest such a thing to Istvan Bathory. I would never betray Czar Ivan. It is a lie." His hands closed convulsively and his eyes smoldered, his shoulders hunched. "If you repeat your suspicions, I will denounce you as a spy. They will flay you for that."

"They might do that in any case, if your Czar takes the notion. It could happen to anyone. He has the power to order your ruin and death, does he not? Now that he has lost his wits, his caprice is endless." Nikodemios examined the backs of his hands as if there were hidden treasures there. "When men are crazed, they think unaccountable things."

He knew that he should not answer these charges, that he should summon the guards and have the Greek taken to prison, but he thought of his cousin, and recklessly he said, "Crazed or not, he is Czar. He is our strength against the Tartars and the Poles and the Swedes. If the Poles were to advance now, Czar Ivan would rally his men and his powers. He would lead us to victory."

"No man would follow him, not the way he is. The soldiers would hear him rave and they would not lift their swords to fight. No troops, not Rus, not Slavs, not Tartars, would follow him now. They would fear for their lives, and with cause." Nikodemios directed his gaze at Shuisky's feet. "Do you think it possible his heir could manage to lead the army?"

"There are many leaders the Little Father might select to lead the army. He need not send his only living son." He stood straighter. "I would welcome command."

Nikodemios laughed, his tone nasty. "I am certain you would. And the Czar would have to be more insane than he already is to give it to you. He would find your sword at his throat before the evening Mass." His laughter turned to a malign chuckle. "Do not protest your loyalty again, Duke. I know what you seek. You seek the sceptre and crown. You intend to rule. That is the goal of all Shuiskys."

"It is my wish to serve the throne," Anastasi insisted, this time with less heat than before, and more craftiness, his mercurial temperament playing with the Greek messenger, enjoying his confusion as it became desperation.

"Though Feodor Ivanovich rings bells and avoids his wife, you intend to support the throne? When Feodor is Czar?" He rose from the chair. "When you come to your senses, Duke, inform me of it. Jerusalem is the best ally you will find in these uneasy times. Your cousin is aware of that if you are not. And if you intend to look higher, you will need Jerusalem with you, or you will fall. For as long as the Church prevails, Jerusalem will be a power to reckon with in Moscovy."

"The power of the Czar is greater, and Ivan Grosny is worthy of wielding it," said Shuisky, deliberately using Ivan's nick-name—Grosny: awe-inspiring.

"Grosny. Perhaps once. But no longer, I think." He fingered the fur lining of his cloak. "Is caressing jewels so much different than ringing bells?" Nikodemios inquired sarcastically. "Be grate-ful that Istvan Bathory has not advanced any farther than he has. The hope you place in Ivan is false. You have seen the Czar, you know how he behaves. You have seen him stare at nothing and claim he sees his son Ivan bleeding in front of him. You have heard him praying in the dead of night, crying aloud at the sky for God to seize him. You know that he is mad, and yet you will not challenge his Right."

"Not while Feodor Ivanovich remains his heir. I have sworn an oath and I will not abjure it." He found it difficult to keep from bragging of his own, complex plans regarding the distressed Czar. It was wrong even to think about it, for Greeks were subtle and might well find a way to discover his thoughts, to use them against him.

"Feodor Ivanovich will not rule," said Nikodemios. "Everyone knows that he will never live to hold the sceptre. He has not two reasonable thoughts in his head. He speaks badly when he speaks at all. Perhaps Czar Ivan will have sense enough to appoint a regent before his madness makes such a decision impossible. Whatever the case, Feodor will never hold power. He is incapable of rule, and everyone agrees that he will not reign. He belongs in a monastery or a farm, somewhere he can ring his bells in peace. Think, Duke. His wife is more capable of ruling than he, and she is nothing more than a woman, and half Tartar to boot. Resign yourself: Feodor will not reign, no matter what Ivan may do. The nobles will rebel before that occurs."

"Saying such things could lose your skin for you, Greek," said Shuisky. "If I were to accuse you——"

"You would not dare do that," said Nikodemios. "I would have a few things to accuse you of, as well. And the rest of your family."

Now Shuisky snickered, a sound like wet leather straps slapping together. "But you are a foreigner and I am a nobleman; my family is noble," he said confidently. "They would not believe you. Foreigners are not guests here, they are strangers. I need only point you out and declare that you have spoken against the Czar and his son. They would start with your feet, taking the skin off slowly so that you will not bleed to death too quickly. They would leave you hanging, your own skin dangling off you in wide strips. It takes a long time to die that way."

"It would not be wise," said Nikodemios, though his brow had gone white and his voice was a little breathless. "I have many secrets that would embarrass more nobles than you and your relatives."

"You mean you would shame the oprichniks? That is nothing to me." He cocked his head. "But perhaps I will not denounce you for a spy. If you assist me, I may be persuaded to keep your confidence a while." His high color had abated now that he was once again in control of his emotions. "I want to know why you think it was I who sent word to Istvan Bathory. Why have you come to me?"

"A . . . a priest claimed he saw such a letter, that it came from this house. Our source was reliable and has never been incorrect before." He was clearly less certain than he had been at first. He had supposed that he would be able to strike a bargain with Anastasi Shuisky and that had proved impossible. Now he was left with no plan to guide him.

"Not the priest who lives in this house," said Anastasi, hoping it would not be true.

"No, not in this house," said Nikodemios, too quickly, which gave him away.

It was possible to smile; his smile was cold. "And how did Father Illya come to see this letter he claims to have read?" asked Anastasi, feeling his way with caution.

"I don't know." He decided to offer some information without having Anastasi ask for it, in the hope that it would improve his position. "But being a true man of God, he sent word to the Patriarch in Jerusalem. He feared that addressing the Metropolitan here might lead to accusations and imprisonment, though he had discovered treason. The power of the boyars—" He was frightened. His faded brown eyes shifted restlessly from one object to another in the room, as if seeking a haven from Anastasi.

"I see," said Anastasi, believing Nikodemios implicitly. It was just what the old man would do. It served him right for permitting a literate priest in his house, he thought. He would know better next time. "He must have entrusted his letter to monks or priests."

"It was brought by a monk," said Nikodemios, nodding several times as if to convince Anastasi more completely.

"And therefore they will expect to remain informed," said Anastasi, his mind working quickly now. Of first importance was to get this worrisome Greek out of Moscovy, to a place where he could be dealt with. "I think it would be best if you returned to my cousin's estate. It would be dangerous for you to be here in Moscovy. You will carry a letter to my cousin and you will wait there for further instructions." He rocked back on his heels. "And if you fail to do this, I will denounce you to the Metropolitan and the Czar, and your life will be worth less than cattle dung."

Nikodemios watched Anastasi with the same concentration that a rat watches a house cat. At last he said, "What of the Patriarch in Jerusalem?"

"What of him?" said Anastasi. "He is nothing to me but an inconvenience. If you contact him, my cousin will make short work of you." He was already planning the letter he would send to Yuri, and the orders he would give that very junior member of his noble family.

"He is expecting reports, the Patriarch is," said Nikodemios. "If he does not receive them, he may—"

"Oh, he will receive them," said Anastasi very smoothly. "He will receive them regularly." He looked directly at Nikodemios, his furious smile growing more pronounced. "It will all be arranged."

Nikodemios was truly terrified. "Duke, it would be a sin if you were to deceive the Patriarch. It would be a sin to harm his messenger."

Anastasi shook his head slowly, his cold smile dazzling as sun on ice. "But I have so many sins on me already. What difference will a few more make? Sin is part of life, stranger, and no man can escape it. Remember that," he added as Nikodemios moved to the far side of the room. "With all my sins, what difference will that deception make? Or murder?" He looked away, his attitude changing to one of languid contempt. "Go to the kitchen. They will feed you. And one of my guards will go with you back to my cousin's estate. Tomorrow." This delay was a concession for the benefit of his servants, not for the Greek messenger. "The chief cook will show you where you can sleep."

"Praise God," Nikodemios said in Greek, and wished fervently that he had gone to the Metropolitan instead of coming here, to the house of this smiling, deadly nobleman.

Text of a letter from Father Wojciech Kovnovski to his sister in Gniezno.

In the Name of the Trinity, my greetings to you, dear Danuta, and to your husband.

I pray that God has protected you thus far through this terrible winter and will bring you to safety and health as spring comes on. The priest who reads this to you will know of the great task the Pope and King Istvan have set for us; depend on him to explain to you what an honor has been bestowed upon the eight of us. I am filled with gratitude for this opportunity to demonstrate my devotion to the Church and God.

For the time that we are gone, I anticipate that it will be difficult for any of us to send personal letters from Moscovy, and so this is to serve as a temporary farewell. Do not despair if there are years that pass without word from me. With God's Grace, we shall meet again in this life, and if not, then we will share the Light of God in Heaven.

I can think of no finer act than the upholding of the Catholic Church in this time of need. To be provided the chance to bring the souls ensnared by the Orthodox Church to the True Faith once again is the greatest joy. I am overcome with satisfaction and thanksgiving. I hear the souls of Russia cry out to me in their need for the Blood of Redemption. We know from the earlier attempt at reunification that there are many Rus who are anxious to embrace the True Church, but who have been deprived of the salvation they seek through the connivance of the Orthodox Patriarch and the Metropolitan of Moscovy. The might of Constantinople is gone, and the city is in the hands of those who follow the Prophet of Islam. The people of Russia know that without Rome they are as lost as Constantinople is, and they desire to turn to us, to become part of the Church and, through the Church, the servants of Christ. This time we will not fail in our task, but will emerge with Russia once again part of the Catholic Christian community, allied to Rome, and all declared against the Sultans and the forces of Islam.

We will travel in the escort of a company of lancers. There will be fifty armed men to guard us to Moscovy, not so much against the Rus, but against the bandits and other outlaws who prey on travelers. We are being permitted servants for our service as embassy.

There is a Hrabia, or Comte or Graf or Prinz—I have heard him called by all those titles—from Transylvania, a countryman of King Istvan's, who accompanies us. It is said that he is an alchemist, but in what little contact I have had with the man, I see nothing of the devil about him. It is the King's wish that this man influence the Czar by presenting him with gifts. It would be incorrect for priests to do such things, and so this exiled Transylvanian will serve King Istvan in this way.

Though it is wrong of me to confess this, I must tell you that I cannot help but hope that if my actions meet with the approval of King Istvan I might be given advancement within the Church. There is so much I could do if I had a more influential position. I have humbly accepted my place within the Church, but with this venture, I have allowed myself greater scope of intention.

Until now I thought it would be my lot to remain a mere priest. I was content to serve God in that capacity. But now I am aware that there might be benefits resulting from the task that has been given to me, and I pray that I will show myself worthy of higher position within the Church, to which my experiences will surely entitle me. No, I look no higher than Bishop, but I cannot see why such advancement is impossible if I comport myself well in Moscovy. I have accepted the rebuke of my Confessor for my pride, but I cannot yet dismiss my hopes as unreasonable and prideful.

May God bless you and your family, dear sister, and may you all thrive in His favor until I return to you. Know that you are always in my prayers, and that as soon as it is possible, I will send word to you. In the meantime, I ask for your remembrance while I am gone.

With the deep affections of a brother,
Father Wojciech Kovnovski
By my own hand, on the Feast of Saint John Chrysostom,
January 27, 1583 At Saint Jerzy of Armenia Church.

3

February was bitter, with blowing drifts of snow that made traveling all but impossible. Istvan Bathory had moved the Court to winter quarters as near the Russian border as seemed wise, and now had his hands full of impatient younger sons and gathering priests who were ready to advance to the east, into the heart of Russia, and were made prisoners by the terrible cold.

"It's bad for the horses, all this waiting. They chew the wood in their stalls and their legs swell," insisted Hrabia Dariusz Zary as he paced the length of the soldiers' hall, relentless as a caged tiger. "They're getting stale, having nothing to do day after day."

"They cannot be taken out in a blizzard," said Istvan testily. He was aching from the cold and had not slept well. "If you want to sweep out the old armory, they may be ridden there."

"Hah!" scoffed Zary with an impatient toss of his head. "What good is it to ride a horse around a room? It bores you and it bores the horse." He folded his arms defiantly and waited for Istvan to castigate him.

He was deprived of that recreation, for the door swung open and four men in snow-crusted cloaks stumbled in, one of them coughing badly. As they rid themselves of their frozen, sodden garments, they were revealed as priests, two of them in the habit of the Jesuits, the other two in pluvials with minimal embroidery.

"Father Casimir Pogner," said the oldest of the four, a tall, weathered man with hard eyes and a thin mouth. "These are Fathers Milan Krabbe, Stanislaw Brodski, and Dodek Kornel." He looked around, seeing only the young Zary and Istvan, who had none of the regalia they expected in their King, and therefore paid him scant attention. "Who else has arrived?"

"Father Aniol Tymon and Father Wicus Felikeno have come," said the young nobleman, striving to show the priests the respect King Istvan required of him in spite of his own low opinion of clerics. "Fathers Lomza and Kovnovski have not yet arrived. We expect them in a day or two, when the weather improves."

Father Pogner nodded slowly. "They have a greater distance to come. With God protecting them, they will make a swift journey."

"Of course," said Hrabia Zary, realizing belatedly that Istvan was testing the newcomers, playing a game with them. He decided to make the most of this opportunity. "Now that you have arrived, doubtless you have much to do. Perhaps you wanted to present yourselves to the King?"

"Yes," said Father Pogner rather distantly. His nose wrinkled at the overpowering odor of wet wool as he spread out his cloak to dry. "After we have seen the Bishop, of course."

Zary glanced at Istvan, who had busied himself with working wax into the saddle set out over the arm of his chair. "Not the King first?"

"The King is our sponsor, and for that we owe him courtesy. As men who were born on Polish soil, we honor him. But we are priests, and our first duty is to the Church," said Father Pogner, with a quelling look at the other three, for it seemed that Father Kornel was about to protest. "So we will present ourselves to the

Bishop and ask his blessing before we bow to the King." His lips widened, but it was not possible to call that a smile.

"The King might not be pleased," said Zary. "Since he is sending you as his representatives to Ivan's Court."

"We go as priests," said Father Brodski, who was a bit younger than the others. He ducked his head toward Father Pogner, clearly seeking his approval.

He did not receive it. "See that you remember that, all of you," said Father Pogner. "Where is the Bishop?"

Istvan answered the question, addressing the Jesuits with a show of respect. "He is in the village, good Fathers; he has been given the use of a house there, next to the church of the Savior. When the wind dies down, it will be much easier to find the place. As it is——"

Father Pogner stood straighter than before. "Surely someone will guide us. We must not delay." He motioned to the priests, his expression resigned but still purposeful. "It might be best to put your cloaks back on, if we must go out into the storm again."

"A messenger could be sent for the Bishop," suggested Istvan, with a covert motion to Hrabia Zary to remain silent.

"That is not appropriate," said Father Pogner. He watched as Father Krabbe picked up his cloak again, coughing with the slight effort. "You may be excused from this obligation, Father Krabbe," he declared. "You must seek the aid of the physician if you are to be fit to travel to Moscovy."

Father Krabbe crossed himself. *"Deo gratias,"* he whispered, and coughed again. His hunched posture and fever-pinched features made him appear older and more frail than he was, for his hair was still rich brown and the lines in his face were not deep, and judging from the way his Jesuit habit fit, he had a good breadth of shoulder.

"Father Kornel, Father Brodski, prepare yourselves," ordered Father Pogner. He regarded Istvan with brief interest. "If there is someone who should inform the King of our arrival, tell me his name."

"I will tend to it," said Istvan. "Hasten to make yourself known to the Bishop, by all means. The King will wait your pleasure," he went on, aware that only he appreciated his irony; the three priests left the room.

Father Krabbe stumbled toward the hearth, his habit showing

wet stains at the shoulder and across the back. For a moment he steadied himself against the stones of the mantle, then he sank down onto his knees in front of the fire and began to pray, interrupting himself with the same tense, hacking cough as before. He was shaking visibly.

"Zary, go find Rakoczy at once. Tell him to come here." Istvan got up from his chair, leaving his saddle half-polished.

Knowing advantage when it stared him in the face, Zary went down on his knee, kissed Istvan's hand. "It is done," he said as he hurried from the room.

From his place by the fire, Father Krabbe stared. His face paled as Istvan approached him, and very hesitantly he said, "Majesty?"

Istvan's joints were too sore to permit him to do more than bend down a little, but he did this, saying, "God give you recovery, good Jesuit. I am Istvan Bathory. You are Father Milan Krabbe, I believe Father Pogner said." As Father Krabbe broke off praying, turning his face up in true shock, the King went on. "I am sorry you are ill. It is not fitting that men in my service should suffer unnecessarily. That is why I have sent for the alchemist who is to travel with you. He will be able to tend you better than the physicians we have here, who are used to binding up minor wounds and cauterizing serious ones but have little skill beyond such treatments. Rakoczy will know what to do to make you better."

"You must forgive them. They intended no insult, Majesty. Father Pogner did not know," Father Krabbe said urgently, masking his cough with his hands. "Truly, Majesty, he did not know."

"That was apparent," Istvan said dryly, who was less certain than Father Krabbe that such knowledge would have made much difference to Father Pogner. "For if he did know, he would have had to pay his first duty to me, no matter what he preferred to do."

"He will be . . ." This time his coughing covered his confusion.

"I suppose he will be embarrassed. He has brought that on himself. Still, it is acceptable to me that he was candid." His leg ached steadily, and he leaned against the stone mantle of the fireplace to provide some relief. "Depending upon how he comports himself when he discovers the truth, I will endorse or end his chagrin. If he is chagrined." He rubbed at his hip. "Winter has

been hard on all of us. Your illness has been prevalent with some
of my men. Four of my captains have been sent to monasteries
in order to recover."

"The monks will cure them, in the Name of Our Lord," said
Father Krabbe with the kind of desperate certainty that comes
with having the same disease.

"Perhaps." He looked up as the door flung open and Hrabia
Zary returned. "Rakoczy is coming, Majesty," he said with a
casual bow. "He begs that you will excuse him for not accompanying me; he asks you to wait a moment or so while he com-
pletes his preparations."

At another time Istvan would have been dissatisfied with this
message, but after the calculated indifference of Father Pogner
the grace of this response was most satisfactory. "If he does not
expect me to wait very long."

"He was loading something into that peculiar oven of his, the
one that looks like a brick-and-stone beehive," said Hrabia Zary
in disgust. "And that manservant of his was sifting through a tray
of little green pebbles. Rakoczy claims that the pebbles would
combine with acid to yield copper." He shook his head at such
nonsense.

"Did you tell him about Father Krabbe?" asked Istvan, just a
touch of condemnation in his tone.

"I said more Jesuits have arrived and one was ill." He tossed
his head, his fair hair brushing his broad ermine collar. "He said
his work would be for nothing if he did not load the oven
properly."

"Then I suppose he has done what is best," said Istvan, though
a vertical line was deepening between his brows.

"You may be certain he will claim so," said Hrabia Zary,
drawing his poignard half out of its scabbard suggestively. "I
could compel him."

"No, you could not," said Istvan bluntly. "Try such a foolish
thing and he would make short work of you."

Hrabia Zary laughed outright. "He? He is past forty and he
dresses like a dancing master."

"It isn't wise to be deceived by his appearance," said Istvan,
looking down with concern as Father Krabbe continued to
cough. The priest's color was muddy and his breath wheezed.

"If you command me to treat him as if he were a soldier—"

Zary began, then broke off as Rakoczy, dressed in a heavy black fur-lined mente over a dolman of red, black, and silver, came into the room and walked directly to Istvan before offering his Italian bow.

"I'm sorry for the delay, Majesty; my athanor is finally hot enough for the work you have asked of me. In three days I will have the talismans I mentioned." He kissed the King's hand, then gave his attention to Father Krabbe. "This is the priest?" he asked as he knelt.

"Yes. As you see, he coughs." Istvan abandoned his place by the fire and returned to his chair. "Is there anything you can do for him?" he asked as he eased himself into the most comfortable position he could find.

Rakoczy did not answer at once. He gave the priest a quick, expert inspection, noting how Father Krabbe strained to draw air into his lungs, and the faint rustling sound in his chest. Only when he had touched Father Krabbe's forehead, neck, and hands did he say, "Yes, I think there is something I can do. He is filled with illness, but there is still a chance to save him." He looked Father Krabbe directly in the eyes, commanding the priest's attention. "There is a compound I can give to you. It is not one of the substances approved by the Church, but there is nothing diabolic about it. You may ask one of the priests who have come with you to bless it, if that will relieve your mind. Will you take it?"

Father Krabbe tried to draw a deep breath and failed. When his spasm of coughing was over, he said, "I will."

"Then there is a good chance that you will be better shortly," said Rakoczy, but made a sign to the king as he continued to talk to Father Krabbe. "What you need now is a warm bed and hot wine."

"I will arrange it at once," said Istvan, and signaled Hrabia Zary, who sighed dramatically and bowed in inelegant imitation of the bow Rakoczy had offered. "A bed and a servant to tend this priest."

"He will need broth," Rakoczy went on. "I will speak to the cooks myself." This last gesture was wasted on Zary, who glared.

"The world is full of Jesuits," he muttered as he left the room.

Rakoczy knelt closer to Father Krabbe. "Tell me, Father, have you had much pain in your chest?"

"A . . . a little," said the Jesuit.

"Pressure?" Rakoczy pursued. "Do you feel as if there is a weight on you?"

Father Krabbe nodded. "Father Pogner says it is the weight of my sins."

Unwise though it was, Rakoczy shook his head and gestured his exasperation. "It is the nature of your illness. Do not blame your sins for it." He placed his small hand on Father Krabbe's neck again, feeling the fast, thin pulse. "I want you to sleep. You have worn yourself to the bone, aside from this illness. Why on earth did you force yourself to travel—" He broke off, realizing full well why Father Krabbe had done so ill-considered a thing. "Father Pogner."

"He has exhorted us to be diligent and firm in our dedication." The last two words ended in coughing again. He stared at Rakoczy out of his dark-rimmed eyes. "Is there anything that can be done? Or are you offering me comfort and an easier death?" As Rakoczy started to answer, Father Krabbe continued, "For if that is what you intend to do, I ask that you will not. If I suffer, I will offer it up, and you will not waste your medicaments to no purpose."

Rakoczy's smile was fleeting. "Very brave, Father. But I fear that there is still enough life in you to justify the treatment." He patted Father Krabbe on the shoulder, then got to his feet once again, moving a short distance away and motioning for Istvan to come with him. "He is going to need constant nursing for the next four days," he said in an undervoice.

"He has putrid lungs?" asked Istvan, who had seen the sickness many times before.

"Yes," said Rakoczy, "but he is not dead yet." He knew how quickly those with putrid lungs were given up for dead, and he wanted to prevent the neglect that would be more deadly to Father Krabbe than his illness. "With syrup of poppies to help him sleep and the hermetic sublimate I can provide, he will recover, if he is well-attended."

Istvan shrugged. "There are monks who—"

"Your pardon, Majesty," said Rakoczy as if there was nothing strange in interrupting the King. "Monks are very well in their place, but that is ministering to the poor. This man requires a greater skill than monks may provide, and more help than simple prayer."

Istvan cocked his head and lifted his hand in warning. "Do not let the Jesuits hear you say that, Hrabia Saint-Germain, for the sake of Father Krabbe, if not your own. Your ancient name and your title would not be proof against them, if they decided you were the servant of Satan."

Rakoczy nodded once, his dark eyes distant, his long memories recalling the zeal of priests for more than three thousand years. From the dread of the High Priest in Nineveh to the jealousy of Denim Mahnipy in the Temple of Imhotep to the hysterical austerity of Ranegonde's confessor to the self-destructive excesses of Tamasrajasi to the denied greed of Savonarola, Rakoczy recognized the breed: they had served many gods, and in a variety of ways, but their mania was the same. "I have learned that lesson, Majesty."

"Have you," said Istvan, seeing something in Rakoczy's face that revealed more than he knew. "Then keep the lesson in mind, my friend."

Rakoczy made a gesture of assent. "In the meantime, there must be two or three squires who would take turns with Father Krabbe. I will send Rothger to watch him in the night."

Hearing the priest cough again, Istvan watched him critically. "Are you certain he will recover? I have seen many another less ill than he who could not be saved."

"He is young and strong," said Rakoczy. He looked around the room as he continued his observations, as if others might overhear him. "He must be kept warm, that is most important. The only true danger to him is continuing cold—the rest I can remedy. Once he is warm and dry he needs hot wine and broth until his cough lessens and the fever is gone. After that, provided he is not forced to leave his bed before he is ready, good food and rest will restore him." He shifted his stance so that his back was to Father Krabbe. "It might be wisest to settle him before the others return?"

"I take your point," said Istvan. "It will be tended to immediately. The man has suffered enough." He returned to his chair and picked up the large brass bell lying by the saddle. As he rang it, he said to Rakoczy, "Do you wish to supervise moving him?"

"It might be best. And with your permission I will give my manservant the task of selecting three squires to assist him in the care of Father Krabbe." He offered Istvan another bow. "Thank you, Majesty." With that he turned and went to assist Father Krabbe to get to his feet.

The priest blinked several times before he realized what was happening, and then he struggled to manage on his own, protesting that it was wrong for a nobleman to aid a priest. Since he doubled over with coughing before he had finished objecting, Rakoczy paid no attention.

By the time the other three Jesuits made their way through the wind and snow back to Istvan's quarters, Father Krabbe was snug in bed under a quilt and fur robe, Rothger supervising the inexpert ministrations of Tomcio. Rakoczy had already given him the first of five doses of the hermetic sublimate that began as moldy bread.

Entering the chamber where they had come before, Father Pogner was a little surprised to see that the older nobleman was still in the room, tending to his saddle. He spread out his cloak before the fire before he addressed Istvan. "What has become of Father Krabbe?"

Istvan regarded the priests with interest, noticing that the other two seemed more cowed now than before. "He has been put to bed where he may rest easy and his illness may be treated."

"Prayer will do him more good than any physic or luxury," said Father Pogner with a gesture of dismissal. "It is for God to heal him."

"That may be, but Scripture instructs us to look for the world's solutions in the world." There was a trace of amusement in his voice and his eyes brightened with a smile. Istvan was feeling better since Rakoczy had supplied him with more of the tincture of pansy, willow, and angelica; his leg and hip no longer ached as if caught in a vice.

"A man in your position may be excused for thinking so," said Father Pogner with hauteur. "Who has been given the care of our companion? It is fitting that we approve him."

"I will send for him, if that would suit you?" He started to reach for his bell.

He was spared the necessity. The door opened and Ferenc Rakoczy came into the room, for once going down on his knee to Istvan instead of bowing in the Italian manner. "Majesty," he said, paying no obvious attention to the three priests, "I have left Father Krabbe with Father Mietek, who is hearing his Confession."

"Very good," said Istvan, motioning to Rakoczy to rise. He saw the outrage in Father Pogner's face, unguarded and blatant for an instant, then gone and replaced with apparent humility.

Father Kornel crossed himself. "Jesus protect me."

Father Brodski stared at Istvan. "You are King?" he asked before he could stop himself.

"By Grace of God," said Istvan seriously, taking satisfaction in the discomfiture of the priests. If only the old Polish nobility could be as effectively influenced. "And this is the man who has made the care of Father Krabbe his business—Rakoczy of Saint-Germain. Like myself, he is a Transylvanian." He motioned to Rakoczy to rise and find a place to stand near him as a sign of favor that the priests would understand.

"Honored, good Fathers," said Rakoczy, ducking his head to the priests and watching them without appearing to notice much about them.

Fathers Brodski and Kornel returned the half-bow, but Father Pogner stood straight and disapproving. At last he spoke, begrudging every word. "Your family name is not unknown to me," he said grudgingly.

"I am from an older branch of the tree than those you mean," said Rakoczy without any indication of pride. "Still, it is pleasant to hear them well spoken of." His smile was swift and disarming.

Father Pogner remained obdurate. "Only a fool puts his satisfaction in the favors of the world, or its pains." He glared at Istvan. "I apologize that we did not do you honor, Majesty, when we first arrived. But there was no one to tell us who you might be, and our concerns are not for courtesy."

This stung Istvan enough to earn a rebuke. "You had better have concern for courtesy if you are to serve my interests at the Court of Ivan. He is one who puts great stock in courtly obligations, according to what I have been told. Neglect to honor him and you might pay for that oversight with your skins."

Father Brodski belatedly dropped to one knee, paying no attention to the quelling look Father Pogner shot him. "It was not my intention to offend you, Majesty. It was only our ignorance that kept us from showing you honor. We ask you to remember that we had never seen you. And given"—he broke off to indicate the worn double-sleeved old-fashioned cote Istvan wore—"that you are not yourself dressed for courtesy, we may be forgiven our misunderstanding."

Istvan nodded decisively twice. "That is more in the line of what I will need in Moscovy. You relieve me, Father Brodski. I was beginning to fear I was sending incognizant men to work on my behalf." This last was intended for Father Pogner, but it was Father Kornel who felt the barb.

He went down on one knee beside Father Brodski. "King Istvan, we will serve you in whatever capacity you require; you have but to tell us what that capacity may be, for it would not be fitting or desirable for us to anticipate your wishes in this regard, and thus risk compromising the very thing you wish us most to do." He lowered his head, and earned a quick glance of disgust from Father Pogner before he reluctantly dropped to one knee with the others.

"It was not my intention to offend you, Majesty," said Father Pogner in a tone that implied the opposite.

"I am not offended, unless you should now forget yourselves." He lifted the bell at last. "There is a meal waiting for you. Since you were not here at mid-day you missed the dinner. There is only a supper planned for the evening, and so the cooks have made something more substantial than that because you are weary from traveling and cold. It was ordered while you made yourselves known to the Bishop, anticipating your return. The servants will serve it in the chamber next to the pantry. That way they will be able to continue their tasks without neglecting you or their work. The chamberlain will lead you there." He waited a moment, then ventured, "Unless you would prefer to speak to Father Krabbe first?"

"It would be my honor to escort you to his bedside," said Rakoczy smoothly.

Father Pogner got to his feet, his pale eyes seeming almost metallic in their sheen. "What graciousness," he said tightly. He stared down at the other two priests as if memorizing the extent of their duplicity in honoring Istvan. "We will pray at his bedside and bless him with holy water," he announced in a level tone, moving back toward the fireplace while Father Kornel and Father Brodski both scrambled to their feet. "Before we eat."

The other two accepted this without question, although Father Kornel licked his lips and looked disappointed as he agreed.

"You will find he is resting," said Rakoczy. He watched Father Pogner without revealing himself; he maintained a polite deference. "It would probably be best if he continues to sleep."

Father Pogner rounded on him, determined to establish his authority over Rakoczy as well as the other priests. "It will be best if he joins us in prayer, for the salvation of his soul and the preservation of his body, if it is God's will he be delivered from sickness." His long hands were clenched and his thin mouth now turned down with the force of his condemnation.

Rakoczy exchanged a swift, emphatic glance with Istvan Bathory before he met Father Pogner's gaze with his own. "You must do as you think best. But you will find the rosary in his hands and his missal on his pillow. And my manservant read to him from Scripture. If you believe you must disrupt the restoration of God's healing sleep, you will do it. But I myself heard him place his soul in the hands of his good angel, and I am not willing to stop the angel at his work."

"What faith you have," marveled Father Pogner with contained fury. "I wonder that you are not in Holy Orders."

"I studied for the priesthood when I was a child," said Rakoczy; it was the truth, but he did not mention that the priesthood had vanished before the Gardens of Babylon were built.

For the first time there was a trace of respect in Father Pogner's manner. "Then why are you not now ordained?"

Again he gave a truthful answer, as far as it went. "I had to defend my native earth. Unfortunately we were not strong enough and enemies overran our country," said Rakoczy, thinking of the hundreds of times armies had swarmed over the Carpathians since his youth, the Ottoman Turks being the most recent in a long line of conquerors.

Father Pogner studied Rakoczy as Fathers Kornel and Brodski slapped at their clothes to neaten them. "How unfortunate," he said at last. "You should have chosen the Church instead of your family. Your lands are in the hands of your enemies, but the Church grows greater with every passing day."

"It is the tie of blood." Rakoczy met Father Pogner's accusing stare with an enigmatic half-smile, all the while preparing himself for what he feared would eventually become another battle, this one a question of power disguised as an inquiry regarding heresy. He knelt to Istvan once more, and kissed his hand.

"We will talk later, Rakoczy," said Istvan, making his voice especially cordial.

"Majesty is gracious," said Rakoczy before he rose.

* * *

Text of a dispatch to Istvan Bathory, King of Poland, from one of his geographers.

To the most gracious Istvan Bathory, by Grace of God King of Poland, the greetings of his devoted servant Pavel Donetski, and his prayers for the fruits of victory to be yours.

I have spoken with fur traders just arrived here from Moscovy. They say that the road is difficult but it may be traveled without fear of being detained for months because of weather. The leader of the traders warned that the rivers are unusually high where the ice has melted and warns all those going into the territories of Ivan Grosny to be on guard against flooding. He also recommends that all river crossings be undertaken on fer-ries instead of bridges, for with such a wet spring, many of those bridges will not be safe.

I have also had the opportunity to speak with a horse breeder, who has said he is willing to set aside two dozen of his strongest young horses for the use of your embassy going to Moscovy. He has named a reasonable price and I have told him that this will be acceptable. Since I understand that your embassy has al-ready begun its journey, I will have to assume that these prepa-rations are part of your plan for their protection, along with the company of Lancers. From what we have been told, they should be expected to reach here in fourteen to seventeen days, provid-ing there is no more rain. The road from Minsk to Smolensk is often wet and marshy but there has been no fighting near it, so travel is not too great a risk.

I must warn you that the first word we have had from Moscovy does not bode well for Czar Ivan, who is said to be caught in the center of his madness, thinking himself haunted by the son he killed. It is cause to be careful, Majesty, for if the Czar is de-mented, then no bargain struck with him will be regarded as having meaning. Your embassy could face tremendous dangers if the Czar is truly gone insane.

We will do what we can to keep you apprised of the changes in Russia as we hear of them, especially all the reports from Moscovy, and we will correct our maps as we gain more infor-mation. What lies beyond Moscovy remains uncertain; we are attempting to learn more of the lands to the east. As geographers we occasionally have the aid of scholars, and they often bring information that a dozen spies could not procure. When your embassy stops here, I will do as you have suggested and avail myself of the knowledge of your alchemist. From what you have said, he is more widely traveled than most men we meet.

God has favored your cause thus far, Majesty, and we all pray that He will continue to bring you the victory. And while we pray, we will also continue to gather the charts and maps you say you need. We have been at pains to obey your orders and keep these maps hidden from all but your appointed deputies, so that others will not be able to turn the tide against you. We are all loyal to your cause and will defend all that we have learned. There is no enemy who can cause us to surrender what we know. If God wills it, you will have no cause to worry about the Russians or the Livonians or the Hungarians or all the might of the Ottoman Turks. As you have said yourself, the leaders with the most complete information will prevail so long as the forces are well-matched.

Until we receive your embassy and report back to you, rest assured of my loyalty and devotion. My skills are ever at your service.

Pavel Donetski
At the library of Anatoli Gritschekov, near Smolensk, April
16, 1583

4

"Why have we stopped?" demanded Father Pogner as Hrabia Zary motioned for the Lancers to halt. The soldiers at once formed a block at the front of the travelers, prepared to fend off anyone who might be ahead of them. Behind him the baggage train mules of the embassy were grateful for the respite. The priests, all but two of them riding mules, gathered around Father

Pogner, with the exception of Father Krabbe, who stayed in the company of Ferenc Rakoczy.

"Because we are not on Polish land anymore, Father," said the young man with ill-disguised annoyance. "We are strangers here."

"We are the embassy of Istvan Bathory, king of Poland, and servants of His Holiness the Pope," said Father Pogner, reciting these credentials with ritualistic fervor, as if they alone could preserve them from any danger. "We are not enemies, we are appointed messengers of two sovereigns."

"The Rus might not see it that way," said Rakoczy quietly, and nudged his grey Nonius forward, approaching the Lancers with caution, for they were suspicious of him. "Whatever the trouble ahead, it is getting late and we would do better facing opposition in the morning. Is there a village near this place?"

"Well, there was a village once, but it was burned in the fighting, years ago," said Hrabia Zary, guarding every word he said where Rakoczy could hear him; no matter what the King had declared, Zary did not trust the elegant and cultured exile from the Carpathians.

"Then there are no buildings we could shelter in," said Rakoczy.

"No," said Zary, becoming nervous as he contemplated Rakoczy. "There are no buildings. It was burned. Razed to the ground."

"I see," Rakoczy responded, and signaled to his manservant. "Rothger, I think we had better attempt some scouting."

Rothger was composed and quiet, a sandy-haired middle-aged man with steady blue eyes, mounted on a raking Neapolitan bay; he rode as if a day in the saddle was a pleasant outing, and the prospect of more travel no more daunting than an invitation to visit nearby. He heard Rakoczy's scouting suggestion without flinching. "Very well, my master. But I would recommend a change of horses. These need rest."

"Of course," said Rakoczy. "There's no reason to ride the horses into the ground." He looked directly at Zary. "Would you like one of your men to come with us, Hrabia? It might be best."

Zary flinched but answered as directly as he could. "I will select one."

"I'll accompany you," volunteered Father Krabbe. "I can ride for a few hours more before my loins give out." He chuckled, and was pleased that a few of the soldiers laughed as well; as a priest he realized that soldiers did not readily trust him. Their laughter gave him confidence.

Rakoczy considered this offer, taking care to show the necessary respect. "If Father Pogner does not object, it is quite satisfactory to me."

Though Father Krabbe was disappointed, he did his best to conceal it. "I did not mean to act without the permission of Father Pogner."

"Since he is in charge of you Jesuits," said Hrabia Zary, "he must give his permission or I cannot authorize you to ride. Where you priests are concerned I must bow to his authority." There was a tinge of irritation in his acknowledgment, an indication of the strain that had developed between Father Pogner and him.

"I will submit my request at once," said Father Krabbe, and wheeled his horse to ride back where the rest of the priests waited.

"Father Pogner will forbid it," predicted Hrabia Zary with anticipatory satisfaction; he had his suspicions about Rakoczy but could give him the benefit of the doubt; he was hostile to Father Pogner. "He does not like the influence you have with Father Krabbe, Rakoczy."

"I am aware of that," said Rakoczy, a quick frown flickering over his features. "He believes Father Krabbe's gratitude for his recovery is inappropriate. Little as he may believe it, so do I, but . . ."

"Father Pogner dislikes you because he has no authority over you, except his authority as a priest. He thought he would be in command of everyone in this embassy and he is not pleased with the way Bathory arranged it. Which I suppose is why the King arranged it as he did." Zary lifted a fair brow and looked sideways at Rakoczy. "Are you surprised?"

"At what you have said, or that you have said it?" asked Rakoczy smoothly, and answered both questions. "I am relieved that you are aware of the disputes within this embassy, and I thank you for your observations." His dark eyes filled with ironic amusement. "Be aware that Father Pogner is likely to clash with you before we go much further."

"I will," said Zary, puzzled why Rakoczy should offer him such a warning.

Then Father Kovnovski rode up on the leggy black Furioso Rakoczy had loaned him that morning. "Father Pogner has ordered me to assist you in your scouting. He has determined that Father Krabbe is not sufficiently recovered to undertake so arduous a venture."

"Indeed," said Rakoczy, his face betraying no emotion whatever. "Then put cheese and bread and water in your bags, and come with us." Next he looked at Hrabia Zary. "Appoint the best scout in your Lancers. We have three hours to sundown and that means he may have to ride at night. If you make a temporary camp here, we will know where to find you." He turned away to Rothger. "We'll need lanthorns, three of them, with spare wicks. Flint-and-steel, one for each of us. And two pitch torches, for when we find a place we can stay. I will rely on you, as always."

"As well you might," said Rothger with amusement, his Hungarian spiced with an accent that none of the others recognized.

Zary did his best to reassert his authority. "You will have to depart quickly if we are not to make camp for the night here, with nothing temporary about it."

"Of course," said Rakoczy in his unflustered way, adding, "While I am gone I request you put three of your Lancers on guard with my things and my horses. The two wagons contain valuable articles, many that are not replaceable and that must remain untouched."

Although Zary himself was consumed with curiosity about the secret things Rakoczy was transporting, he wanted to ally himself with the other nobleman against Father Pogner. "Certainly," he said at once, determined to find out later what those two wagons contained.

There was a faint smile in Rakoczy's compelling eyes, as if he guessed Zary's desire. "That is very good of you, Hrabia."

Father Kovnovski heard this out with apprehension, for he was aware that there were tensions in the embassy that could not be ignored. He shifted in the saddle just as Rakoczy dismounted and handed his reins to Rothger. "I will get my food and return, Rakoczy." Like most of the others he was unsure what title to use with the black-clad alchemist and so generally avoided using any at all.

"Excellent," said Rakoczy, then told Rothger, "The five-year-old Furioso—the blue roan."

"This saddle?" his manservant asked.

"Yes, but change the pad. I fear after so many hours this one is matted." He watched his manservant lead the horse away.

There were forty horses and a dozen mules on the remount lines, and ten of the horses and four of the mules belonged to Rakoczy, much to the annoyance of the company of lancers. Hrabia Zary's objections to so many horses had been overcome when Rakoczy announced that he would provide care and feeding for all his animals, leaving Zary no reasonable grounds to protest.

Father Kovnovski glanced at Hrabia Zary, then spoke decisively. "We will need to have gold, as well. In this region we may have to purchase a place to sleep. We are at the limits of the Church."

Rakoczy looked up at him. "I have gold," he said calmly.

This was not what Father Kovnovski had planned, but he did his best to use the unexpected opportunity to his advantage. "It would be best if I carry the gold, as a priest."

"Your pardon, Father," said Rakoczy with a slight bow. "In these regions the priests are poor. If you carry gold, there are many who, should they discover it, would assume you are not a priest and would treat you badly for what they would regard as a pretense."

Father Kovnovski did his best to scoff. "It could be made clear to them. How could the people like it any better if soldiers or noblemen carried gold?"

"It would be what they expect," said Rakoczy tranquilly. "That we are foreigners is dangerous enough; if we do not attempt to accommodate their sense of the world, then we will not live to reach Moscovy, and the cause of Istvan Bathory will be compromised."

Hrabia Zary laughed angrily. "You have the right of it there, Rakoczy. We must not let this embassy fail."

"We will succeed," said Father Kovnovski, his teeth tight.

"Let us hope so," said Rakoczy, and bowed to the other two. "I am going to tend to my horse. I will return shortly." He strode off, leaving Father Kovnovski and Hrabia Zary to glare at each other.

More than an hour later the scouting party at last came upon a high-walled monastery with a few huts clustered around out-side. In the fire-tinted rays of the setting sun the stone appeared gilded and the huts seemed roofed in hammered brass. Seven women in enveloping, shapeless garments and elaborate head-dresses gathered around the fountain in the center of the tiny village, taking turns drawing water up from the well. They stopped this task and stared in terror as the four men rode out of the forest toward them, carrying lanthorns to light their way.

One of the women held a baby in her arms, and she screamed, prepared to run.

"Halt," ordered Rakoczy, holding up his hand to signal the other three. "And keep your hands away from any weapons." He let his horse stand, reins hanging on the neck. His hands rested on the high pommel of his saddle. When the other three had done the same thing, he called out, "We mean no harm, good women." He said it in Polish and then in Russian, hoping that they would understand one of those languages, for he had very little command of Livonian.

"Hah! That is what all soldiers say!" answered the oldest of the women in a version of Polish. She spat and crossed herself Orthodox style.

"There is only one soldier here," Rakoczy said to her. "There is a priest, my servant, and myself."

"There are soldiers," said the old woman with grim certainty. "You would not be here if you came without soldiers, not with ermine on your collar."

The woman with the baby bolted from the well toward one of the huts.

Rakoczy tried again. "We are part of an embassy from King Istvan of Poland to Czar Ivan of Moscovy. There are eight priests, a company of Lancers—"

"Soldiers," said the old woman with utter condemnation.

"Twenty-six soldiers," said Rakoczy at once. "Surely there are more than twenty-six of you in this village. How many monks are at the monastery."

"Forty-seven," said the old woman, calculating the odds. "Our men are working. They will be back soon. They have pitchforks and flails, and they will use them. The monks can fight, too."

Rakoczy shook his head. "We do not wish to fight. We need a place to sleep for tonight and tomorrow night. We are tired. And we are willing to pay for our beds and any food."

"Pay how?" asked the tallest woman; her voice was harsh and loud, as if she spent the day calling to the men in the fields.

"With gold," said Rakoczy, and drew a few coins from his wallet that hung on his belt. "Here." He flung the coins at them, watching them spatter into the damp earth near the fountain.

The old woman went to gather them up, taking care to bite each one before she whispered something to the tall woman, who listened and nodded before she called out, "Two coins for each man, for each night," she said, looking very nervously at what was to her a gigantic sum.

"Done," said Rakoczy before either the sergeant or Father Kovnovski could speak. "I will give you twenty coins now. My manservant will bring them to you." He signaled to Rothger to dismount and come to his side. "Watch," he told the women as he counted out the coins into Rothger's gloved hands. He made sure they were satisfied with his count, then called to the women, "You saw. There are twenty coins. My manservant will bring them to you." He motioned to Rothger to walk forward as he took charge of his horse.

"Keep your weapons sheathed," ordered the old woman as Rothger approached.

"I will," he said as he came up to them and held out the coins. "Count them for yourselves."

As the women took the coins, Rakoczy went on, "We must lead the rest of the embassy to this place. And there are preparations to be made while we do this. There isn't much time to do what has to be done. My manservant will help you deal with the priests and soldiers who are coming, as will Father Kovnovski. The sergeant and I will return with the others."

Father Kovnovski glowered at Rakoczy. "It would be more fitting for me to inform Father Pogner of what we have found, so that he may decide if it is correct of us to remain here."

Rakoczy regarded him evenly. "Fitting or not, it is the only village we have found in our searching. If we want a roof over our heads tonight, it will be this place or none. I think it would be best if you remained. They are wary of soldiers, not priests."

"Are you certain?" Father Kovnovski demanded.

"Yes," said Rakoczy, his mouth grim. "Have you noticed? There are no children here, except that infant. That would mean soldiers have been here less than two years ago, and they stole or killed their children. So it is better to leave you and Rothger than a soldier; they would probably slaughter the sergeant. But you'd be wise to be careful. This village is tied to the monastery and the monastery is not Catholic, it's Orthodox. Look at the crucifix over the gate—three cross-pieces. You will have work to do."

"Orthodox," whispered Father Kovnovski, and crossed himself, noticing as he did that the women stared at him in shock for his Roman blessing.

"I think you had better speak to the Superior, or whoever is in charge of the place. Give him the particulars of our embassy, and make it convincing. We don't want to be met with rock-throwing monks, do we?" Rakoczy's bow in the saddle was practiced and ironic.

"And what if these women change their minds as soon as you ride away? What if they decide to keep the money and drive us out?" Father Kovnovski glanced at the women as if he expected them to come after him with cooking pots and kitchen knives.

"I think they want the rest of the money," said Rakoczy. "For that money, I assume they are willing to put up with us for a day or two."

This was not what Father Kovnovski wanted to hear, and he would have defied Rakoczy, but he realized that the sergeant was regarding him with contempt, doubtless thinking that because he was a priest it followed that he was also a coward. He did his best to recover his self-command. "I wish you both to keep in mind that I advise against this reckless action. It is ill-conceived and without proper dignity. But if it is what I must do to accomplish the mission entrusted to us, then I will comply with your orders."

"How very good of you," said Rakoczy.

Father Kovnovski decided it was best not to argue with Rakoczy. He tapped his horse—or rather the mount Rakoczy had loaned him—forward, and swung out of the saddle as he reached the well. He offered the women his blessing, and was shocked when one of them spat and turned her head away. "I am grateful," he said, speaking very slowly so that he would be understood.

Rothger pointed to the nearest of the huts. "Will one of you be good enough to tell me? Whose house is that?" He managed the dialect better than Father Kovnovski did, and he treated the peasants with respect. "Is it possible for me to speak with the woman of the house? So we can make the appropriate arrangements?"

The tall woman bobbed her head. "That is my husband's house, and his father's." She clutched four of the coins as if she expected them to vanish.

"How many men would you be able to make up beds for?" He managed to be cordial without being ingratiating, a skill that Father Kovnovski coveted because he could not achieve it. "And is there a stall or two where we might tie our horses and mules?"

The tall woman smiled, showing that half her teeth were gone although she was not over twenty-five. She liked to bargain, and she was now in her element.

"There is a fenced pasture. We could drive the sheep out and let you turn your horses out there for the night. But it might cost another gold coin, for the grass they eat." She said the last with less certainty than the rest, afraid that she might press too far.

"That's reasonable," said Rothger. "And perhaps we could purchase a sack or two of grain for our animals?"

The tall woman grinned at the word *purchase.* "We do not have much, but I think we can spare some, if the price is agreeable." She knew the other women were watching her closely, and she almost preened. "If we have to kill animals to feed your men, then we must charge for them, too, as if we were going to market." It was her boldest move and the other women held their breath.

"It is what we expect," said Rothger before Father Kovnovski could speak.

"That is robbery!" the priest exclaimed.

"Nonsense," said Rothger at once, directing his attention to Father Kovnovski as if he had authority to oppose him. "My master is willing to pay them for what they provide us. As it is not your money, why do you object?"

Father Kovnovski blustered, but could find no defense for his indignation, which served only to make it worse.

Rothger once again addressed the tall woman. "Would you be willing to be the bargainer for all the village? I do not want to deprive any of you of what is due you, but if I can deal with one instead of many, the arrangements will be made more quickly, and in a way that is fair for all because everyone will receive the same price."

Most of the women nodded, but the old woman shook her

head. "I know that Aniela is clever and good at sums. But what if I do not like the terms she accepts, what then?"

"Discuss the matter with her first, so that she will bargain to your satisfaction," said Rothger, his manner deferential.

"Well." The old woman glanced at the tall one. "I will listen and if I don't like what I hear, I'll speak up."

"That is reasonable," said Rothger, ignoring Father Kovnovski's whispered insistence that bargains with women were worthless.

By the time the Lancers and the priests came into the little village it was deep twilight. They rode out of the woods with lanthorns burning, as awesome and spectral as the Huntsmen of Saint Hubert. The villagers who saw them were struck by the vision, and a few of them made the sign against the Evil Eye.

The men had returned from the fields and now lined the one street, holding their pitchforks and shovels, their faces set as they sized up the embassy. Their women were nowhere to be seen.

"Not very promising," said Hrabia Zary to Rakoczy.

"They're worried for their women," said the alchemist softly. "And not without reason." He nodded toward the lean, habited figure in the tall, straight hat at the entrance to the monastery. "There is the one you will have to address. Unless I am mistaken, the village will do whatever the Superior tells them they must do. He is the final authority here."

"An Orthodox monk is hardly a monk at all," said Father Pogner.

"Do not say that if Czar Ivan can hear you," Rakoczy advised. "Not all the world is Jesuit."

Father Pogner did not deign to answer.

The Superior took a step forward and the embassy stopped at Hrabia Zary's signal. He approached them slowly, holding up his pectoral crucifix as if to banish devils. As he came near them he intoned prayers in a strong, deep voice that commanded the admiration of the villagers.

"God give you a good night, Superior, and keep you safe from the demons of the air," said Rakoczy in Polish as he dismounted.

"And to you, priests and soldiers," he replied with great dignity though his eyes shifted nervously.

Rakoczy glanced at the peasants lining the street. "I regret that we have been forced to make a stop here, for it imposes on your hospitality, but as my manservant and Father Kovnovski have told you, we are on urgent orders from the King of Poland. For several weeks we have been on the road and now we need to rest for a day, not only for ourselves but for our animals. The road to Moscovy is very long; we cannot get there if we are already exhausted. I hope that the sum of two gold coins for each man, each night, is sufficient for housing us?"

The superior coughed. "The women of the village have said they will accept that sum. If their husbands and fathers do not demand more, then it is satisfactory. But that speaks only for the village and its people, even though we rejoice for them in their good fortune. For the monks in my charge, there is no such payment. But the monastery is a poor one, and we are dependent on the charity of Christians to maintain it."

Rakoczy bowed, thinking he should have foreseen this. He put his hand to his wallet. "It would honor my family to provide a donation to you," he said, and thought of the six sacks of gold coins hidden in his wagons. "Would fifty gold coins be too small a token?"

The Superior stared, as if he did not correctly understand the figure. "That is . . . generous," he said. "A noble gift."

"In the name of my father," said Rakoczy with a fleeting smile. "Who lost his kingdom before his life."

"God will be merciful to him," said the Superior, and looked at the company of Jesuits with apprehension. "So many."

"There are eight of us," said Father Pogner, raising his voice as if that would compensate for the lack of understanding of the dialect.

"Eight Jesuits to treat with the Czar," said the Superior as if puzzling out a questionable passage of Scripture.

"It is the wish of the King of Poland," declared Father Pogner as he got off his mule. "On behalf of Istvan Bathory and Pope Gregory, we journey to Moscovy."

The Superior's eyes narrowed. "And Lancers."

Rakoczy broke into their talk before it became open confrontation. "We are all tired and hungry," he remarked, indicating the soldiers and the priests with a sweep of his arm. "If we might see where we can feed our mounts and tend to them before eating? And then establish our sentries for the night?" He paused and added, "I and my manservant will take the watch until the darkest hour." He did not add that neither he nor Rothger required much sleep and were, in fact, capable of staying up the entire night; such an admission would give rise to speculation that might become dangerous. "Let one of your monks and a Lancer keep watch with us until then."

The tension of the moment faded. The Superior nodded, his tall hat making the movement significant. Along the street the peasant men set their tools aside and lowered their heads apologetically to the Lancers and Rakoczy. They avoided the priests except to show them which of the houses would shelter them.

Rakoczy was gathering the lead reins of his remount horses when the old woman came bustling up to him. "I have told your manservant you and three others may sleep at my house. At my age no one will think it wrong for me to have you sleep in my house. After you have served as our guard." She shook her head, marveling. "That such a fine nobleman as you would guard our village."

He looked over his shoulder at her, thinking that at most she was fifty, which to him was nothing at all. "Thank you for such consideration."

She grinned. "They'll all be purple with jealousy, but I have the right by age, and everyone knows it. None of the others can claim you for their guest, not while I have my husband's house to live in and places for beds." Her faded blue eyes brightened. "I will be able to talk about you and your manservant for a year, and they will all have to listen."

At this Rakoczy chuckled once, enjoying her innocent, malefic delight. "I will do my poor best to provide you with interesting things to say."

"Oh, you don't have to do that if you'd rather not," she told him, walking beside him to show him where he could turn the horses out, her wrinkled face creased with mischief. "I will make up what you do not tell me, in any case."

Text of a letter from Ferenc Rakoczy, Hrabia Saint-Germain, to Istvan Bathory, King of Poland.

To my gracious Transylvanian countryman who reigns as King in Poland, my greetings from Mozhaysk.

The Lancers, with the exception of Hrabia Zary and four of his soldiers, were turned just east of Vyazma where a company of mounted bowmen in the Czar's army encountered us. They have taken over our escort, and our journey has been much more expeditious: no more searching for villages to sleep in, and no more need for night-long sentry duty. The bowmen tend to all that. They commandeer country houses on large estates and demand respect for us, in spite of our position as foreigners.

For the Rus are wary of foreigners. They do not show the hospitality and welcome you would expect in Hungary or Poland or Austria. Instead they take great care to avoid dealing directly with us, for fear that we will contaminate them. While they are generous with food and beds, they keep themselves separate from us. Hrabia Zary believes it is because we have not yet presented ourselves to the Czar and are therefore of uncertain position, but I know it runs deeper than that. These people do not trust any outsiders. They wash their hands and faces after speaking with any of us, to insure they have no taint of that-which-is-not-Rus. I have done what I may to respect their ways, but I know that what they do rankles the Jesuits.

We are told that we are within a week's journey of Moscovy, which I suspect is an accurate estimate, since there are signs that indicate we are approaching the capital: houses are finer here, and the owners of the estates dress with greater distinction than those we have seen thus far, and maintain their homes more splendidly. And the domes of the churches are gilded. These Rus have a great love of opulence and grandeur, some of it undoubtedly learned from the Mongols who ruled them for so long.

Spring has come to the land, and there are orchards still blooming everywhere. Yesterday we passed through a forest of apple trees, and this morning I saw out my window mountains of berry vines, their blossoms just fading. There were men laboring in the field and the farmyard, and women working at tending livestock; all animals are under the women's charge here.

The bowmen say that the peasant laborers follow the planting and the crops throughout the year, gathering together in makeshift villages through the winter. Our host here is one of the new nobility—oprichniks; the old nobility are boyars—and he favors the reforms that would bind the peasants to a region or estate. The captain of the bowmen claims that far too many of them die of cold and starvation in the winter and that only when landowners are ordered to care for them year-round will they thrive. They could also be given better religious instruction, which this captain thinks is long overdue, for he claims that most of them still offer sacrifices to the earth and the storms by killing their children at midwinter, which is to him a sin more than a crime. Without attaching the peasants to the land, terrible abuses will continue, such as abandoning peasants to die during famines or droughts, and refusing them protection in war. According to what this man has said, Czar Ivan was once in favor of this reform but no one can now be certain if this is still the case. The very careful way he speaks of the Czar, and the things he does not say at all, make me believe that the reports of his state of mind are not as exaggerated as was first supposed.

I will entrust this to the Hrabia Lancer Captain Zary appoints as his messenger and will use those Lancers as long as they remain available. When they are gone, I will do all that I can to find another means to send these reports without recourse to the Jesuits.

In all duty, and by my own hand,
Ferenc Rakoczy, Hrabia Saint-Germain
28 May 1583, on the road to Moscovy (his seal, the eclipse)

5

At dawn the brazen song of the Kremlin bells drowned out the keening of the Czar. From all over the city came answering peals until the air shook with ringing. As the bright June sun touched the many clusters of golden onion domes of Moscovy's churches and cathedrals, the dark city blossomed in splendor.

In his chapel, Grand Prince Ivan IV, Czar of all the Russias, lay back against the closed door, blocking out the rest of the world, one large hand tangled in his white beard. Above him the martyr-brother Saints Boris and Gleb awaited their assassinations passively. He put his other hand to his eyes to shut out the sunlight that had just touched the high east window of the chapel. He whispered to himself, "No sunlight, no sunlight," repeating it with the same fervor of his earlier prayers.

His personal servant, an aged eunuch with a squint in his right eye and a beautiful voice sweet as a child's, rapped on the closed door, waiting until the bells quieted before calling out, "O Czar, listen to your slave. I bring you the reminder you wanted, in duty and love. You charged me to summon you at the proper time. There are foreigners who have come to your court. You have said that you will receive them today."

"Foreigners came last week," said Ivan after he thought about what Yaroslav said. "I have seen them."

"Those were the English, Little Father," said Yaroslav, fear closing its grip on him. "They are from the London Company of Merchant Adventurers, sent to join Sir Jerome Horsey, who is the servant of your friend Elizabeth of England. You have shown them great honor already. These other foreigners are from Istvan Bathory in Poland. They arrived two nights ago."

"Poland!" Ivan burst out, for once ignoring the hated light and opening his large blue-green eyes in outrage. "What does he dare to send me?"

Now Yaroslav was so frightened he found it difficult to speak. "Eight priests and an alchemist from Transylvania. They have arrived with a few Lancers—five of them, four soldiers, and a noble captain—and the alchemist has a manservant. That is their entire company." He knew from long experience that Ivan demanded absolute correctness in a report; if only he had bothered to learn the ranks of the Lancers.

"Lancers," muttered Ivan, dragging himself to his feet and brushing off his food-spotted gold-brocaded kaftan. "Istvan Bathory sends me Lancers."

"No, no," protested Yaroslav. "He sends you priests, Little Father, priests: eight Jesuits, and an alchemist with a manservant. There is no army, Czar, there is only a very small escort. Five Lancers, Little Father, fewer than the priests."

"Istvan Bathory has attacked me," said Ivan, but with some confusion. "He has attacked me."

"In another time, he has. But he is not attacking you now," said Yaroslav desperately. He wished Ivan would open the door and let him in, so that he could ascertain what was necessary to do to bring Ivan to a point he could appear in public without creating more rumors. With only the sound of Ivan's voice, Yaroslav feared he would fail in assessing the Czar's condition this morning.

"You say there are priests," said Ivan, sounding more attentive now. "Jesuits."

"Eight of them," Yaroslav reminded him. "They are to be recognized today. And you have your duties. The council expects to see you, and there are peasants gathered even now beneath the Petitioners' Window of the Gold Room. All of them seek your wisdom. Let me in, Little Father. You have been at your prayers all night. You may want my assistance."

"Yes, I prayed I prayed I prayed I prayed all night, but God would not hear me; I am still alive. And my son accuses me. He stands before me. He accuses me!" The last was a shout. He leaned against the wall, then released the bar holding the door closed. "Very well," he said in a more ordinary tone as the door swung open. "Tell me more of these foreigners."

Yaroslav had served Ivan long enough to permit no expression to cross his face when he caught sight of the Czar, but this time it was more of an effort than it had been before. He bowed low before Ivan and then hurried toward him. "Little Father, how much you have prayed."

"I prostrated myself. I! I flung myself at the feet of God. I begged with the abject humility of Judas at the Cross. But God has refused to take away the vision. I saw Ivan lying on the altar, blood from his wounds, his voice naming my sin—" He raised one arm to block out the sight again. "It is futile. It is futile."

Yaroslav moved nearer. "Little Father," he said as if he were soothing an angry wolfhound, "come with me. There are matters you must attend to. Many await you. You should eat something, and bathe before receiving the foreigners. The court is ordered to assemble after mid-day Mass."

"Why then?" demanded Ivan with sudden acuity. His eyes sharpened and some of the old cleverness returned to his ravaged features.

"Because it was the hour you set," said Yaroslav. "You declared that this would be the time you would be willing to see these foreigners. That was three days ago, Little Father, before they were given permission to enter the city. You had your bowmen keep them outside Moscovy's gates until you knew what was best to do. Everyone has been at pains to obey your summons."

"Yes," said Ivan in a low voice. "Of course. Everyone."

"Little Father." Yaroslav recognized Ivan's returning despair and did what he could to distract the Czar. "It is seen as a good sign that Istvan should show such honor to you, Little Father. The patriarch has already declared that he has seen God's hand in this work, and it brings new times to Russia."

"New times." Ivan held out his hand, staring at his hideously bruised knuckles. "How can there be new times while my son's blood is on me?"

"Perhaps because merciful God will cleanse it away," said Yaroslav as he tried without touching Ivan to get him to move out of the chapel.

Reluctantly Ivan moved through the door, then paused before the tremendous ikons that flanked the chapel entrance; two gigantic golden angels stood guard, one holding a stylus, one holding a spear. Below the angels were a number of smaller ikons of the Prophets, each lavished with gold leaf.

"This is the Third Rome," Ivan said emphatically as he crossed himself three times. "This is where Christ will reign when He returns."

Wisely Yaroslav crossed himself. "The Mass will be at the Cathedral of the Dormition." More properly it ought to be held at the Cathedral of Saint Mikhail, but since killing his son Ivan had refused to set foot in the building where all the rulers of Russia were to be buried, claiming he would go there soon enough.

"A pleasant place, the Dormition," murmured Ivan as he permitted Yaroslav to lead him away through the corridors of the Terem Palace to his private quarters.

By the time Czar Ivan emerged again, he was dressed in one of his grandest kaftans, jewel-encrusted and gold-embroidered so that it glistened, appropriate to the occasion of welcoming the Polish embassy. His beard and hair were washed and combed and he wore the fur-bordered crown of his father. At first glance, his appearance was excellent; only those who had watched him through the last year would recognize the telltale shine in his eyes and the tremor in his hands.

Inside the entrance of the Terem Palace, Yaroslav handed Ivan off to the care of his son's wife's brother, the energetic and canny Boris Feodorovich Godunov, with the whispered warning, "He was up all night, in the chapel."

"I see," said Boris with immediate understanding, and at once directed his attention to Ivan, bowing deeply and offering a gesture of submission. "Good morning, Little Father. May our gracious God send His blessings to you this day." He stopped to cross himself before the ikons at the door, then signaled the guards to open the door.

Ivan stood as if transfixed by the ikons. "They are always watching. No matter what we do, they are always watching."

"To remind us that God is always watching," said Boris smoothly. "Come, Little Father. The Patriarch will not begin the Mass without your presence."

"No, he would not do that," said Ivan, and straightened himself as he regarded the soldiers on either side of the door. "These men are the might of Rus. There are no other men as strong as they are."

"True enough, Little Father," said Boris, managing not to sound as if he were placating the unpredictable old man. "They rode with you from Kazan to Pskov. They showed their devotion and loyalty in a thousand ways each day."

"Yes," whispered Ivan. "They were loyal."

Not far away a group of peasants prostrated themselves at the sight of the Czar; they remained on their faces until Ivan was at the entrance to the Cathedral of the Dormition, his escort trailing him with arms at the ready.

The inside of the cathedral was crowded and smoky. Censers filled the air with incense, and scores of priests made their way around the cathedral blessing the hundreds of ikons in anticipation of the Mass.

Ivan was guided to his place, and the Patriarch intoned the opening words of the Mass, to be echoed by the choir. As the procession to the ikonostasis began, the congregation parted to give the clergy room to pass, for there were no benches or other seats in the cathedral; Russians stood in the presence of God. The Chrysostom liturgy was long, ending almost two hours after it had begun. In the whole service Ivan lost his composure only once; during the Veneration of the Virgin he wept wretchedly.

Boris Godunov was at Ivan's shoulder before the last *omeen* had died away, saying respectfully, "The foreigners have been brought, Little Father, and they are waiting for you in the reception hall of the Granovitaya. They have been there some little time. Let us announce your coming to them."

"The foreigners should wait while we give thanks to God," said Ivan lucidly enough. "It would be more fitting if they were to worship with us."

"The Jesuits are not allowed to do that," Boris reminded him. "It would be against their religious teaching."

Ivan glared at him, his face darkening. "Then their religion is at fault. We would allow anyone to come into our churches and sing the praises of God. If they are not allowed to do this, then their religion is not true religion."

"Very possibly, Little Father," said Boris quickly to forestall another outburst of temper. "But let them find their own way to God. You have said yourself that it is the only way any man can worship."

"Ah." Ivan considered this and nodded. They were approaching the Granovitaya now, its splendid Renaissance Italian front still catching the eye. The Palace of Facets had been the creation of Marco Ruffo and Antonio Solario not quite a century before and was still reckoned to be one of the most impressive buildings within the Kremlin walls.

"These foreigners are not sent in war but in peace," Boris went on, watching Ivan covertly but very closely. "They are men of the Church and they do not want our soldiers to fall in battle."

"Still, they have fallen many times, all because those Jesuits were eager to bring their false Christianity to Russia." Ivan reached up and squared the crown on his head. "I will listen to what they have to say, and I will do what I decide is best with them."

"Your wisdom is always excellent," said Boris as they entered the Palace of Facets. "And we will all be glad to learn of you." He bowed deeply again; being a noble he did not have to prostrate himself completely.

Another escort of soldiers framed Czar Ivan at the entrance to the cavernous reception hall while the Court of nobles in their golden kaftans took their places in their appointed seats.

"In which room are they being kept?" asked Ivan of the nearest guard.

"The Red Chamber," said the nearest guard.

"A great honor," muttered Ivan, who often denied his own nobility access to this waiting room because it was too beautiful for most visitors to see.

"To show the Pope of Rome there is no insult given," said the guard. "It was the suggestion of Vasilli and Anastasi Shuisky."

"Shuisky!" said Ivan with a mixture of contempt and approval. "Those cousins show the foreigners too much respect."

"The Patriarch himself said it would be wise," one of the other guards pointed out very softly. "Because the Pope of Rome is a Christian Prince."

"Ah." This was reasoning Ivan was more willing to accept. He nodded, fingering his beard, and watched carefully as his nobles took their places in the huge hall. The elaborate pattern of the floor held his attention briefly, and then he watched his nobles more closely. "Where is the basin and cloth?"

"The servants will bring them," said the nearest guard. "They wanted to be certain that Czareivich Feodor Ivanovich was in his place before they brought the cloth and basin."

Ivan looked away, his nostrils pinched as if he had suddenly smelled fresh urine. "I hadn't thought . . . of course." Only the year before Feodor had disgraced his father by playing with the water in the basin at another such reception of foreigners. At the time everyone had done their best to make light of the dreadful gaffe, as if Feodor were performing an entertainment like the skomorokhi who sang and put on puppet shows on market day. But such a lapse could not be tolerated again.

"Once the Czareivich is in his place, we will be ready." The guard's voice came from somewhere behind Ivan but he felt as if it came from overhead, from the elaborate patterns of the ceiling and perhaps from God's sky above.

There was a sudden flurry of activity in the reception hall signaling the arrival of the gentle, foolish Feodor; Anastasi Sergeivich Shuisky, resplendent in a red-and-gold kaftan and tall fur hat, slipped into the Red Chamber, bowing respectfully to the Polish embassy. "We are almost ready for you now," he said in Greek, motioning them forward.

Father Pogner, who understood Greek but spoke it badly, said to Ferenc Rakoczy, "Tell him that we are ready as well."

Rakoczy spoke in Russian, and added after relaying Father

Pogner's message, "Tell us, what are we to do? No one has said."
He was dressed in a sable mente—which in the warm June
weather was uncomfortably hot—over a dolman of cloth-of-
silver embroidered in black and red. From a silver collar de-
pended a pectoral of raised, displayed silver wings, surrounding
a circular, glowing dark gemstone.

Anastasi was relieved not to have to continue in Greek. "You
are not to touch the Czar. You are to approach him only when
you are told to; otherwise you must stay at a distance. After he
has washed his hands, you must leave the palace. You need not
prostrate yourself when you are called before him, but you must
bow to him as you would bow to your King Istvan. Is that
understood?"

"I believe so," said Rakoczy. "What else?"

"So long as one of you understands Russian, I think we will
manage well enough. The Little Father is versed in many languages, but he is pleased when foreigners speak the language of
Rus." Anastasi looked around the room. "My cousin Vasilli will
do what is necessary to present you."

"Not you?" Rakoczy asked in some surprise after he had translated the bulk of this for Father Pogner.

Beside him, Father Krabbe looked apprehensive, and
smoothed the front of his habit for the dozenth time, fingering
his pectoral crucifix as he did.

"I am not of sufficient rank, I fear," said Anastasi with an angry
smile. "No matter which noble family presents foreigners, they
must always be presented by the family member of the highest
and oldest rank. That is our custom." He folded his arms. "My
cousin is taller than I am, thinner, and not as fair, but otherwise
we are much the same in appearance." He looked at Rakoczy. "I
presented him to you earlier."

"Yes. I will know him again," said Rakoczy, not bothering to
glance at Father Pogner. "Where do we go once the presentation
has been made?"

"You will return here and wait for me. I will then take you
where the Little Father decides you would best present yourselves to the Court. Remember, do not touch anyone unless they
offer their hands." He bowed slightly, turned abruptly and returned to the reception hall.

As soon as Anastasi was gone, Father Pogner hurried forward, his face set with outrage. "Who are they to tell us how we are to behave?"

"They are the people we will have to treat with," said Rakoczy gently. "And if that means we pluck chickens for them, then we will do it." He looked at the other seven priests. "You are here for Poland first, good Fathers. It is safer."

Only Father Kovnovski looked truly enthusiastic about their coming presentation; Fathers Tymon and Felikeno were apprehensive to the point of fear. Father Krabbe was more nervous than frightened. Fathers Brodski, Lomza, and Kornel were trying to be remote, each keeping silent though none of them made a pretense of prayer. They were in their habits, their sashes laced with gold, their crucifixes large, golden, and jeweled. Against the opulence of the Russian court they would appear paltry.

Father Pogner was prepared to argue with Rakoczy, but his opportunity was lost as two tall guards carrying Tartar battle-axes came into the Red Chamber and bowed to them, indicating the door leading to the reception hall. There was no sign of Anastasi Shuisky's taller, leaner cousin Vasilli.

The Court was intended to impress from the huge reception room to the smallest detail of Court clothing: every noble wore a kaftan worked in gold with wide jeweled collars. Their tall fur hats were trimmed with uncut gems and pearls. Several hundred men sat around the room, all of them looking at the straight-backed, fierce old man who occupied the center of the rear of the hall, who was more magnificent than any of the rest. In silence the small Polish party approached the tall, white-haired figure in the fur-trimmed crown.

Without Vasilli Shuisky to tell them, Rakoczy had to guess how close the Polish embassy could come to Czar Ivan without causing offense. As they drew within two arm's lengths of him, Rakoczy stopped and went down on his knee, removing his black velvet hat as he did. "Most exalted Prince Ivan, Czar of all the Russians," he began in a voice that carried throughout the hall before all the priests had dropped to their knees as well. "We come in the name of Istvan Bathory of Poland, who greets you in the brotherhood of Princes and prays that it will be possible for you and he to set aside your former arguments in order to preserve the Christian world from the Ottomites."

Ivan cocked his head to the side, looking narrowly at Rakoczy. "You are no Pole," he said at last.

"No, I am not. I come from Transylvania, of ancient blood, as does King Istvan. Until my lands were conquered I held the title of Prince. Now I am a Count, and an exile. I am here at King Istvan's personal behest." Rakoczy said it clearly, and saw Ivan's expression vacillate between fury and sorrow. What about his answer had caused the Czar such distress, he wondered. And how would he avoid such errors again.

"The priests are Polish," Ivan accused them.

Father Pogner answered in Polish, which Rakoczy translated. "We are from the Church as much as King Istvan. Father Krabbe is Bohemian. Father Kornel is Prussian. I am Galician. Each of us owes worldly fealty to King Istvan as we owe the faith of our souls to the Church."

"That was a fair translation," said Ivan when Rakoczy was finished. "It pleases me that you did not change what the priest has said. Those who change the words of priests are damned." He looked around, his eyes lingering on his moon-faced son Feodor before sweeping over the Court.

A dark-eyed, handsome courtier whose features had an angular, Asiatic cast, a man of some privilege from his demeanor, approached Ivan and whispered something to him. Rakoczy watched the courtier with interest, noticing how skillfully he dealt with the unpredictable Czar.

"Godunov is right," announced Ivan when his daughter-in-law's brother moved away. "They are deserving. It is an honorable greeting they bring. The ritual must be done or there will be disgrace for the Court." He sighed deeply. "And I have so much to answer for." Reluctantly he stepped forward and placed Rakoczy's hands between his own. "God protect you in Holy Russia."

Rakoczy ducked his head and murmured "Amen" before looking up at Czar Ivan. He said nothing, but he stared directly into Ivan's large, troubled eyes, where madness flickered.

Ivan repeated this gesture and phrase with each of the priests, and then stepped back with apparent relief. He clapped his hands and two guards carried a large basin of water to him, holding it while he washed his hands. Another servant brought him a towel. When he had finished drying, he gave the towel back to the servants and held his clean hands up for the Court to see.

Czareivich Feodor whooped once, but otherwise the Court was silent.

Then Ivan did something unexpected, and the men gathered in the reception hall of the Granovitaya watched in appalled fascination as the Czar turned back and approached Rakoczy again, moving as if propelled by forces beyond resistance, reaching out to touch the silver-winged pectoral he wore.

"Czar?" Rakoczy asked, aware that this was a break with custom and ritual.

Ivan touched the cabochon stone that served as the heart of the eclipse. He stared as his fingertips caressed the polished gem; his middle and first finger lingered on the stone. There was a passion in his eyes now, an emotion beyond mere covetousness or greed. At last he looked at Rakoczy. "I do not recognize this jewel," he said very quietly.

Rakoczy answered in a low voice. "It is a sapphire, Great Czar."

"A sapphire?" Ivan took a step back, pulling his hand away as if the gem could burn him. "But it is black, glowing black."

"There are black sapphires, Great Czar," said Rakoczy, and gambled, adding, "Would you like one?"

Ivan reached out for Rakoczy's pectoral, and was shocked when he drew back. "Is there a price?"

"Not on this," said Rakoczy. "It is very old, and of my . . . kin. I could not part with it without disgrace." He had made it as a gift for Ranegonde, nearly seven hundred years ago. He paused in the hope that Ivan would continue to listen. "But I have others, and you may choose the one that pleases you the most, if that would be satisfactory."

"How many do you have?" demanded Ivan, his face working with fierce emotions.

"Eleven, as I recall. Not all are as dark as this; they range from darkest blue to black." He paused. "I have emeralds and amethysts and rubies as well. And black pearls." This last was a dangerous admission, for many believed that black pearls were malign and predicted mourning.

"I will see them," Ivan declared, looking around toward Boris Godunov. "Arrange it. I will see this prince in my study. And you." He rounded on the Jesuits, one hand extended, pointing. "You will assist the prince. He is the deputy of your king. You will follow his orders as if they were the orders of your King Istvan." He fell silent, staring at Rakoczy's pectoral as if caught in a trance. "Eleven dark sapphires. And emeralds. And amethysts. You will bring them all. Including the black pearls."

There was a slight, shocked sound from the Court but no one dared to question Ivan's orders. The whispers would begin later, when the Czar could not hear them.

Ivan clapped his hands to signal that this audience and reception had ended, and before the nobles could rise and bow to him, he strode down the length of the reception hall, his step as firm and energetic as it had been twenty years ago. His escort of soldiers hurried to keep up with him.

The susurrus of distressed whispers began as soon as Ivan was out of the Palace of Facets; in their positions at the front of the hall, Rakoczy and the Jesuits were left scrupulously alone.

And then Boris Godunov came up to Rakoczy, bowing slightly. "They are upset because the Little Father did not wash his hands after he touched your sapphire," he explained, and motioned to the Jesuits to rise. "Two years ago he would not have forgotten."

Rakoczy got to his feet and studied Boris' clever face. "I take it that some of the nobility will consider it a bad omen?"

Boris watched the Court, the gold-clad men beginning to mill, most of them refusing to look at the Polish embassy. He chose his words carefully. "Between that and the black pearls, I'm afraid so."

Text of a letter from Father Milan Krabbe to Archbishop Antonin Kutnel, found by servants and stolen.

In the Name of the Trinity, my greetings to you, Excellency, and my prayers and blessings in all your endeavors.

It is now two months since the embassy has arrived in Moscovy, and we continue to be shunned as if we brought plague with us. The nobility here are deeply superstitious, and they are convinced that we have tainted the Czar with our presence, and so avoid us. Only the English embassy are willing to talk with us for more than a few minutes. The clergy are not averse to discussing passages of Scripture, but they will not consider that any of their writings are incorrect, and take every opportunity to question our Latin rites. We are constantly being told that we will shortly be given better reception by the nobility, but thus far it has not proved to be the case. There is one note of encouragement: Rakoczy of Saint-Germain has been given some welcome, and he is fast becoming the confidant of Czar Ivan. Father Pogner has insisted that Rakoczy must convince Ivan to extend his welcome to all of us, but thus far he has had no success.

The people here have learned to make houses that can be assembled from prepared lumber in less than a week. A man need only say the number of rooms desired and state the sizes they are to be and the lengths of lumber are sent to the building site. I am told there are many fires in this cold, wooden city, and the houses of this design are necessary if the people of the city are not to freeze. The houses are heated with angular, enameled stoves that provide much heat but occasionally lead to fires, hence the need for the prepared-to-assemble houses in the first place.

Rakoczy already has a house in the district near the goldsmiths, not far from the Kremlin, and he has set about decorating it in the Russian style, earning him the favor of such nobles as the Shuisky cousins and Boris Godunov, who is reckoned to be the man who will serve as regent for Feodor, should he ever become Czar; Godunov is not the favorite of the nobles here, for all the Czar approves him. I am informed that his mother is Tartar and that is sufficient for many of the high-born to suspect him of treachery. I have told Rakoczy of this, but he has said that it has no bearing on our mission, for Godunov is the Czar's right hand and therefore our most worthwhile ally.

You had said that among the Orthodox there are no Orders as we have them within the Church. They have but one Rule of Brotherhood for monks, one rule for priests and higher authorities. A few have said they believe that Orders are divisive and are not in the spirit of the teaching of Christ. While I could see some reason in such a position, little as I agree with it, I was distressed to learn that few priests and fewer monks can read, or are encouraged to learn. They tell the Gospels as they tell the stories of their Prince Igor and the long-dead princes of Kiev. When I questioned the wisdom of this, I was informed that reading would inevitably lead to controversy, and for that reason it was discouraged in favor of memorizing Scripture and repeating it in faithful humility. Many priests here believe that if we Catholics did not read, we Jesuits would not exist. They fault us for counting the years from the birth of Christ: the Orthodox Church reckons their calendar from the beginning of the world, which they believe to have been more than seven thousand years ago. They claim that to do otherwise is to place Christ above God the Father in importance, which is heresy. When I asked for a clarification, they promised to have Father Grigori explain it to me, although this has not occurred yet.

To such an end I must report that I have found few books to send you but a handful in Greek. I have been informed that the writings of Russians are kept for Rus and not for those outside her borders. It is as if they fear their thoughts would wither and die transported from their native soil. When I mentioned this to Rakoczy, hoping that he would be able to assist me, he remarked that ideas were not the only things that withered without their native soil. I am still not certain that he spoke in earnest, or in jest.

All that you have heard of the central market of Moscovy held in the square immediately outside the main gates of the Kremlin pales when the thing itself is seen. There is abundance from the fields that I have never seen in Bohemia or Poland—there are berries and melons in quantity here that are wholly unknown to me, but which these Moscovites treasure. There is a profusion of apples and other fruits brought long distances. Grain of many kinds is offered at the market, and blooming flowers. They even bring fish, alive, in great wagons that drip salt water from the Black Sea to Moscovy. There are linens and silks for sale, although the finest fabrics are not displayed here; only the nobility are permitted to purchase them. Aside from knives and axes, few weapons are sold, for such enterprise is carefully supervised by the army. There is wood everywhere, from the lumber for the houses I have mentioned to carved chairs and cabinets to scraps to burn for heat. And outside the eastern gates of the city the market for livestock flourishes. They say that on a busy market day there will be as many as five thousand horses sold.

We have as yet met very few noble Russian women. They

are kept secluded for the most part, although there are occasions when they appear before the Court to mark events of special importance. Peasant women have few restrictions upon them and they may be encountered in the marketplace and working beside their husbands in shops. But boyarinas and other well-born ladies live much the way the women of the hareem do, in their private quarters, under strict supervision. There are constant rumors of rivalries and crimes, but I have not heard a direct accusation made against anyone. The women remain a mystery. Yet on those occasions when they are present at Court, it is considered essential by every noble household that one of their women attend, for to do otherwise, the family so unrepresented would give offense to the Czar. Therefore most noblemen living in Moscovy have at least two or three of his female relatives in residence with him against such occasions. We have been told that most of these noblewomen excel in needlework.

The English have shown us some hospitality and we have been happy to accept their invitations, all of being strangers in this country. They are a disrespectful lot, toasting their Queen's Grace with a freedom that would lose a Pole his head. Still, I find I am in accord with Rakoczy in this instance and if I am not permitted to learn from one set of foreigners, I will avail myself of the opportunity to learn from another. It may be that when this embassy is recalled, we will return with more knowledge of the English than the Rus.

It has been very warm, and the air is close. Often there are thunderstorms at night, and we have heard that when these occur the Czar cries aloud to Heaven for redemption. There have been two minor fires caused by lightning, but they were quickly put out and already new houses are rising on the ashes of the burned ones. The worst of this weather is the vermin— there is nothing to stop the bites, the constant itching, and the unwholesome feeling that comes with the biting. There may be hermits who regard lice as seals of purity and mortification of the flesh, but I cannot believe that God intended His servants to be the supper for such vileness. I have decided to accept Rakoczy's offer of a tonic to use against the lice. He rid me of putrescence in my lungs—perhaps he will banish the lice as well.

In all duty and with the assurance of my devotion to you and to the One True Catholic Church and Our Savior Jesus Christ. By my own hand in acquiescence to your instructions.

Milan Krabbe, Society of Jesus
August 9, 1583, at Moscovy in the Goldsmiths' Quarter

6

Rothger stood at the head of the stairs blocking the door to Rakoczy's alchemical study; his austere features, catching the light of oil-lamp flame, were creased with concern. Around him the large house was silent but for the distant sigh of the wind and the sound of night-hunting birds.

As he started up the flight, Rakoczy glanced at his manservant and shook his head, saying with a sardonic smile, "Were you worried, old friend?"

Rothger's silence was answer enough.

"You needn't be concerned," said Rakoczy as he climbed slowly upward, his action revealing that his black woolen kontush was torn at the sleeve and a second rent ran from his hip-slung belt to the hem, a handsbreadth below his knees.

"It is near dawn," said Rothger. He did not mention the state of Rakoczy's clothes.

"Yes. Yes, I know," said Rakoczy softly, and sank down on the stairs about half-way to the top. "And I said I would return before Vigil prayers, which are long past." He patted the Dutch watch hidden in his torn sleeve as he pulled off his fur hat and raked his small hand through the short, dark waves before rubbing the back of his neck. Gradually he straightened up. "Don't upbraid me; I've done enough of that for both of us." The light of the lamp shone on the clean line of his left brow and cheek, the line of his strong, angled nose, the left side of his upper lip; otherwise his face was in shadow.

Rothger came down a few steps. "I was troubled."

Rakoczy nodded. "So was I." He braced his elbows on the stair above him and leaned back, facing down into the darkness. The tread pressed against his waist. "It was . . . more difficult tonight."

"Worse than before." It was not a question; both men knew how dangerous their position was.

"Yes. She very nearly woke while I was with her." He cracked a single, sad laugh. "I should have been more alert. But her dream was sweet, and she gave herself to her joy. She was magnificent and I was as much filled with her passion as I can be when they sleep. Afterward I thought . . . I thought she was ready to release me to deeper sleep. I was not aware of her need for companionship as well as passion. As I started to leave she clung to me, not for gratification but loneliness." He shook his head again, more slowly; he thought fleetingly of Estasia in the days before she lost herself in religion. There had been an echo of her longing in Ludmilla tonight. "Perhaps I ought to have anticipated it, planned, but—" He shrugged.

"Were you recognized? Did she know who you are?" asked Rothger, keeping his voice emotionless with effort.

"How could she? She has only seen me in dreams, and then her vision of me was masked by her desire for another. If she supposes—" He broke off and when he went on he sounded weary. "Even if she has heard of me, she would never assume that I have heard of her. How could I? She is a Russian boyarina, living a sequestered life and not part of the outer world." He stared down into the dense shadows of the lower floor. "It would have ruined her to be found with me. Worse than ruined—they'd kill her for it."

"And you," Rothger pointed out.

"At least they might have some reason to kill me," Rakoczy said quietly. "By their lights I have done a thing deserving death. But she? She has only had a dream. To die for that . . ." He looked away before going on. "I had to induce sleep in her again, and wait until she was lost in another dream before I could leave without risk."

"You mean without risk of discovery by her," said Rothger.

"Um." He made a fatalistic gesture.

After a brief silence, Rothger said, "Can't you make some arrangement within this household?"

"Foreigners are not supposed to keep concubines," said Ra-koczy. "It smacks too much of the Golden Horde. And I am hardly in a position to arrange a marriage. Even if there were a woman in this household for my . . . benefit there is the danger she might tell her confessor something that would prove to be embarrassing."

"Would that be any riskier than what you are doing now?" asked Rothger, letting the question hang between them.

"You mean that the accusations of a woman might be ignored? Why would I want such a woman? Or she me." Rakoczy got slowly to his feet, swinging his shoulders as if to work stiffness out of them. "Still, you might be right." He looked down at the ruin of his kontush. "Do you think this can be repaired?"

"I'll make sure the servants don't see it. Set it aside and I'll look at it in the morning; if there's any doubt, you decide," said Rothger, accepting the lack of answer he had received. He, too, rose. "Do you want to bathe, or sleep?"

"Bathe," Rakoczy said at once. "I can feel mud drying on me." He went a few steps upward, then said, "I wonder why it is that I find this earth so offensive yet my native earth is anodyne to me." He expected no answer and was surprised when Rothger spoke.

"You seek sustenance and nourishment, as do all living things." He faltered. "You need touching and more than touching. You are bound to life."

Rakoczy wore a wry smile now. "I deserve to hear my own words given back to me. Very well. I accept them. I won't foist any more of my maundering on you, not tonight, in any case." He tossed his fur hat to Rothger. "We can save this, at least."

Rothger caught the hat. "Your clothes: what happened?" He indicated the tears in the kontush.

"Oh, nothing worrisome." His smile faded. "One of the carvings on the lintel snagged me as I was leaving. The roof was steep and the purchase poor; I mistimed my jump."

"Both tears from the lintel? The hem *and* the sleeve?" asked Rothger in reserved disbelief. "The cut on the sleeve is cleaner."

"Suggesting a blade, is that it?" Rakoczy met his manservant's steady blue eyes with his dark ones. "There are robbers in every city in the world. One had the folly to come after me." He looked away. "They will find him in the river, if they bother to look for

him, and if he has not drifted beyond the city walls on the
current. He didn't drown; his back is broken." As he said this last,
his jaw tightened in distaste.

"He had a knife," said Rothger.

"An axe, actually." He turned toward the lamp and for the first
time Rothger saw a long gash on Rakoczy's right cheek.

"An axe," he repeated.

"One of those long-bladed ones, like a short pike." He
touched the edge of the cut where blood had caked. "It will
heal."

"And you are certain he was a robber?" Rothger asked as if the
question meant nothing more than a quibble about proper dress.

"What else would he be?" Rakoczy countered, not challenging
the question but not willing to accept the underlying reason
Rothger had asked. He turned his small hands palms up to show
that there was little he could do in any case.

Rothger said only, "I will see that the bathhouse is heated."

"Thank you," said Rakoczy, turning to regard Rothger, his
expression rueful. "On top of the rest, I have been churlish. And
you have been good enough not to tax me with it. Let me
apologize. For all I have said nothing, I have noticed." He was
almost at the top of the stairs, the injured half of his face lit by the
lamp, his wound black in the light.

With a slight bow, Rothger went down the stairs toward the
rear of the house where the bakery and bathhouse were located.

By the time the bathhouse was heated the sky overhead was
pale grey, the sun a brilliant smear in the massing clouds. The
household was already up, the two cooks busy in the cavernous
kitchen where the banked coals of the open hearths were prod-
ded to life before the ovens were fired. Another three servants
put plank tables up for the workmen employed to finish the
interior of the house; the carpenters were expected to arrive as
soon as first Mass was over.

Rakoczy knew that he was being watched, that all his activities
were monitored by his servants as efficiently as if they were all
paid spies; he remembered to bless the ikon of Archangel Gavril
before entering the bathhouse. Once inside he removed the
enveloping, hooded robe and stood naked in the cramped dress-
ing area. The wan morning light showed the wide, white swath
of scars from beneath his ribs down to the base of his pelvis; the

scars of his death-wounds were the last scars to mark his flesh; no injury since then had left any lasting talisman on him.

The bathhouse was one of the few places in the house where he had been able to put his native earth beneath the floor, and the solace he felt as he walked into the steamy bath room was more from the presence of his native earth than the caress of the heat. He lowered himself into the deep, square tub, sinking up to his waist before his feet touched the bottom planks. With a silent sigh, he settled into a corner of the tub and leaned back, letting the sitting wedge support him. It was not as large or as elegant as the baths he had had at his Roman villa, but it was better than he had hoped for in Moscovy. Gradually the ache eased from his compact body.

His bedchamber was small and austere as a monk's cell, his bed hard and narrow, little more than a thin mattress atop a trunk filled with his native earth. Rakoczy returned there in his hooded robe, leaving the damp impression of his small, high-arched feet on the stairs. Restored in the bath, he lay back in comfort on his bed with a single lined blanket for warmth. In a short while his dark eyes closed and his breathing slowed.

The third Mass of the day was finished when Rothger came to rouse Rakoczy, standing by his bed while the exiled Count returned from that dreamless depth that seemed almost a twin to death.

He woke quickly and completely, passing from one state to the next without so much as a yawn. "When is Godunov expected?" Rakoczy asked as he sat up. He had set his Dutch watch on a red lacquer chest of ancient design that stood just outside his bedchamber door.

"He is supposed to be here within the hour," said Rothger, watching Rakoczy closely. "You are better," he approved as he inspected Rakoczy's face. "The gash is little more than a scratch."

"All the easier to account for its disappearance," said Rakoczy as he rose. "I suppose the kontush will have to be turned into rags."

Rothger nodded, noticing how Rakoczy anticipated him. "I've done it already. The sleeves were sectioned for the carpenters and carvers, for rubbing the wood with beeswax. The back was cut in half and given to the priests at Saint Alexander's, to make into smocks for poor children." The kontush used a great deal of fabric in its pleats.

"Very good," said Rakoczy as he drew on the fine Italian camisa with the narrow ruff on a standing collar Rothger brought. He rubbed the cloth between his fingers before fastening the rosettes at the wrists, enjoying the superb softness the weavers had achieved. "How many of these do I have left?"

"Five," said Rothger, offering him the deep red woolen dolman and a wide silver belt to go over it. "I've brought the red leggings as well."

"Excellent." When he had finished buttoning the ten cabochon garnets into their loops, he fastened the belt around his waist, taking care to center the link with the eclipse emblem. He reached for the leggings next, and as he pulled them on, he watched Rothger with attention. "What is it?"

Rothger adjusted the mente he held, smoothing the black-velvet-and-silver fabric. "I was thinking about Lo-Yang. I remember how much had to be left behind because foreigners were suddenly suspect."

"And you think something of the sort can happen here," said Rakoczy, standing with his leggings in place. "If it is any consolation, I know how you feel."

"It isn't much consolation," said Rothger, not quite amused. "But I am relieved that you are aware of the dangers."

Rakoczy reached for the mente and eased it on. "And you question the decision to come here." He cocked his head toward his manservant. "Aside from curiosity about the place, where would you have preferred? Would it have been safer to remain in the Carpathians, waiting for the Ottomites to find us? For it is certain they would. It would have led to greater slaughter, and I've had more than my share of that." His dark eyes, usually enigmatic, shone with loathing at the thought. "I've had more war than I can stomach. Would it have been wiser to venture to Italy? The Pope might have a few questions to ask me if I returned there now. Or France? There's still a price on my head in Troyes and the Catholics are looking for an excuse to declare war on the Huguenots. How long will it be until the streets are ankle-deep in blood? Or the German States? Half of them are already at one another's throats. Do you think it would have been wiser to visit Olivia in England? Or cross the ocean to the New World?" He secured the last of the lacings and patted them. "Satisfactory?"

"As always," said Rothger.

Rakoczy nodded, his expression distant. "You think that I ought to have refused the summons of King Istvan, or refused to be part of this embassy." He reached for his boots—black, with thick soles and heels lined with his native earth, decorated with red leather stitching—tugging on the right one first, a habit left over from Rome, fifteen hundred years before.

"I think you would have been able to, if that was your wish." Rothger said this without approval or condemnation, his manner not quite deferential.

"Do you." Rakoczy considered this while he slipped two jeweled rings onto each one of his middle fingers. Sapphires and amethysts set in gold smoldered on his small, beautiful hands. "I suppose I might have," he said at last, quite seriously.

Rothger said nothing as Rakoczy ran an ivory comb through his hair, then remarked, "The second athanor is almost ready to put into use."

Understanding took the sting out of Rakoczy's remoteness. "Good. Czar Ivan will want another sapphire or amethyst before the week is out; that has been his pattern."

"It would be useless to say that presenting gifts to the Czar adds to your danger, would it not," Rothger ventured as he offered a short bow. "I'll be certain the cooks have something ready to serve Godunov."

Rakoczy's smile this time was singularly gentle. "I am grateful. Believe this." Both of them knew that his thanks were for more than one service.

Boris Godunov arrived to be met with an extensive, makeshift display of fruit and pastries set out in the main reception room, the second room in the house to be completed. Not all of the ceiling had been painted, but Rakoczy was pleased to show Boris the sketches the artists had made.

"Very satisfactory," Boris pronounced after he had completed the ritual of blessing the household ikons of the Archangel Gavril and Saint Feodossi of the Caves, as he looked at the representation of the Four Evangelists. His manner was cordial and forthcoming, qualities Rakoczy had rarely encountered among the boyars. "Your selection of Saint Feodossi is most interesting, for a Saint from Kiev honors both Russia and Poland. Apt; very apt. It is the same throughout. Acceptable to any Moscovite but with a foreign flavor to it. Very elegant." He made a sweep of his arm, indicating the reception room and the dining room beyond. "You have done a great deal."

"The workers have done a great deal," Rakoczy corrected him affably. "I have paid them."

"Admirable modesty, as well." Boris reached over and snagged another spiced pastry filled with apples. "These are excellent. Are you sure you wouldn't like one?" As he took a bite, he added, "You men from the West are too thin. We Rus know that thinness is ugly and take care to avoid it." He patted his own girth—quite moderate by Russian standards—as if to make the point more clearly.

"I have observed it is often a matter of custom, what is beautiful and what is ugly," said Rakoczy, wanting Boris' attention shifted to other matters. "There are those who do not prefer red to other colors, and some who favor woolens to silk. One man rides horses with white markings, and another spurns them. For every man who chooses fair women, there is one who would rather have dark ones."

"You don't eat enough to keep meat on you," Boris went on, unwilling to be shunted to other topics. "You have a deep chest and enough bone in you, but you need more than that."

Rakoczy spoke more firmly though his manner remained affable. "I respect your ways and the customs of the Rus. But among those of my blood, dining is a very private thing, an intimate thing. We do not often do it in public."

"It is a silly custom, if you will think about it. Do not defend it to me. All foreigners have customs that we Rus find strange." He reached for a bowl of small, deep-red berries mixed with thick sour cream, then retrieved his fork and spoon from the folds of his waistband. "What is more noble a gesture than to offer food? It is the first thing a mother does for her child. It is the offering we leave on the grave. Jesus Christ fed the hungry and it is fitting for Christians to give food in His Name. And what is—" He broke off as hammering came from another part of the house. "Your workers are busy."

"I trust they are," said Rakoczy, trying to fathom where this was leading. Perhaps Rothger had been right, and their hazard was increasing.

"Have them knouted if they are not. If they live they will serve you faithfully the rest of their lives." Finally Boris reached for one last pear preserved in honey. "I don't know how best to broach this, Rakoczy. It has been troubling me since yesterday." He looked around at the tall, carved chairs that lined the room. "Let us sit and I will explain."

"I wish you would," said Rakoczy with feeling.

Boris decided he could laugh at that, and let a chuckle rumble through him as an afterthought. "It is two weeks since you have seen Czar Ivan, is it not?" He selected one of the most intricately carved chairs.

It was seventeen days since Rakoczy had been admitted to Ivan's presence, but all he said was, "About that, yes."

"Truly." He continued to eat. "It is unfortunate, but for the last five days the Czar has . . ." He chewed noisily as he tried to select an appropriate word that would not be viewed as treason. At last he found it. "The Czar has suffered a great deal because of the visions he has had. It is his son, Ivan Ivanovich. He claims the mace he struck him with hovers over him as the spectre of his son hangs before his eyes. He has been unable to break their hold on his soul."

"That is a tragedy," said Rakoczy.

"Your Jesuits have been three times to the Terem Palace, and every time the Little Father has refused them entrance." This time his hesitation was more awkward than before. "It has been suggested to him—by whom, who can tell?—that the Jesuits are performing rites to strengthen the visions. The demeanor of the Jesuits is severe. They are not at all like the English. It is the unhappy truth that Czar Ivan is beginning to believe those who have told him this thing against the priests."

"That the Jesuits are behind his visions," Rakoczy repeated to be certain he understood Boris correctly. "And who implies this?"

Boris sighed. "As I have told you, it saddens me to disappoint you but I am not able to say, not with any certainty. I have my suspicions, for everyone at Court has suspicions about everyone else. Rumors of conspiracy are as common as maggots in old meat." His expression grew somber.

"Boris Feodorovich, what do you want of me?" It was improper of Rakoczy to ask so bluntly. He inclined his head, an elegant gesture that removed some of the sting of his question. "I do not intend to give offense; I am here to serve Istvan Bathory in Czar Ivan's Court. To do that, I must understand clearly what is expected of me."

But Boris had not taken umbrage. He leaned back, regarding Rakoczy with his bright, black eyes, measuring him with approval. "I hope that Istvan Bathory knows how fortunate he is to command your service, Rakoczy. Two or three of you loyal to me and I would not fear anyone at Court, including the whole Shuisky tribe." He slapped the arm of the chair with his left hand, still sticky with honey.

Rakoczy bowed again, more deeply. "I am flattered, Boris Feodorovich, but I am not answered."

"No, you're not," Boris agreed, fixing his gaze on the far side of the room. "Let me put it to you this way: it would be useful to Bathory's Jesuits if you had another . . . gift you might present Czar Ivan just now."

"Jewels," said Rakoczy, taking Boris' meaning.

"No diamonds or topazes, nothing light. He claims such gems would strike him blind now." He licked the last of the honey from his fingers.

"I have three large garnets, rose colored, one slightly flawed, the others perfect," said Rakoczy. "And turquoise, nine smooth stones the size of my thumbnail, to match the stones in Czar Ivan's Kazan crown." He had made them a month ago, anticipating this request.

To Rakoczy's surprise, Boris shook his head slowly. "Hold them; no doubt they will be welcome later." He drummed his fingers on the arm of the chair. "What else? Have you darker jewels? Not jade or lapis, but ones holding light?"

Rakoczy did not answer at once. "I have a beryl, a tiger's eye, of a true, dark gold color, translucent, with a single spear of light through it. The stone is about"—he held up his thumb and first finger curved together—"this size." He said nothing about the four attempts he had made before achieving this stone.

"Dark gold," mused Boris. "How dark?"

"Darker than wild honey," said Rakoczy, a slight smile tweaking the corner of his mouth. "If the jewel were not full of light an ignorant man might mistake its color for brown."

Boris laughed his approval. "Yes. That ought to hold the Czar's attention for a time. Be sure the Jesuits are with you when you present it, and make them kneel to kiss the hem of the Little Father's kaftan. He will not listen to the tales of their enemies so readily, at least not for a while." With a sudden, energetic motion, Boris was on his feet. "I knew you would be wise."

Rakoczy bowed, but continued to watch Boris carefully. "Tell me: why do you confide in me? It honors me and puzzles me at once. The Court mistrusts this embassy, yet you visit here when it might be better to stay away."

Boris pursed his lips, walking back to the table where he pretended to be considering another helping of nuts preserved in malieno spirits. "You ask because you understand that I am not trusted at Court. You suppose this might tip the scales against me." His laughter this time was curt and unpleasant. "No one is trusted at Court, but I am trusted less because of my Tartar mother. So you think it strange that I come here. But who better? Already they suspect the worst, so I use their suspicions to my advantage, and strive to learn as much as I can in order to offer wise counsel."

"I see," said Rakoczy, who knew better than to pursue this partial answer. "You are gracious to tell me."

"I have reason to want your good opinion, as the English say," declared Boris with the assumption of candor. "If you can still say that a year from now, we must both count ourselves fortunate." He swung around to face Rakoczy squarely. "I will arrange an audience for you on Tuesday, after the fourth Mass of the day. Bring the dark golden beryl. And tell no one you bring it at my recommendation. If you are asked, say that it is King Istvan's wish, not mine."

"If that is what you—" Rakoczy began.

"It is what you will do," Boris ordered curtly, turning abruptly on his heel and striding toward the ikons flanking the door, crossing himself in front of the Archangel Gavril. The ikon had been made by a master and long ago, judging from the style of the writing identifying the Archangel, whose wings of blue and green feathers hung behind him like exotic armor; there was a long, curved brass horn in his hands. Boris stared at the grave, long, other-worldly face of the ikon surrounded by a halo of hammered gold and topazes. "Why do you choose Gavril, of all the Archangels?"

"His feast is at the dark of the year, as was my birth." It was the truth, as Boris' answers had been the truth. He bowed to his guest.

"The Archangel of the Resurrection," murmured Boris as he went to cross himself before the ikon of Saint Feodossi of the

Caves. "A strange choice, for all the feast coincides with your birth."

This time Rakoczy's smile was genuine. "Indeed."

Text of a letter from Father Pogner to Ferenc Rakoczy Hrabia Saint-Germain, delivered by Father Krabbe.

To the exiled Transylvanian who abuses the trust of King Istvan Bathory, I am unable to send my blessing.

By what authority do you order us to appear with you at the Palace of Facets tomorrow? It is not your place to decide how the affairs of this mission are to be accomplished. What you call your consideration for us is nothing more than a display of most un-Christian pride and for such sin you must beg the pardon of us all before you can be received as a true Catholic again.

You inform me that the purpose of this meeting is to present the Czar with yet another bauble for his treasury on the pretext of providing him with sovereign remedies for his madness. You deceive no one with such obvious ploys. Everyone knows that this is nothing more than a bribe given for the purpose of persuading the Czar to honor the treaty he has made with Poland and Sweden. To claim any other cause for your actions serves only to convince the Russian Court that their suspicions regarding foreigners are correct, and that we are nothing but deceivers who deal without integrity or steadfast purpose. Full well do I recognize your desire for aggrandizement and Courtly influence. Hrabia Zary has revealed his worst fears to me, saying that he is convinced that you are here to make yourself a fief in your exile, a place where you would once again have position and respect instead of the empty titles and lost estates that now are your lot. You would carve for yourself a position between the Polish and Russian thrones where you can be the only mediator, dictating to these worldly Princes. It is madness to trust in madness, Count. You bow to Czar Ivan, placating him with this gem or that, and have a day's favor for it. What does it matter that the treasures offered to God and His Church must be sacrificed? And how many more of these precious stones have you secreted away?

This gesture also fires greed in the Russian Princes, who are eager to have such treasures for themselves. How long will it be, do you think, before the Nagoy and the Shuisky and the Romanov families demand jewels to gain their favor? Perhaps the Kurbskys as well will seek baubles from you. You may have spawned a monster, and at the expense of King Istvan and the Pope, who cannot forever provide such riches to you. This ridiculous fiction you are minded to spread—that the jewels are of your manufacture—has been accepted by a few of these ignorant Russians, but others are less credulous than you assume, and they, just as we, scoff at your claims and know you for an opportunist and a charlatan who abuses the confidence and the wealth of Pope and King.

Does that word offend you, Count? Charlatan. Fraud. Deceiver. Perhaps traitor is not too great a condemnation, for you have shown yourself willing to bargain with the treasures of this world for the merit of the soul. Unless you are lost to all honor, each condemnation should lie on your conscience like a hot brand. The burning of your soul should sizzle and stink, for I tell you now that vice marks the man as much as the hazards of life. Does it horrify you to know that these stains are on your soul—your soul, Count? If it does, you must examine your conduct and reform it so that my disapprobation is no longer deserved. I am not easily convinced of amended purpose, and to that end I warn you that no display of piety or pretended virtue will satisfy me. You must fully abjure this chicanery and publicly acknowledge your contemptible schemes. You must formally apologize to the Czar and King Istvan, making restitution to them for all you have done. To the Church you must be truly penitent. We Jesuits are trained to be alert to just such sophistry as remorseless men employ, and we uproot it as a farmer uproots encroaching vines, knowing that without such measures his crop is lost. An insincere admission will deliver you into the hands of the Russian authorities and the justice of the Czar.

Yet even the most rigorous of priests occasionally falls prey to the wiles of the very thing he should most abhor, and your suborning of one of this embassy is ample proof of your determination to implicate all of us as your accomplices. That one of our number has been taken in by your machinations saddens me but it does not astonish me, for it is apparent that you have also fooled the Rus who flock to you, either for your riches or for your skills. Given the love of luxury we see everywhere in this barbaric city, it is not difficult to guess which attracts these Rus the most.

When I have received word that you have made a start in returning to virtue and humility, then I will answer such an arrogant summons as the one you have sent. In the meantime, I will pray daily for the salvation of your soul and hope that God's mercy is greater than His patience.

In the Name of the Father, Son, and Holy Spirit,
Casimir Pogner, Society of Jesus
September 27, by the new calendar, in the Year of Grace
1583, by the hand of Father Dodek Kornel, S. J., at Moscovy.

7

Vasilli Shuisky's palace was inside the Kremlin walls, halfway between the Savior Gate and the Annunciation Cathedral, in a triangular plot that included stables and a small barracks as well as a proper terem. It was here that Vasilli received his cousin Anastasi on a dank morning in early October.

"I suppose you've been told?" Vasilli asked when he and Anastasi had finished blessing the ikons. He rubbed his hands together to keep off the chill.

"You mean the great embassy presentation?" said Anastasi with a nasty smile as he shrugged off his enveloping sheepskin shuba. "Yes, I have been told. Full Court, all regalia. Banquet for eight hundred, half of whom are foreign." He looked down at his hands as he tugged off the heavy gloves he wore. "Women, too, at the presentation, according to the summons."

"Women, too," said Vasilli heavily. "Ivan Vasilleivich is losing all sense of propriety along with his wits, ordering women to attend the presentation. Does he want to compare his jewels to theirs, I wonder?" This sarcastic question needed no answer.

"Such an occasion is for envoys and diplomats, not females. And there is no reason for full Court." He clapped his hands and said to the two servants who came and bowed deeply to him, "My kinsman and I will be in my study. We will want hot tea and visnoua. At once." He clapped again and his servants backed out of his presence as Vasilli led the way up the stairs, looking at Anastasi and shaking his head in disapproval. "A pity you should see them so lax. I will have to correct them. They're not as attentive as they ought to be, the household. They are waiting for word about the Little Father and they neglect their duties. Every time Ivan screams, it is reported throughout the city."

"Everyone neglects duties; it isn't just your household," said Anastasi. "Never more so than when the Czar is failing." He looked around quickly, as if he might be overheard; he was able to appear amused.

"There is nothing to bother about, Cousin," said Vasilli. "Everything said in this house is reported to me, even the things whispered in the terem." He made a gesture of dismissal, the brocaded sleeve of his kaftan shining in the subdued light. "Women are very foolish."

"But very necessary," said Anastasi. "Your father and my father were agreed on that, if nothing else." His smile was ingratiating but it fooled neither man. "Why do you bother with the babble of women?"

Vasilli shrugged. "They hear things. They see things. Most of it is nothing, but occasionally they discover . . ." He made a sweep of his arm. "Who can say."

"Your terem may serve you well, but Galina and that infernal daughter of hers—Xenya!—have never been so useful to me, except in these instances, for Court. They hear nothing, not even gossip while on those errands of mercy," Anastasi complained as they reached the second floor. One direction was blocked by a large, ornate metal door guarded by a tall, burly man in a rust-colored kaftan holding a pike. Beyond was the women's quarters where Vasilli's wife, mother, mother-in-law, and two daughters lived with a full staff of women servants. "They are not at all like your women."

"You do not live inside the Kremlin walls," said Vasilli as if that settled the matter. He opened the door to his study, a large, gold-and-red chamber with a ceiling like a tent, painted in intertwining vines surrounding medallion ikons. "We came very close." He stared toward the Czar's Terem Palace.

Anastasi paused in the entrance to the room. "Close?"

"To that." His heavy gaze moved from the Terem Palace to the onion domes of the Cathedrals. "It should have been ours."

"Cousin." Anastasia wisely closed the door before crossing the room to his cousin's side. "It may still be ours," he said after a short silence; his tone was light, capricious. "If I take your meaning."

"You take my meaning," said Vasilli, his eyes hardening. "Oh, yes, you take my meaning." Slowly he moved away from the window. "Galina will be at the presentation?"

"And Xenya. She hasn't agreed to become a nun yet, so she will have to attend or Ivan will be offended."

"Why isn't she in a convent?" asked Vasilli. He stopped and crossed himself before the ikon of Saint Vladimir. "Under the circumstances, she ought to have retired there long ago."

"She claims she is not suited to the life, that God has not sought her as one of His own." He turned his hands palms up to show his exasperation. "What can I do? She is not my daughter, and I have not been awarded a father's authority: I cannot compel her. She says she is content to be unmarried and care for her higher-ranking relatives in the terem until God invites her to the convent."

"How much more of an invitation does she need?" Vasilli demanded, slapping his hands together once. "She should have been given to the nuns the day her father was buried."

"Her mother was so despondent . . . and the convents were filled with women the Golden Horde had . . . ruined . . . and the dying . . ." Anastasi no longer pretended he sympathized with Galina Alexandrevna. There was a short, miserable silence between the cousins. Then Anastasi coughed delicately. "It is still possible for her to marry, you know."

"Possible?" asked Vasilli. "To what man?"

"One who was content to be ignorant; one who was ambitious enough to let the past remain past. One who did not know and would not ask." Anastasi dropped into one of the four uncomfortable chairs that stood near the slant-topped stove. "She says she does not want a husband."

"She's an idiot," Vasilli declared. "She will be nun or wife, or she will starve."

Anastasi took a turn around the room, noticing four new ikons near the door. Automatically he crossed himself once for each of them. "Which do you think it will be?"

Vasilli did not answer the question. He strode to the trestle table that served as his desk and sat down. "I've learned that the occasion for the Court is not just to receive letters from the King of Poland, but the Transylvanian, Bathory's alchemist, is presenting the Czar with yet another jewel. I forget how many he has given the Little Father already. This one is supposed to be very large and dark and rare. Rumor claims it is a fine beryl." He frowned, his eyes distant. "One of the servants of the Jesuits overheard two of the priests talking, and that is what they said, according to the servant. I want to learn more, but so far I haven't been able to discover anything—"

There was a rap on the door that brought the two cousins to attention.

"Who is there?" Vasilli rapped out the question hard and fast.

"Serkha," answered the servant. "With tea and visnoua, as you ordered."

The two cousins exchanged glances and Vasilli said, "Bring them in at once and leave."

The servant bore a large tray, moving gingerly; the samovar was boiling and it hissed when it shifted. A pear-shaped glass bottle filled with a translucent liquid stood beside the samovar. Four cups were on the tray, jiggling as Serkha brought them to the table. Once he put them down, he bowed deeply to Vasilli, then slightly less deeply to Anastasi before he backed out of the room, crossing himself once as he passed the ikons.

"Do you worry about him?" asked Anastasi as he heard the doorlatch slip into place.

"Serkha? No, his tongue would be slit if he was caught revealing private things. And besides. What can he say?" He reached for one of the smaller cups, and then for the bottle. "Come. With arms linked." He was already pouring out the visnoua into the cup. "Fill your own and drink with me."

"Gladly," said Anastasi, accepting the proffered bottle as he picked up the other smaller cup. "I always like your visnoua better than Dmitri's."

The mention of his brother made Vasilli expressionless. After a brief stillness, he forced a smile to his thin lips. "It is a question of taste; even Ivan says so." He nodded as if his older brother's name was not personally offensive.

Anastasi was grateful for the respite Vasilli offered him. "Yes," he enthused. "That's precisely it." He spilled a few drops of the strong cherry liquor before he put the bottle down and held out his right arm. "To the prosperity of our family, the success of our plans, and the returning health of the Czar."

Vasilli stood up and linked arms with Anastasi across the table, both men having to lean over in order to drink from the cups. Their beards brushed together, dark brown and wheat-blond; they drank their cups empty and stepped back. "Not a bad blessing," said Vasilli as he sat down and refilled his cup. Once again he gave the bottle to Anastasi.

"Not too bad," said Anastasi, who was pleased with what he had said. He refilled his cup and offered the blessing to his older, higher-ranking cousin. "May our fortunes thrive."

This was not an uncommon blessing and Vasilli paid little attention. "Let us get on with it. This Transylvanian—is it true what I have heard, that the Polish priests are not willing to support him?" He opened a studded leather case on his writing table and pulled out a vellum sheet. "According to what I have been able to learn, the leader of the priests, Father Pogner— what unwieldy names these foreigners have!—has ordered the Jesuits to avoid his company, and the five Lancers are not permitted to provide him any protection or escort. Here is the report." He tapped the sheet. "What do you know of this?"

Anastasi glanced at the document, then lowered his head, unwilling to meet his cousin's eyes. "I have spoken twice to Father Krabbe, who is the only one of the Jesuits who appears to defy Father Pogner." It was not the answer he had wanted to give Vasilli, but he knew better than to lie to his cousin; stretching the truth was risky enough. "He claims that Hrabia Zary has protested Father Pogner's orders, but is afraid not to obey them."

"These Jesuits are not made of the same cloth as Father Possevino," said Vasilli, "no matter what they claim."

"Father Possevino is not Polish," Anastasi reminded him.

"It is more than that," said Vasilli. He drained his cup and filled it again. "Who else has approached the foreigner?"

"Grigori Nagoy invited him to take a meal with them, but Rakoczy refused. It is said the refusal was gracious, but he is here at the behest of a King—what else would it be?" Anastasi did not mention the other thing he had learned from the Nagoy servant: that he had been told all invitations to meals had been unsuccessful. There might come a time when such information would stand him in good stead.

"Perhaps he does not want to favor any noble over the Czar. It would be a sensible precaution," said Vasilli slowly, his eyes narrowed and measuring. "And yet. And yet. I am sure this man Rakoczy is subtle and sly. He is more dangerous than the priests. Listen to him speak. He says everything and nothing."

Anastasi drank half the visnoua in his cup, regarding Vasilli as he did. There would be a service he could do for his more august cousin that would also benefit him in days to come, freeing him from the tyranny of Vasilli's patronage; it was bad enough they were cousins. "I will do what I may to learn more of him, if the Czar does not forbid it."

"Worry more about what Godunov forbids. He is the one who has decided to extend friendship to the exile. He will be the one who will decide who among us is worthy of Rakoczy's favor." Anger marked Vasilli's face now. "That Tartar is foreigner enough by himself. That he could support this alchemist—"

"He endorses the English as well," Anastasi pointed out. "He says that they will buy more than rope and gold and furs from us if we are prudent."

"We are not merchants!" Vasilli burst out, then swung away, rising from his chair and pacing back toward the windows; he still held his cup tightly in his hand. "It is despicable to put trade above the safety of this country, but Godunov is determined to do it." He tugged at his beard with his free hand as if the tension would pull the rage out of him.

"If his sister were not married to Feodor Ivanovich . . ." Anastasi shrugged heavily. "But as Feodor Ivanovich's brother-in-law—"

"That may not mean what it did. There are whispers, whispers. I have heard that the Little Father forgot himself a short time ago, and tried to add Irina Feodorevna to his unofficial wives. Apparently Boris Feodorovich stopped it before it went beyond the bounds the Church could excuse, but the whispers are that Czar Ivan in his shame and wrath is no longer willing to leave everything to Godunov, and Godunov is wary of the Little Father as he was not before." Vasilli hesitated, as if tasting the words he wanted to say before he spoke them, relishing them. "If Irina falls from favor, what will become of her brother? Feodor Ivanovich is not one to defend his wife, is he? He will ring another bell. And if he will not defend his wife, then certainly the wife's brother must be lost." He chuckled twice, the sound as ominous as a death rattle.

"And about the alchemist?" Anastasi prompted.

"The presentation has been postponed twice, and both times the ceremony of presentation has become grander for the delay," said Vasilli quietly, his features turning contemplative as he came back to his writing table. "If Godunov cannot serve as sponsor of the presentation, then it could be possible to use the occasion to show the Little Father how great our concern for him is. Godunov will not permit us such an opportunity, but perhaps—" He looked at Anastasi, renewed speculation in his demeanor. "Perhaps you might be able to gain the foreigner's good-will. Surely he senses that all is not well with Godunov; he might welcome your intervention?" He poured himself another cupful of the cherry visnoua. "Don't you think?"

Anastasi nodded at once, pleased to agree unreservedly with Vasilli. He downed the rest of his visnoua and held out his cup for more. "I will find some plausible reason to know him better."

"You will find a plausible reason to assist him, to show him that you, unlike Godunov, are indispensable to his success in Moscovy," corrected Vasilli. "You want him in your debt."

"But surely," said Anastasi, and Vasilli paused in refilling his cup. "It would not be wise to present him with obvious motives. He would know the ruse for what it was at once."

Vasilli shook his head. "No, no. You don't comprehend. You're not one to prate about foreigners and the changes coming to Russia, as Godunov must have done. You will present yourself as one who can assist Rakoczy with Czar Ivan while Boris is compromised. You will show that you have something to gain. It will be a reasonable agreement between reasonable men. It is disarming to foreigners when they are given such opportunities."

Anastasi licked his lips and shifted uneasily on his feet. "He may suspect that there is more."

"Certainly he will suspect it," said Vasilli. "But you will disarm his suspicion. Show him openly all you stand to gain by taking his part. Tell him that you seek to free yourself of the shadow that hangs over me and my brothers, that puts all Shuiskys under the same pall. As our cousin, you have cause to want to establish yourself beyond our damaged reputations. What better way than through the aid of this foreigner?"

So close was Vasilli's proposed scenario to Anastasi's actual plans that he had to put his cup down to keep from revealing how badly his hand shook suddenly. He made himself say, "I'm confused, Vasilli," as he crossed the study away from his cousin. "How will the foreigner be convinced?"

"Oh," said Vasilli lazily, "you and I will quarrel where he can see and hear it, and he will accept what you tell him." He placed his hands together, very satisfied.

And then Anastasi said, "And I will confess to the Patriarch—"

"The Metropolitan," Vasilli corrected.

"The Patriarch," Anastasi repeated with heavy emphasis, "is what he is being called now, and so I will call him that. It is only a matter of time before the Czar declares the Church in Russia to be supreme over the Church in Jerusalem. Constantinople is lost to Christians and Czar Ivan is right to call Moscovy the New Rome." His mercurial smile lit his face. "We rise from the ashes here in Moscovy. The city burns and thrives anew. The Orthodox Church survives here, not in Jerusalem, surrounded by those who scorn Christ." He crossed himself.

Vasilli slapped the flat of his hand on the table. "You will keep silent with such thoughts. They have no bearing on our success in this. The foreigners need not know that there is dissension in the Orthodox Church."

"Why?" asked Anastasi, feeling a heady pleasure in speaking his mind. "It is what I know to be true, Cousin." He came back to the table and picked up his cup to drink. "What am I to confess to the Patriarch? That you and I are at odds? I may do that with a clear soul." He tossed off the potent visnoua and poured more. "If that confession will aid the purpose, so much the better."

"And you will profit twice?" jeered Vasilli, his derision making Anastasi long to throttle him.

"If I may," Anastasi admitted through clenched teeth. "As would you, in my position." He stepped back. "I will confess tomorrow. Before the second Mass. That way the priests can gossip with the servants, and by the time the beryl is given to the Little Father, everyone will know my mind, and that will open the door to Rakoczy." He bowed much lower than courtesy and rank demanded, delighting in the insult this offered Vasilli.

"Be careful, very careful," Vasilli said softly. "You and I have the same purpose to serve now, but there may come a time when we do not."

At this Anastasi laughed. "You need someone who can read and speak Greek as well as Latin who will serve you without deceit, with intelligence. I am the only cousin who can, save Igor, and he is no use to anyone, with his whoring and drinking; so you must have me if you will have Latin and Greek, with a few words of English now that Sir Jerome is here. You must have someone who is beholden to you, who must serve you well for his living; we both know my circumstances. Therefore I am willing to be your tool, but not your dog." He grabbed one of the larger cups and filled it with boiling tea from the samovar.

Vasilli silently did the same. He sweetened his tea with a generous amount of honey, then scowled at Anastasi. "They say that Nikita Romanov has visited the alchemist. They say he spent an hour in his company."

"Nikita Romanov wants to take Godunov's place," said Anastasi. "He intends to become the regent for Feodor Ivanovich when the Little Father is called to God. Everyone knows it. He is too obvious to deceive such a one as the Transylvanian. We need not concern ourselves with him, or any of the Romanovs. They are nothing." The tea was too hot to drink, but the fragrant steam helped clear away the haze of visnoua. He inhaled deeply and felt his fair cheeks flushing. "What of Grigori Nagoy? If he has invited Rakoczy to dine with him, what is he seeking?"

"The Nagoys are powerful in their way," said Vasilli. He sipped his tea, paying no heed to the scalding of the roof of his mouth. "They will strive to gain more power."

"They might," said Anastasi, becoming guarded.

"If they can convince the merchants of Moscovy that their wealth lies in the west, then they will have the support they seek to strengthen them sufficiently to topple us." He clenched his fist. "It is not acceptable that they should do this."

"And a pity we did not think of it first," said Anastasi in false commiseration. "We could turn it to advantage faster than they can."

Vasilli was affronted; he felt himself sulk. "You forget what you are saying."

"Not I. If anyone should woo the merchants, it is Shuisky," said Anastasi, his square face suddenly very bland. "We will return to prosperity with Novgorod. Now that Ivan has brought them to heel, they should be eager to open the portals to the west for us. We have only to remind them of the slaughter that was visited on their city when they defied the Czar."

"We are not merchants. We are Princes." Vasilli put his hand to his shoulder as if to reassure himself that the image of Saint Ephraem of Nisbis was still there.

"I am a Duke, not a Prince," Anastasi reminded him, laughing as if it were a joke. He drank a long, hot sip of the tea. "Excellent."

Vasilli put his cup down and folded his arms. "If you are planning mischief, Anastasi Sergeivich, you had better abandon your stratagems or suffer for them. You know what I require you to do."

"And I will do those things, I've told you so already," said Anastasi. "I vow to serve you. Because I must." He had the rest of his tea, watching Vasilli over the rim of the cup, his eyes bright with furious humor.

It was a short while before Vasilli trusted himself to respond. "If ever I discover this is not the case, no estate of yours, no matter how remote, will be far enough for you to escape me. Your family will be forfeit to your gamble, Cousin, all of them—wife, children, household—will answer for you. My vengeance is as sure as my arm is long."

Anastasi put the cup back on the tray. "I would stay for more, but there is an alchemist whom I do not know well enough yet." He bowed too deeply and backed to the door like a household servant. "Yours to command, Cousin," he assured Vasilli before he left the room.

When he was certain Anastasi was out of his palace, Vasilli took the cup his cousin had drunk his tea from and smashed it against the end of his trestle table, swearing steadily as the thin metal crumpled under his assault.

Text of a letter from Benedict Lovell to Ferenc Rakoczy, Hrabia Saint-Germain. Written in English and Latin.

To the most excellent Count, Ferenc Rakoczy, of Saint-Germain, late of Transylvania and now attached to the embassy of King Stephen Bathory of Poland in Russia, through the good offices of introduction arranged by Madame Clemens, currently resident near Harrow, my sincerest greetings.

It is with the hope of good-fellowship that I take pen in hand to write to you as Madame Clemens recommended I do almost a year ago; your reputation, with gratitude to Madame Clemens, preceded you, and before Moscovy was dazzled by you, I had heard of your remarkable skills and talents long before I set sail for this most puzzling country. Pray do not let my awkwardness in this epistle count to my discredit. If it were possible for more regular dealings, I would undertake them gladly, but given that foreigners have many restrictions upon them and spies set to watch them, I have resorted to this irregular communication, in large part because I suspect that your accomplishments are more comprehensive than the Czar and his servants realize. In England Madame Clemens assured me that your abilities are unique and without equal in the world. She informed me that you have some knowledge of English but that your Latin is almost that of a Roman of old, and for that reason I provide these two versions. Further, she ventured that you will not be put off by this proffered hand of friendship from the English, or this one Oxford scholar, in any case, though it comes improperly.

Because Madame Clemens has already provided me with your name, I take the liberty of addressing you directly instead of seeking your attention through the Jesuits who are the masters of your Polish embassy. It might be otherwise if I had not her admonitions to guide me, but given the circumstances, I can see that you are remarkably suited to your position and therefore need not apply to your small escort for protection, nor need you obtain the approbation of other high-ranking nobles in order to complete your mission. It is not required of the priests that they extend their courtesies to you. If it is not impertinent, I must tell you that I am aware of a growing friction between you and the priests of your embassy. It appears likely that they would forbid contact between us for the satisfaction of such denial, and excuse it as a stand against the Church of England. If I err in this assessment I hope you will forgive me for telling you of my misapprehensions. Therefore I make bold to direct my attentions to you without other considerations, and I thank you in advance for those services you might well be able to extend to me and the tasks with which the Queen's Grace has charged me. I do not believe that anything I may require will compromise your mission. All foreign missions may well benefit from the favor I ask of you.

Count Rakoczy, I ask you, for the sake of all foreigners in Russia, to address Czar Ivan on behalf of all of us. It has been said that he suspects foreigners of causing his malady, but any reasonable man must know it is not so. If the Czar is willing to listen to you, then I beg you will intercede for all of us and make it clear to Ivan that no foreigner has the strength, either of arms or magic, to bring him to such a pass as he now finds himself protecting. Neither the Poles nor the English, nor the Germans, nor even the Swedes, for that matter, are able to influence so mighty a ruler as Ivan Grosny. His fears are more phantoms than his vision of his son is, yet it is apparent that he thinks he is the victim of some mischief. With such terrors upon him he also cries aloud to Heaven to forgive him for his sin of murder; his son's ghost is with him night and day. That is not the doing of any sorcerer or magician.

You, being an alchemist, may be able to persuade him to regard his foreign visitors with less distrust and suspicion. He appears to accept you. He has certainly shown you greater favor than any of the other foreign dignitaries living in Moscovy. He might be willing to hear you if you would vouchsafe to inform him of the innocence of our duties here. Ivan Grosny has long corresponded with Queen Elizabeth, and has—or so Sir Jerome has informed me—offered to enter into a pact of mutual government in exile, so that each would be assured of protection at the Court of the other if ever they were brought into danger by conspiracy and treason. With your voice to add to ours, it may be that Czar Ivan will accept our position and our obligations without his concomitant assumption of malign intention toward him. I freely acknowledge that my request is beyond the bounds of charity or the courtesy due fellow-strangers in foreign places; if there were other means at my disposal to address the Czar without enhancing his distrust of us, I would avail myself of it, but no such remedy has been discerned. Therefore I make bold to send this, desiring that you will agree to address our plight.

With your permission I will do myself the honor of speaking to you at the banquet following your presentation tomorrow night, and I beseech you to consider what I have said to you; with your help we may all serve our countries and the Czar in just duty. With my prayers for your aid and my appreciation for your thoughtful decision, I remain

Your most obedient servant,
ever yours to command, etc, Benedict Lovell
Doctor of Philosophy, Fellow of Brasenose College, Oxford
At Moscovy, October 9, 1583, by the English calendar.
Carried by Nicholas Bower, secretary to the English Embassy,
with the express permission of
Sir Jerome Horsey, the Ambassador

8

Snow delayed the beginning of the presentation of the beryl; all of Moscovy shivered in the first serious storm of the coming winter. From the outer wooden gates of the city to the stone walls of the Kremlin, the city moved slowly, hunched and bundled together against the razor cold of the wind, the sting of snow.

There were Guards at every step leading to the reception hall in the Palace of Facets, armed men with battle helmets in place, their Court kaftans as shiny as their weapons. Members of the Court filed upwards, their kaftans glistening gold and red, jeweled collars and tall fur hats showing the formality of the occasion. All the Court went unarmed, for to carry any weapon into the presence of the Czar could be seen as a sign of treason.

The women, brought in curtained wagons, went to the terem entrance where they were received by Czar Ivan's current appointed wife and eunuchs, who took them to their place in the Palace of Facets. Glimpsed as they made their way from wagon to palace, these women were dressed as grandly as the men they complemented: their red silken sarafans falling from their necks to their ankles, sewn with pearls and golden thread; their outer sleeves stiff with embroidery and gems; heavy, bright cosmetics made pretty masks of their faces, which were framed in the peaked kokoshniki like halos of pearls.

Boris Godunov had shown Ferenc Rakoczy to an antechamber on the lower floor of the Granovitaya when the alchemist had arrived somewhat earlier. "It cannot begin until the Court is seated. We will be informed."

"And you?" asked Rakoczy. "Must not you be seated then, as well?" He was dressed in full Hungarian court dress: his dolman was cloth-of-silver bordered with silver-and-red patterns of raised wings; the mente worn over it was sable with frogging in silver cording, and the high collar ended in a narrow ruff of brilliant red silk. His leggings were black, sewn with a raised wing pattern of pearls and small garnets, and his thick-soled boots were silver. He wore his single pectoral, the same circle of black sapphire framed by raised, displayed wings. There was a large ring on his first finger, a dark cabochon ruby with the same eclipse pattern incised into it. A silver coronet studded with rubies circled his head.

"I will go up ahead of you," said Boris, using both hands to adjust the wide jeweled collar he wore. "You and your escort will—"

"My escort?" Rakoczy interrupted. "What escort is that?" He sounded nothing more than mildly curious, though he was filled with apprehension. Soldiers in this setting meant greater risks; Ivan had always been capricious, and since the killing of his son, he had become more extreme. It was not impossible that the Czar would order him killed or taken to prison after receiving his jewel.

Boris turned and looked at him, surmising his thoughts. "The one the Polish priests sent: that Polish officer. Hrabia Zary. He is supposed to accompany you, because you carry valuable gifts to the Czar. At least, that is what Father Pogner informed us two days ago. He worried that such jewels would be a great temptation, and that the Court must know that the men of Istvan Bathory know the worth of these gifts." As he reported this, his frown deepened. "What is it?"

"Nothing," said Rakoczy, a bit too quickly, and added, "I

wasn't aware that Father Pogner was so concerned about the jewels." He did his best to make light of it, all the while wondering what Father Pogner hoped to gain by this sudden concern. "It seems that I do not hold the beryl in sufficient reverence for the Jesuit's good opinion."

"Why is that?" Boris put the question sharply.

This time Rakoczy was prepared to answer. He smiled. "I suppose because I make them." His tone was still conversational, but there was a change in his enigmatic dark eyes. "I care more for them in the making and less in their . . . reputation."

Boris considered this answer. "And their reception?"

Rakoczy was able to dismiss the question. "There is so little I can do. They are received as they are received." He held out the pale-green chalcedony box that contained the beryl. "Czar Ivan treasures his jewels, but not as many others do. He does not want them for wealth or adornment, but for the power he believes they hold. Speak to anyone at this Court and each will have a different reason to want jewels, and a different response to them; where one might accept a donation like this with happiness, another might accept it with fear, another with anger, and another with lust."

"You speak as if you had seen all that," said Boris, his black eyes narrowed and measuring as he looked at the chalcedony box.

"And more," Rakoczy assured him in a manner that did not encourage more questions.

"What are the carvings on the box?" asked Boris, knowing better than to ask to examine the box himself.

"An ox, a lion, an angel, and an eagle," said Rakoczy, pointing to the sides. "A twelve-pointed star on the lid."

"The Evangelists and the Apostles," Boris approved, not quite able to conceal a sigh of relief. "Excellent choices, all of them. The Little Father will like your conceit."

"I trust he will." He took a turn about the small red room, stopping before the two medallion ikons of Saints Boris and Gleb. He crossed himself and studied the long-nosed, narrow-chinned faces. "I have seen Greek ikons, in Adrianopolis, and some in my native land, but these are not quite the same." He did not add that he had seen the Greek ikons eight hundred years before, or that he had owned many when he had lived in Trebizond on the Black Sea while it was still a Byzantine city.

"Unlike the Christians in the west we know the importance of ikons here," said Boris sharply, then looked up as Hrabia Dariusz Zary came through the door, adjusting his ankle-length gold-colored wilczura so that the short wolf-fur cape fell properly around his shoulders.

"They took my lance," he complained without greeting Rakoczy or Boris Godunov. "Just took it away from me. They said it wouldn't be needed."

"No one carries weapons," said Rakoczy before Boris could speak. "It isn't allowed at Court, for anyone but the Guards." Had they been alone he would have told Zary to master his ill-humor before any of the Rus noticed; with Boris in the room with them, such a warning was futile.

"Well, that's a stupid idea," said Zary, his mouth hard with disgust. "What kind of escort doesn't carry a weapon?"

"One inside the Palace of Facets," said Boris, and made a formal bow to Zary as if to bring the young Pole back to his senses. "Where you are very welcome, for yourself and for your King Istvan." He spoke as if Zary had stepped through the door and presented himself in form. "This is a most auspicious time for the Czar, and for you here at the behest of King Istvan. You have the opportunity to heal old wounds and forge new bonds. It is almost the hour to begin. Let me give you your instructions now, so that there will be no error in the reception hall." He saw Zary stiffen.

Rakoczy intervened in what was about to become an argument. "Boris Feodorovich knows the way of the Court, Hrabia. Neither of us is above learning from him. You may be prepared for this, but I am not, and I seek his instruction."

"God of the Prophets," muttered Zary.

Boris went on as if the young Hrabia was cooperating. "When you are summoned, you will walk three paces behind on the right of Rakoczy. You will bow when he does and will remain no more than five paces from him until the Little Father dismisses you."

"If that is the way it's done," said Zary, making no attempt to disguise his disapproval of the arrangements.

"It is the way we have done it for centuries," said Boris, permitting his pique to show. "Say nothing, and speak only to Rakoczy if he addresses you."

Hrabia Zary shook his head. "I might as well be a servant."

"You *are* a servant," said Boris sternly. "All of your embassy are servants, to your King and to Czar Ivan. Let your conduct reflect that." He looked toward Rakoczy. "It is not long. Listen to the footsteps on the stairs. Most of the Court has arrived."

Rakoczy had been aware of the lessening of footsteps for several minutes, and he took advantage of the opportunity Boris provided to say, "I suspect Hrabia Zary is as nervous as I am. This simple gift has become an occasion of state importance. Czar Ivan has surprised us. None of us were quite prepared for it." He motioned to Zary to bow.

Boris acknowledged the bow, and returned the one Rakoczy gave him with greater courtesy. "You do not strike me as a man who is nervous, Rakoczy." He cleared his throat. "And if you are, it must not affect your appetite. Custom must be observed." He smiled with practiced enthusiasm. "This is a great occasion, and the Czar is marking it with every distinction. At the banquet, you must eat everything served. Otherwise the Czar may decide you are afraid of poison, and he will be deeply insulted."

There was a moment of silence, then Rakoczy said, "Your pardon, Boris Feodorovich, but I thought I had told you that when I make jewels, I fast." He had spent the greater part of an hour with Boris only a few days ago, and had tried to explain then that he had special requirements in regard to food. "I assumed you understood: I cannot eat."

"Yes, when you are making jewels. That was very clear," said Boris, sensing there was more at stake. "But you are not making jewels now." He waited, standing as if listening for whispers instead of Rakoczy's words.

The qualms that shook him were ignored. Rakoczy spoke steadily, knowing how much might depend on his explanation. "It appears I did not make myself clear. There are disciplines that are demanded of the alchemist if the jewels are to remain true. If I end my fast too quickly, the jewels become cloudy and dull," said Rakoczy seriously, for there were many alchemists who taught such things as truth. "It could mean that the beryl would no longer have the single spear of golden light through it, or there would be more, and the beauty would be gone." He glanced at Hrabia Zary. "Surely he is a worthy deputy for King Istvan. You do not want me to risk such a change in the stone, do you?"

Boris shook his head at once. "No. I would be a fool to do that." He paced around the antechamber once, looking from Rakoczy to Zary and back, one hand stroking his beard. Suddenly he stopped, his face set. "I will do what I can, but it may not be much. So much depends on the . . . demeanor of the Czar tonight."

"Truly," said Rakoczy, who had seen Ivan fall to the ground in a fit, his mouth foaming like a mad dog's. That had been a week ago.

Boris bowed again. "I will do what I can," he repeated before he left the antechamber.

"I don't trust him," Hrabia Zary said as soon as Boris was gone.

"You had better," warned Rakoczy, his dark eyes giving weight to his words. "He is the only possible ally we have tonight."

There was a crisp order given from outside the room, and both Rakoczy and Zary looked up.

"Our summons," said Zary sarcastically. "Three paces behind you on the right, he said. I will take up the position now."

Rakoczy nodded, and stepped out of the room, bowing slightly to the Guard who had called them. "May God show you favor," he said, and started toward the staircase, not looking to see if Hrabia Zary was obeying Boris' orders. As he climbed the stairs, he sensed the Guards watching him, not with the hard look they reserved for the Rus but with a grudging curiosity mixed with awe.

Court was assembled on a grander scale than when Rakoczy had been there previously. All the chairs around the tremendous chamber were occupied; on three walls the majesty of the Court was assembled, and at the far side of the hall the women were seated, the current Czarina at the front of the splendid gathering. They were flanked by a squad of Guards. The foreigners—English, Polish, German, and Greek—were required to stand, and their place was near the main staircase, which was the greatest distance from the Czar. They, too, were surrounded by Guards.

Czar Ivan no longer waited at the end of the chamber but was seated in his gem-studded ivory throne at the foot of a great gold-and-red pillar decorated with the double-headed Byzantine eagle that Ivan III had adopted as his own. He held the jeweled mace of state and was crowned with the filigreed-gold-and-turquoise crown of Kazan. His kaftan was cloth-of-gold with red lacings and garnets; his collar was studded with a fortune in diamonds.

Rakoczy walked directly to the throne, stopped six paces from Ivan, and dropped to one knee, as if to King Istvan, instead of prostrating himself as the Czar expected. He was black-and-silver in a hall of gold-and-red. "God show you favor and bring you victory, Czar," he said, pitching his voice to carry throughout the huge room.

Czar Ivan gazed at Rakoczy, his blue-green eyes brilliant as if with fever. "It is for your honor that you are welcome here, Rakoczy of Saint-Germain. You have provided many reasons for recognition. Word will be sent to your King of your accomplishment. He has shown good judgment in sending you." He looked around as if unable to remember what he had to do next. "I will write of this myself. You"—he pointed the mace at Hrabia Zary—"will carry the message for me, and report its truth. At once. Before nightfall tomorrow."

Zary looked shocked. "Great Czar, it is almost winter," he blurted out from where he knelt, three paces behind Rakoczy.

"You will carry the message," said Czar Ivan in a tone that brooked no opposition.

"Bow, you idiot," whispered Rakoczy in Polish. "And agree."

It took a moment before Zary was able to say, "It is more honor than I deserve, Czar."

Ivan nodded. "Yes. Yes. But Istvan Bathory will know that, and he will see that I am magnanimous. He will know that I will not prevent messages from reaching him, even messages from his Jesuits." He returned his hungry stare to Rakoczy. "You have something to offer me, alchemist."

"Yes," said Rakoczy, holding out the chalcedony box as he went on. "The jewel and its container are both gifts to you, Czar, to show that the position of Czar and the man Ivan are both held in highest esteem by my lord. They also demonstrate that religion is the haven of the soul. They are freely given as tokens of respect presented to you by King Istvan of Poland through me, his deputy in Moscovy." It was a formal, rehearsed speech, and it made a good impression on most of the Court.

A shine of spittle was on Ivan's mouth; he gestured to Rakoczy. "You may bring them to me. On your knees."

Awkwardly Rakoczy did as Ivan ordered, the hem of his dolman catching under his knees so that he had to stop and tug the silver fabric free before reaching Czar Ivan on his ivory throne. When he was close enough to reach Ivan's outstretched hand, he stopped. "Accept this gift, O Czar."

Ivan leaned forward and took the chalcedony box, holding it up to examine it. "Is this your work, as well?"

"It is, O Czar," said Rakoczy.

"You have rare abilities, alchemist," said Ivan, his expression suddenly guarded and suspicious. He held out the box to Rakoczy. "You made it. You must open it."

There was a concealed gasp in the Court, for such an order meant that the Czar was afraid of treachery. At his place along the wall, Anastasi Shuisky turned to the old blind war hero Piotr Grigoreivich Smolnikov and very softly told him what had happened.

"A bad business," muttered Piotr. "It is a direct insult to Istvan of Poland."

"Yes," hissed Anastasi, as much to quiet Piotr as to concur.

If Rakoczy was aware of the affront, he gave no sign of it. He took the box back into his hands and held it up so that Ivan could watch him open it. "The lid has the Apostles' Star," he explained. "If you place a candle behind it, the color will change so that the star will glow like an ikon."

Czar Ivan leaned farther forward in his throne, his hand tightly closed around the mace. "I will see that done," he vowed.

Rakoczy offered the lid back to the Czar and tipped the box so that he could see the contents before he lifted the tiger's eye out. "The beryl, Czar. Saint Mikhail's Sword." He had decided to give the gem a name just two days ago and now he saw that his impulse had been wise. Holding the tiger's eye out to Ivan, he added, "It is light in the darkness."

Czar Ivan grasped for the jewel, staring at it with an expression bordering on awe. "It is very powerful. Very powerful. No woman could touch this jewel, and no unclean man." He opened his fingers in order to stare at it. "There is more dark than light, but the light is the greater because of that." His words were sing-song and he paid no attention to anything but the stone. "It is the enigma of the soul, where all is dark, but for the mercy of God." He looked up suddenly. "It is well that it is the sword of the Archangel. A jewel of this power, with such darkness, would

be a mighty tool of damnation if it were not given to holiness."
He lifted up the beryl, holding it so the light caught the single
pale-gold flash through it. "There is passion here, with purity.
With this jewel a man could read the human heart. If his heart
were without sin." With that Ivan howled, clutching the tiger's
eye, tightly pressing it to his forehead under the fur rim of his
crown. He began to sob, his whole body shaking with each
breath.

Rakoczy remained on his knees; he felt dangerously exposed,
as if he were running naked on a battlefield. "Great Czar—" he
began.

The mace slammed down on the inlaid floor, missing Rakoczy
by less than a handsbreadth. "Say nothing!" thundered Ivan.
"Nothing!"

Hrabia Zary almost lurched to his feet.

"Hold," Rakoczy ordered, his voice low. He did not turn; his
eyes continued on Czar Ivan.

The Guards standing behind the pillar lifted their pikes.

Czar Ivan lolled back against the ivory, his shaking turning
now to convulsive spasms. His eyes rolled and froth appeared at
the corner of his mouth.

Then Czareivich Feodor came running forward, his moon-face
creased with anxiety. He rushed up to his father and flung himself on Ivan, calling to Ivan and God; his tall hat fell from his
head, rolling toward Rakoczy. Feodor took hold of Ivan's beard
and tugged as if pulling a bell rope.

The Czarina was crying openly, her tears marring the heavy
cosmetics she wore; several of the women clustered around her,
a few of them weeping in dread and sympathy. Their Guards
moved to screen the terrible sight, for it was known that witness-
ing tragic events could render women barren.

From their seats along the wall both Boris Godunov and Nikita
Romanov sprang up and hurried forward, Nikita reaching for
Feodor, Boris for Ivan. Not far from Nikita, Vasilli Shuisky settled
back to watch, his dark eyes thoughtful. The Court buzzed with
urgent whispers and a few of the other boyars took a chance and
stood, prepared to assist if an opportunity presented itself. Anastasi Shuisky gave blind Piotr a running account of what was
transpiring.

The Guards moved nearer but did not attempt to impede

either Godunov or Romanov. Their leader seemed anxious to be relieved of his position; he did not want to be the target of the Czar's favor at a time like this. He held his pike with the point down and signaled his men to do the same. Rakoczy remained on his knees, unmoving. He made no attempt to speak to anyone.

As Nikita drew Czareivich Feodor away, the Czar's heir reached out and pulled the coronet from Rakoczy's brow, crowing with delight at his trophy. He permitted himself to be led away while Boris tended to Ivan.

At last Rakoczy broke his silence. "If I may?" he said to Boris. "I have some experience with . . . disorders of the mind. If you would permit me?"

"God and the Archangels, if you can do anything—" Boris declared with feeling as he struggled to hold Ivan on his throne.

Rakoczy rose, coming the last few steps toward Ivan. He reached into the wallet hanging from his dolman's belt, and drew out a small bottle of clear liquid. "This is a composer," he said to Boris. "It will help relieve him."

Boris glowered at him, all his Russian distrust of foreigners reasserting itself as he stared at the vial. "If it is anything but what you say, you will not leave this room alive."

"Rest assured," said Rakoczy with a faint, ironic smile, "I will leave this place as alive as I am now." He removed the carnelian stopper. "If you will help me? I must tip this into his mouth."

"He'll choke," said Boris, panting a little as Ivan attempted to thrash free of him. His face was shining with sweat.

"No, he will not," said Rakoczy. "I have done this before, Boris Feodorovich. I will not fail now." He waited, showing no distress as Ivan began to wail and spit.

Boris relented. "Very well, Rakoczy. But if there is any—"

"Hold his jaw open, will you?" said Rakoczy, unwilling to listen to more threats. He braced himself against the throne, then slipped the open end of the vial between Ivan's lips, letting the liquid run out very slowly. When the vial was empty, he stepped back. "Here," he said, offering the vial to Boris.

The Guards now surrounded Rakoczy, but he paid no attention to them.

"I can't hold him," Boris protested, still restraining the Czar.

"He will be calmer shortly." He watched Ivan, looking for the pulse in his neck, nodding once as it began to slow. He motioned the Guard to move aside so that he could return to his place on his knees.

Czar Ivan shuddered twice, then coughed, bringing his arm up to wipe his mouth afterward. His movements were as clumsy as a child's, but he was no longer shrieking and his limbs were not rigid. "God protect me," he muttered.

There were new whispers in the reception hall of the Palace of Facets, and those boyars who had stood now sat down again, a few in genuine amazement.

Czareivich Feodor looked up from contemplating Rakoczy's coronet and suddenly smiled. He pointed to his father, observing to Nikita, "Look, Uncle, the Czar is awake. He is awake."

Boris stepped back from the throne, a puzzled frown marking his brow. He looked over at Rakoczy, then back to Czar Ivan. "Little Father?"

Czar Ivan yawned hugely and stretched. "My sweet soul. I did not think— What has come over me?" he asked sleepily. "My head aches. My sinews hurt." He sat up, adjusting his kaftan and loosening the hold he had on the tiger's eye. "A potent jewel. A very potent jewel. It plumbs the soul. No wonder it is Saint Mikhail's Sword. You have spoken truth." He directed his attention suddenly and intently at Rakoczy.

"It is an honor to serve you, Czar," said Rakoczy.

Boris stared at him while he signaled the Guards to return to their posts.

"It is great service." Czar Ivan's voice rose. "This man has done what none of the rest of you have. He has brought clarity to me when the devils are raging. This jewel is most powerful. Therefore let all men respect him and show him the regard due a boyar." He looked directly at Rakoczy again. "I vow that I will reward you, Rakoczy, for the magnificence of your gift, and I will relate fully to King Istvan your achievements."

"You are gracious to a stranger, Czar," said Rakoczy with care.

Ivan struggled to his feet, hefting his mace at the same time. It was impossible to believe he had been locked in a fit only minutes before. A motion of his hand brought the huge room to complete silence. "You are deserving of honor, Rakoczy. You will be rewarded, when I have thought of what is suitable to give you."

This time Rakoczy only bowed his head while thinking in sudden desperation how he might avoid the Czar's favor. He caught sight of Boris and read apprehension in his black eyes. "The jewel is the heart of all treasure," Ivan declared, then sank back onto the throne. He signaled to Boris. "Pick up the box for me, Boris Feodorovich. I myself will place the jewel in its case."

As Boris did as he was ordered, he gave Rakoczy an inquisitive glance, then prostrated himself before handing the box to Ivan.

Ivan caressed the box before returning the tiger's eye to it. "You will have a great reward, a great reward," he promised again, very softly.

Rakoczy, still on his knees, stopped himself from protesting the Czar's promise. He made himself incline his head and say, "Such favor is not necessary, Czar. To serve you and King Istvan at once is all the reward I could want."

There was satisfaction in Ivan's face, a satisfaction that bordered on gloating. "What man would not wish for so diligent a servant as you are?" He caught sight of Czareivich Feodor, still playing with Rakoczy's coronet. "That will be returned to you."

Rakoczy answered quickly. "It is unnecessary. He may keep it as my gift." But even as he said it he realized that Czar Ivan was not listening.

Text of a letter from Anastasi Sergeivich Shuisky to Father Pogner, written in Greek and delivered by mute servant.

To the revered Jesuit who leads the Polish embassy in Moscovy, sincerest greetings from one who proposes a pact to our mutual benefit.

Certainly I cannot doubt that you share my sentiments regarding the alchemist Rakoczy who has come in your company to Moscovy, for I have seen the distress you cannot conceal at the flagrant behavior of the Transylvanian exile. What man of character could not be deeply shocked by what has transpired? I am appalled that the Czar, no matter how decrepit he has become, has been taken in by this man and his endless tricks.

This most recent outrage—bringing on a fit through presenting the Czar a poisoned gem and then offering the antidote as the means of displaying his so-called powers—no doubt causes the severest shame to one of your calling and dedication; that this man is an embarrassment to your embassy is beyond question. You, in your sacred calling, are compromised because of the tricks a clever deceiver commits in the shadow of your worthiness. I believe that your indignation has been earned by this man's chicanery, and for that reason I address you in this manner, to offer what assistance I can to aid you in revealing the fraudulent activities of this Rakoczy.

You must appreciate how delicate our positions are while Rakoczy enjoys the Czar's favor and attention. Ivan will not look kindly on those who seek to discredit a man he has decided to approve, at least for the time he approves; he has sworn that if any man attempts to harm Rakoczy he will be knouted to death. It is necessary that we work in complete secrecy if we are to circumvent the Czar's ill-deserved favor. Therefore I will not yet reveal my identity to you until you indicate you wish to know it, so that you may have some protection if the Czar questions you in this regard. You will have no name to offer; your ignorance will protect you, far more than your Jesuit's vows will.

I have heard some rumors of the reward Ivan is contemplating, but I cannot be convinced that even now Ivan is capable of so great an outrage. Lamentably, the Czar is afflicted in his reason, and for that we pray to God for his deliverance and the return of his former greatness. He is determined to shower greater honor on Rakoczy, but in his demented state he is not capable of distinguishing what is appropriate. Yet even now, I cannot think he could contemplate so egregious a thing as I have heard whispered he intends to do, for it would not be a reward but the severest punishment, and would reflect adversely on him as well as bring calamity to others. It would also serve to add to your disgrace, which imposition, when so much has been heaped upon you through the faults of Rakoczy, must surely be intolerable.

But perhaps that punishment would serve your purpose, good Jesuit, and perhaps it would serve mine as well. To compel Rakoczy to serve two masters would put his head twice in danger, and that can be turned to advantage. We will know in time, if the thing comes to pass.

In the meantime, let me advise you to prepare to celebrate the

Nativity with grandeur, for such courtesy would be viewed favorably by the Czar and by most boyars; you have little over a month to arrange a suitable feast. Such a show of joyous respect and religious zeal will earn the good opinion of those who disapprove of the antics of Rakoczy.

From one who shares your concerns.

9

Their horses were protected from the cold by winter tack, which included a saddle pad that wrapped around the horses' bellies, held in place by the girths, and a breastplate that was two-hands wide and lined with lamb's wool. Rakoczy rode one of the black Furiosos he had brought from Hungary, a fine, strengthy mare with a long trot and mettle. Beside him, Benedict Lovell rode a square-headed dun gelding he had purchased in Moscovy several months ago. The third member of their company, Anastasi Shuisky, was mounted on a prized red roan with a fine arched neck; it was he who had suggested the outing.

"So these oprichniks are not newly created nobility?" Lovell asked Anastasi in his excellent, English-accented Russian. "I had thought they were."

"So had I," said Rakoczy. "Until recently."

"Nothing like that, not as boyars and Princes are," said Anastasi as they neared the southern gate of Moscovy. "They were a special force, very fierce, sworn to uphold the rule of the Czar. They went about the country, carrying brooms and the heads of dogs for their talismans, rooting out evil and corruption as the Czar wished. Or so they claimed." He wiped at his beard to brush away the first flakes of snow. "They exceeded their position, and eventually had themselves to be stopped from evil and corruption."

Lovell nodded. "A lesson most are slow to learn," he observed, drawing his Russian shuba more tightly around him. "So they are gone now?"

"Most of them; there were many executions. But a few were loyal and have advanced, and they are now very powerful, those few," said Anastasi darkly. They had almost reached the gate, and the crush of traffic slowed them to a walk. The narrow streets in this southern quarter of the city were filled with people going to the last horse market of the season.

Rakoczy was aware that they were on very unsteady footing with these questions, and so he said, "Czar Ivan is fortunate indeed. Many a ruler has been brought down by the very guards he has trusted to protect him." He drew in his mare to let the others go ahead of him through the massive wooden gate.

Anastasi, taking the lead, made sure to cross himself beneath the massive ikon of Saint Alexander before he gave the Guard his name and the names of his companions.

"I do not like this idolatry, all these painted-and-gilded saints. It's worse than Popish display," said Lovell very softly to Rakoczy in English as he turned in the saddle to face the Transylvanian. "You cannot go in or out of a door without endless rituals in front of these endless ikons. It is a practice that we English could not accept."

"Cross yourself anyway," Rakoczy advised as he blessed himself and the ikon. "These are not my saints, but I will honor them while I am in this country."

Lovell shrugged once as he copied Rakoczy. "All their worship is graven images," he protested softly.

Rakoczy nudged his mare after Lovell. "Think of it as you might think of a relic," he suggested, for he saw little difference between them.

"More idolatry, done by those who bow to the Pope of Rome," said Lovell with feeling, inadvertently raising his voice with the emotion he felt. "It is not what is done in England."

"It used to be," said Rakoczy sardonically. "Never mind the ikons now: we're here for horses. We can talk about gilded saints later, and attract less attention." He nodded in the direction of the Great Field where the horse market was conducted. Although it was late in the year there were huge herds brought to this place. There were horses tied and tethered everywhere there was room on the field.

Lovell drew in his horse, staring. "How many do you think there are? I have not seen so ample a—"

"Probably two thousand or so." Rakoczy moved his mare up next to Lovell's gelding and sought to avoid the deepest mud holes in the road. "Speak Russian here," he advised in that language. "We are already suspect for being foreign. If we are noticed speaking another tongue it will be presumed that we are plotting."

"Surely not," said Lovell in surprise, although he obediently switched languages. "It is clear to everyone that we are foreigners. They must know that foreigners do not speak Russian, that they have languages of their own."

"Nevertheless, speak Russian if you do not want to be seen as an enemy." He indicated where Anastasi rode ahead of them; his voice was low. "And be very careful around that man."

"Of course," said Lovell, dismissing the matter with a motion of his gloved hand. "He must provide reports on what we do. He is the Czar's servant."

Rakoczy studied Anastasi's broad back. "I wonder," he said after a long moment of consideration.

Anastasi swung his arm to encourage the two foreigners to catch up to him. "You must press on," he chided them. "Here we do not wait to seize our chance when it is presented. Hurry along, or others will take the best horses. Come up to me." As Rakoczy and Lovell reached him, he pointed to one group of Tartars in their heavy leather-and-silk garments. "These are the traders you seek. They have the horses I mentioned to you, Rakoczy. You will find them everything I have described, and more. And they are as honest as any men selling horses." He shouted to one of the Tartars as they approached. "How many head have you brought with you, Khelmani?"

The Tartar answered promptly, bowing lavishly and grinning. "Not too many. Six hundred. It is the end of the season." He made an enormous gesture of resignation. "Most of these are two- and three-year-olds."

"Thinning the youngsters before you have the spring foals," said Rakoczy as he swung off his Furioso, his high, fur-lined, thick-soled boots sinking in the frosty mud. "Very sensible." He did not add that it was also a way to be rid of unpromising animals before they could breed their undesirable points back into the herd. "And it makes our coming here worthwhile, to see the best of your younger horses."

"You have a knowledgeable man in Hrabia Saint-Germain; he is expert in many things," Anastasi promised with relish and good-fellowship.

Khelmani regarded Rakoczy narrowly, unconvinced by Anastasi's endorsement. "Why would you say so? That we would thin the young ones?"

"Because I have raised horses myself, from time to time," said Rakoczy, remembering with a mixture of fondness and repulsion the extensive stable he had maintained to the east of Rome, fifteen hundred years ago, and the villa at Trebizond, a few centuries more recently, where his estate was home to more than eight hundred horses; he had arranged for Olivia to take most of them when he was forced to leave, turning them over to her personal servant Niklos Aulirios before he and Rogerian fled east-by-south. He handed his reins to the Tartar and faced him. "I understand you have a breed we have not seen in the West."

"There are many breeds you do not know in the West," said the Tartar with scorn. He pointed to the nearest group of young horses, most of them dark-coated and compact. "You do not know these. Don horses," he said. "The greatest horsemen in the world ride them."

"They are Cossack ponies," said Anastasi as he swung out of the saddle. Like many portly men he was light on his feet and graceful. "Good in battle and light keepers. But they are not the ones I told you of."

Rakoczy had dealt with horse traders for centuries and he knew that it would be a mistake to appear too eager, so he strolled over to the Don horses and gave them a careful perusal. "Good legs, by the look of them, and a steady eye. But they do not hold their weight in winter, do they? The cold robs them of flesh."

The Tartar started a long, involved explanation of the hazards of travel and the youth of the animals to account for their prominent ribs. He ended saying, "In time they become used to the cold."

Rakoczy's smile was very polite and his manner bordered on the diffident, but his dark eyes were implacable. "I doubt that. They haven't the coat for it." So saying, he motioned to another group of horses. "Tell me about these."

"Ah, they are a long way from their home. They dwell beyond

Sarai." The mention of the Mongol city brought a scowl to Anastasi's face, but Rakoczy paid no attention to this and Khelmani offered the Russian an evil grin.

"What breed? They look very tough." He approached the small, well-formed horses. "Desert horses, aren't they?"

"Yes." Khelmani studied Rakoczy, clearly reassessing him. "They are strong and hardy. They are called Karabair."

Rakoczy went closer to the herd. "How large do they grow? These appear to be small for two-year-olds."

Khelmani spat. "They are not big, they are strong. In horses this is best."

Lovell watched this sparring with interest. He dismounted and tugged his horse after him, making his way after Rakoczy rather than waiting with Anastasi. He looked at the Karabairs with some interest. "There is a breed that Madame Clemens has in her stable that are not unlike these."

"Her Barbs, you mean?" Rakoczy said. "Yes, there is a resemblance." He turned to face Lovell. "Perhaps you would like to send her a pair of these three-year-olds? There are some handsome animals here. That filly with the lead-colored coat is a promising one, and the liver-chestnut. Olivia might find them of interest."

Lovell shrugged, his fair British face growing rosy, and not entirely from the cold. "I fear my purse will not allow such a gift, no matter how much I might wish to give it. It is regrettable that—" He looked away from Rakoczy, pretending to be fascinated by one of the Don yearlings as he used his free hand to tug the flaps of his fur hat more snugly over his ears. "And if I could afford them, how would I get them to her? No one is leaving for the West until spring, and if the war with Poland starts up again, it would not be possible to send them across Europe. The port our ships use is closed with ice, and will be until late in April, when the White Sea becomes passable. And the road will not be clear of ice and snow soon; no one wants to travel to Novo-Kholmogory. So we could not move horses north now, in any case. In the spring . . ." He faltered, searching for words that would be reasonable and save face at the same time.

"I will stable them for you, if you would like," offered Rakoczy. "Purchase what you wish. I will answer for your selection." He smiled slightly, a suggestion of sadness pulling down the corner of his mouth.

"Oh, no; Count, you are most gracious. But I must not accept. It would not—" Lovell protested in English.

Rakoczy overrode him in Russian. "I will make an appropriate arrangement with you, Lovell. But I think it might be wise if there were a few horses in reserve for . . . foreigners. In case we must ride for Poland or your Novo-Kholmogory port." He regarded the Oxford scholar evenly. "What do you think?"

Lovell looked around rather awkwardly. "I should not accept."

"But you will," said Rakoczy, his compelling eyes lending weight to his words.

"It . . . not for kindness alone, but, yes, if it strikes you as necessary." He looked about, feeling embarrassed for no reason he could easily explain. Whatever Rakoczy's purpose for this unexpected generosity, Lovell knew it was not the one he had volunteered. He was about to question the alchemist when Rakoczy's quelling glance silenced him.

"Show me some of the other horses you have while Doctor Lovell makes his selection of these," said Rakoczy to the Tartar in an off-handed way, as if his interest in the Karabairs had vanished.

Watching this interchange, Anastasi had to stifle his own urge to coax information from Rakoczy. He followed along behind the two foreigners, doing his best to appear only mildly curious while he listened intently to glean any item of use from their conversation. At last he said to Khelmani, "Where are your treasures, your moon-horses?"

The Tartar gave Anastasi a startled look, as if surprised that Anastasi should mention these animals where the strangers could hear. "I have brought only twenty with me," he said at last. "Three-year-olds, all of them."

"Ah," said Rakoczy with sincere anticipation. "Then let me see them, for the love of God. This man"—he indicated Anastasi— "has been telling me about these moon-horses with coats pale as silver and I do not know if I can believe what he says."

"There is nothing like these horses in the West," said Anastasi, his square face set with determination.

"So you have assured me," said Rakoczy with a polite show of disbelief; he had seen the so-called moon-horses before, but not for nearly a thousand years. He had ridden the Chinese cousins of the breed more than three hundred years before; he thought it ironic that in China they were called Celestial horses. The Tartar bowed again, more lavishly than the first time. "Then come with me, worthy foreigner, and see for yourself."

Even with their fuzzy winter coats, the twenty horses were glorious, their pale hair shining that polished silver the Poles called ermine-dun, a shade between palest blue-grey and paler tan. Their long manes and tails were sadly in need of grooming. They were somewhat larger than the other breeds the Tartars were selling, and they moved with the elasticity of acrobats. "The Moon-Horses of Heaven, the team of the Chariot of Death," said Khelmani grandly. "The Akhal-Teke."

A warmth entered Rakoczy's smile that had not been there a minute before. He walked toward the tie-line where the horses waited, holding out his small, gloved hand to the nearest inquisitive nose. He rubbed the next on the forehead and then moved down the line, patting each horse in turn, watching the response of each animal closely. As he made his way back toward Khelmani, he said crisply, pointing to certain of the horses as he passed. "These three colts, and these six fillies. I want to examine them."

Khelmani stared at him, for never had a high-ranking foreigner made such a demand of him. He looked to Anastasi for guidance. "Greatness?"

Anastasi bustled up to Rakoczy's side. "He's foreign, Khelmani. He doesn't realize what he is asking." There was no way to conceal his sudden nervousness, but he made light of it. "There is no offense offered here. And he is not forbidden, exactly, to have so many." He saw the guarded look in Khelmani's face and decided to change his manner. He bustled forward. "But nothing is wrong in those the Czar favors."

"May God forever protect and guide him, and send him mercy in his trouble," said Khelmani at once.

Anastasi crossed himself, noticing that Rakoczy did so as well. "If this were not the last horse market before spring, it would be another matter . . ." He tried to think of what Vasilli would do in this situation, and discarded his conclusions at once: if Vasilli wanted to decide for the foreigners, he ought to have come with them. As it was, he, Anastasi, would trust to his own judgment.

"The Czar is about to honor Hrabia Saint-Germain. He has declared it openly. I do not think he would forbid him the purchase of a few horses. It is not as if he is a fighting man with soldiers around him." He waved a hand in the direction of Lovell, who was still trying to select two of the Karabairs. "And he is a teacher, a scribe. He must have a horse to tend to his duties. There will be no objections."

"If it is the will of the Czar, it is the will of Heaven," said Khelmani, making it plain that he accepted no responsibility for anything that resulted from this arrangement.

"The Czar will praise your good sense, Khelmani," said Anastasi. "You will be given the thanks of the Little Father—"

But Khelmani had held up his hand. "It is not fitting that I should take anything from the Czar," he said very quickly, looking around as if he expected the horses to repeat what he had said in their clarion voices.

Anastasi did his best to look concerned. "But you have done much to—"

"It is not fitting," Khelmani repeated emphatically. "If there is honor, take it for yourself and do not wish it on me." He turned away more abruptly than he had intended, almost slipping on the mud underfoot.

Rakoczy reached out to steady the Tartar, only laying his hand on Khelmani's back briefly. "By nightfall it will be solid," he said without emphasis. "It is always difficult to find the right footing."

Khelmani turned and looked at Rakoczy with curiosity. "Yes," he said after a brief hesitation. "That is very true."

A faint, ironic smile played at the edge of Rakoczy's lips, but he spoke without a trace of amusement. "I am pleased we understand one another." He gestured to the line of Akhal-Teke. "May I see the horses I selected?"

When Khelmani bowed this time there was great respect in his manner, and he made no attempt to extol the virtues of his horses. "Inspect them as you like, foreigner." He stepped back to watch, refusing to let anything distract him.

Rakoczy pulled off his gloves, flexing his fingers against the cold. He approached the first colt he had wanted to see, reaching for the rope halter and pulling the head down to examine the head, eyes, and ears of the horse. Satisfied with what he saw there, he pulled back the upper lip and opened the jaw.

The colt, surprised and nervous, began to champ.

"No, no," whispered Rakoczy to the young horse. "You are not with a stranger. You will not be hurt. My word on it." He patted the pale neck, noticing the texture and length of the pale mane, and the horse dropped his head, his nose tucked into the bend of Rakoczy's arm. "Good. Very good," said Rakoczy.

Anastasi was a serviceable horseman who took no part in the care of his horses—those tasks were left to his servants—but even he recognized that there was something remarkable in the way Rakoczy dealt with the colt. There might be something worth learning here, he decided. He took a step nearer, watching with interest as Rakoczy continued his inspection.

"A pity there isn't room to see him run," he remarked when he had finished with the first colt. "He is quite satisfactory. I will deal with the others."

Khelmani did not quite sigh, though he looked up at the low, grey clouds scattering their snowflakes like gelid petals over Moscovy. It was already turning colder and in another two hours the sun would be gone. He wanted to be back in the inn before night came.

In an hour Rakoczy had approved all but one of the mares and was aware that both Anastasi and Lovell were waiting for him impatiently. When he had taken four perfect diamonds from his wallet, he studied the two men who accompanied him. "It wasn't necessary for you to wait with us, Duke," he said to Anastasi. "But I am grateful for your courtesy."

Anastasi was begining to ache with cold, but he forced his icy face to smile. "There is no reason to say so, Hrabia. As the man who brought you here I could scarcely leave you without causing great distress to Khelmani." He, himself, was unsure what distress this might be, but he plunged on. "How was he to know that you would deal honorably."

"It is a risk with strangers," said Rakoczy seriously.

"Truly." He crossed himself. "And yet all has come to a satisfactory conclusion. You and Doctor Lovell have your horses and Khelmani has been very handsomely paid." As he said this he thought again of the great beryl Rakoczy had given Czar Ivan, and envy rose up in him, so powerful that he feared it would be visible to everyone.

"It would not be wise to do anything else," said Rakoczy as he watched Khelmani finish tying all the horses to the same lead, which he then handed to Rakoczy; Lovell already held his two Karabairs on a lead, where they danced and feinted with each other in an effort to keep warm.

Anastasi decided to make the most of this opportunity. "Come. I will have visnoua and malieno brought, with cakes and fried meats."

Rakoczy had just got into the saddle and was bringing his restive Furioso to order, holding her with calves and steady hands. He took the lead from Khelmani and said to Anastasi, "That is very gracious of you, but I think it is growing too late to impose on you. These horses must be put into their new quarters as soon as possible, and given warm mash against the cold." He stared directly into Anastasi's shiny blue eyes. "Perhaps another time."

"Very true, the horses must get out of the weather as soon as possible," agreed Lovell, his teeth chattering a little. "And so must I." This confession was offered merrily enough, but with a note of underlying desperation that made Rakoczy look sharply in his direction.

"Are you all right?" he asked in English.

"Just a bit chilled," answered Lovell, too uncomfortable to notice the change in language.

Rakoczy switched back to Russian. "Come along with me. I'll see that your horses are stalled. My manservant will prepare a bath for you, and that will warm you." He offered Anastasi a wide smile. "I regret we will not be able to accept your kind invitation." He bowed in the saddle and half-saluted before starting his horse back toward the gates of Moscovy.

Lovell was quick to follow after him, tugging on the lead to bring his new horses with him; he was still not sure how he had come to buy them, or why Rakoczy had wished it.

Watching them go, Anastasi was tempted to spur ahead of them and inform the Guards at the gate that these foreigners were to be refused entrance. The notion was sweet. But if Czar Ivan ever learned of it, Anastasi's head would hang over the Beautiful Market Square just outside the Kremlin, and his cousins would laugh at him until all the flesh was gone from his skull and only his empty grin remained to mock them. It was not worth the brief satisfaction to risk such a result. There would be other times, Anastasi reminded himself as he started back toward the southern gate. As long as the foreigners were in Russia, he would find a way to exact the whole price of his humiliation from them, as he would claim it from his more noble relatives. For the time being, he had one chance left to him still to bring Rakoczy into his hands, and he would remind Vasilli of it before nightfall, so that it would be fresh in Vasilli's mind when he attended Ivan's council tomorrow morning. He mused on this last possibility in greedy anticipation as he entered the city walls and nudged his red roan in the direction of the Kremlin, where Vasilli was waiting for him.

By the time Anastasi reached the Beautiful Market Square, Rakoczy had at last put all the new horses into fresh-bedded stalls and supervised their first feeding. His groom, a taciturn Livonian, listened to Rakoczy's instructions with no change of expression but with increasing doubt in his grey eyes.

"What is it?" Rakoczy asked when he had finished. "Nemmin, what is the matter?"

The groom required some little time to frame his answer. "I do not wish to interfere. You are master here."

"And you are groom," said Rakoczy at his most reasonable. "What is it that troubles you?" He looked steadily at the man, and although the groom was more than half a head taller than Rakoczy, the alchemist was not disadvantaged by this.

In order to escape the keenness of Rakoczy's eyes, Nemmin stepped back, looking toward the stalls with their new occupants. "It isn't right, treating horses like that."

There was a lessening of tension in Rakoczy's face, a subtle shift of expression that indicated that this was the least of his worries. "You do not approve of the mashed grain for supper and the potion for their hooves," he guessed. "You think they are too pampered."

"It makes them weak," muttered Nemmin. "They will have no strength when you need them to carry you through the cold."

"It will not harm them," said Rakoczy patiently. "I may be foreign and have a title, but I know a few things about horses. I rode here from Poland, and to Poland from Bohemia and Transylvania." He did not mention the places he had been before that: India, China, Africa, Europe, Egypt.

Nemmin nodded twice in agreement. "And may God not pun-

ish you for permitting the horses to pass one day without tasting
the whip." He set his lantern jaw. "They will turn on you if you
do not whip them each day. They forget their stripes and then
they cannot be controlled."

Rakoczy made a gesture of dismissal. "I have told you before:
I will not tell you again. I do not want my horses cowed. I do not
want them beaten. They are to be treated with respect."

"You are—" Nemmin spat and made a sign against the Evil
Eye.

"I am an alchemist," said Rakoczy with weary patience. "And
I am foreign. I do things in foreign ways." The way of raising
horses he had learned so long ago in lands where the Ottomites
now held sway. Those memories were not so painful as many
others, more recent and more distressing.

"It will shame you if it is learned." Nemmin kicked at the loose
straw underfoot with a force that revealed his emotions more
truly than his voice. "They will know you are a sorcerer."

Rakoczy spoke gently. "And who is to tell them, if I do not and
you do not?"

Nemmin was already four more steps away from Rakoczy. "I
will tell nothing. I will not bring infamy on this house, though it
is foreign."

Listening to Nemmin lumber away, Rakoczy realized that the
groom might yet change his mind. For as long as Czar Ivan held
him in favor, Rakoczy knew that he was safe; as soon as that
favor ended, all the suspicions and loathing that had been silent
would become a relentless cry. He made a last check of his new
horses and the two Karabairs, then took the covered hallway
back along the side of his house to the side door where Rothger
was waiting for him.

"The English scholar is almost finished with the bath," Rothger
informed him as he stepped into the muted lamplight of the
antechamber.

"Good," said Rakoczy a little distantly. "Is there food to offer
him?"

"It's been arranged," said Rothger. "And I have set out a kontush for you, so that you can sit with him while he eats."

Rakoczy paused, looking directly into his manservant's eyes.
"Do you think that is . . . advisable?"

Rothger answered obliquely. "You tell me that this scholar

was for a time a companion of Madame Clemens'. He may not have your secret, but he must be aware that those of your blood are . . . idiosyncratic."

With a rueful chuckle Rakoczy acquiesced. "Very well," he said, knowing that someone would report this to the Czar and all the others who were at pains to watch him. "Bring me the kontush; I will change clothes in my chamber and I will spend an hour with the English scholar."

Proclamation issued by Czar Ivan in Russian, Greek, and Polish.

At the time of the Nativity when we reward the service and prayers of our servants, I, Ivan the Fourth, called Grosny, Czar of all the Russias, wish to show gratitude to the foreign alchemist Ferenc Rakoczy, Hrabia Saint-Germain, of the embassy from Istvan Bathory, King of Poland.

Be it known that it is my intention to show thanks to this remarkable man in a way appropriate to all he has done and how I have come to value him. Let no man say that there is any reason beyond this for what I have decided.

It is my decision that Ferenc Rakoczy, Hrabia Saint-Germain, will, on the 27th day of January, the Feast of Saint Janis Chrysostom, in the Cathedral of the Dormition, marry the noblewoman Xenya Evgeneivna Koshkina, of the household of Duke Anastasi Sergeivich Shuisky.

The wedding is to be celebrated with all pomp and finery, and there will be a banquet to celebrate the marriage that will serve a thousand men. A thousand women will be permitted to dine behind screens for this splendid occasion.

Word of this glorious union will be sent to Istvan Bathory of Poland as soon as the way is clear in spring, at which time he will certainly rejoice in his servant's good fortune.

This is my will and the will of Heaven.

Ivan IV
Czar

PART II

XENYA EVGENEIVNA KOSHKINA

Bride

Text of a letter from Father Casimir Pogner, S. J., to Ferenc Rakoczy, Hrabia Saint-Germain.

Thou pernicious traitor:

Not content to ignore the warning I have sent you in the hope that you could be recalled to some sense of honor, you now seek to complete the disgrace of yourself and this mission by carrying through with the ludicrous marriage you claim the Czar has forced upon you. How can you contemplate so egregious a union as this one? Your insistence that the Czar has demanded it can have no bearing on you, for you are here at the behest of Istvan Bathory, your countryman and King. The orders of the Czar cannot bind you, especially one that smacks so much of subornation. By taking this bride you have shown yourself to be Ivan's lick-spittle.

Your protestations of your innocence ring false, Rakoczy. I have it on excellent authority that you sought this marriage to ensure your position at Court and to claim for yourself estates and lands in compensation for those taken from you by the Turks. How can you seek so putative an alliance? You are succumbing to something worse than treachery in this perfidy, you are embracing apostasy if you go through this wedding to one who is of the Orthodox rite. I will have no choice but to excommunicate you for this action if you undertake this felonious marriage. As it is, I can no longer regard you as a trustworthy part of this embassy. Through your actions you have

137

shown you are not one of us any longer, if ever you were. It is most distressing that I, as a priest, must inform you of certain things about your bride: you know the woman is compromised, don't you? You claim you know nothing of her except her name, but I have information that convinces me this is not the case. You have made a point of finding a woman who could not be expected to refuse you. Did you realize how great her sin is? Or have you made that a part of your filthy bargain? Was it your intention to find a woman who could not complain of you, no matter what indignities you heap upon her? Did you seek a woman who could not object to your courtship and whose family would be forced to welcome you because it allowed the woman to preserve some little dignity in the face of the loss of her honor? What sense have you abandoned that you could consider taking such a creature to wife as this one? And how have you overcome the family's scruples to permit her to wed you in the first place? Has another of the Pope's jewels gone to further your ambitions? I know certain of her relatives are overwrought at this forthcoming marriage for they dread the return of the shame she has brought to them. That you would use so unworthy a weapon as her disgrace to win this bride is beneath contempt. Your continued protestations that you did not seek and do not want this marriage lack true conviction, and your claim that you cannot defy the Czar without drawing the entire embassy into danger is surely a scurrilous lie, told to frighten us into acquiescence. We are assured by those of the Court who have made it their business to inform us that neither of these things is true and that you have misrepresented your desires and our dangers in order to gain your ends without opposition.

As soon as the roads are passable and Hrabia Zary is ordered to depart, it is my intention to inform Istvan Bathory and Pope Gregory of your actions and to seek redress for the humility you bring on this mission, on Poland and the Catholic Church.

Casimir Pogner
Society of Jesus
January 9th, by the reformed calendar,
in the Year of Grace 1584.

1

Blizzards had howled over Moscovy for more than a week but with the morning of the wedding the sky had cleared, showing a world so cold that the brilliance of sunlight made it seem the sky was in danger of cracking. Wind as penetrating as blades cut through the stout wooden walls of the houses of Moscovy, and smoke from the thousands of chimneys was quickly swiped away. Peasants set to clearing the Beautiful Market Square between the Cathedral of the Virgin of the Intercession and the tomb of the Holy Fool Vasilli and the Savior Gate of the Kremlin went to their work muffled in shubas as engulfing as snowdrifts, yet even then the cold ate through the heavy sheepskin and gnawed at their bones.

Within the Kremlin priests and monks labored in the Cathedral of the Dormition, trying to put the gorgeous royal church to rights in time for the Nuptial Mass which was scheduled to start in late afternoon. Sweet evergreen boughs had been tied around the pillars and were strewn on the floor; incense perfumed the air.

At the ikon of the Virgin of Vladimir, the Czar himself lay prostrate, repeating prayers that begged for mercy. Occasionally he raged at the Holy Mother, demanding that she use her influence to gain him some redemption before his death. His heavy silken kaftan was stained and threadbare from his long hours of lying prone before this ikon when he was not in the Czar's Chapel of the Annunciation Cathedral, fifty steps away from the Cathedral of the Dormition.

Yaroslav waited a short distance away, fretting as he watched over his charge. He crossed himself from time to time and whispered a few words to the ikons, hoping that the Virgin would be able to hear him over Ivan's endless supplications.

Before the second Mass of the day, Father Simeon approached Yaroslav, pulling him aside for a moment. "We must have access to"—he indicated the area where the Czar lay—"the whole of the place, if we are to perform the wedding as well as the regular Masses here today."

"Of course," said Yaroslav, and went to urge Ivan to go to the Annunciation Cathedral for the rest of his petitions.

Father Simeon crossed himself as he watched the Czar being led away. "May God be merciful," he said, then hurried to join the others as they readied the altar.

Out in the shattering sunlight that turned the ice to diamonds, Ivan shaded his eyes. "God is warning me, showing me the way," he said to Yaroslav. "He is sending His angels to guide me."

"Yes, Little Father," said Yaroslav as he motioned for the Czar's armed guards to accompany them.

A short distance away, in the palace of Vasilli Shuisky, Anastasia had just arrived with Galina Alexandrevna Shuiskaya-Koshkina and her daughter, Xenya Evgeneivna. For once the women were not taken directly to the terem, but were led into the study of their host.

Vasilli accepted the women's deep reverences without any more formal acknowledgment than a wave of the hand. He stood back and inspected Xenya, his mouth pursed in distaste. "Well," he said at last, "you're too thin and too pale, but there's not much we can do about it now. Have my wife and her women tend to your hair and face. We can't do anything about your body, but they can make your face more satisfactory." He indicated a carved wooden box sitting on his trestle table. "Your bridegroom has very properly sent you a gift, a necklace of . . .moonstones set in silver." He said the last with puzzlement, for these milky, luminous jewels were not often seen in Russia and rarely given as wedding gifts. Pearls were considered the most acceptable jewels for women. "He is a foreigner, as you already know. You will wear it, of course."

Xenya tightened her hands into fists. "Of course."

Galina, seeing the expression in her daughter's pale brown eyes, tried to avert any unpleasantness. She moved a little nearer to Xenya and attempted to signal to her. "She is very nervous, Vasilli, my fond friend."

"That is because I would rather not marry," said Xenya in a voice that was as clear and steady as her mother's was tremulous.

"For your guardian angel's sake, girl," said Anastasi solicitously, "think of what you are saying. You are going to be married. All things considered, you ought to be on your knees in gratitude, both to your kinsman Vasilli and to the Virgin for delivering you from disgrace."

"If the Virgin wanted to deliver me from disgrace, she should have done something twelve years ago," said Xenya defiantly. Her large honey-colored eyes filled with tears, which she dashed impatiently away. "Oh, I am resigned to this. I do not wish to marry, but I will. You needn't fear I will say something to remind the Court of my shame."

Galina pressed her hand to her lips to keep from speaking. She was a once-beautiful woman who had found a certain security in its wreckage and her widowhood. Of all the things she had learned to protect herself, silence was the most valuable. She prayed her daughter would be wise and follow her example.

"No more of that, girl," said Anastasi to Xenya; his tone was light but the set of his mouth demanded compliance.

"You are not to say anything," Vasilli warned her. "Just as your mother has ordered you, you are to say nothing. You have accepted our story for a dozen years, and you will endorse it to your grave or you will pay a higher price than you know. You will not only bring black shame on yourself, you will forever destroy the memory of your father, and the family will not be able to escape the stain of his sin or yours. We have succeeded in saving your reputation thus far, but if you break silence now it would defile the Shuisky name and you might well be banished."

Xenya folded her arms. She was not yet dressed in the magnificent wedding sarafan Anastasia had provided as his gift, in white and gold to suit her foreign bridegroom; her garments were plain and utilitarian, suited to the work she did with the poor each day. She made no apology for her appearance but regarded Prince Vasilli directly. "What do I tell to this foreigner who is to be my husband, and who wants me pale as a corpse?"

"You will think of something, if he has any questions to put to you. If he does not, you need tell him nothing," said Galina quickly, deeply grateful to have a suggestion to offer. "I have several notions that might account for . . . for the clean sheets."

"I don't want to know, whatever you decide upon," said Vasilli with distaste.

Galina made a reverence to Vasilli and Anastasi, then nudged her daughter's arm for her to do the same. "We are thankful to you, august kinsman, for sparing Xenya the stigma of spinsterhood."

Vasilli dismissed the notion. "It was more Anastasi's doing than mine. Indeed, he was the one who suggested the match to the Czar; all I did was endorse it. But I am pleased you are aware of how great an achievement this is." He looked critically at Xenya once again. "They will give you more color when they paint your face, but it would help if you made some effort to smile. If you were to wear red, that would help, for it is so splendid a color that you could not help but smile." If he had expected to cajole Xenya this way, he was disappointed.

With a sudden toss of her head, Xenya reached out and grabbed the wooden box. "Let me see this, since the foreigner sends it to me."

Anastasi and Vasilli exchanged uneasy glances as Xenya opened the box, paying no heed to the soft protests Galina made. Xenya pulled the necklace from its housing and flung the box aside, stretching the necklace out between her hands. It was nearly as fragile as lace, an interlocking pattern of raised wings, with moonstones where they intersected. There were more than forty of the jewels and the necklace itself was glossy with shine. Xenya, who had been ready to scorn it, now stared in fascination, her face softening as she lifted the necklace higher. "Where did he get this? There is nothing like it. No Russian silversmith made this." She turned the necklace, letting the light gleam.

"He claims he made it himself, as part of his alchemical skills," said Anastasi, making it plain that he did not believe this.

"It is lovely, very lovely," said Galina, seizing on the one thing Xenya had shown any favor for in regard to her marriage. "A wonderful gift for you, my daughter."

Xenya rounded on her mother. "Unfortunately, I cannot have the necklace without the man," she said, and added to Vasilli, "We might as well get this done, since you are all determined to have it."

Vasilli shrugged and clapped for a servant. "Take my kinswomen to the terem. My wife is waiting for them."

Not far from the Shuisky palace, Boris Godunov had just come to the reception hall of his palace to greet his guest, his wife

Marya Skuratova for once accompanying him; she was noticeably pregnant and moved with great care.

"How fine an occasion to welcome you to my house," Boris assured Rakoczy as his guards escorted the Transylvanian to the reception hall.

Rakoczy bowed in the Italian manner as deeply as his heavy wolf-fur kontush would permit and indicated his manservant, saying, "My Rothger has my wedding clothes. If you will direct him to the place he is to prepare them?" Then he managed a quick, fleeting smile. "What a churlish thing to say to someone who has opened his home to me. I ask you to think of it as an oversight, brought about by my nerves."

"You are nervous?" asked Boris in some surprise; he did not present his wife, for that would have been insulting to her since Rakoczy was not Boris' kinsman. "You haven't the look of it."

Rakoczy nodded once. "But I am. Very. You see, I have never been married."

"And you are ten years my senior, or so I judge." Boris' black eyes shone with genuine sympathy; he was thirty-two, which was old for a man to marry. "It is the fate of the exile, I fear. All the more reason to rejoice in your good fortune here." He signaled to one of his servants. "Take the Hrabia's houseman to the room we have prepared for my guest. Be certain the mirrors are clean."

"Mirrors." Rakoczy could not keep the irony from his chuckle. "I think Rothger and I can manage without them." It had been more than three thousand five hundred years since he had seen his reflection in any surface; not even clear water could show him his face. "But thank you," he added.

"Do you practice humility this way?" asked Boris as two of the servants led Rothger away, one of them carrying the two large cases Rakoczy had brought with him. "Let us drink to your bride, and to the happiness of your marriage," said Boris enthusiastically.

Rakoczy held up his hand, his expression rueful. "My good friend, for all the kindness you offer me, I appear always to refuse. Do not let me take drink now. I am certain that it would not be wise for me to fog my wits; they tell me the Nuptial Mass is almost two hours long. I will need to keep my head."

Boris laughed outright. "Always so prudent, you foreigner.

You must learn to be more Russian now, and forget your circumspection. You must embrace life, my friend, clasp all of it to your breast and hold it fast, though it eats the heart out of you for your pains."

"I must," said Rakoczy enigmatically.

With a laugh Boris gestured his concession. "Very well. But when the wedding is over and you are feasting, then you and I will drink until the stars wobble in the sky."

"Certainly," said Rakoczy at once, hiding his inner trepidation with a bow that also freed him of his heavy fur cloak. As he draped this over his arm, he said, "And if I am to be ready for the wedding, I fear I must shortly turn myself over to my manservant. I fear it will take time to dress." This was not wholly the truth, but he wanted to escape Boris' cordial probing.

Boris glanced at his wife, then asked, "Tell me, is it the custom for those who marry in your country to wear white?"

"Occasionally, yes, if it is a first marriage," said Rakoczy; he chose his words carefully now, sensing that Boris was probing for something more.

"Then you will wear white, too?" It would have been intolerably rude to ask this of a Russian, but Boris excused himself with the certainty that a Russian would be wearing proper red for his wedding.

"White edged in black, with rubies," said Rakoczy, adding, "To honor my blood."

This was a satisfactory explanation to Boris and he rubbed his hands together vigorously. "The Czar will approve when I explain it to him." He signaled for more servants. "Well, then, into your clothes. I will tend to the Little Father before the Mass begins, so there ought to be no unpleasantness. If he is not told of your plans, he might decide to take offense that you do not wear red." He hesitated. "You have been honored twice," he warned Rakoczy as the alchemist started out of the room.

"Honored? How is that, Boris Feodorovich?" asked Rakoczy.

"Czar Ivan has ordered three of his hymns to be sung, in addition to the Nuptial Mass, two in veneration of the Virgin, the other an anthem of salvation." Boris held up his hands, palms outward. "They are very good hymns, my friend, but they are very long."

"I see," said Rakoczy. "I'll keep that in mind." He was almost to the door. "And when you speak to Czar Ivan, thank him for me for so gracious a gift."

Boris' smile glinted. "Most assuredly." Only when Rakoczy was out of the room did he turn to his wife and ask her opinion.

Marya considered her answer, trying to sum up her impressions. "He is astute, as you have said. But there is something about him, cherished Boris. I pray that Xenya Evgeneivna has the skill to command his affection. If she can do that, she will need fear nothing but the loss of him for the rest of her life."

"*You* are always astute," Boris approved. "You have expressed my own thoughts, and better than I could."

When Rakoczy came into the chamber Boris had given them, Rothger had most of Rakoczy's clothes laid out. He silently took the plain mente from Rakoczy, then waited for the dolman.

"I was thinking this morning as we rode here," said Rakoczy as he pulled off the dolman and unfastened his leggings from his under-belt, "that it has been a long time since I have worn white."

"The last time was in Fiorenza," said Rothger, giving the city its older pronunciation: it was now more commonly called Firenza.

"Nearly a century; I claimed Hungarian alliance then, too, and to be my own nephew." He stood still for a moment, half-naked, his dark eyes distant, recalling the flames and Estasia.

"My master?" Rothger prompted.

Rakoczy blinked. "Oh. Yes. You're right." He finished undressing, standing naked long enough for Rothger to sponge and dry and perfume his body, then gratefully slipped into the fine black silken camisa he would wear under the white. As he fastened the front lacing, he said, "What sort of woman do you suppose this woman is?"

"Her father was killed when the Mongols last attacked the city," said Rothger. "She and her mother have been living with Anastasi Shuisky ever since. They say she is over twenty."

"In other words, they are poor relations," said Rakoczy. "That much was clear. But that tells me almost nothing about Xenya Evgeneivna. I'm still not certain why Czar Ivan selected her." He gave a short sigh. "I wish I knew something useful about the woman. As it is—" He took the silver-shot white leggings and drew them on, securing them to his underbelt.

"Czar Ivan was probably persuaded by Anastasi Shuisky," said Rothger, holding out the glossy white dolman edged in black and closed with black lacings.

"Very likely," agreed Rakoczy. "But who is she?"

Rothger took the ankle-length mente from its case; it was ermine and the front was studded with rubies in the pattern of Rakoczy's device—the eclipse with raised wings displayed. "This will complement their two-headed Byzantine eagle," he remarked, only his pale-blue eyes revealing his amusement.

"Let us hope," said Rakoczy, and looked for the white boots he would wear as he held out his hand with the ruby signet ring. "At least it complements this."

An hour later the Court began to assemble at the Cathedral of the Dormition, most trying to get as near to the golden Coronation Throne as possible without appearing more interested in the Czar's favor than in the ranks upon ranks of gilded ikons soaring to the ceiling. The afternoon sun slanted in through three windows in the enormous frescoes filling the entire west wall depicting the Last Judgment. Hero-saints glowed on the pillars and a forest of candles blazed before the Virgin of Vladimir.

There was a flurry of activity as Czar Ivan arrived with the Czareivich Feodor in tow; the moon-faced young man was beaming, having been promised an opportunity to ring bells after the wedding was over. Their Guards stationed themselves around Ivan as he went from ikon to ikon, prostrating himself and praying. Feodor followed after his father, smiling gently, his brow encircled by the coronet Rakoczy had given him.

Father Simeon returned to the Cathedral, now vested in a pearl-sewn omophorion instead of his usual black habit, and because this was a wedding, he was crowned with a pearl-and-agate-studded kamelaukion. He could not prostrate himself before Ivan without profaning his garments, so he made a deep reverence instead. "Little Father, the Nuptial Mass ought to begin. What do you want me to do? Shall I signal a delay?"

Czar Ivan looked around, his blue-green eyes dazed. "No," he said after a short hesitation. "No. The wedding must take place, to honor the jewels I have received. Now the foreigner will receive a Russian jewel." He laughed loudly, then struggled to his feet. "Have the bride and groom arrived?"

"Both are here," said Father Simeon. "Their sponsors are waiting. The procession is ready."

"Ah," Ivan muttered, getting to his feet and moving toward the ikonostasis. "Then it must begin." He stared around in satisfaction. "Yes, it must begin." Slightly distracted, he made his way toward the front of the Cathedral, remarking to his amiable, slow-witted son as he went, "I have been informed they are going to wear white, like shrouds; it is the custom in Hungary or Poland or some such place." He crossed himself twice, once for Rakoczy and once for Xenya. "May God be merciful."

Once the Czar had reached his place of honor, the concealed choir broke forth in twelve-part harmony, extolling the mercy of God. The procession of the priests began, followed by the bride, led by her sponsor, Anastasi Shuisky; behind them came two more priests and then Boris Godunov accompanied Ferenc Rakoczy toward the ikonostasis.

This was the first sight Rakoczy had of Xenya; she was almost as tall as he, unfashionably slender, her gold-threaded white sarafan hanging in heavy gathers around her, more like a Roman stola than a Russian gown. She carried herself well. There was no way to tell much about her kokoshnik-framed face, for her cosmetics were heavily applied, making her brows black, her skin a pale golden rose, her mouth a crimson bow. Her clear, golden-brown eyes met his without flinching.

The choir soared in ecstatic praise and the priests intoned the first blessing of the couple, extolling the blessing of matrimony.

By the time the Nuptial Mass was finished, it was twilight. The Court, having stood in worship for the last three hours, was now ready for the extensive banquet that waited a short distance away in the Palace of Facets. Ably assisted by the Czareivich, the priests were ringing the Cathedral bells to celebrate the wedding.

Ivan had lingered in the Cathedral after the Court and newly married couple had left it, prostrating himself to pray at the ikonostasis before summoning his Guards to escort him from the Cathedral; the Court and the wedding party would be waiting for him in the courtyard outside, for they could not depart from there without his permission. He stepped into the frozen evening, favoring the bride with a nod of his crowned head. "God is merciful," he announced, raising his head to indicate that the skies were still clear. And he shrank back, his features a rictus of fear.

High overhead, out of the east, a comet streamed.

Slowly, in confusion, various nobles of the Court looked up, and crossed themselves in awe, a few sinking to their knees in spite of the freezing mud and their fine clothes.

The ringing of bells grew in intensity, the air trembling with their enormous song.

"God and His martyrs!" exclaimed Boris as he caught sight of the comet. He crossed himself twice and looked at once to Rakoczy and the woman he had just married. "You cannot stay here," he said with conviction. "Leave. Leave while you can."

Xenya had turned away, not quite cowering but gripped by fear; Rakoczy stood looking upward, compelling curiosity in his dark, dark eyes.

"Cross yourself, fool!" shouted Boris, knowing that he could hardly be heard over the bells. He nudged Rakoczy and repeated himself.

Rakoczy nodded once and did as he was told.

Czar Ivan had fallen supine, still pointing upward at the heavens, foam on his lips as he screamed and drummed his heels on the icy Cathedral steps.

Some of the Court were praying now, their mouths moving as they stared at the comet and rocked with the swing of the bells. The priests who had performed the Nuptial Mass withdrew into the sanctuary of the Dormition, seeking the protection of their ikons; a few of the Court followed after them.

The Czar had bitten through his lip and now his beard was spattered with blood. The crown had fallen from his head and lay like a bauble in the banked snow at the side of the Cathedral steps. His guards milled around him, most of them refusing to look at the comet while the Czar shrieked and thrashed and spasmed at their feet.

Boris leaned very close to Rakoczy. "Take your wife and leave," he insisted. "Leave now. Who knows what the Little Father will do while he is like this? I must attend him at once. Do not put yourself in danger." He shoved Rakoczy in the shoulder. "It's a pity the clouds cleared, after all," he added, then made his way toward the Czar, not looking back.

Rakoczy watched him go, then turned to his wife. "Xenya," he said as gently as he could to be heard over the bells, "Xenya Evgeneivna, will you come with me?"

She stared at his extended hand, and the ruby signet ring. "If I must," she said as she put her hand into his, lifting her chin as she did.

"Good," said Rakoczy, and led the way through the growing hysteria of the Court toward Boris Godunov's palace, where his new curtained wagon could be made ready for them. Under the baleful light of the comet, Rakoczy took his bride to his house.

Excerpt from a report by Father Milan Krabbe to Archbishop Antonin Kutnel, entrusted to Hrabia Zary.

. . . Regarding the occasion of the marriage of Hrabia Saint-Germain to the Russian woman, the event was marred at the end by the appearance of a great tailed star in the sky that struck all the people with dread and awe. I have been told that the Czar himself was sent into a fit at the sight of it. Because of this apparition, the banquet that was to follow the wedding did not take place and all the meats that were to be served to the Court were distributed to the poor that very night and prayers were ordered at every altar in the city of Moscovy.

It is said that the Czar has sent for Lappish witches, to have them tell what the tailed star portends. They are supposed to arrive in a matter of days, and all the Court is filled with rumors, for you must know that among the Rus, Lapps and Finns are considered to be powerful magicians.

Because of this occurrence, Rakoczy has not been much at Court, although he has sent two magnificent amethysts to Czar Ivan for his recovery. I have heard that the Czar accepted them, but is not willing to admit Rakoczy himself to his presence. If the Lapps declare that it is not dangerous to have the Transylvanian near them, then he will be permitted to address Ivan directly once again.

I trust this will happen, for since the coming of the star, Ivan has not been willing to speak to any of us. He is certain that the presence of Catholics has lessened God's favor for him, and therefore he is unwilling to recognize our embassy. We have been informed by Duke Anastasi Shuisky, who has somewhat befriended us, that this is certain to pass and that it will not be long before Czar Ivan realizes that he must speak either with us or with Father Possevino.

Although Father Pogner distrusts Rakoczy and believes that he has turned against King Istvan, I am not convinced this is the case. He himself told me that he had not sought the marriage and that the Czar had required it of him, as a way to ensure a continuing supply of jewels. I have been told that Ivan has ordered other members of his Court to marry women he has chosen for them, and so I have reserved judgment in regard to this event, for it appears to me that Rakoczy never behaved as if he wanted such a union. I realize this contradicts what Father Pogner has said, but in conscience I must inform you that it may not be as it appears, and King Istvan may still have a steadfast servant in Hrabia Saint-Germain.

There was a small fire in the Bakers' Quarter, and it has been attributed to the tailed star, as has every misfortune since it appeared in the sky. We saw it for two nights only. Another storm blew clouds over the sky and since then the star has not been seen. Some say it has fallen to earth and others say God has recalled it to Heaven. Whether this is true, only the wisest of men can know. In the meantime, we will await the prognostications of the Lappish witches.

In regard to the wagons used to bring fish from the Black Sea, I have not yet had the opportunity to see how they are caulked, but I am told that most of them are tarred like ships and then lacquered in order to keep water within them on the long journey . . .

2

Their garments were made of wolf skin and reindeer hide and were embroidered in strips from shoulder to hem. Their boots, too, were embroidered and turned up at the toe, as did the peaks of their leather caps. Their eyes were light but their faces were Asiatic, with high, flat cheekbones and broad foreheads. There were sixty of them, ranging from youth to old age, and they refused to prostrate themselves before the Czar when the Guard escorted them into Ivan's Golden Chamber.

In the last three weeks, Ivan had deteriorated. He had refused to bathe since the star appeared and he wore the same kaftan he had donned for the wedding. His beard and hair were a tangled thatch and his eyes, always prominent, now seemed to start from his head. He pointed to the Lapps with his mace and demanded without ceremony that they use their powers at once to tell him when he would die.

The most senior of the witches, a man with deep seams in his face and few teeth, heard these orders without dismay. His Russian was accented strangely and the rhythm of his speech was equally strange, but he was comprehendible. "We must see into the fire," he explained. "Let us have fire."

"Why fire?" demanded Ivan, extending his finger and pointing at the Lappish witches. "You come to burn me to show me Hell."

The senior witch shook his head. "We do not. Hell is your teaching, not ours." He turned and spoke to the others, then went on, "The star was a fire in the sky. To know its meaning, we must consult fire."

The sense of this penetrated the miasma of fear that held Ivan captive. He signaled to his Guard. "Tell them to build up a fire in front of Saint Mikhail's. The cathedral will protect us if there is any work of Satan in this." He gestured wildly. "Do it. Do it!"

A number of the witches chuckled at this desperate display, but they were quelled by the stares of the Guard.

"Make the fire!" howled Ivan, swinging his arms as if they were weapons.

The Guard hurried out into the courtyard, where they summoned servants to bring wood and set it alight; they worked quickly and forced the servants to hurry in order to avoid the Czar's wrath. Ivan stayed in his Golden Chamber, his face pressed to the milky windows, staring down as his orders were carried out. He prayed constantly and would not look at the Lappish witches who crowded around him for fear of their enchantments.

When the fire at last was blazing, the senior witch signaled the rest to follow him, and they trooped down, out into the courtyard. They circled the fire, making themselves a human container for the flames. Under the watchful, apprehensive gaze of the soldiers, the witches made reverent gestures to the fire and began their slow, repetitious chant, shuffling from one foot to the other as they circled the flames, occasionally throwing bits of dried plants into it, sniffing the smoke and pointing to the way the wood broke apart.

Ivan watched with such intensity that he was not distracted

when Vasilli Shuisky entered the Golden Chamber unannounced and prostrated himself.

"Great Czar," said Vasilli when he had been doubled and prone for some little time. "I have prayed to God to send you succor in your hour of need."

Instead of looking around, Ivan only waved Vasilli to silence, his manner abrupt and annoyed. "I cannot speak to you now. This is more important. They are at their work."

"Who, Great Czar?" asked Vasilli, taking a chance in speaking. "What are they doing?"

"The Lappish witches have come. They will read my fate." He turned at last, revealing tortured features. "If only they can tell me what I must do to expiate my sins. I am willing to renounce all, you have heard me declare it, but the Metropolitan has refused to let me. He says it is God's Will that I continue as Czar while living in guilt, because my poor boy Feodor is not competent to do anything other than ring bells. But God cannot have cut me off from mercy. It cannot be. I have besought God and the Virgin, but they are silent to me. And so I have found those who can hear, who can read the signs the heavens leave for us. The witches will know. They have ways to learn these things."

"Speak to the Metropolitan, Czar. He will instruct you." It was the sort of advice he would have given a child, and he offered it in a kindly spirit. "You do not need these un-Christian people to bring their sorcery to you in your misfortune."

"They are wise, and their skill is known everywhere," Ivan insisted, his face hardening. "And the Metropolitan is obdurate. He will not grant my petitions. So I must deal with these witches. They are able to find out the secrets. They will know, and they will tell me what I must do. My jewels cannot tell me. The priests are all fools, slaves of the Metropolitan. But they"—he pointed down toward the courtyard—"they have true wisdom. They will know the truth and they will reveal it to me."

Vasilli's smile was faintly condemning. "How wise can they be? And how will you know it is the truth?"

"I have sent for Rakoczy. He will tell me if they are truthful," declared the Czar.

"And how will you know that foreigner is not lying?" asked Vasilli with asperity. "He seeks your favor, since his own embassy wants no part of him. The distrust of the Jesuits should serve to alert you, Czar." He took a chance and got to his feet, approaching the Czar with the look of a man wishing to impart special information. "This man is not what he appears to be; the Poles have told you that. He abuses your trust, Czar, taking treasures for himself that you have not denied him, and all for the price of a few gems. He has gained far more from you than you from him. Yet you continue to show him favor." He shook his head, his expression turning sorrowful, as if he was only concerned for Ivan's welfare. "You cannot trust men who are so wholly dependent on you, Great Czar."

"Everyone is dependent on me," declared Ivan with heat. "Without the Czar, there is no Russia. From the lowest serf to the highest Prince, all of you come to me for guidance and protection. That is the work of the Czar." His eyes were wide again, and as he spoke foam coated the corners of his mouth.

The chanting in the courtyard was louder, and the witches moved more quickly around the flames.

Vasilli changed his attitude immediately. "Yes, yes, Little Father. And everyone who is Rus knows it. You are the heart of all Russia, and nothing happens here but that you desire to happen, and anything that is against your will is treason to the country. But Rakoczy is not Rus."

Ivan listened attentively; his demeanor was more forbidding than ever. "You say he is not dependent upon me?"

"How can he be, sworn as he is to Istvan Bathory?" Vasilli inquired in exaggerated sympathy.

"He is married to your cousin now, Vasilli Andreivich. You have him as one of your own. He comes to Russia as a Shuisky now that he is married. And that assures me of his devotion." He folded his arms as he watched the witches. "He is a good man, trustworthy. He only gains through my good-will. He is not like the rest of you, with lands and titles and ambitions."

Vasilli knew that he was taking a chance now. "But he is an exile, Czar, and he has nothing to lose if he—"

"Stop!" ordered Ivan, his face darkening and his eyes too bright. "I have done what a Czar must do to those who are loyal. You want me to dishonor myself. I will not do it. I will not. *I will not!*"

"No. No, you will not," Vasilli said quickly, hoping to soothe Ivan before he became too overwrought and needed the help of his priest once again. He decided to approach the matter one more time, from another stance. "But as a Shuisky, you cannot blame me for my concerns for you. With my cousin married to a foreigner, I am afraid that it could come to pass that we would be blamed for any actions this exile might take."

"He will not act against me. Not he. He is my strong support and he will not—" He broke off as the Lappish witches gave a high, shrill cry, stopping their shuffling around the fire and staring upwards as sparks mounted toward the leaden clouds.

Vasilli came nearer. "Do not trust him, Little Father. Lest he bring disgrace on all the Shuiskys."

"You speak to him," said Ivan, and pointed toward the door of the Golden Chamber. "I do not want you here, Prince Vasilli. You will leave."

There was nothing Vasilli could do but withdraw. He bent over so that his tall hat almost brushed the ground, and he let his caftan drag around him as he backed out of Ivan's presence, irritated with himself as much as Ivan at his failure to compromise Rakoczy. He was still nursing his insults when he saw four Guards approaching from the other end of the corridor, Rakoczy walking in their center. At least, thought Vasilli, Boris Godunov was not providing Rakoczy's escort; that was a welcome change. Rakoczy had been in Boris' company far too often to suit the Shuisky fortunes. As they drew abreast of him, the Guard stopped and reverenced Vasilli.

"God send you a pleasant day, Prince Vasilli," said Rakoczy, who knew better than to use the more familiar patronymic form with Xenya's highest-ranking kinsman.

"And to you, Hrabia Saint-Germain." This was a deliberate and unkind reminder of Rakoczy's foreign status, and his inferior rank. "How is my cousin?" To inquire about a man's wife at Court was offensive and often led to angry confrontations; Vasilli longed for an argument so that he could give voice to some of his inner fury.

Instead Rakoczy bowed slightly in the Italian manner. "I hope that she is well, Prince. She was so when she left my house this morning, in the company of two of my servants. She is with the Sisters today, giving food to those who are injured and abed."

"Still at her charity." Vasilli's faint smile was contemptuous. "And you intend to allow her to continue these works now that she is your wife?"

"Why should she not?" asked Rakoczy.

"For your honor," exclaimed Vasilli, truly shocked that Rakoczy would ask such a question. "Now that she is married, she should never leave the terem but for your pleasure, to tend to her children, and the order of the Czarina." He paused. "And at her death, of course."

Rakoczy regarded Vasilli in momentary silence, then gestured his deference. "Because that is the way of Rus?" he asked gently. "But, Prince, I am not Russian, as you have been at pains to remind me. And so, since she is my wife, and the only female of my household, save the baker, I believe it would be best if she lived as if we were in Transylvania still, and the Turks were not. I realize that my ways are not yours, but she is my wife now. We do not keep our women in terems, married or unmarried. Since it suits her purpose to render charity and she does not endanger herself in the process, she may conduct herself as she wishes within reasonable bounds. I trust her good sense to protect her better than guarded doors." He bowed again, his manner impeccable. "The Czar awaits me, Prince, and it is discourteous to delay."

Vasilli could not resist one last parting barb. "If she is not to your liking, beat her until she is."

Something burned in Rakoczy's dark eyes, and then it was gone. "I will remember you recommended it, Prince." He signaled to the Guard and they continued down the corridor.

Watching after Rakoczy, Vasilli had the odd notion that the Polish King's charlatan could be more dangerous to him than he was to Rakoczy.

Ivan was once more pressed against the window as if he wished to fly through it when Rakoczy came into the Golden Chamber, properly blessed the ikons at the door, and went down on his knee in the Polish manner; he was willing to remain there until Ivan recognized him. The Czar took no notice of Rakoczy's presence; he was lost in tangled prayers, addressing saints and God alike while he stared down at the Lappish witches.

"Great Czar," said Rakoczy when he had waited a considerable time.

Ivan swung around with a cry, as if he expected to see Archangel Gavril standing before him. He blinked, dazed and filled with questions, then made an effort to recover himself. "Ah. You are here, Rakoczy."

"As you wished, Great Czar," said Rakoczy. He remained on his knee, aware that the Guard were still watching him, ready to cudgel him if they decided he was not respectful enough to the Czar.

"As I wished; yes, yes, yes," Ivan agreed. He crossed himself twice. "The Lappish witches have come."

"I saw them in the courtyard, Czar," said Rakoczy, his tone carefully neutral for he recognized the hold of madness that was steadily growing in Ivan. "There is a fire burning."

"They are there, with the fire that was lit for them," Ivan said at once. "They are there to learn my fate."

Rakoczy hesitated, aware that Ivan expected something from him, yet having no notion what it might be. He chose a careful response, given Ivan's chaotic condition. "Are you certain you wish to know?" There was a remoteness about him as he asked, "Might not knowledge be worse than your uncertainty?"

"Nothing is worse than uncertainty. If I were as other men, what you say might be true." He tapped his chin with his finger, then hooked it into his beard. "But I am Czar, and my fate is the fate of all Russia. So I must, perforce, know what is to become of me so that Russia will not be left to the mercy of the Mongols or the Catholics."

Rakoczy crossed himself as Ivan did, as if he shared the Czar's fears. "And these Lappish witches will reveal what you wish to know? Are you certain they will? It is a difficult matter to interpret oracles, Great Czar."

"I hope they will reveal whatever they see, no matter how terrible," said Ivan, suddenly beginning to weep. "I am desperate, Rakoczy. I am not able to think as I must because of my desperation." He coughed once. "I must have the truth. God is merciful and the font of perfect peace, and He will not abandon all Russia to ruin for my sin." He sank onto the steps leading to his throne. "I must ask these un-Christian witches because my Metropolitan will not learn what God desires of me. He is stubborn, the Metropolitan. I would declare him Patriarch, but not if he will not bend his faith to my will."

"Great Czar, you are the only one who knows what to require of your Metropolitan, or whether he must be elevated to a higher position. My King is Catholic and has told me nothing in regard to your Patriarch." While this was all true, Rakoczy was also troubled that he might become more embroiled in the internal struggles of Russia than he was already, and the very notion distressed him. The brief exchange with Vasilli Shuisky had made it apparent to him that the stakes were high for everyone.

"Always so reticent about religion," said Ivan distantly.

Rakoczy saw the hectic shine in Ivan's eyes. "I am not so wise that I seek to understand God. And what man can read the faith of another?"

"With your darker jewels, it is possible," said Ivan with great solemnity. "Faith is the heart of every man."

"Or so the priests would like to believe," said Rakoczy, re-membering priests from his childhood to Babylon to Egypt to Rome to Spain to India; each priest had been certain he—or she—knew Rakoczy's inmost heart. Only one had, the first one, who had shared his blood.

"It is blasphemy to deny it," said Ivan in sudden wrath. "It is only that you are foreign and have lost your lands that I will not order you beaten for saying such things." He was on his feet again, but reached out to his throne in order to steady himself as he swayed. "But I must not raise my arm again, no, no. I must not. It is sin, a great sin." He was weeping once again, this time in such wretchedness that Rakoczy took a chance and went to his side.

"May God send His good angels to guide you, Czar," he said, knowing that Ivan would accept this.

"Yes, I pray so, I pray so." He crossed himself and tottered back to the window, staring down at the fire. "If it were night, they would be dancing in Hell."

Rakoczy thought of the many implications of this remark. "The witches will be strengthened by your prayers, and your faith may clarify their visions," he said carefully, aware of how quickly Ivan could turn against them. "It takes great courage for men to look into the flames."

"Yes," whispered Ivan. "Yes, yes, yes, yes." He wiped his hand over his face, banishing his tears as quickly as they had overcome him. He concentrated on the scene in the courtyard. "They are skillful witches. It is known they are the most skillful. I will reward them."

Rakoczy watched Ivan, measuring him. The Czar was growing steadily worse, he realized, and because of that, the danger he represented continued to grow. "To be called to serve you may well be reward enough, Great Czar," he said, wanting to forestall Ivan's unpredictable notions of deserved payment.

Ivan rounded on him, one arm extended. "What you say is very true, foreigner. You understand this more than those around me, for I have granted them privileges that they turn to their advantage. You, being without bounty from my hand, you are . . ." His words straggled off and he frowned. "You are not beholden to me."

"Except for the wife you have graciously bestowed on me," said Rakoczy quickly, not wanting Ivan to decide he was ungrateful or taking advantage of the Czar's generosity; either of those courses could be dangerous in Ivan's current state of mind. "Surely a faithful wife is the greatest treasure any man can know. For that I am in your debt for many years to come."

"Most certainly," said Ivan. "A Russian woman is a treasure, even a skinny one." He made an impatient gesture to the Guard. "You must wait in the hall. I do not need you in this place. I will summon you if you are needed."

The four Guards bent double at the waist and left immediately, exchanging uncertain glances as they went.

A high shout went up from the courtyard, and Ivan at once rushed to the window, staring hungrily out. "They know something," he whispered. "They know something. Something. Something." He remained there in silence for several minutes, then looked around, fixing Rakoczy with his gaze. "And you will tell me if they are revealing what they know."

"I?" Rakoczy asked, taken aback. "Great Czar, surely there are those at Court who are more learned in the ways of these people. One of them will be able to report far more than I."

But Ivan would not be put off. "You have humility, and that is a wise gift in an exile, who must rely on the good-will of others. But you have the secret of the jewels and through them you can read the human heart." He looked away. "I was able to do it, before Ivan Ivanovich died. I could have discovered for myself, in my jewels, the truth of these witches."

A thousand years before Rakoczy might have challenged this assertion, but now he only said, "I am not worthy to do this, Great Czar."

"True, yes, it is true," said Ivan. "But you are the only one I trust, Rakoczy. You are the one who will hear what these Lapps say, and you will inform me if they speak the truth."

Rakoczy offered Ivan an Italian bow and set his objections aside for the moment, not wanting to anger Ivan. "If it is your wish that I do this, I will try to please you to the best of my ability. But I warn you, Czar, that the ways of these witches are not my ways, and I may err through my lack of understanding." There were few other responses Ivan might accept; Rakoczy hoped that the Lapps would be sufficiently obscure in their predictions that he would not have to verify much in order to please Ivan.

"They will return here," said Ivan darkly. "They will come and tell me what I must know. It is their task."

"May God send them true sight," said Rakoczy, as much for himself as for the Lapps.

Ivan crossed himself several times. "I do not sleep, you know. If I do not drink until I am in a stupor, I do not sleep."

"Sleep is a blessing, Great Czar," said Rakoczy, who had rarely slept more than two hours every night for well over three thousand years.

"Sleep comes from the angels, and my angels have deserted me for my sins," said Ivan mournfully. "Death is the sleep of angels, so the Metropolitan has said, and if he is right, I will sleep before the year is gone. When I know God's will, then I will find my angel again, and perhaps then I will sleep." He looked down in the courtyard. "They are putting the fire out."

"Then they——" Rakoczy began.

"They will come and tell me what they have learned, and you will inform me if they are lying," said Ivan, filled with renewed energy.

"I will do my poor best, Great Czar," said Rakoczy uneasily.

The sharp orders of the Guard announced the witches before the formal request for admission to the Czar's presence. He was very nervous and revealed it by speaking too quickly and at a high pitch.

Ivan signaled to Rakoczy to open the door to the Golden Chamber. "Move aside. Stand where they will not notice you. Give them plenty of room. They must not be crowded. It is unwise to crowd witches."

Rakoczy did not respond to this except to do as Ivan required.

The senior witch prostrated himself before Ivan's throne as the

Czar took his place upon it. Ivan smiled with satisfaction, but Rakoczy, seeing this, knew it meant very bad news.

"We have divined, Czar," said the senior witch, not rising from his place.

"Yes. And tell me what your oracles have revealed to you." It was a blunt statement, but Ivan was growing impatient. "Tell me at once."

The senior witch cowered. "We could find no answer but this, Czar: that God will take you to Him on the eighteenth day of March."

The Golden Chamber was very silent. All the witches seemed to have stopped breathing, and the Czar might have been carved in ice. Finally he looked directly at the prostrate senior witch.

"Are you certain?" He asked it very quietly, and then pointed to Rakoczy. "What do you say, foreigner?"

Rakoczy shook his head once. "I do not know if what he says is true prophecy, but I know that the man is honest. He may not have a true vision, but he has told you what he has seen. He does not lie, Great Czar." He held up his cabochon sapphire pectoral, aware that he needed to add to his credibility. "By the power of this dark jewel, I say this."

Ivan accepted this endorsement with a blessing, lowering his head in apparent submission. "It must be done again, so that there will be no error." He leveled his right hand at the witches. "You will have another bonfire, and you will reveal your auguries to me."

The senior witch lifted his head from his hands. "Czar, if we implore our gods again, they may be angry."

"Nonetheless, you will do it," said Ivan, accepting no dispute. "You will do it, and I will hear what you say again." He clapped his hands, summoning his Guard. "You will build up another bonfire. At once."

The Guard officers faltered for only a moment, then left the Golden Chamber and set about following the Czar's orders.

"And you," Ivan continued, staring at Rakoczy. "You will go down to the courtyard and watch them. You will observe all that they do, so there is no taint of Satan in it."

There was no point in questioning Ivan, and Rakoczy did not bother. "If that is what you want, Great Czar," he said, wishing he had been permitted to leave. He was certain there was nothing the witches could tell Ivan that he would be satisfied to hear.

"It is what I demand of you, foreigner," said Ivan. "It is my wish that you protect me from any wiles of Satan. If God will speak through these witches, then I will know my fate is sealed." He raised his hand to block whatever sight had come upon him. "It was sealed when Ivan Ivanovich fell. I gave him his death, and he will have mine."

The senior witch had risen to his knees, and as Ivan collapsed in convulsive sobs, he regarded Rakoczy with frightened eyes. "You are to watch us at the fire?"

"It is what Czar Ivan has ordered me to do," said Rakoczy quietly.

The senior witch looked back at Ivan. "It is a very difficult thing, reading the signs for this man. There is too much around him."

"I do not doubt it," said Rakoczy. He moved closer to Ivan, who now buried his head in the crook of his arm, refusing to raise his head when Rakoczy spoke his name.

"He is there, my son is there." He shuddered and brought his hand to his lips. He bit at his nail, tearing it off below the quick and letting it bleed. "He watches me and he rejoices in my suffering. He does not heed my prayers. I have begged him, begged him, begged him to show compassion, but he only stands before me, his face red with his blood, the side of his head cracked so I can see his brains, and his eyes like burning embers. He waits for my death, to throw me into Hell."

The senior witch made a series of gestures. "This is to banish evil spirits, Czar," he explained as he repeated the gestures.

Ivan motioned the Lapp to stop. "My son is not an evil spirit, and you will not be able to banish him. He has never been far from me since the hour I struck him and only God Himself can call him away." He rose slowly, as if carrying a yearling colt on his shoulders. "Nothing I have done has moved God to spare me."

"We will pray for you," said one of the witches. "Perhaps our gods will—"

"No!" bellowed Ivan. "None of your prayers. No. No. No, you will not!" He took two hasty steps toward the witch, then stopped. "I will not have Ivan Ivanovich taken away from God and His peace. It is my sin that keeps him here, and God will take

full measure from me to ransom my son's death. He will be in Paradise while I am in Hell. You will not change that."

The senior witch intervened, soothing and apologetic. "No, we will not. None of us want to harm your son, and we do not want to take him from your God. We do not seek to try that, Czar. We seek to serve you, to answer your questions if our skills are great enough. None of us wish any harm to Ivan Ivanovich. We speak his name in our rituals. We ask the spirits we serve to protect him."

"The angels of God protect him," said Ivan sullenly.

Rakoczy had brought some of the composing liquid with him; he felt the vial tucked in his belt where most Russians carried their forks and spoons. He was about to draw it out and offer it to Ivan when the senior witch approached him.

"I do speak the truth, do I not?" he asked of Rakoczy, leaning close to him to add, "What does the man want of us?"

"What none can give him, I fear," Rakoczy answered softly, then made a point of studying the Lapp's face. "He speaks the truth, Czar. As he understands it. He intends no harm to you or your son."

Ivan nodded several times. "Just as well, just as well," he muttered as he wandered toward the window. "The fire is burning."

The senior witch bowed deeply and wearily. "We will consult the fire again."

"And you will tell me everything it reveals to you. I will not accept less than the complete revelation." Ivan was quite erect now, and his face had the stern command that had earned him the appellation Grosny, for he was awe-inspiring as he stood before the Lappish witches and charged them with their task.

The witches offered him reverences before they left.

"Wait," said Ivan as Rakoczy turned to follow them. "I want to speak privately with you, foreigner."

"Very well," said Rakoczy, his manner circumspect. These lightning shifts of temperament Ivan displayed made dealing with him difficult. "I am at your service, Great Czar."

"I do not believe that these Lapps will lie to me, but they could work their magic on me, put enchantments or curses on my head. I want you to watch for such tricks, and inform me of them. If any of them, witches or not, should do such a thing, I will have them knouted to death on the Savior Gate." He glared at the window. "If they have no better answer for me, they will have to consult the flames again. I will not tolerate such inadequate answers." He made a gesture of dismissal, then added, "If you see Godunov, tell him that Feodor Ivanovich is not to be allowed to know of this. His mind is not stalwart: these witches could—" He had no way to describe what the witches might do to his mild, childlike heir.

"As you wish, Great Czar," said Rakoczy with another Italian bow. "I will watch for malign actions." There had been many times in his long, long life when he had encountered the sort of magical craft Ivan so feared, but there was no trace of that destructive obsession in any of the Lapps; he doubted Ivan would believe him if he tried to convince the Czar of this. He backed out of the Golden Chamber and was escorted by two Guard officers down to the courtyard where the second fire was quickly turning the banked snow to muddy slush.

The witches were again moving around the flames, repeating the ritual they had already performed. Rakoczy took up a position in the shadow of the Terem Palace where the watery, oppressive sunlight would not leach his strength any more than necessary.

All through the afternoon and into the evening there were fires lit and the Lappish witches strove to give Czar Ivan some message other than the one that the flames had provided at the first: that Ivan would die on the eighteenth day of March.

Text of a letter from Boris Godunov to Sir Jerome Horsey, English Ambassador, written in Latin.

To the most honorable servant of Elizabeth of England, her ambassador in Moscovy, my greetings.

Sadly, I must agree with your observations of yesterday and inform you that I share your concerns. It is true that Czareivich Feodor is not likely to perform the duties of the Czar very well when his father is no longer able to. As deeply as we pray for the returning health, in body and mind, for Ivan, he is now fifty-three and no longer possesses the strength of his youth. To place our hopes in Czareivich Feodor would be folly. I say this without

*any treasonous intent; rather I renew my loyalty to Russia by
stating that Czareivich Feodor will need the guidance and care
of others if he is to survive at all. He is my brother-in-law, and
I hope that for my sister's sake he will permit me to assist him.
Ivan has indicated that he intends Nikita Romanov to be guardian to Czareivich Feodor, and so you may rest assured that there
will be two dedicated nobles to watch over Feodor.*

*About the incident with the Guard officers: Feodor Ivanovich
is still more a child than a man, and he has a child's curiosity.
He did not intend to commit any sin when he asked to inspect
the nakedness of the officers. He sought only to see in what way
they resembled him. Had he the sin you describe, he would be
walled up in a monastery for it, no matter who his father might
be. The Orthodox Church is very strict in this regard, and sins
of the flesh as you describe are punished with death. I understand that this is true in some of the Catholic countries as well.
But those who are as simple in their souls as Czareivich Feodor
are not prey to these sins. Indeed, he takes more pleasure in
ringing bells than in the flesh, either his own or my sister's. For
Feodor Ivanovich the duties of his rank are arduous and alarming, and never more than when he is with Irina. The Metropolitan himself has declared that the Czareivich is as untainted by
fleshly desires as any haloed saint.*

*It is true that continuing our trade with England is essential
to our progress. Through your industry and determination we
have achieved some success that must be strengthened and
enlarged upon if Russia is to receive the full benefit of the trade.
This is not to say that England cannot profit as well. You have
remarked yourself that Russian furs are considered to be among
the finest in the world. To be able to provide these furs in exchange for access to your market cities brings profit to you as
well as to us, both for carrying our goods and for what you can
sell here. Doubtless we can come to some understanding that
will make it possible for us to enlarge the scope of our mutual
enterprises.*

*Because Czareivich Feodor has no aptitude for these matters,
it might be wisest if we conduct our dealings together and present what arrangements we have made to him when our agreement is final. Certainly you can see the benefit in such methods,
for then there would be fewer delays in implementing our vari-*

ous plans. For the sake of prompt action we need to have as little uncertainty as is possible when the Czareivich is consulted.

By all means, let us meet again in a week when we will both have had the opportunity to reflect on our recent discussions. At that time we may arrive at ways by which we can promote the well-being of both our countries. In the meantime, let me advise you that it would not be very wise to approach Czar Ivan, unless you intend to present him with a gift on behalf of your Queen. He has allowed himself to be persuaded by the predictions of the Lappish witches and truly expects not to live beyond the eighteenth day of next month. That is still more than three weeks distant. Until that day has come and gone, he has divided himself between the luxury of his wife, the austerity of his prayers, and the comfort of his jewels. I do not think he will receive you at Court.

I regret to disappoint you, and I ask that you not allow these momentary distractions of the Czar to turn you from the goodwill you bring to Russia. May God show you favor and bring you long years of prosperity and happiness. May you thrive while you are here in Moscovy and may your return home be sweet.

Boris Feodorovich Godunov
Brother-in-law to the Czareivich Feodor Ivanovich

3

Not long after midnight Rothger found Rakoczy in his alchemical laboratory, a large room that took up almost half of the second floor of his house. There were two athanors, both quite new, on the far side of the chamber and one was heating for use.

"Another jewel?" Rothger inquired, cocking his head toward the athanor.

"The Czar wants a topaz, darker than the others he has." He shook his head once. "No jewel can protect him from his fear."

"Because of the witches' prediction?" asked Rothger.

Rakoczy carefully drew up one of the tall stools set at a high table, perching on it as he answered. "Not really; not entirely." He reached for a small stack of paper and pulled it to him. "No, the prediction is not significant by itself. But the man is in agony of spirit and his body will pay the price." He selected a stick of charcoal and began to figure the ingredients for the topaz.

"He will die," said Rothger. His expression was distant.

"Everyone dies," said Rakoczy, looking away from his manservant; he bent over his work. Both men spoke in Imperial Latin. "In time."

"In time," echoed Rothger. He was content to remain quiet while Rakoczy went on with his computations. Through the night-silent house only the grating of the icy wind made sound as it scraped through Moscovy. And when Rakoczy looked up Rothger spoke as if there had been no suspension in their conversation. "Have you been in here all evening?"

Rakoczy's quick smile was wry. "What you mean to ask, old friend, is have I visited my wife yet? And the answer is no." When Rothger said nothing more, he went on. "I've been to her chamber twice since our wedding; she might not knowingly accept what I am, but I supposed I could visit her in her sleep, as I have with others." His dark eyes grew somber. "When she has started to respond to what her dreams offer, she becomes frightened and wakes. She has almost discovered me. Whatever troubles her is a greater influence on her than any gratification I can offer; she does not trust me. Her agitation has not faded yet. That is dangerous for both of us, so—" He turned his small, beautiful hand over to express his dilemma.

"What does she think of your conduct?" Rothger wondered aloud, concern for his master revealed in his frown.

"My reticence, you mean? I don't know," said Rakoczy after a minute hesitation.

"That is unfortunate," said Rothger. The wind was rising, sounding like iron scraping ice, and he glanced around the laboratory as if he expected the interior shutters to break. "Should the fires be built up?"

"Not yet," said Rakoczy, then added quietly, "It is unfortunate. For her as well as for me." He rose and paced the length of his laboratory, his black fustian gown a garment more often seen in Rome or London than Moscovy, marking him a stranger as much as his clean-shaven face and manner of bowing. "I have sworn in church to protect this woman, though she is not one of my blood." He stopped at a large trunk and put his hand on it. "How many more of these are left?"

"Four," said Rothger, accepting this change of subject with aplomb. "And the earth in your mattress and soles."

"I will send a request for more with Zary." He saw the shock in Rothger's countenance. "That's Boris Feodorovich's doing; he does not want the Hrabia and his Lancers to die in the snow. He has been able to persuade Ivan that Istvan Bathory would not like it. So Zary's departure has been postponed yet again."

"And how will you explain your need for Transylvanian earth?" Rothger asked. "Istvan Bathory is likely to wonder why you need it."

"Because he, too, is Transylvanian and knows the legends?" Rakoczy suggested. "I am an alchemist. I require Transylvanian earth for my . . . transformations. He will believe this."

Rothger was about to question this when a single, high scream, thin as the crying wind, rent the air.

Rakoczy was off his stool at once. "Xenya," he said, and gestured toward Rothger. "Fetch something hot from the kitchen— mead, visnoua, wine, it doesn't matter. Bring it to me in Xenya's chamber." Then he was out of the door and rushing down the hall, hoping that his household servants would not be wakened by his wife's screams.

There were three rooms allocated to her use, the smallest set aside for two clothes presses and a formidable bed. Xenya had pulled the curtains close around it, as if sealing herself in a chamber of cloth. As Rakoczy reached to draw them back, she screamed again, this time higher and in greater distress.

Rakoczy saw that she was half-awake, her honey-colored eyes open but her mind still in whatever nightmare had tormented her. He stood quite still, and when he spoke, his voice was soft and low, his Russian nearly perfect. "Xenya Evgeneivna. Xenya. Do not be frightened. You are safe here."

A third scream, barely louder than a whisper, broke her free of the dream. She stared up at him, trying to keep from shuddering at the sight of him. "Husband," she made herself say.

"What is the matter?" he asked, sympathy in his compelling eyes.

The wind drubbed the side of the house as if it sought to break in.

She looked away from her husband. "I . . . I had a dream." This was all she wanted to say; her discomfort was clearly increasing and her behavior was not calculated to cause him to remain with her. "A nightmare."

"Yes, I realize that," he said, his voice low and gentle.

"It was only a dream. I was an idiot to cry out." This last was more defiant than self-deprecating. She drew her covers closely around her, securing herself against his presence. Her plaited hair hung over her shoulder, a bronze rope; the silken night rail he had given her as part of his wedding gifts was tied all the way to her chin.

Rakoczy's concern did not fade; he regarded her with sadness in his eyes, wishing that she would trust him. "What was it, Xenya?" It was not a demand but she knew he would not be put off; tonight, tomorrow, next week, next year, he would find her out.

"A nightmare, as I've told you, a child's fright," she answered evasively. "From time to time I have them."

"What is your nightmare?" he persisted kindly. "Tell me."

Her laughter was brief and forced. Her gesture was quick, as if discarding a rag. "Childish fancies." She stared up at him, then looked away. "Nothing."

"If it had the power to terrify you, it is hardly nothing," said Rakoczy, opening the hangings enough to be able to sit on the foot of the bed, although he was aware she was apprehensive about him. He leaned back a little, his small hands linked around the front of one knee. "Please tell me what you dreamed."

There was a clatter on the side of the house as the wind at last succeeded in pulling a loose shutter off its hinges. The shutter battered its way onto the stable roof and then slapped onto the stout wooden wall surrounding Rakoczy's house and stables.

Xenya shook her head, more scared of Rakoczy now than her nightmare. "It is not right to speak of dreams. Satan comes in dreams. It is not fitting—"

"Isn't it." He made no move to leave or to approach her.

Xenya watched him with suspicion, her vexation increasing. She tried changing the subject. "Are you going to make me your wife tonight?"

He gave her a long, measuring, kindly stare. "Is that what you expect? To be frightened into submission?" He gave her a chance to answer and when she did not, he said, "Xenya Evgeneivna, we are strangers, you and I. We have barely met. Neither of us sought the other. We are married because Czar Ivan had a whim and a determination to assure himself of my loyalty. You have endured his caprice already. You will not have to endure mine."

She stared at him. "You do not want me?" Her voice was hardly more than a whisper and her eyes were huge. "Do I offend you?"

"No," Rakoczy said at once, then went on more deliberately. "No, you do not offend me. But I suspect I might offend you: I am very foreign. The ways of my blood are not your ways." He disengaged his fingers and stretched out his hand only to see her flinch at the simple gesture; he drew his hand back. "There. You understand?" It was more difficult for him to say this than he had anticipated and the last word caught in his throat.

"You will repudiate me," she said miserably.

Rakoczy was very still. "Why should I do that? I know of no reason to repudiate you."

There was panic in her eyes now, and something else Rakoczy could not quite read. "No. Oh, no. They told you, didn't they? God and the angels! Anastasi and Vasilli, they said they would not, but they did."

"They told me nothing that would offend me," said Rakoczy, growing more aware of her profound, contained distress. "You have my word."

She was no longer listening to him; she dashed tears from her eyes. "Did they tell you the truth, or the lie? Did they tell you my father ran and left me to them? Or did they repeat the myth? Did they say he stopped them before anything happened?" Her agitation increased with each question.

"They told me only that your father was killed by Mongols when Moscovy was attacked twelve years ago. They told me he was a hero." He spoke very calmly, keeping to his place at the end of the bed. "They did not tell me very much about your father. He was the son of a poor nobleman and had no fortune, nor did the rest of that branch of the family. Thus, you have only one uncle who is very old and lives on his country estate who cannot leave his children much and has nothing for you; your mother is provided for by Anastasi Shuisky, and she lives in his Moscovy house. You and she constitute the women of the terem. Am I correct thus far?" Was it fear of penury that had brought about her nightmare? he asked himself inwardly. She had been married out of hand to a foreigner. She had no relatives to provide for her. Perhaps she worried that he might desert her.

Her features were set and her hand gripped her blankets like talons. "If you wish the lie as well, so be it."

Rakoczy shook his head, taking care to keep the challenge out of his question. "But what lie is it, Xenya?"

"You know." She pulled her covers higher in an effort to bury herself in their depths. "I can see it."

"What lie is it?" he repeated gently.

Before she could speak—if indeed she was going to—there was a tap on the door and Rothger announced himself.

"I have brought spirits of wine, my master, heated." He held a lacquered tray in his hands with a single golden cup on it, a length of red linen wrapped around it to protect Xenya's hands. "And I told the baker and the cook that they heard the wind. They have gone back to bed without questions. On a night like this, it might well be the wind."

Xenya's dread increased; she shrank back and averted her face.

Rakoczy saw all of this, but said only, "My manservant is going to bring the cup to you, Xenya." He nodded once to Rothger, and waited while Rothger presented the cup.

"Better to have the cup from me," said Rothger in his determined but badly accented Russian. "Keeps this meeting private."

"Thank you," Xenya whispered, breathing too fast as she reached out and took hold of the golden cup by the cloth tied around it. She would not take her eyes off Rothger as he bowed to her and his master, then withdrew. "There should be no man but my husband in the terem," she muttered.

Another shutter began to bang, flailing against the side of the house somewhere in the vicinity of the kitchens.

"Doubtless that is true," said Rakoczy with practiced diplomacy, as if he were speaking to a nobleman of high rank instead of his reluctant wife, "if there were a terem in this house. But we agreed there would be none. Why establish a women's quarters for just one woman and her personal servants? In this house, who is to decide what pleases you but you? You said that you did not wish to live in isolation with two maids and your needle-work, but wish to continue your charities and your religious activities." His smile was speculative. "You told me that life in the terem was boring."

"It is," she said emphatically. "But it is . . . protected." To forestall any explanations, she drank some of the spirits of wine, blinking at the potency of the hot liquid.

"Would you like to have a bodyguard, Xenya?" He asked it as if he were asking her what dish she wanted to eat at noon.

". . . I . . ." She lowered her eyes. "It is not fitting. And if you gave me one," she said, trying to rally her pride, "there are others who would guess the reason, because some of them suspect . . . and everyone would know . . ."

"Would know what?" Rakoczy asked when she faltered.

She did not answer. "How could they not? And my father would share my disgrace. Cousin Anastasi would not permit my mother to remain in his household—how could he? No. You must not give me a bodyguard." This last was supplication; she took a deep, reckless swallow of her spirits of wine. "Tell me you will not. I couldn't bear my shame being displayed."

"I know nothing shameful about you, nothing." Rakoczy did not move from his place at the foot of the bed. "I swear by all the lost gods, Xenya, that neither of your kinsmen has told me any-thing to your discredit but that they think you are too thin and you married later than is fashionable. And at the order of the Czar. What shame are you talking about? Tell me, and I will help you."

Her eyes were filled with hopeless anger. "Why?"

"Why should you tell me, or why should I help you?" he inquired, his voice steadying and tranquil. "The answer would be the same: you are my wife. And while I have never been married before, I understand my obligation. I respect bonds, Xenya, even ones such as this."

"You can have none to me," she said, her voice now hardly audible.

"There, I fear, you err." He let her have time to drink more of the spirits of wine, both to bolster her courage and to loosen her tongue. "Whatever you have done, Xenya, it makes no differ-ence, I promise you."

The silence between them was vast; the shutter had stopped banging, either secured or whipped away on the wind.

She drank the last of the spirits of wine. Her hands were shaking as she reached out and gave the cup to Rakoczy. "They say my father was killed when the Mongols entered the house. They say he held them off. They say he was defending . . ." She ran out of words.

"They say?" His voice low and gentle, Rakoczy said, "And what is the truth."

It was more than she could do to look at him. She trembled. "He ran. It didn't matter. Others caught him. They killed him. I think I heard him screaming. But there were eight of them. With me." She doubled over, her arms clenched at her waist. She tried not to sob.

Rakoczy had expected this answer, or something like it, nevertheless it stunned him; he had been unable to resign himself to that human ferocity since he left Babylon. "Eight of them. How old were you?"

"Eleven," she answered when she could control herself enough not to weep.

"And your mother?" Rakoczy asked.

"She was at the Convent of the Mercy of God, where they had taken the pregnant women and babies. It is on an island, and there were bowmen to defend it. She . . . my mother was pregnant then, but she miscarried." She looked away, whispering, "God punished her for my sin."

A thousand years ago Rakoczy would have condemned such assumptions roundly without hesitation. Now he went carefully, unwilling to open old wounds. "Did she say so?"

"When we prayed for the soul of my father. She told me that if I had not shamed her she would have delivered my father's son, to live to bring honor to his father's memory. As it is, all five of her children are dead but me. Most of them never finished their first year. My mother says now that she was given a warning that she did not heed, and now my sin stains her as well. She has begged God and the Virgin to keep me from sinning again." She was still breathing too fast, but not with panic. "And Father Illya has warned me many times that those who sin once are more likely to sin again. If I had not been the cause of my father's death, I—"

Rakoczy was no longer content to withhold his response entirely. He said as rationally as he could, "You were not the cause of your father's death. Mongols were the cause of his death. Mongols killed him, not you. You owe nothing to him for that."

She started to protest, to defend her dead father; then tears filled her eyes. "He left me." Her thin wail was as sharp and penetrating as a poignard. her hands locked together, all red and white. "A wagon was being readied for us. We were going to escape. He said he would wait in the wagon, but he didn't. He saw them break into the house and he left me." Her voice dropped even lower. "He was afraid. Oh, God, my God. Most of the servants were gone. No one stopped them. They carried bows and pikes and axes. They killed the maid—they said she was too old."

"And they raped you because you were a child," said Rakoczy. Xenya crossed herself. "It is my shame," she murmured.

"No, it is not," said Rakoczy. He bent to put the golden cup on the floor beside the bed. "Xenya, no. You have no shame in this. It should be the shame of those who raped you, and those who permitted it to happen, and those who wished shame on you, but it is never yours."

She stared at him as if he had suddenly run mad. "Don't you understand what happened to me?" She grabbed the blankets more tightly, no longer able to restrain her weeping; her whole body shook as if with feverish chill. "Those eight Mongols. They took turns with me, all of them. They—"

"Raped you," said Rakoczy evenly.

She refused to look at him. "I must never say it."

"You may say it to me," Rakoczy assured her.

"No. No. I must keep my silence. It cannot be discovered. It must never be discovered." She gasped as a wind-flung object struck the side of the house, then dropped noisily downward. "No one must ever know. No one."

"But you know, Xenya Evgeneivna," Rakoczy said with compassion in his dark eyes.

Xenya crossed herself again. "I must forget it. I must put it from my mind."

Rakoczy watched her as he said, "But you haven't been able to, and your family have not let you, because they insist on being ashamed and command you to bear it with them."

"I am defiled," she whispered.

"No. You were raped," he said. "It may seem to your family that you have sinned, but I do not believe it of you. I have seen too many women take the burden you carry; you are innocent, Xenya." He concealed the anger he felt toward the Shuiskys and Xenya's mother for what they had done; he feared that Xenya would believe that anger was directed at her.

She wailed, shaking her head in denial. "They want to spare me greater shame." She tried to wipe her tears away, with little success. "I shouldn't have told you. I ought not to have—"

He would not let her continue this way. "You may say anything you wish to me, Xenya. You will not offend or shock or disgust me."

"But I will," she said. "My family warned me and warned me: no one must ever know and I must forget." This was a litany for her, repeated like a prayer. "It can never be revealed or discussed. It must be forgotten. By everyone."

"Then why do they constantly remind you of it while requiring you to deny it happened?" he asked with far more tenderness than ire as he looked at her mottled, drawn face. "Xenya, Xenya, what they have done to you—the Mongols and your relatives— is a double betrayal. You have suffered twice. To force you to accept a burden you are not permitted to acknowledge is an outrage."

She stared at him through her tears. "They have protected me," she told him unsteadily.

"No. Your father did not protect you and your family have not protected you." He made the effort to say this without condemnation. "And now they have relinquished the right to protect you. But I will, if you will grant me that privilege."

"Privilege?" It was as if she did not comprehend the word.

"Yes," he said at once, then sat back, deliberately calming himself and giving her the opportunity to talk. A short while later as Xenya tried again to dry her tears, he said, "Will you give me your hand, Xenya?"

"My hand?" she asked him blankly, then slipped into her elusive manner. "It is yours for the taking, my husband."

Rakoczy shook his head once. "That isn't what I asked you, Xenya Evgeneivna. I asked if you will give me your hand." He lay his right hand on the quilted coverlet, palm up.

"If it is—" she began only to be cut off.

"If you want to take my hand, it would please me. If taking my hand is a painful duty, then spare us both," he said, his voice deep and soft. He remained unmoving, his dark, compelling eyes on her hands instead of her face.

A muffled crash from the stable followed by a frightened whinny and the sound of kicking hooves brought Xenya erect in the bed, the rosy mottling fading from her cheeks. As the distant, sleepy voice of one of the grooms strove contrapuntally with the storm, the terror went from Xenya's eyes; she blushed. "I am very foolish. Forgive me."

Rakoczy did not change his attitude. "There is nothing to forgive. Nothing."

She pulled on the covers, drawing them closer to her chin once again. "God has not forgiven me. Father Illya said so."

It was tempting to revile the priest, or to select examples in Scripture that would counter what Father Illya had said, but he was a stranger—a stranger challenging her most deeply held beliefs. So he kept his hand in place and he said, "Xenya Evgeneivna, I will make an agreement with you." He could feel her wince. "You need not fear my wishes and my whims, now or ever."

"And what do I agree to do?" Her face was stubborn now. "You are entitled to the use of my body for the birth of your children. Your agreement might not last long, and then I would be at the mercy of—"

He turned his eyes on her and for once did not disguise their impact. "I will not use your body in any way but to house and clothe and feed it until and unless you wish me to." She turned away from his gaze, but he continued. "If that time should come, I will tell you then what you may expect of me." It was the truth to a point and he offered himself the inward consolation that it was not likely that she would ever reach a point where she would want to know more about his nature than she knew now.

She did her best to look relieved. "I will pray for you," she said quietly.

He started to bow and withdraw when he decided to take another chance. "I am grateful for your prayers, but I would prefer that you talk with me."

She was startled enough to stare at him once more. "Talk with you?"

"Yes," he said gently. "You are alone here, but for your two maids. You've already admitted that the terem is boring. I am a stranger and know little of Russia beyond what I have learned on behalf of the King of Poland. It would be most useful for me to know more." He spoke easily, lightly, as if they were chatting after a meal. "Your charity work must have shown you many things about Moscovy that most who live here do not generally learn. Therefore I request the chance to talk with you. We will learn to know each other better and you will assist me to become a more capable emissary."

"I suppose this . . . is possible," she said, her eyes suspicious but her face smiling.

"Good," said Rakoczy with what he hoped was the right combination of enthusiasm and distance. He had no wish to frighten her; he wondered if she would come to trust him. Once more he started to bow European-fashion as he prepared to leave the room.

She made a sound in her throat. "I don't know what to call you," she complained as he looked back at her.

"My . . . ah . . . Christian name is Ferenc. My father's name—" He broke off, remembering his father who was called a King because he administered a district that took more than five summer days and double that number of good horses to ride across. "I suppose Nemo would be one way to call him," he said, his face remote: both Greek and Latin meanings were applicable, although his father had never heard either tongue. In Greek *nemo* meant "from the grove" and it was in the sacred grove at the depth of the year that he had come to the blood of his god. In Latin *nemo* meant "no one".

"Ferenc Nemovich," she said shyly but with the first sign of easing tension.

"Yes, Xenya Evgeneivna?" He was being deliberately playful now, taking pleasure in the first, tentative gesture she made toward him.

"Why do you want to know about the charities I do? It is wrong to boast of such service." She was no longer clinging to the blanket but her fingers continued to move restlessly over the quilted wool, wary as siege sentries.

"I am a foreigner here," he said directly. "There are not many ways for me to learn about this place. The servants here say nothing, and what they say I suspect is reported to Skuratov. If

Boris were not willing to show me favor my situation would be much more difficult." He resumed his place on the end of the bed. "But it is my task to learn what I may about Moscovy, not for King Istvan alone, but for those who seek to know more of Russia. They say that anyone who treats with England in these times must also be ready to treat with Moscovy. When my embassy returns to Poland—and you need not fear that day, Xenya—part of what I will take with me to make my way in the world, as exiles must, is my knowledge of Moscovy." He smiled once.

She would not look at him. "When do you go? When will you leave?"

"I don't know," said Rakoczy with simple candor. "I serve at the wish of two rulers: Czar Ivan and King Istvan. Either of them may command me, and I must in honor obey."

Xenya nodded twice. "I see," she said. "Very well."

He could not see her averted features; there was no way to read her thoughts, her fears. "Will you talk with me?" He asked it gently, easily, as if they were old friends.

She said nothing.

The roof near the crest shrieked at the raking of the wind. Driven by the four tremendous gusts, the alarm bell in the inner courtyard clanged just loud enough to be heard in the house.

There was a wild look in her eyes; she reached out blindly and took his hand.

Rakoczy looked at her hand and closed his small fingers gently, not pressing or confining her. He adjusted his posture sufficiently to allow him to remain in position in comfort. They sat that way together, speaking rarely, for the rest of the wind-haunted night.

From Hrabia Dariusz Zary to Ferenc Rakoczy, Hrabia Saint-Germain:

Worthy foreigner and deputy to our Polish King;
Our delays are at last exhausted. We have been ordered to depart at the end of the week, with escort as far as Vyazma, barring serious fighting to the east of Moscovy.
We were ordered by Father Pogner not to include your dis-

*patches and reports in the documents we carry, but my man-
date comes from King Istvan, not Father Pogner, and for that
reason I will do as my King commands me. I will also warn you
that the priest is determined to discredit you and will do everything in his power to bring you down.*

*If it were not that you are the chosen servant of the King, I
would not place myself between a priest and a foreigner. But
King Istvan has been constant in his approval of you, and he
charged you with a task you have been at pains to honor and
to carry out. As long as you proceed in honor, how can we
refuse to assist you without forfeiting our honor?*

*Therefore, I am offering you this last opportunity to entrust to
us your reports and letters and dispatches. You have my word
as a man of rank that we will do all that Heaven allows us to see
your words delivered into the hands of Istvan Bathory. There are
three leather dispatch cases, both with double flaps and buckles
for securing the contents. These will not permit your writing to
drown or be lost on the wind, as some have said when giving
excuses for their failures. You may fill them with reports or
whatever material you think is needed in order to bring about
a successful representation of all you have done thus far.*

*I must inform you that Father Pogner has written an excoriat-
ing denunciation of your marriage and has impugned your
motives for undertaking it. As I do not share his opinion, I have
taken it upon myself to report what I know of the case. If King
Istvan banishes you while you are here, you will find it difficult
to enter Poland now or anytime Istvan reigns. If you cannot
enter Poland, you must take your chances with the Turk, the
Hindu, the Chinese, or the White Sea. I will do what I can to
spare you dealing with any of them.*

*Have your servant bring the dispatch boxes to my house in the
Fancy Bread section of the city by sundown tomorrow night.
You know the place we soldiers live. I will be gathering together
all the materials we need for our journey.*

*Your offer of more horses is most gratefully accepted, and the
mules, too. Four of each will mean the difference between an
arduous trek and a difficult one. Now, if among your other
talents you possess a way to lessen snow and prevent mud, we
can hurry along as if it were July and not March. We do not
require more wagons. We have sufficient for the trip and we*

have followed your advice and made sure all the wheels are interchangeable. We have half again as many wheels as we have places to put them.

Also the purse of gold coins is very welcome. I suppose it will not much matter whose likeness is on them if they are good quality. It is not always a pleasant task for a man like me to accept so extravagant a gift as the coins, so I will make a provision to my gratitude: when you return to Poland, this amount will be waiting for you, increasing by one-third each year. That way, should King Istvan not prevail, or should the new King not honor Istvan's donations, then you will not be without deserved recompense. Poland has a hard history, but we who are her nobles have held her honor dear and her cause sacred. You will not be cheated at Poland's benefit while I live, and I will tell my son to take up my obligation to you when God orders me to put it down.

It is my fervent wish to be with my wife and children again. They have been much on my mind while we have sat through this interminable dark and cold. I want another son for my wife to dandle, and another. I will not get them sitting here in Moscovy. And soldier's games get no children.

The bowman will bring back letters—that much has been arranged. So I will inform you of everything I have learned once we reach Vyazma. But I will be at pains to keep my address general and unremarkable, for it is a certain thing that someone will read the dispatches. Enough of the boyars know their letters to do that. If there is reason to suppose that there have been great changes or that you would be wise for a change in orders, I will inform you that there are many blossoms in the fields and that crops ought to be good. If there is present danger, I will say that there is evidence of flooding. Do not forget these words, for they will be the only safe way I can guard you as I swore to King Istvan I would.

You have been an uncomplaining companion in travel—a rare thing in those who are not used to the rigors of campaigning—and you have done much to save us all from unknown hazards. You have ministered to those who were injured or unwell. You have provided for our needs when they outstripped our resources. For that I thank God for giving you the perspicacity to do it. You have been resourceful here, for without your skills at conjuring or alchemy, the Czar would have made short work of us, I fear. I am not as certain as Father Pogner is that you are only a clever mummer, but it may be that I do not worry about folly the way he does.

May God watch over you in this perplexing country. May He strive to bring you peace and send the light of His good angels to guide you when the night is deepest. May He protect you when the Czar is most desperate and give you succor when there is none other to give comfort.

Hrabia D. Zary
Embassy of Istvan Bathory of Poland in Russia

4

For the last three days priests had released hundreds of white doves over the Kremlin as they prayed for the life of the Czar. The birds were everywhere, and were given the same blessing that ikons were, in the hope that the Holy Spirit would hear them through the doves. All the hymns Czar Ivan had composed were sung repeatedly, their deep, twelve-part harmonies reminding God of Ivan's piety. In the cold March winds the poignant sonorities quickly vanished.

Ivan's previous night had been torturous, and he had come away from it with his face pasty, his breath fast and reeking, and his hands so palsied that he was nearly unable to lift his jewels as he tried to take strength and courage from them. At fifty-three he looked seventy. He was hoarse from shouting and he stank. He ordered that no one was to approach him any closer than seven paces.

"Little Father," said Boris Godunov as he prostrated himself before Ivan in the treasure room of the armory toward the end of the afternoon. "Let us summon your physicians again. And the Metropolitan, to pray for you."

"The witches said that they would protect me," he declared

with emotion. "They are very powerful, but today is the seventeenth. Their prophecy was specific and they repeated it more than once. Tomorrow is the last day." He clutched an enormous ruby against his chest, pressing as if he wanted the great red stone to penetrate his ribs and take over the work of his heart.

"To believe that, Czar, is to believe that God cannot grant mercy," said Boris, going very carefully, for he had not assessed the current state of Ivan's madness. Over the last week the Czar had become even more unpredictable than he had been and his moods shifted more quickly with less reason.

Czar Ivan fixed his son's brother-in-law with a hard stare. "God listens to priests, who want me dead. I know that their prayers ask my death. Yes! They petition God to destroy me. He hears the Metropolitan say that I promised he should be a Patriarch and I have not granted it yet, so he has persuaded God to abandon me. God no longer hears my prayers for mercy; they are drowned out by the priests."

Boris did not change his posture or contradict anything Ivan said. He waited in silence as Ivan put down the ruby and took up a medallion of jasper, letting the light play over the surface. When he was certain that Ivan had placed his thoughts on his treasures, he said, "Your faithful foreigner, Rakoczy Saint-Germain is here. He has brought a jewel for you."

"A jewel. For my salvation and redemption," said Ivan with a hint of hope. "It must be for that."

Taking advantage of this reaction, Boris said, "I don't know what it is for. I know only that he has asked to present it to you in this time." He hoped that the two Guard officers in the treasure room would remember what he said if there was ever any question about this last gift. He knew as well as any Tartar or Russian that a conspiracy often took years to reach success; he wanted no such hints made of him. If Rakoczy truly were a poisoner sent by Istvan Bathory to kill Ivan as many of the courtiers suggested, there was no better time than this for him to accomplish his work and escape undetected, and Boris, much as he enjoyed the Transylvanian's erudition and ironic wit, did not want to appear allied with him: that would lead to disgrace and death.

"If it is a good jewel, I will accept it. The might in all these jewels might bear a man to Heaven if he were saintly and innocent. If it is not a good jewel, if it is a curse, I will have him beaten with the heaviest knout until the marrow runs from his bones," said Ivan, caressing a long strand of rough emeralds, allowing them to slip through his fingers and catching them to let them fall again. "Tell him that, and if he still enters the room, I will show him honor. Perhaps."

Boris sighed as he got to his feet. He wanted to dust off the front of his gold-embroidered kaftan. But that might offend Ivan, make it appear that Boris expected some evil from the Czar, and the consequences would be swift and unpleasant. "I will tell him, Little Father."

Ivan waved him away, the greater part of his attention on a tourmaline, pink and green at once.

For once Rakoczy was dressed entirely in black: dolman, mente and kontush, leggings and boots. His black sapphire pectoral gleamed, and the ruby signet on his hand seemed to have taken on the darkness of his garments. "What do you have to tell me?" he asked without any of the elaborate forms of address and conduct that were usually seen at Court.

Boris made a palms-up gesture of ignorance. "I don't know what to say. If he decides the jewel is good, you may receive a reward—although I won't vouch for what that reward might be—or, if he thinks the jewel is cursed, he will have you knouted." He looked down, studying the tips of his boots.

"What do you recommend?" Rakoczy asked, unflustered by this news.

"I?" Boris sighed. "I don't know. I look at him, and I can no longer anticipate him or his madness."

"I see," said Rakoczy. He nodded once. "Then it must be on my head." He walked down the narrow hallway between the dozen Guards who had been placed on duty, then turned on his heel and came back to where Boris stood. "You'd better take me to him. If I do not present the jewel, he may decide that is an indication of my untrustworthiness and . . . who can tell what he might do then?"

"You could flee," Boris suggested with an unhappy laugh.

"Certainly," Rakoczy agreed with false joviality; his next words were bitter. "But how? Without escort? Without authorizations? Over roads that are crusted with ice and hip-deep in mud where the ice is gone? And where would I go? There are Russian soldiers all along the road to Poland. If I went south to the Black Sea, the

Cossacks would hold me for ransom or sell me to the Turks. And to the north all the ways are blocked with snow, and the rivers and bays filled with ice. Eastward, there is trackless wilderness and unknown peoples. I have met two Samoyeds, but no others from Siberia." He achieved a thin smile. "And I have a wife I am sworn to protect. I cannot abandon her, and I will not drag her to places you would hesitate to take seasoned troops."

Boris lowered his head. "You're probably right," he said with a trace of regret in his voice. "Still, it could . . ." The encouragement faded.

"Let's not keep Czar Ivan waiting," said Rakoczy, settling the matter. "Announce me, then leave if you wish."

At that Boris shook his head. "No. I will remain with you." They had almost reached the treasure room. "You may encounter Nikita Romanov while you are with the Czar. It is Ivan's intention that Nikita Romanovich should provide guardianship for Czareivich Feodor, as I am to give him direction in his rule."

"Is this perhaps an awkward disposal of power?" suggested Rakoczy as he paused outside the treasure room door.

"It may be. Ivan Vasillievich believes that conspirators will be less able to strike Feodor down with two families looking after him." Boris was eloquent in the short silence that followed his explanation.

Rakoczy nodded. "For how long has he entertained this notion?"

"Too long, worthy exile. He has not wavered in his intention to do this since it occurred to him last autumn." He put the tips of his big, square fingers together. "Any who try to speak of it are seen as jealous and treacherous."

There were many questions Rakoczy wanted to ask Boris— Did he suspect treachery? Where? From whom? Was Feodor actually safe? Were any of them safe?—but he would have to pursue them later. For the time being, he had Ivan to deal with. He squared his shoulders and lifted his head. "All right; open the door."

Boris made a sign of agreement and swung back the iron-strapped doors, indicating the ikons inside so that Rakoczy could bless them properly. "Little Father, your foreign servant, the Transylvanian exile who is your alchemist and adviser, has come."

Ivan had been leaning back against a large, lapis-clad chest encrusted with agate and turquoise, two ropes of freshwater pearls tangled in one hand, a golden ikon two or three centuries old and as tall as Ivan's forearm, painted in enamel and studded with topaz and diamonds in the other. "It is the Apostle Bartholomaios." He lifted the ikon a short way, then let it drop, for it was heavy. "I have been praying to him, asking him to support my life. They say he was mild and innocent, never deceiving anyone, never doing ill. I have tried to tell him that I did not want to do ill, but there is much evil in the world, much evil, and the most just and righteous of rulers is often surrounded by dangerous men. As much as it may offend a good man, he has his duty, and he must . . ." He stared muzzily at Rakoczy as if slightly drunk. "You have a jewel for me?"

"I do, Great Czar," said Rakoczy, going down on his knee.

"If there is anything evil in it, you will answer for it," Ivan warned him, fixing him with blood-shot eyes.

"If there is anything evil in it, I will gladly surrender myself to your judgment, Great Czar." He reached into the capacious sleeve of his mente and pulled out a small box covered in glorious brocaded Persian silk, which he held out to Ivan.

"No. No. Do not give it to me, Transylvanian. I know what they say of you, all of you, that you are more skilled than the Italians at poison. So. You open it, and put your face low to it, to breathe the poison or take the venom of the insect or demon." Ivan rapped out the order as bluntly and crisply as he had ordered his men forward at Kazan, so many years ago.

"If that will please you," said Rakoczy, opening the box and all but pushing his nose into it. He looked up. "Nothing has bitten me and I still breathe, Great Czar. In this box there is silk and an amethyst dark as Hungarian wine, and as potent. Nothing more or less than those things, Great Czar." He offered the box a second time. "The jewel is larger than a child's fist." When he had made the last series of jewels he had done all that he could to make them as large as possible. Of those nine he made, this was the best; the color was pure and glowingly intense; it was regular in shape, without flaw, capturing inward light better than a raindrop, and big enough to impress even Ivan. "It is my gift to you, Great Czar, and the gift of the king of Poland, to show respect and admiration."

Reluctantly Ivan took the box, examining it suspiciously as he pulled it toward him. He lifted it up so he could look at the underside. He ran his finger along the edges of the box as if seeking out pins or cutting wires. Then he stared inside, and a strange expression came over his ravaged features as a harsh cry escaped him.

Guards appeared in the door at once. "Czar!" four of them shouted as they rapped the floor with the butt of their pikes.

"Leave!" Ivan thundered at them, watching them withdraw in hasty disorganization.

"What are we to do?" asked the nearest Guard of Boris.

"Leave," he said with a hitch of his shoulder. "Now."

The Guard straightened, barked an order, and the four left the treasure room in good form, slamming the door emphatically behind them.

Ivan reverently lifted the gem from its box, holding it tenderly. Softly he began to croon to it, singing a bit of one of his own hymns to the Virgin. "Rejoice, O Gracious Lady, the Lord is with thee, grant us thy splendid mercy." He fondled the stone. "It is the soul of woman, I think, yes, yes, it must be, for it is darkness and light, darkness and light," he said, never looking up from the amethyst. "Tender, so tender, and yet no man may read it except when he is a little child. After that, it is purity and mystery and sin. This is worthy of the grandest crown." He kissed it, then licked it once, twice.

Rakoczy did not move from where he knelt. He was afraid to draw any of Ivan's attention now that the Czar had become entranced in the amethyst. He wondered how long it would be until he was permitted to get off his knee.

Some little time later Ivan tottered to his feet and began to circle the treasure room, moving as if he were striving not to step on nasty things. He paid no attention to Boris and behaved as if Rakoczy were not there at all. During one of his slow, dancelike turns, he dropped the amethyst Rakoczy had presented to him, and now it lay away from the rest of the treasure. Ivan continued to ignore Boris and Rakoczy.

Then the door slammed open and Nikita Romanovich Romanov came in abruptly, blessed the ikons, then prostrated himself at once and so hurriedly that Rakoczy could hear his fork and spoon clink together in his belt, his large, bulky frame blocking the doorway even prone. "Little Father, the people of Moscovy are sending their prayers to God for your recovery. They are praying for you at the Virgin of the Intercession, as many as can stand in the cathedral. All the merchants in the city have come there to supplicate the Virgin to add her prayers to theirs. At sunset all bells will ring for an hour, to bring God nearer to us." He was a little out of breath by the end of this, but he had the desired result: Ivan stopped perambulating and looked at him.

"You are very industrious, Nikita Romanovich," he said to Romanov. "You are to teach my son to apply himself, so that he will not fail at his tasks. You must show him how a man proceeds in the world."

Since Ivan had not given him permission to rise, Nikita remained where he was. He knocked his forehead lightly on the slates. "May God show me the way, Little Father."

"Yes, yes," said Ivan, starting to move off again, leaving Nikita on his face and Rakoczy on his knee. "It is the waiting that is the most troublesome. But the witches must be right. If they are not right, I will have them knouted and left in the snow where the wolves will find them before they die." His ferocity was sudden and malign. "Everyone who has brought me suffering will be made to suffer ten times what they have done to me. Ten times! A *thousand* times! And I will exact that from all their families, so that the deadly plant is rooted out and lost." He lurched toward Boris, then clutched his head, crying out incoherently.

Boris had started toward Ivan, then hesitated, knowing that he did not have the Czar's permission to assist him. "Little Father, please, for the Grace of God, let me help you."

Ivan struck out with his arm, then swung away from him. "Yaroslav! Bring me Yaroslav!"

From his place on the floor Nikita cursed softly.

Boris stayed where he was. "Alas, Little Father, have you forgotten? Yaroslav had the . . . had the misfortune to fall down the main stairs in the Palace of Facets. He went into a sleep from which we could not wake him, no matter what was done. He slept four days. And he died, passing from his sleep into death as gently as a mother guards her infant." He said it so tentatively, as if he feared that at any time the Czar might take his wrath out on him as he had on Yaroslav.

This time there was no raging outburst. "Yaroslav is dead?" Ivan asked in bewilderment. He looked toward Nikita for confirmation.

"Yes," said Boris.

"Yes, and as he described," Nikita seconded.

Ivan rounded on Boris. "Who killed him? *Who killed him?* Tell me, that I may have him flayed or set all his hair afire." There was a little froth on his mouth now, and his eyes were glazed and staring.

"Keep silent," Nikita whispered to Boris. "Don't let him know. The state he's in, who knows——"

"He fell, Little Father," said Boris, attempting not to sound desperate. "He fell. He was not killed; it was an accident, an unfortunate accident." How could he inform Ivan that the man who had shoved Yaroslav backward to his doom was the Czar himself?

"He could not fall. I would not permit him to fall. I would save him," said Ivan bluntly. "He must have been ki——"

"He fell," Boris insisted calmly. "Backward. Down the stairs."

From his knee, Rakoczy said, "It is true, Great Czar. Yaroslav fell. You were not able to save him." In a skewed way—a way as skewed as Ivan's tormented mind—what he said was accurate. He hoped it would be enough to keep the Czar from pressing until he remembered what he had done.

"Yaroslav dead," said Ivan softly, his big hands clenching and unclenching.

"God have mercy on him," said Nikita and Boris together; Boris blessed himself, but Nikita, still lying on the floor, could not.

At last Ivan signaled to Rakoczy and Nikita to rise. He was already wandering back to the pile of caskets and trunks and loose gold and jewels heaped in the middle of the treasury room floor. He dropped onto the lid of an ivory cask bound in hoops of gold studded with diamonds. "So many are dead," he said, his tone almost conversational. "So very many."

"It is a misfortune for Russia," said Boris, knowing that such an assertion was probably acceptable to Ivan. He approached a little nearer. "Little Father, give me a task. Let me show you my devotion by fulfilling your commands."

Listening, Rakoczy thought this was a very dangerous offer, for in his current madness Ivan might order Boris to murder his wife and children, or to leave Moscovy forever. He said, very respectfully, "Such loyalty is rare, Great Czar. None knows it better than one who has lost a kingdom. Treasure faithful men, for in all your reign you will see very few of them. No monarch can afford to lose even one such man as Boris Feødorovich is."

"There is merit in that," said Ivan after he had thought it over. His face was glistening with sweat now, making the grime more apparent. He breathed with difficulty and from time to time raised his hand to press his forehead or shield his eyes. "It is a sign of loyalty, as you say," he announced to Rakoczy. "No wise ruler wishes to fight with men like Boris. But there is the desire for combat. It is in all great leaders, a need to prove—" He broke off and grabbed his head, grimacing.

"Little Father," said Boris, his apprehension growing.

Ivan waved him away and forced the travesty of a smile onto his mouth. "We will play chess!" he announced. "Yes. We will play chess. And you may move first," he added, in an attempt to be magnanimous. He signaled to Nikita. "Run ahead and tell them to make a chessboard ready," he said, his movements becoming frenetic. "That must be done. Yes."

Once again Nikita prostrated himself; Rakoczy heard him sigh as he stretched out on the cold slates. "It will be as you wish, Little Father," he announced, then got back to his feet and took the time to bless the ikons before leaving the treasure room.

"Chess," repeated Ivan, growing pleased with the notion. "We will play. A good game will . . . will banish the evil words of the witches." He turned on his heel. "They are great liars. All those who are not Christians are liars. And half the Christians are liars, as well, and lost in sin. It was God come to earth that made men learn to be truthful." He was pacing rapidly and with great purpose, without any of the meandering and turning of a short time before. "Therefore I put their words behind me." As he said this, his foot struck the amethyst where it lay at the edge of the shadows. Ivan gave a howl of anguish and knelt to pick it up.

"Little Father . . ." Boris said, once again uncertain if he would be wise to approach the Czar.

Ivan had picked up the jewel and cupped it protectively in his large hands, as if shielding a single flame against a blizzard. "It is heart and soul, and I have wounded it. All of woman is within it, and I have struck it down, as my Anastasia was the first struck down." He did not often speak of his adored first wife, but it appeared that her memory now worked a calming influence on him. "Soon I will see her glorious face, if God shows me mercy.

No man has ever had such saintliness as Anastasia Zakharina-Romanova; man was not made capable of the goodness of woman. How often God reminds me of my pride and my guilt." Rakoczy could sense another burst of rage welling in Ivan and strove to circumvent it. "Or it may be that God is showing you that He sees your heart is injured. Your late wife must have praised you and pleaded for your salvation; God would listen to such a woman as she. Perhaps He is showing you the promise of mercy, not the fires of Hell."

Ivan stared at him. "Is that in this jewel?"

Rakoczy knew that he was taking a very great risk now but none of his apprehension showed in his tranquil exterior. "The Great Art is the same as all art, Czar. I am only an instrument; the full extent of what these jewels can do are for greater souls than mine to know. If devout prayer and the fruits of learning are pleasing to God, then that jewel must be filled with compassion as well as the magical properties of amethysts."

It took Ivan a short time to respond, and when he did, he looked pleased. "You are a modest man, as exiles must be," he said, then swung back toward Boris. "Chess. We must play chess." He went and knelt before the ikons at the door, the amethyst still clasped in his hand.

Boris sidled up next to Rakoczy and whispered. "What did you tell him?"

Rakoczy's half-smile faded almost before it had begun. "Ambiguities, with a little truth for seasoning."

"A hazardous game," Boris warned, watching Ivan praying.

"Not so hazardous as chess might be," Rakoczy pointed out with serious concern.

Boris acknowledged this with a scowl. "Are you going to watch the play?"

"I think not," Rakoczy said in a measuring tone. "Father Pogner has informed me that he has an audience with the Czar later this evening, and he does not wish to have any dealings with me. I am ordered to absent myself." He caught the impatient twitch Boris gave to his kaftan. "I think it might be best if I passed the evening with my wife."

"The game, Boris Feodorovich," Ivan interrupted from the doorway; he had finished his prayers and was determined now to have his chess match.

"At once, Little Father," said Boris, and without any further word to Rakoczy went and blessed the ikons before leaving the treasure room, calling to the Guard that Rakoczy was still within and was to be escorted out at once.

The blessings of the ikons Boris and Rakoczy offered were perfunctory as they left the treasure room. The Guard in the hall watched them leave and made a careful show of closing the tremendous doors, locking the massive iron crossbolt into its staples.

"What do you think?" asked Boris very softly in Greek as they left the armory.

"Of the Czar?" Rakoczy replied in that language. "He is getting steadily worse. If it is not tomorrow, it cannot be much longer. You need only look at him to see that his body is worn out and his mind has slipped into realms of fancy."

"Is he dangerous?" Boris asked.

"He is Czar," said Rakoczy sardonically.

"But such a Czar," Boris prompted. They were almost at the door, and Boris deliberately slowed his step, taking advantage of this to dust off his kaftan at last. "He was great, truly he was. He forced the Mongols and the Tartars back to Sarai and he brought Novgorod into Russia for good and all. We no longer pay tribute to any power but our own. Without Ivan Grosny, this would not be true."

Rakoczy remained discreetly silent. He looked through the open doors into the silver sunlight beyond; the sky was white with high clouds and fused with the snow-covered buildings of the city. "And now he raves for the son he killed; if an army should rise against Moscovy now, how would you defend her? You cannot expect Czareivich Feodor to lead men in battle, can you?"

"There are boyars and generals—" Boris broke off.

"Who wish to be Czar," Rakoczy pointed out. "And with an army could claim the throne." He stepped into the sunlight, grateful for the thick layer of his native earth in the soles of his thick black boots.

Now that they were out of the armory, they could hear the sound of the choirs at Saint Mikhail's and the Annunciation Cathedrals. The two ecstatic hymns clashed with one another, dissonant and jarring. Both Cathedrals were full, with many people standing outside the doors to listen and pray.

Boris frowned as he listened. "A bad business," he muttered in Russian.

"The singing?" Rakoczy guessed, also in Russian.

"Not exactly," said Boris. "They are singing at Saint Mikhail's. The Czars are buried there. Ivan might think it a bad omen." He rubbed his hands together, more from worry than against the cold. "I'd better hurry, before he changes his mind about chess."

They walked a few more paces together, then Rakoczy looked over at Boris; though he was half a head shorter than the Russian-Tartar, he gave the impression of being the taller of the two. "Be careful, Boris Feodorovich. The favor of a man like Ivan is more deadly than a tiger in the house."

Boris crossed himself. "My good angel and the mercy of God protect me," he said with feeling. "My sister is Feodor's wife. What can I do but strive to guard her and that innocent she has married. As you have already acknowledged, there is no escape, so I must—" He nodded in the direction of the Terem Palace. "Well. And I ought not to keep Ivan waiting. Remember me in your prayers?"

Rakoczy's half-smile was enigmatic. "When I pray," he assured Boris, and made him a reverence and was about to leave him when he remarked, "Why have the bells stopped ringing?"

"It is Ivan's order," said Boris. "He has said that he wishes no bells to sound until the eighteenth is over, when they are to ring in victory to signal that the Czar has prevailed over the witches. Masses are to begin at midnight and continue constantly all through tomorrow, but no bells are to sound before midnight tomorrow. If they ring before then, it will be to announce his death." He looked toward the old bell tower. "Feodor is upset about the silent bells. I don't think he understands why his father has given the orders and assumes he is being punished." He looked toward the Terem Palace once again. "How can we explain it to him?"

Boris did not expect an answer and Rakoczy had none to give. He nodded a bow as he pulled on his black Italian gloves. "And if the witches are right?"

"As great a risk Russia has with Ivan mad, she will have a greater one with Ivan dead." He said it in Greek, then looked about to be certain they were not overheard. With that he turned on his heel and hurried away toward the Terem Palace, his golden kaftan looking rusty brown in the lowering grey afternoon.

Text of a letter from Sir Jerome Horsey, dictated to his secretary, to Elizabeth Tudor of England.

To the Queen's Grace, Defender of the Faith, Elizabeth Rex, in duty the report of her ambassador to the Court of the Caesar of Moscovy, Feodor Ivanson.

As may be surmised by my salutation, gracious lady, Ivan IV, called Caesar of all the Russias, has at last succumbed to his many ills. Life departed his body late on the evening of the seventeenth of March by the calendar here, which agrees with England's; it was less than six hours before the time predicted by the Lappish witches, which has terrified many of the ignorant for they believe that the prophecy caused Ivan's death, not his wretched state and distracted mind. I was among the foreigners who were called to his side shortly before his death, and I must report to you that I have never seen a man so deeply suffering as Ivan was. His face was like one who has been tortured. While they say it was because of his madness, I must suppose that his body was also profoundly tormented.

The Rus are in mourning now, and the echoes of single bells tolling from their towers is continuous. There are also continuous prayers and Masses sung to Ivan's honor and memory. These are strange to English ears, for the Rus, like the Greeks, allow no music but the human voice in their churches, and their harmonies are stirring and distressing at once. I myself have attended Russian Masses for the repose of Ivan's soul, both at the Cathedral of the Dormition within the Kremlin itself and at the Cathedral of the Virgin of the Intercession on Red Square. Half of Moscovy have come there to pray at the tomb of Vasilli the Holy Fool, who is said to have been blessed by God with visions.

I have taken it upon myself to approach Boris Godunov, who has become the adviser to Caesar Feodor, and he has assured me that Russian dealings with England will not be imperiled by this new Caesar. He is brother-in-law to Feodor and through his sister is protected. Guardianship of Feodor, who much requires one, is Nikita Romanson Romanov, whose sister Anastasia was Ivan's first wife and the mother of Feodor. This uncle has kept away from the Court until last year. Such an irregular arrangement may well lead to dangerous rivalries, but it is according to Ivan's disposition and none in this country dare challenge it.

I have recently been contacted by Prince Vasilli Andrewson Shuisky. He is of great importance in this Court, and his influence is significant. He has urged me to consider extending our trading contracts to direct dealings with merchants of Novgorod, for shipping might be less hazardous from a Baltic port than from Novo-Kholmogory, which is filled with icebergs throughout the year and unreachable from November to April. While there is some good sense in his suggestion, I am reluctant to be beholden to this Prince Shuisky, for I have heard he is one who aspires to the throne himself and it would not do to give the appearance that England supports one ambitious noble more than another. The Rus fear foreign intrusion as they fear nothing else in the world. To them all strangers are nothing more than tolerated enemies, and although they are courteous and hospitable, neither Rus nor English ever forget that we English are foreign, a consideration that over-rides all other factors.

My decision in regard to this Shuisky has been seconded by Doctor Lovell, who has studied these men more closely than I have, and is particularly aware of the crosscurrents at the Court. Many of the nobles speak to him with greater candor than they speak with me, for he is less obviously the servant of the Queen's Grace and therefore less subject to scrutiny.

It is my intention to conclude as many contracts as possible when the Hercules *arrives at Novo-Kholmogory, so that if there is greater disruption at court—as I suspect there will be—England need not suffer because of it. We have the advantage that many of our treaties of trade, such as the one for rope, is of many years' standing and therefore less likely to be challenged. The more recent arrangements may prove more difficult to maintain, and so it is on those agreements I plan to turn my energies. This is the third year in which we are successfully trading Norwich wool for Russian furs, and with proper measures taken there is no reason to end this mutually profitable venture.*

I will make every effort to keep you currently informed on

*developments here. This report will be carried by messenger to
Novo-Kholmogory as quickly as may be. I have secured the
necessary documents for the courier and will start him on his
journey at dawn tomorrow with an escort of Russian bowmen
as far as Kargopol, where he should encounter the escort for the
newly arrived English ships' cargo bound for Moscovy. The bowmen will then return to Moscovy and serve as guards for the
goods while the courier continues to the north with the English
sailors and the Russian guides. This arrangement is acceptable
to the Russians and the English seamen as well.*

*In the hope that God will smile on our efforts here to enable
us to serve the Queen's Grace with honor and achievements, I
sign my name to this and include it with all other embassy
dispatches bound for the* Hercules *and passage to England.*

*The most obedient and faithful servant of
Elizabeth Tudor, by Grace of God, Queen Regnant
Sir Jerome Horsey, Ambassador to the Court
of the Russian Caesar
On the 13th day of May by the English Calendar
in the Lord's year 1584*

5

Brilliant morning light filtered through the thick double-win-
dows in Rakoczy's alchemical laboratory, striking the two athanors and half the trestle table where he worked, dressed in
unrelieved black, perched on his tall stool, measuring two vials
of opalescent liquid into an alabaster jar with a jasper lid. He was
engrossed in his task and did not look up when Rothger rapped
once on the door and let himself in, tugging one of the servants
after him.

"My master, I need your attention," Rothger said after he had
stood quietly for a short while; his manner was deceptively calm.
"It is important: it may be urgent."

"May be?" Rakoczy said, turning to look at Rothger and the servant.

The pale young man was more defiant than frightened, although there was no disguising the white line around his mouth or the shiftiness of his sea-blue eyes. He did not reverence Rakoczy, keeping his head up; he stood with his legs slightly apart, prepared to run or fight.

"This is Yuri," Rothger began.

"Yes, I know," said Rakoczy. "He came in January, after Klavdi left. He's the footman or doorman—whatever they call them here. He carries messages and admits visitors." He looked directly at the young man. "That is correct, isn't it. Those are your duties."

It was warm for May and the harshness of winter had given way to the excesses of spring. The very air smelled green with growing things. Grasses and exuberant weeds sprang up everywhere, even between the paving stones in the Beautiful-Red Market Square. From one of the two open windows in Rakoczy's laboratory the sound of courting birds vied with the distant bells of the Monastery of Saint Ivan Baptist.

Yuri said nothing. He returned Rakoczy's stare as long as he dared, then fixed his gaze on the floor between his feet.

"I discovered him reading the message sent over from Father Krabbe," said Rothger, almost apologizing. "I didn't realize before that he could read, let alone Polish." He moved aside, leaving Yuri to face Rakoczy.

"That is surprising," said Rakoczy very softly. He regarded Yuri with curiosity. "Reading Polish. I presume you have Russian. What other languages do you know?"

"Master is mistaken; I am ignorant. I cannot read. I tell you: the letter came open and I only looked at it. I wanted to see what it was. It meant nothing to me, only marks on the page. I thought they looked strange, not like Russian writing." He realized he was talking too much but could not make himself stop. "That's all it was, master. I do not know how to read; I only wanted to see what Polish looked like."

"You cannot read, and yet you knew the letter was in Polish?" Rakoczy said politely. "What made you think that."

Yuri stared at the athanors to avoid looking at Rakoczy. Only then did he realize that he was unprotected by Rothger. "I do not read," he insisted stubbornly. "Common servants do not read, Master."

"It is certainly an unusual ability," Rakoczy said, setting his vial aside. "In a common servant, who knows Polish when he sees it."

"But it is not true that I read the letter. I guessed it was Polish because it came from the priests, the ones of the embassy. They are Polish. The messenger said it was from them," Yuri protested rather wildly. "Your manservant is mistaken that I read it. He is wrong. I wasn't reading. I am a servant, a servant. I do not know how to. Truly."

"Truly," Rakoczy mused. "And yet Rothger is not a man to claim such a thing if he were not certain. And you say the letter was in Polish, not Latin, which I would expect of priests. Even you Orthodox know Roman priests speak Latin." He rose from the tall stool and came closer to Yuri, measuring him through narrowed dark eyes. He glanced once at his silent manservant as if seeking some response. When he spoke his voice was light. "Either Rothger is mistaken or you are not a common servant."

"He is mistaken," Yuri insisted.

Rakoczy did not respond to that. "I wonder," he said, walking around Yuri slowly. "Your clothes are not the ones I've provided, are they?"

Yuri looked down at his full rubashka of heavy linen. "This is mine. I brought it with me. It was a gift from my mother. She made it for me." He fingered the embroidery at the collar, doing what he could to force himself to smile. His forehead and upper lip were wet and he licked his lips once. "She presented it to me at the Nativity, when I left home to come here."

"Very commendable," said Rakoczy gently. "It is a fine thing when a son takes pride in his mother's work."

"She *did* give it to me," Yuri said desperately.

"I have not argued that," Rakoczy pointed out. "Nor will I. Although I am curious why you should set out for Moscovy in winter, when so many of the roads are unpassable and traveling is a hardship." He stepped back and returned to the table. "And do you know, it puzzles me that a common servant should have a mother who sews such excellent linen. I was under the impression that few common people could afford such fabric. Doubtless because I am a foreigner I do not understand how she came to have the flax to make so fine a shirt for you." His genial smile terrified Yuri.

"She lives in the country, near Tver. The boyar is generous, very generous," he said with increasing apprehension.

Rakoczy heard this out without changing expression. He motioned to Rothger to close one of the windows so that the birds would not distract them. "How strange, that he did not keep you with your family."

Yuri blinked, his face turning very white. "It . . . it was . . ."

"Perhaps," Rakoczy suggested kindly, "you had reason to want to leave. If the boyar was generous, as you say, he let you come to Moscovy."

"Yes!" Yuri seized on this explanation at once; his cheeks now harbored two bright spots as if he had a fever and his eyes were hectic with fright. "Yes. You have it exactly. That is what happened. I asked for permission to leave. And it was granted to me by the boyar."

Rakoczy listened in cordial attention. "He must be very generous indeed if he was willing to let a strapping young man like you leave his lands to come to Moscovy, for you are strong and clever. There are few boyars who would be willing to permit a man like you to come to Moscovy. Most would insist that you remain to work the land." He gave Yuri a bland smile. "But perhaps there were other considerations?"

"He told me to come here, to seek out his cousin," Yuri declared. He was not quite so scared now, for he had not been struck or sent off in disgrace as he expected to be; he stood straighter, his hands hitched in his wide belt. "He helped me to find work."

"Yuri arrived with a servant from the Nagoy palace," said Rothger, adding, "They said that Grigori Nagoy thought you would have a place for him here."

"I won't make you strain your inventiveness to explain that," said Rakoczy dryly, and Yuri realized that his black-clad master had not been deceived by any of his claims. "One of two things is true of you: either you are illegitimate and an embarrassment to your father, or you are merely posing as a common servant. I regret that I suspect the latter." He gave Yuri no chance to interrupt. "Which means that you are a spy."

"Master is mistaken," said Yuri with passion. "I am not—"

"You are not the first we have discovered in this household," said Rakoczy, his voice tinged with weariness. "And probably you are not the last. Foreigners attract spies."

"No. No, I am not a spy," Yuri protested.

Rakoczy held up his small, elegant hand. "No more mendacities, please. I haven't an appetite for them." He leaned back a little. "You are an unexpected difficulty. What are we going to do with you?"

Yuri went pale as whey. "Master—"

"I would like to make a bargain with you, Yuri." He broke off and motioned to Rothger to bring his box of writing implements and vellum. "Let us abandon this pretense of common servitude. What is your patronymic?"

"I—" Yuri gave in. "Piotrovich."

"Very good," said Rakoczy. "Yuri Piotrovich, you know that you could be condemned for spying. You would be killed."

"On the word of a foreigner," said Yuri with patent disbelief mixed with bravado. "How could it happen?"

"On the word of this foreigner, it most certainly could." There was repugnance in what he said next. "One of the spies discovered in this household was knouted to death on the order of Nikita Romanovich Romanov." Rakoczy did not add that he suspected Nikita had done it because the spy had been Romanov's own and in need of silencing. "Ask the other servants."

Rothger set the writing-box down beside the alabaster jar and returned to his station near the door.

"Servants are always gossiping; it means nothing." Yuri's scoffing rang false. "Let a servant overhear a few words, and he will weave fables from them."

"Gennadi was his name," said Rothger. "He came from Vladimir where his father and brothers make saddles and harness. He was in the employ of the Metropolitan. We discovered three other spies before him."

In the three and a half millennia of his life Rakoczy had been beaten many times, but the thought of the knout with the iron claw at the end of a heavy iron ring attached to a cable of tight-braided leather sickened him. The knout was designed to do maximum damage, to lacerate skin and muscles and break bones. "His death was appalling," he said quietly, his dark eyes pained and distant.

"That is an empty threat," said Yuri with what nerve he could muster. "You say it but you do not dare do it."

"Because your father is a Nagoy?" inquired Rakoczy, once again smooth-mannered. "I have not met Piotr Nagoy and no one has mentioned him to me before now: an odd omission if he is ranked with the rest of his kin. But it is possible he keeps to his country estates, being rich in land instead of gold, or burdened with some disgrace. The son of such a father might learn to read, and would seek the patronage of more highly placed relatives, wouldn't he."

"What are you saying?" Yuri burst out, frustration and bluster combining to make him bold. "I cannot read. I did not read that letter. You know nothing. You can know nothing."

Rakoczy shook his head. "When you have lived as long as I, perforce you learn." He looked once at Rothger, then back at Yuri. "I mentioned a bargain, Yuri Piotrovich. If you are telling the truth I will honor it. If you lie to me, that is another matter. I will spell it out for you, this bargain, though you tell me you cannot read; I will write it down so that it cannot be questioned. Listen well and consider before you answer: if you are telling me the truth about reading you will remain here, in my employ. You will continue to report to Grigori Nagoy, or whichever of your relatives you work for, but you will serve in the same capacity for me. You will report the activities of your family to me as you report mine to them. In exchange, you will continue to be paid your servant's wages and will not be turned over to Skuratov for judgment. If you acquit yourself well, you will be rewarded with gold. If you attempt to deceive me, then I will denounce you before the Court. And you may be certain that your relatives will not protect you then, not at the risk of exposing themselves." He paused. "Foreigner that I am, I am still the safer course, Yuri Piotrovich."

"You expect me to betray my family?" he asked in astonishment.

"Why not?" Rakoczy answered coolly. "You have betrayed me, haven't you."

Yuri's denial was heated. "I am not a spy. You are mistaken. It was not betrayal."

"Wasn't it." Rakoczy directed his attention to the alabaster jar. "Perhaps I have not understood you." He reached out for a sheet of vellum and drew his inkwell nearer. "I will put down our terms." As he set out the vellum, he continued. "Do you think that your devotion to your family or your desire for advancement excuses what you have done here? Because I am a foreigner?" He selected a trimmed quill and set it in the ink.

"I have done nothing that was not—" Yuri began.

"Bear with me for a while longer, Yuri Piotrovich. You may protest later." He wrote a few words on the vellum, then set the sheet aside to dry. "I will show you my good-will. Here." He took two gold coins from the wallet hung from his belt and held them out to Yuri. "Take them. So you will have something to show for my good faith when I assure you that there is reason to believe what I say to you. As you are honest, I will be honest."

Yuri took the coins eagerly, his wide, strong features turning vulpine. "What do you require of me?" he asked.

"That you deliver a message for me, as a gesture to show you accept our bargain and to demonstrate your veracity. It is no great task, to carry a message; you have done it often before. Surely this is little enough to ask of you." He took a second sheet of vellum and wrote on it. "You are to take this to the palace of Boris Godunov within the Kremlin and wait for the answer. It is a simple message." Rakoczy held the second sheet out almost negligently. "You may read it if you like."

"I cannot read," said Yuri again, after a brief pause. "You wish to believe that I can, but it is not true. I recognize a few words in Russian, but that is the extent of it, master."

"Look at it in any case," Rakoczy insisted.

Yuri shrugged and glanced at the vellum with studied indifference.

Take this faithless servant and imprison him at once, Rakoczy had written in Polish.

With a sudden cry Yuri stepped back, letting the vellum drift to the floor. He crossed himself, then realized that Rakoczy was regarding him with composed attention. "May you be trampled to death by elephants!"

"It would surely destroy my spine," murmured Rakoczy in the Latin of Imperial Rome. "And that is the true death." From Yuri's abrupt change of expression, it was apparent he had understood part of what Rakoczy said. "So, you are able to read. And understand a little Latin."

"God will punish you for this," Yuri vowed in harsh tones.

"And the Court may punish you." He let Yuri consider the implications. "Yuri Piotrovich, what is it to be?"

"You are a devil," Yuri said sullenly.

"Oh, I doubt that," Rakoczy answered easily. "An exile, yes, but hardly a devil." He favored Yuri with a long, thoughtful stare. "You are not willing to serve me. That much is apparent. But your masters—your real masters—have set tasks for you. You have not outlived your usefulness to them if you can continue to inform them of the activities in foreign households. Your learning is your greatest asset to them, and they expect you to employ it on their behalf." He cocked his head. "But clearly you cannot remain here."

The fear was back in Yuri's eyes. "I will sign your bargain," he said grimly. "I will do as you order me. I will swear fealty to you."

"I think not," said Rakoczy very gently. He reached for a third sheet of vellum and began to write on it. "Since you know some Latin, you may follow, if you wish." He moved his arm so that Yuri could see his note.

"I—" Yuri had the good sense not to go on.

"Precisely," said Rakoczy, as he continued his letter. "If you will deliver this, there is a good chance you will find work in that establishment. After all, a servant who can read is a treasure, particularly to an embassy. Doubtless you will find ways to make yourself useful to everyone. Your Nagoy relatives should be satisfied, for you will be able to tell them about the Poles, and you will not have to be openly disgraced or punished. And I will have one less spy under my roof." He frowned before he wrote the next line. "You would do well not to speak directly with Father Pogner, not that he is likely to speak with a servant in any case. Deal with Father Krabbe; Father Pogner is as opposed to me as I must suppose your family is." He signed the letter and reached for sealing wax. Rothger had already lit a taper and this he held out to Rakoczy. When there was a large drop of wax beneath his small, neat signature, Rakoczy fixed the impression of his signet ring on it. "There," he said, offering it to Yuri.

But Yuri refused to touch it. "You want to trick me," he said, moving two steps back. "You are playing games with me."

Rakoczy handed the letter to Rothger. "See that Father Krabbe gets this when you escort Yuri to him. And tell him for me that caution is required with this man. Speak to him privately, and candidly." He intended this last for Yuri, not Rothger.

"You are wrong about me," said Yuri a little wildly. "I am no spy. I serve you well, Master, I do not—"

"I will explain it to your kinsman," Rakoczy said, his patience growing thin. "I will not blame you."

Yuri's angry laugh was eloquent. "And you think any Nagoy would believe you? You? You had that debauched Koshkinya woman wished upon you by the Shuiskys. What man would trust your judgment?"

Rakoczy did not move; when he spoke his voice was very soft and astuciously conversational, but there was something in his manner Yuri had not seen before which frightened him more than anything else about the elegant stranger, something ancient and dangerous, as contained as a banked fire. "Would you care to repeat that?"

Now Yuri faltered, wishing he could take back what he had said, or claim it was a joke. "It is nothing. Nothing. Only that . . . that there are rumors about . . . about the woman you married, about her father dying to save her. They say that she was ruined by the—"

"If," Rakoczy said with great precision, his voice still low, "if there is any tale repeated about Xenya Evgeneivna, you will answer for it: you, and those of your blood who seek to compromise my wife."

"But everyone has heard the story," Yuri said, more in desperation than defense. "Her father was killed trying to save her." He repeated himself vehemently, as if that would give him more credibility. "Everyone has heard the story! Everyone. The man was dead. The Mongols were in the house, and all the servants were gone but her maid, and they killed her. We know what Mongols are. The girl must have been used. And," he went on, trying to bolster his argument in order to escape Rakoczy's fierce attention, "she has given her life over to charity. Everyone knows what—"

"She seeks to honor the memory of her father," said Rakoczy.

"Oh, yes. That is what the Shuiskys claim, and the Koshkins," jeered Yuri, too much afraid of Rakoczy to measure his words carefully. His dread made him reckless. "They would have to claim she never—" Then he realized how great his transgression was and fell silent.

For well over a minute no one spoke. At last Rakoczy turned his compelling dark eyes on Yuri. "You had better go. At once." Rothger moved to stand beside Yuri, who was fidgeting with the hem of his rubashka. "I will arrange for his things to be carried to the Polish embassy house."

"Excellent," said Rakoczy, who regarded Yuri one more time. "Keep the coins I gave you, and remember how you came by them, that they are true coin for false." With that, he turned away and did not move again until Rothger and the servant had left the laboratory.

Bells were ringing for sunset Mass by the time Rothger returned from his errand. "Father Krabbe sends you greetings," he told his master as he made sure the door was securely closed.

"Thank you, old friend," said Rakoczy distantly; he was occupied with a handful of small topazes, examining them for flaws and discolorations. He set two aside, dissatisfied with their quality. He continued his critical examination of the rest. "I trust you gave him mine?"

"Most certainly," said Rothger. "And I informed him of the reason for our actions, privately of course."

"And what did Father Krabbe say?" Rakoczy asked, his face looking drawn.

"He would be very careful." Rothger's austere features shifted into a faint smile. "There are already spies in the embassy, of course. They have come to expect subterfuge from their servants, but Father Krabbe is a sensible man. He is aware that a literate footman is a valuable addition to their household, familial loyalties aside. And knowing that Yuri is already suborned makes his position easier, for none of the embassy need spend time trying to guess where his allegiance lies."

"I suppose it is a blessing of a kind," said Rakoczy. He held out three of the topazes so that the light from the oil lamps could touch them; little fingers of flame danced in the jewels. "Czar Feodor does not have his father's obsession with rare stones, but Nikita Romanov knows their value, and will not disdain a few baubles like these. I am going to ask Boris for the opportunity to present them to the Czar."

Rothger had no comment to make about those plans. He watched Rakoczy put the jewels into a small ivory box. "I am concerned, my master. Yuri is not one who will honor you for sparing him. He is more likely to seek vengeance for what you have done. He considers himself shamed. If you will not act against him, you must be prepared for him to act against you."

"I fear you're right," said Rakoczy. "He will expect retaliation for his insults. It is what he would do. But it is not what I will do; I will not be made cruel to suit his notions of noble conduct." He strode across the room to the athanors, both of which were cooling now. The oil lamps cast puddles of light that threw his face into half-shadow.

"My master," said Rothger, hearing the note of finality in Rakoczy's words.

"And you do not approve," said Rakoczy with irony flavoring his amusement.

"It is not my place to approve," said Rothger more stiffly than he wanted to. "You are master."

Rakoczy's single crack of laughter masked his inner dejection. "And fine deference you show, my friend." He motioned his implied rebuke away in a single gesture. "You are worried, and I do not make light of that. For what consolation it may be, I also worry."

"And yet you remain here," said Rothger.

Rakoczy touched the little ivory box. "What is there to go back to? War? Famine? In Russia or Europe, what does it matter?" He asked the question as if he were inquiring about the weather.

"But what is there here to remain for?" Rothger's question was fast and quiet, his steady faded-blue eyes unflinching.

The answer did not come at once. "You may be right, and I am being foolish." Rakoczy rubbed his brow.

"Not foolish," said Rothger at once.

"Oh, there is no reason to spare me," said Rakoczy. "I do not seek to spare myself." His gesture included all the laboratory. "I am aware that my situation here is precarious, all the more so because those at Court seek my skills. Yet without this, I would be at the mercy of spies and Court machinations. As it is, the jewels buy me a measure of peace; the boyars are as Pyrrhonic as they are greedy, and they are reluctant to tamper with someone who might be to their advantage."

"Father Pogner would gladly release you from your obligation," Rothger observed.

"My obligation is to Istvan Bathory, not Father Pogner; if it were to Father Pogner I would have been cast off long since,"

Rakoczy reminded him. His manner changed, becoming remote. "How many times have I lost my native land to invaders? And how many times have I been taken from it." He did not expect an answer and got none; he went to a tall, locked cabinet where all his books were stored. The light from the nearest oil lamp angled across his features. "Istvan Bathory has honored me in exile, and that is rare in kings, as we both have cause to know. For that alone, I shall discharge my duties here for as long as I am capable of it."

Rothger had seen Rakoczy in this state perhaps a dozen times in the sixteen hundred years he had served him, and each time it had troubled him. "Surely King Istvan does not expect you to remain here in the face of danger."

At that Rakoczy smiled, a sardonic glint in his eyes. "Of course he does, and with good reason. He requires someone at this Court who has nothing to lose but the King's good-will. That is why he did not leave this embassy entirely to priests." He leaned on the cabinet, his arms folded. "But you're right; precautions are in order. I suppose it would be best to alert the servants; they will have to be told that Yuri has left and is not to be admitted again without my permission. That will lead to just the sort of speculation we want to avoid, but there is no other course open to us."

"And your wife?" asked Rothger, his tone made noticeable by its neutrality.

"Xenya." Rakoczy's eyes seemed to be looking a great distance. "I'll try to persuade her to . . . to trust me." It was an effort to say it so directly.

"Should she be guarded?" Rothger anticipated the answer, adding, "And which of the servants do we assign to protect her?"

"That is a perplexing question, isn't it." Rakoczy's solemn demeanor did not match his light tone. "And I have no answer to give you. Her greatest risk comes from her family, and I cannot stop them from seeing her without causing her distress. It may be necessary to find new servants, and that increases the chance of bringing new spies into the household." He moved away from the cabinet. "I dislike being coerced."

"You could confine her to the house as most wives are confined, in the terem. No one would think it strange if you do this. It is what you are expected to do," said Rothger, but without much confidence that Rakoczy would order it.

"I could; and hire eunuchs to watch her," he allowed as he paced down the room, the heels of his boots clicking smartly on the bare wood. "And that would destroy what little faith she has in me."

"It might become necessary," Rothger said.

"Yes," said Rakoczy.

"The Shuiskys and the Nagoys are powerful rivals," Rothger persisted.

"Yes," said Rakoczy.

"Father Pogner is determined to discredit you."

"Yes," said Rakoczy. "He is."

In exasperation Rothger turned on his heel and left Rakoczy alone in his laboratory.

Text of a letter to Istvan Bathory, King of Poland, from his cousin Tibor Bathory, written in Hungarian.

To my Heaven-favored cousin who reigns as King in Poland, my greetings from the beleaguered city of Trieste.

It is with reluctance that I take pen in hand to write to you, for certainly what I have to impart will cause you concern. Much as I have hoped that another means to end this shame would manifest itself, I have not perceived it in spite of many long hours of prayers for guidance. Nevertheless, you must be informed of these occurrences in order for some action to be taken to correct what has become a very difficult situation within our family. It is essential that you be warned of certain damnable events before word reaches you through the offices of those seeking to discredit the name Bathory.

I fear I must inform you that a number of very troubling reports have been provided me that suggest that my half-sister, your cousin, Erzebet Bathory, has been seduced by a servant of the Devil himself, a woman who is one of her housekeepers. This woman practices vile witchcraft and has drawn Erzebet herself into the despicable practices and godless rites of those who turn their back on the Salvation through Christ Jesus. Erzebet has made herself an acolyte of this malignant creature and claims to have abandoned Christian worship in favor of making hideous offerings to the gods of her instructress.

If only Erzebet had children, for they would keep her thoughts away from such practices. How often we are warned that idleness in women leads to sin. With children to claim her attention she would bend her thoughts to their welfare and learning, filling her hours with the pious sacrifices of motherhood. But it is nine years now since she and Nadasdy married, and they have nothing to show for their union. It is said by uncharitable people that there exists an antipathy between husband and wife. Nadasdy spends much of his time away from Castle Bathory, often marching with the army against the Turk, but more frequently seeking out entertainment of other sorts in Vienna and other cities known to cater to secret vices. Although many hold him in high esteem, others speak of him less favorably, comparing his actions to those of a wayward and feckless youth.

You may see how sin had led to sin. The absence of her husband has left Erzebet with time to brood and nothing but folly to occupy her hours. There is little for her to do; Castle Bathory does not boast much society, and Nadasdy has not encouraged Erzebet to surround herself with her own friends. Thus has she fallen prey to the reprehensible housekeeper, striving to fill her empty days and isolated life with the promise of power in the world, which is the lure of Satan.

I must ask you, Majesty, to consider the damage that may well be done to the honor of the House of Bathory if the activities of Erzebet go unchecked. It will do you, nor your brother, any credit to have it known that your cousin is the willing slave of the Devil and studies spells whereby she may gain ascendancy over those around her. It is not possible that you could endorse her dedication, and therefore you must oppose it; for otherwise suspicion may well spread to you, and in these times no man may consider himself immune to the taint of diabolism.

Let your justice be swift and sure, Royal cousin. Let it strike out the heart of the evil and cleanse the name Bathory of all implication of sin. You have the authority to require her to confess. If you cannot act, you must relinquish the governing of Erzebet to the Church. Do not abandon her to the temptations she has pursued. I will pray for God to give you the wisdom and courage to turn Erzebet from her disastrous path.

In the sure and certain hope of the exoneration of the honor of Bathory, I sign myself with all sincere dedication,

> *Your cousin,*
> *Tibor Bathory*
> *On the 29th day of May, in the Year of Grace 1584.*

6

After blessing the ikons at the front door of Rakoczy's house, Anastasia Sergeivich Shuisky asked to see his "so-sweet-cousin Xenya." His cupid's-bow mouth, framed by his wheat-blond beard, lent the phrase a sensuality that Rakoczy recognized with misgiving. "You will permit me to have a word with her in privacy, won't you?"

"Certainly," said Rakoczy after a moment as he rid himself of disturbing memories: Cornelius Justus Silius watching Olivia with the lovers he sent to her, Pentecoste at her spinning, the inextinguishable hunger in Estasia's eyes. He clapped his hands twice and said to the servant who answered the summons, "Please inform my wife that her cousin has arrived."

The servant reverenced both men and left the reception hall.

"You no longer have a doorman," Anastasi observed, brows elevated.

Rakoczy shrugged. "Yuri is more suited to work for Father Pogner and the embassy; I am at their service." His black dolman was open at the collar, revealing the red-embroidered Italian camisa beneath. "In time I will find someone to replace Yuri."

It was a warm, close afternoon, oppressive and thunderish. In the market squares throughout Moscovy vendors were sluggish and buyers surly; animals drooped in harness; the white doves that usually littered the sky kept to their perches. The moat around the Kremlin stank and spread its miasmic presence over half the city.

"Graciously said," Anastasi told him, and looked around the

room, perusing the contents and at last nodding to show his approval. "You have made this very nice, especially for a foreigner."

"Thank you," said Rakoczy, and indicated the withdrawing room behind the reception hall. "Let me offer you the use of this chamber. And I will ask my cooks to prepare something for you, if that would please you."

Anastasi rubbed his hands together. "I admit that fancy breads would go well just now: fancy breads and a little fruit, and something substantial to drink. Yes, that would be the best fare in prickly weather like this. You're a considerate fellow, Rakoczy, and have taken to our ways fairly well: better, certainly, than your Polish priests." He took a turn about the reception hall, his bright eyes revealing his interest in the heavy draperies from England. He chose to comment only on things Russian. "The lacquer-work on that chest is very striking; the battle against the German Crusaders, isn't it? A strange topic for you, I would have thought, you being foreign. That lantern is from Ratcatcher Street, or I do not know good Moscovy brass. The carving on the beams is very good. You must have found excellent workmen to do it for you."

"I trust I have," said Rakoczy, and turned as Xenya appeared at the top of the stairs.

Xenya was flushed from the heat; without cosmetics she looked very young, an impression made more forceful by her long, bronze braids falling down her back without ribbons or binding. Her camisa was sheer linen—a gift from Rakoczy—and she wore her lightest sarafan. She watched Anastasi intently, then lowered her head to greet him. "May God show you mercy and favor, Anastasi Sergeivich."

"And to you, Xenya Evgeneivna." He waited until she had reached the bottom of the stairs.

"I trust you are well," said Xenya nervously; she spoke as if she barely knew Anastasi and distrusted his reason for his visit.

"God is very good," said Anastasi, and in a sweeping motion took in her surroundings. "Your prayers have been heard at last, have they not? To have achieved this at your age is remarkable. Not many women who wait as long as you did to marry are so rewarded for their patience, but I see He has favored you. How fortunate that after disaster there is redemption."

Rakoczy disliked the manner and tone Anastasi took with Xenya, but he made no outward show of it and spoke pleasantly enough. "Marriage is hardly redemption, Anastasi Sergeivich."

"Well," said Anastasi, accepting the mild reprimand with an engaging grin, preparing to press his advantage, "perhaps it is salvation, at least. Don't you think so, little cousin?" He enjoyed his own witticism as much as he liked placing Rakoczy at a disadvantage.

Xenya was not able to join in her cousin's laughter but she did manage to smile. "Certainly it may be," she said, looking once toward Rakoczy.

As if he were not aware of the jibes aimed at him, Rakoczy chuckled once as he opened the door to the withdrawing room a bit wider. "If you will excuse me, I will order your refreshments."

"Of course, of course," said Anastasi with a blithe wave. He paid no more attention to Rakoczy but turned his full attention to Xenya as he guided her into the withdrawing room.

It was a pleasant chamber, with four cushioned chairs around a low shelved table, Italian hangings on the walls, and a shocking painting hung over a rack of unstrung hunting bows, an Italian painting in the style of the last century, of a naked, fair-haired woman out-flung at the feet of a massive man in draped golden clothes whose head was wreathed in a crown of lightning; Jupiter and Semele represented by the artist's two favorite models: a larger-than-life Giuliano de'Medici and Simonetta Vespucci.

Xenya waited until Anastasi had chosen one of the chairs before she asked his permission to be seated herself. She folded her hands and waited for Anastasi to speak, fighting down her certainty that she had committed some great error.

"I am disappointed, Xenya," Anastasi announced, losing no time in pleasantries with her.

She swallowed against the fear that threatened to stifle her voice. "What have I done now?" It took all her will not to beg his forgiveness.

"It is two months since you have sent me any word regarding your husband. That is a long time for a new bride to be silent, and surely you have learned more about him. You have been lax. You have not attended to your duty." He loomed toward her, his elbows braced on the arms of the chair, his head lowered like an angry bear. "You were charged with discovering the full extent of the man's fortune, and you have yet to inform me of anything but his claim—which I already know—that he makes his jewels himself. He must take us all for credulous fools!"

"He has not . . . he has told me very little of himself, but that he comes from the mountains of Transylvania." Her voice was low, unintrusive.

"Surely he has revealed more than that," said Anastasi, deciding to try reasonable persuasion first. "You are not to hold things back from me, Xenya. You are under obligation to me, my girl, and it is suitable that you render service for all I have done. Remember that I sheltered you when many another would have turned you into the streets. I did everything in my power to protect your name and the memory of your father. I arranged for you to marry, which all of us had lost hope of happening. I had not anticipated you would be a wife, but since you are, you will not forget what you owe to your family for all they have done for you. And your mother." He examined the back of his right hand. "She sends you her blessings and prays that you will bear a child by Christmas."

Xenya looked away from Anastasi, confusion in her eyes. "Tell her I thank her, and bless her, and I pray, too."

"Yes, you must do," said Anastasi with sham approval. "Your prayers for a child will drown out your mother's, doubtless. Every woman longs for her children. You more than most, with a foreigner for a husband." He sat back a little, but continued the intimidating hunch of his shoulders. "But you must also wish to serve your husband, as you serve your family."

"I do, Anastasi Sergeivich," she said in an undervoice. "I wish—"

"Wishing is not sufficient," Anastasi said with force. "Wishes are scraps of linen in the wind." He raised one admonitory finger. "You cannot think of yourself as other women, but you must forget what is past and give yourself to your husband as if you knew no other men, and sought only his seed, and his children. At least you were spared that—you bore no Mongol young. No one could have guarded you against that. And your foreign husband would never have given you a coin in the street, had that happened. We must be glad you were too young." He coughed for emphasis. "You will want to be certain that he never knows what degradation you have suffered, or he will have to deny the marriage. If I am kept informed of everything you know about him, there will be no cause for concern. You will be safe."

"He will not be safe." Xenya had risen, and now stood trembling. "I have no wish to dishonor him. He has——" She stopped, unwilling to confide more. It was so tempting to shout "He knows! I told him! He doesn't care!" but she held back, sensing that this knowledge was her one bastion against her cousin. As long as Anastasi thought Rakoczy ignorant of her past, she could not be compelled to act against her husband.

"Made complaints of you?" suggested Anastasi, his expression darkening.

"No," she said, trying to steady herself. "He is foreign, as you warned me from the first and continue to warn me, and his ways are . . . are strange to me. I do not understand him, Cousin." The last was the truth.

"Then you must learn," said Anastasi, permitting her no leeway. "You must ready yourself to study him, and discover everything that you can about him. I cannot permit you to remain here if you will not do as you are told. You are charged with the task of discovering his secrets, and so you shall. It is necessary for us, for Shuisky! to know this man. If he is harsh, steel yourself. You have known worse."

She pressed her lips firmly together, her hands clenched; she shivered as if she were standing in the snow. Finally she was able to say, "He has not been harsh with me." She could not reveal that he had never used her body, for such failure would expose her to every disaster she had sought for so long to avoid: without doubt Anastasi would repudiate her marriage and the truth of her disgrace would follow.

The door opened and Rothger came into the withdrawing room bearing a tray laden with a variety of fancy breads, two plates of peaches covered in honey, a dish of almonds, and an opened bottle of Hungarian wine beside two golden cups. "With the compliments of my master," he said, his Russian falling in Latin cadences. The odors of cinnamon, ginger, and pepper were strong as incense.

"Very satisfactory," Anastasi approved, looking over the food offered. "It is very welcome." He moved forward in his chair so that he could reach the tray as Rothger set it on the central table.

"I will convey your acceptance," said Rothger with a reverence, and backed out of the room.

"He is a good host, I will say that for Rakoczy," Anastasi observed. He reached out for one of the fried buns stuffed with sweetmeats. He held this in his fingers, sniffing it. "He allows his cook a free hand with spices. You must enjoy that, Xenya."

Xenya remained standing, rigid so that she would not shake. "He treats me well," she said, once again speaking the truth.

Anastasi devoured the bun in two large bites, chewing vigorously as he poured a generous amount of wine. "The Hungarians pride themselves on this," he said, the words muffled by food. He drank deeply, swallowing the bun with the wine. He wiped wine and sweat from his upper lip when he lowered the cup. "Does he give you meats every day, Xenya? You are so thin. You must eat, become beautiful. How can you expect to have a child when you fast all the time?"

"I am fed well, cousin," she said, unmoving.

"You should eat more then. Have some of this. These breads are filled with cream. Have one, have more. You hardly need my invitation; you are in your husband's house." Anastasi smiled nastily and took more wine. "For now," he added as he refilled the cup.

"It would not be proper," said Xenya. "With my husband gone from the room."

"Perhaps I will summon him," said Anastasi, beginning to enjoy himself; he often found indulging envy exhilarating. "First I want you to discover for me—and I want you to discover it within a few days, not months—what the Poles would do if the Czar breaks off dealings with the Patriarch of Jerusalem and makes the Metropolitan Patriarch of the Orthodox Church in Russia."

"You are not serious." Xenya studied Anastasi, trying to anticipate when he would attack, and for what reason. "I know nothing of these things, only to say my prayers and to do acts of charity for the expiation of sin."

"Well said," approved Anastasi. "But it changes nothing. I must know these things, and quickly, if I am to secure my place in the Czar's favor."

"Dear God," whispered Xenya, crossing herself.

"By all means pray for me, Xenya Evgeneivna. The advancement of Shuisky ought to have your whole loyalty, for my kindnesses to you. Therefore you will do the things I ask of you, and you will do them with a thankful heart. I meant what I said, Xenya. If you fail in the tasks I set you, I will not be able to continue to protect you. Married as you are to a foreigner, you will not find many well disposed to you if it is learned you were despoiled." He finished the bun. "And what is visited upon you will also touch your children."

"But I have no reason to learn about the Roman Church, or the King of Poland. If I should ask about either, he will suspect that I am doing so at your order. You could learn more from others. Speak to the Polish priests, for they must know something. What can I learn from my husband that you cannot find out for yourself, with less difficulty?" She knew it was folly to challenge him, but once she began, she did not have the will to stop. "How am I to do this? You set me impossible tasks, Anastasi Sergeivich, for the satisfaction of having me fail."

His eyes narrowed and the smugness left his lips. "If that were so, you would still be obliged to me. Never forget that." He had a bit more of the wine, pointedly offering none to her. "Your behavior is very poor."

"That is for my husband to say," she countered, feeling giddy with terror.

"Your husband is an exile who knows nothing. You say he treats you well, and you reward him with stubbornness. You pretend to be loyal to him so that you need not serve your family. Is that the ways of his people? We Rus know better. We Rus do not tolerate obstinacy in our women." He made a movement with his hand as if he were swinging a belt. "We realize that the devil must be driven out of women's flesh."

Xenya stared at him, her fear increasing as she listened. "How could you expect me to learn such things from him? Even if you beat me, I have no right to question him."

"I leave it to you," said Anastasi with a wave of his hand as he reached for another little bread. "Just find it out."

"But why should he know this? And why should he tell me?" Her voice had risen and she lowered it once more, not wanting to let Anastasi see how badly he had frightened her.

"A man tells his wife many things, many things. You have only to find an occasion when he is in good humor and ask him to speculate. You know nothing of the Roman Church, as you admit. You might begin there." He smacked his lips as he drank, then set the cup aside. "It is important to me to know this, Xenya Evgeneivna. I will require it."

Although she was still afraid, she found the courage to defy him. "I will not compromise him, Anastasi Sergeivich."

Surprised, Anastasi looked up directly at her. "What is this, little Cousin?" he asked sweetly. He smoothed his beard as he watched her, knowing that his measuring stare would trouble her. "What have you said to me?"

She found it difficult to answer, apprehension gripping her. "I will not compromise my husband."

"You will not oppose me," Anastasi corrected her. "You have no right to oppose me, Xenya Evgeneivna, on the honor of your dead father."

Her teeth were chattering, but she said, "No. You will have to use another of your spies to ruin him." She moved a step backward. "I will tell you what he tells me, but I will not lure him into danger."

"Surely you do not intend to expose yourself to . . ." He let the words trail off and occupied himself in choosing another little bread, this one studded with currants and coated in honey. "Even a foreigner would be disgraced if it were ever known what happened."

"It would shame you as well," Xenya declared.

"True. The dishonor would be felt throughout the family. And your mother would have to withdraw to a convent in order to be rid of the stigma of your sin. Who knows what your husband would have to do, but I could not permit you to return to my house, and I am not certain that the nuns would welcome you, not given your crimes." He nibbled at the bread in sharp, precise bites. "You might have to beg your bread on the streets, go to the houses-with-no-names, become one of the unfortunates you now provide with charity."

"Stop it," she said, but without force. "You cannot—"

"I cannot what?" he went on in the same mellifluous tone. "Do you tell me I have no authority over you? You will find you are wrong, with an exile for a husband. If you had married a boyar, I might have to be content to allow him to school you. But

Rakoczy is not Rus, he is Transylvanian." His laughter was low.

"He is of an ancient house," said Xenya with more feeling, able to defend Rakoczy better than herself. "He told me his blood is very, very old."

"No doubt," said Anastasi flatly, "and no doubt before the Turks over-ran his land he dined off gold platters every day, and sat on a throne with two hundred diamonds in it, and held a sceptre topped with pearls the size of a pigeon's egg, and kept an army of ten thousand, all armed and horsed from his purse." He poured another measure of wine. "But here, he has this house and the things in it, his jewels, a few horses, and you. That is the extent of his wealth in Russia."

Xenya could not stop twisting her hands. "You should not demand this of me," she said quietly.

"Because you dislike it? Because you have forgotten to whom you owe fealty?" He lifted his right hand to reprimand her. "Do you think this ploy will work, my girl? Do you suppose that your husband will approve your betrayal of us because you wish him to believe you do it for his benefit? He will know that you are nothing more than a perfidious whore, prepared to sell the appearance of good faith for favor?" He slapped the arms of the chair and almost tipped over his wine. "What foolishness is this, that you embrace it? You are not a child fresh from the terem, you have done charity in the churches and you have seen what life is for women who do not serve the bidding of their families."

This time Xenya was able to say nothing. She could not bring herself to meet Anastasi's eyes. As much as she wanted to scream defiance and scratch at his eyes, her terror of him kept her cold and trembling.

Anastasi reveled in her fear. He shoved himself out of the chair, grabbed the wine, and took a turn about the withdrawing room. "Look around you, Xenya. You are in a foreign country. That painting"—he gestured toward the Botticelli—"should make it clear to you. What decent Rus would have such a painting where an ikon ought to hang? What foreigner can stand against the Court? If you are disgraced, his disgrace will be greater, no matter how much the Czar enjoys topazes. Do you think this exile would intervene for you, if the Court allowed him to speak? He will be too busy trying to salvage his position to devote any time to the futility of guarding you. And he will not have the ear of the Court. *I will*. And you will answer to me, Xenya Evgeneivna, as we all will answer to God." He drank the wine and filled his cup again; the bottle was more than half empty.

"Cousin—" she began, and her throat grew tight. She was determined not to cry, to let him have the satisfaction of seeing her weep.

"What is it, Xenya?" he asked with false concern. "You really ought to have a taste of wine. It will enhearten you." He paused to pour a little of the dark red wine into the second gold cup. He held it out to her. "Take it, Xenya. Drink."

Much as she hated to take anything from Anastasi, Xenya reluctantly accepted the cup. She muttered something that might have been thanks before she lifted the cup to her lips.

"There. It will help you master your passions, little Cousin. You must certainly wish to do that." His smile flashed once more. He saw that her hands shook and his smile broadened into a grin. "The Roman Church, little Cousin, that is what is most pressing. We must know what the Pope in Rome will say if we elevate the Metropolitan. Those Roman heretics could start another Crusade, and this time we cannot hope that Saint Alexandr will rise from his tomb and defeat them once more."

The scent of the wine filled her head; Xenya thought it would make her tipsy without tasting a drop. She did not want to listen to Anastasi, for his words seemed to cling to her, slippery and clinging, contaminating her. At last she tasted the wine.

"Why are all those Polish Jesuits here? They claim they are here at the behest of Bathory, but that may be a convenient lie, to lend them position while they go about their real tasks. And Rakoczy will know it. He will have orders, too. And you will find out what they are, Xenya. And when you find them out, you will tell me. At once." He spoke low, insinuatingly, coming closer to her until he could reach out a large hand to stroke her hair. "It is essential, Xenya Evgeneivna. You must do it."

She drank again, recklessly this time, letting the liquid fill her mouth.

"Speak to him soon, Xenya, and learn something of worth, or I will be forced to speak to him myself of other matters." He circled one braid around his finger, then let it fall away.

There was a discreet cough at the door, and Rakoczy said, "I hope I do not intrude?" He came toward them, offering a slight, European bow to Anastasi. "I did not want to neglect a guest too long."

Anastasi moved away from Xenya, scowling as he moved. He disliked being interrupted and he had the uneasy feeling that Rakoczy had been in the room longer than it appeared. He dismissed the notion at once as impossible, but the scowl did not fade from his features. Lifting his cup to cover this, he remarked, "A very good wine. You should have some."

Rakoczy favored him with an enigmatic smile. "I do not drink wine."

"Weak-headed, are you?" Anastasi did not keep the sneer out of his tone. He finished what he had and poured most of the rest of the bottle into his cup. "I didn't know that those from Transylvania had such weakness. Unless you got it from the Turks—they do not drink, do they?"

Rakoczy paid no heed to Anastasi's studied insults and answered directly. "They are not supposed to, according to their holy books." He shrugged. "But where is the living person who always does what holy books require?"

Anastasi laughed at that. "Clever, and true." He turned quickly and a little of the wine sloshed over his fingers. "As the priests are forever reminding us."

Xenya had moved closer to Rakoczy and now stood at his side. She took one more sip from her cup, then set it down on the tray. "My cousin . . . has been saying many things. I had not realized how long it had been since I . . . spoke to him. I should have visited my mother before now."

"Invite her here; I will arrange proper escort," Rakoczy suggested, adding to Anastasi, "If it suits you?" He watched his guest, faint, angry amusement lurking at the back of his dark eyes. He indicated the tray, suggesting, "I think you might want to eat a few more of the breads, Anastasi Sergeivich. It would keep your head from aching in this sultry weather."

"A wise precaution," said Anastasi, and reached for another of the cream-filled pastries. "You have a very good cook."

"So I have been told; it is gracious of you to compliment him." Rakoczy could feel Xenya's distress, and knew that it would not end as long as Anastasi was present. "Perhaps you would be willing to bring Xenya's mother to dine with us in your company? I will provide you a number of times that would be convenient in this household, and you may choose the one to your liking."

"I would want Piotr Grigoreivich Smolnikov to accompany us. The poor fellow has little enough to fill his days since he lost his sight." Anastasi gave his best personable smile. "With my wife and children in the country, I need to take care not to neglect my dependents in Moscovy."

"Commendable," said Rakoczy dryly. He paused a moment, then said, "I do not wish to hurry you, but I must leave in a short while, and it is not fitting that you remain when I am gone."

"Another of your Transylvanian customs?" Anastasi stuck a cream-covered finger in his mouth and licked it clean. "I'll have another of these—they're truly excellent—and then I will leave. I'm glad to have had a talk with my little cousin. She is much missed in my house, much missed." He bit the next cream-filled bun in half and busied himself cleaning the overflow off his mustaches. That done, he had the last of the wine and put his cup aside. "In Czar Ivan's time, cups like these were given as gifts to those who attended his banquets. I myself have three of them."

Rakoczy smiled sardonically. "If it would not lessen the worth of the Czar's gift, take this cup, too, by all means." He bowed to Anastasi. "As the kinsman of my wife, to show my regard."

Anastasi nodded several times, as if his head, once set in motion, could only stop with difficulty. "Very pretty." It was not possible to tell if he meant the cup or the gesture. "I will keep it on the shelf below the Czar's cups," he announced as he chewed the rest of the bun. "Yes, that is the correct place for it." He held out the cup, turning it over to let the light play over it. "Very satisfying. I am pleased to have it."

"Thank you for accepting it," said Rakoczy, drifting toward the door as he went on; without obvious force he was compelling Anastasi to follow him. "I take some pride in the things I make."

Anastasi had drunk just enough wine to make him feel bold, not reckless, and so he did not actually laugh. He gestured extravagantly. "That is what it requires, is it? You have the means to make these, and when it suits you, you make more?"

"Precisely," said Rakoczy, holding the door to the withdrawing room wide open.

"You simply cook up gold, the way you cook up jewels," said Anastasi with a mercurial smile. "How clever of you. How many of the Polish embassy actually believe that?"

"Not many," said Rakoczy honestly enough. "But ask yourself

this, Anastasi Sergeivich: how did I bring so much gold into Russia without anyone noticing?"

"I have an answer to that," said Anastasi, pressing his sleeve to his flushing, damp brow. "You arrived with chests. Many chests, closed with leather straps and locks. That was how you brought your gold and your jewels."

Rakoczy bowed slightly, seeing Rothger standing ready by the door. "I do not know what to say." He motioned to his houseman to open the door. "You have answers to everything."

"Or I will have," promised Anastasi, giving a half-reverence to Rakoczy as he reached the door. "I will come again."

"Of course you will, when you permit me to prepare you and my wife's mother and that blind old soldier a meal, the way the Florentines do it." He offered Anastasi another European bow.

Anastasi waggled a finger at him, not quite scolding. "We know something of Italian ways; the architects who worked in the Kremlin and Father Possevino have shown us much. We are not gullible fools who will believe any fable, you know. If you do not show us Florentine manners, we will—"

"Duke Anastasi, I have lived in Florence," said Rakoczy, but did not add that was almost a century ago. "And Venice; and Rome."

"Such is the fate of exiles," said Anastasi with a sage expression as he signaled for his horse. "We will dine soon. Before the month is out."

"It will be my pleasure to receive you," Rakoczy lied.

Anastasi blessed the ikons by the door, chuckled, and sauntered out of the house.

As soon as the footfalls of Anastasi's horse had faded from the wood-paved courtyard, Xenya appeared in the doorway of the withdrawing room, her honey-colored eyes huge. "I didn't tell him anything, my husband," she said softly, desperately.

Rakoczy was at the foot of the stairs, about to go to his alchemical laboratory. "I didn't suppose you would," he said kindly. "Did you want to?"

She let out a thin, high wail and rushed to him, dropping on her knees beside him. "No. No, I swear before Christ Jesus and the Virgin, no, I did not want to tell him anything." She looked up at him. "Do not be angry with me, I pray you. If you are angry, and Anastasi as well, what will I do. Do not be angry."

"Xenya," said Rakoczy very gently, and knelt down beside her. "Xenya, you have nothing to fear from me. And I give you my word you have nothing to fear from your cousin."

She shook her head violently, unwilling now to look into his dark, calm eyes. "He can ruin me, and he would ruin me. He would do it, I know he would."

"He would not ruin me, and he is not so foolish that he will ruin himself," said Rakoczy, keeping his voice level. "Your cousin Anastasi is too ambitious to compromise himself that way."

Her eyes met his, then slid away. "I didn't tell him you knew. I didn't let him find out. I kept it to myself."

"Very good," said Rakoczy, touching her shoulders so that he could lift her to her feet as he rose. "There is no reason to tell him, unless you decide to."

She began to tremble suddenly. "He frightens me." It took all her faltering courage to admit this, and she tried to prepare herself for the condemnation she knew was certain to follow such a confession.

Rakoczy touched her face with one small, beautiful hand. "I know."

With a shaky sigh Xenya moved close to him as if seeking the haven of his body and his self-contained strength; she rested her head on his shoulder.

Slowly and carefully Rakoczy enfolded her in his arms.

Text of a letter from Father Pogner to Istvan Bathory, King of Poland, written in Latin.

To the revered Transylvanian who reigns as King in Poland, sincerest greetings from your embassy in Moscovy.

From the inception of our mission it has been foremost in my purpose to serve the interests of the Throne to the limits that the Church will permit, and I have spent many months attempting to acquit myself honorably in your cause. The other priests have generally emulated my purpose and have been at pains to see that this mission accomplishes the goals you have set. I have had to remonstrate their actions rarely, with the exception of Father Krabbe, who has his sights on other goals than the ones we are mandated to pursue. So it is that I am reluctant to permit him to continue with the mission.

If you are willing to issue your permission for such action, I will order Father Krabbe to return to Poland before the snows fly, or at the first true thaw next spring. I do not want him to travel in severe weather, for he continues to be somewhat less hardy than the rest of the mission since his lungs suffered putrid fever. During the winter he was ill twice, and both times insisted that the charlatan Rakoczy be brought to treat him, which I permitted only because what I have seen of Russian physicians convinces me that Father Krabbe is in no worse hands with Rakoczy than with one of those men, who are little better than herb women.

Since his marriage, Rakoczy has spent very few days with us at our house. He has said to the English that this is because I have forbidden him to come here, but that is not wholly accurate, and I confess that I resent such implications as this statement creates in other foreigners. I would not prevent him from being here, but we do not recognize his wife, of course, and I do not allow him to speak of what he has called the Great Art, that is, the false teaching of alchemy.

In spite of the favor shown to him by Czar Ivan, Rakoczy continues to live in isolation, as do most foreigners in Moscovy. The laws of the city are such that it is difficult for us to abide by them; we are all at the mercy of our servants in a way that no Russian is. For that reason we are very cautious of the men we hire, and take only those with skills. I will say this much for Rakoczy—he found a servant for us who is literate and willing. We have taken on Yuri Piotrovich as our chief footman, and have found him to be very cooperative with our goals. Only Father Krabbe has given any credence to the claim Rakoczy made that this Yuri is a spy for one of the Russian nobles. It is typical of the Transylvanian that he would seek to keep us from making the best use of such a capable servant.

Certainly Hrabia Zary has long since reported to you the situation in Moscovy as he left it. In the time since the death of Czar Ivan, the Court adherents of Boris Godunov have been constantly at odds with the adherents of Nikita Romanov. Both these men were appointed by Czar Ivan to guide and guard his heir, Czar Feodor. It is regrettable that these two men were not in accord from the first, for their positions have diverged sharply in the last few months. I foresee continued difficulties between the two that will last as long as the young Czar is incapable of ruling wholly for himself.

That day, I fear, will never come, for without God's Grace, the young man will remain as innocent and simple as a child of four. He is perfectly amiable and affectionate in nature, but it is with the fondness of a child, not the deeper dedication which marks great men. This Czar Feodor continues in his passion for ringing bells and for all Courtly displays. But his patience is not great, and so all Court occasions have been made as brief as is possible, and ambassadors are received rarely. Of course, the true matters of diplomacy are conducted with Godunov on occasions apart from the Courtly events.

Father Kovnovski has taken it upon himself to become better acquainted with Nikita Romanov, positing a day when Romanov's star may rise higher than it is now. He believes that we may maintain worthwhile contact with both Godunov and Romanov, and is working toward that end. I am not so sanguine and I do not believe that it is wise to court Romanov at a time when Godunov is making the decisions that will affect Poland. Nevertheless, until such time as Kovnovski fails to gain some benefit from his task, I will permit it as his own project. I will do all that I can to keep this embassy above suspicion.

Let me assure Your Majesty that it is necessary for the mission to continue to hold Rakoczy at a great distance. He has shown his perfidy in marrying the Russian woman, and he has not followed my recommendations in regard to the Court. I am more convinced than before that he has gone over to the cause of the Czar and will disgrace us if given the opportunity. It is no longer a question of personal animosity, but of rigorous protection. The exile has found another country where he intends to establish himself. If that is the case, then we who are loyal to Poland and the Church must break with him in order to preserve our mission and our integrity.

With the adamant prayers that God will continue to give Poland the victory over her enemies, and that He will provide you with sound judgment and wisdom, I sign myself your most devoted ambassador,

With God's care and guidance,
Father Casimir Pogner

Society of Jesus
Ambassador to the Court of Czar Feodor at Moscovy
July 12th, by the reformed calendar,
in the Year of Grace 1584

7

They met in the Savior Gate, Vasilli Shuisky bound outward on foot, Boris Godunov returning on horseback with his twelve-man escort of Lancers from a four-day inspection of small fortresses on the west side of Moscovy; he had just reined in on the bridge over the moat to bless himself when Boris noticed Vasilli watching him. Each reverenced the other enough to satisfy convention, neither showing any real deference to the other.

"By what fortune do you return early from your tasks, Boris Feodorovich?" asked Vasilli with a hint of condemnation in the question.

"Good fortune," said Boris shortly; he had been in the saddle six hours that day and his back was almost as sore as his buttocks. "The Poles have kept their bargains and there has been no trouble from Novgorod. The Swedes have been content to remain where they are."

"Surely you did not expect any trouble?" asked Vasilli, holding back his desire to offer a scathing response; he would do that later, where fewer people could observe them.

"In these times one cannot be certain," said Boris. "That was the reason I went to the fortresses. We can report on the state of the fortresses to the court; I now have their requests for winter supplies, and in good time, so that they may be provisioned before the weather turns."

Vasilli made a gesture, indicating the hot, windy day. "Surely you need not bother for a month and more."

"September is almost here, and in the countryside the leaves are beginning to turn. Those boyars on their country estates have warned that winter is going to come early and be hard this year.

All the signs warn of profound cold. We will have to move quickly to supply the fortresses before the first winter storms come." Boris was aware they had attracted an audience; he suppressed his aggravation.

Vasilli made a gesture that combined gracious acceptance of Boris' assessment with the superior knowledge he possessed by right as a Shuisky. He looked over Boris' escort. "Not a very formidable force to take with you on such an errand, if you expected difficulties."

"Then you ought to realize that I expected none, and I did not want to offend the commanders of the fortresses by questioning the quality of their soldiers." He hitched his jaw in the direction of the men behind him. "These are experienced troops, and I took them with me for more than protection; I have listened to them as well as to the commanders of the fortresses, and I value all they have recommended. I have included their observations with the requests of the fortress commanders."

"So you trust them?" said Vasilli, facing Boris directly, although it put the sun into his face and made him squint. "One would think you were Rus." The barb was deliberate and he had the gratification of seeing the pain of it in Boris' black Tartar eyes.

"They are good men, true to the Czar, tested in battle," said Boris, aware that he had to speak up for his men or risk offending them. "For that all Russia can be grateful."

Vasilli smiled, his good-looking features becoming handsome. It was a deliberate ploy, one he had used often in the past. He looked around to see how much attention they had attracted and was pleased to see a number of men had gathered to listen to them. "And when do you intend to present your findings to Czar Feodor?"

"Tomorrow," Boris snapped. "It is to be a simple occasion. In the Golden Chamber, with the advisers." He was about to signal his men to move on, but Vasilli was not through with him.

"And what do you expect the Czar to do? Feodor Ivanovich will not be interested if there are no bells to ring, Boris Feodorovich." He was still smiling, encouraging others around them to smile with him.

"I expect the Czar to hear me out," said Boris. "You may come and listen, Andreivich, if that would reassure you that the Czar is given a full report." He flung this last at Vasilli, as annoyed with himself for being dragged into this impromptu confrontation as he was angry with Vasilli for starting it. He urged his weary horse forward, turning his thoughts to the bathhouse and relief for his aching muscles.

"And how am I to know what I hear is the truth?" challenged Vasilli, unwilling to give up the advantage he had.

"You will ask these soldiers. Or you may visit the fortresses yourself, if you believe we have not performed our tasks well enough." He decided to strike back once at Vasilli. "But the Czar might not understand why you wish to go about the countryside with armed men; it could appear to him to be an act of sedition."

Shuisky ambition was well known in Moscovy, and this last jibe of Boris' served to turn the crowd; now their laughter was more knowing and guarded. Vasilli's smile vanished and he offered another slight reverence to Boris, signaling their encounter had ended.

From the saddle, Boris returned the gesture, then said very quietly, "Feodor Ivanovich may be simple, but we who swore to Ivan to guard him are not." With that, he clapped his heels to his horse's sides, setting the mare into a short, bounding canter that scattered the people near them and cleared a way into the main avenue of the Kremlin.

The Lancers followed Boris, horses at the trot.

Vasilli remained still, watching Boris go, unwilling to be driven from the place by Boris' departure. When the last of the Lancers had turned and were out of sight, Vasilli continued on his way, pausing to bless the huge ikon of Christ in Glory that gave the gate its name.

The Beautiful-Red Market Square was very busy this day, with buyers bustling from one stall to the next, purchasing the bounty of summer before it was all gone. Those with fruits and berries were especially busy, charging the highest prices of the year as they neared the end of their crops. Apple sellers had just begun to bring in their bounty, and their prices were moderate, and would remain so for the next month. Farmers with cabbages and onions did not do as well as many of the others, but they knew they would prosper as the year wound down, when there were no other vegetables available.

Vasilli made his way around the merchants, past the platform called the Brow of the World, the Czar's zoo, and a small chapel devoted to Saint Piotr Chrysologus, and went down one of the narrow streets that ended at the enormous square. He continued through a maze of alleys and pathways until he arrived at a cooperage. There was a small yard for loading and unloading wagons, and opposite that a workmen's inn dispensed kvas and raw Crimean wine. Vasilli went directly into the taproom and found himself a place in the shadows, away from the few patrons seated near the door and the landlord's kegs. There he waited, listening to the hammering and shouts of the coopers vie with the ringing of the bells from the nearby monastery.

A short while later a blond young man in servant's livery came into the inn, his wide, Russian face fixed in an ingratiating expression. He removed his cap, twisting it between his big hands while looking around the taproom cautiously, as if prepared for trouble. He came further into the inn, blinking at the gloom. Then he shoved his cap into his belt and stood straighter.

"You have come to see me?" asked Vasilli, moving out of the darkness.

"Prince," said Yuri at once, making a reverence promptly. He glanced at the four draymen who sat hunched over big wooden cups, and making up his mind, approached Vasilli directly. "I did not know if anyone would come."

"Your note interested me, because it *was* a note." Vasilli did not bother to smile at Yuri, knowing that the young man was his already and needed no urging. "It is not often that a servant elects to make such an offer, and in such a manner." He regarded Yuri speculatively. "How is it you learned to read, and how did you manage to get the note into those saddlebags?"

He answered promptly. "You were moving very slowly, Prince, and the crowd was jostling . . . all I had to do was——"

"Enterprising; and for the moment we will set aside how you came by your skills," Vasilli approved without allowing Yuri to finish. "I have no reason to know more of that yet. You accomplished your aim, and have my attention. That is what matters for the moment, isn't it?" He folded his hands on the rough plank of the table. "Why do you think I want to know what goes on among the Polish priests?"

The question was not one Yuri had anticipated. He rubbed at his arms through the sleeves of his rubashka, glowering in concentration. "You are a Prince, and there are few Princes in Russia. What the foreigners do must be interesting to you."

"There are others of high rank who want to know this, as well. Have you approached them?" he asked in a stinging tone.

He looked away, then met Vasilli's eyes briefly. "I am . . . related to Piotr Nagoy. I have been asked to report to—"

Again Vasilli interrupted. "Piotr Nagoy, Piotr Nagoy," he said dreamily as he tried to place the name. "Is that Piotr Ivanovich or Piotr Mikhailovich?"

"Piotr Mikhailovich," admitted Yuri reluctantly.

"Dear me," said Vasilli. "A *very* poor relation."

Yuri's face darkened. "He has a bad reputation, I know."

"And lacks the fortune to make up for it," said Vasilli with distaste. "Piotr Mikhailovich is a libertine, a boor, a coward, a squanderer, and a drunkard. There are places in Moscovy where speaking his name would bar you from good society." He studied Yuri. "He sired you, I would guess."

After taking a deep breath, Yuri said, "Yes, and a dozen others I am certain of." He tapped the tabletop with the flat of his hand. "He treated me better than most, and my mother as well. She persuaded him to educate me and to send me away. He agreed so long as my . . . my brothers and sister remained on his lands." There was a sound in his voice that held Vasilli's attention, a slow-burning fury that Yuri himself did not recognize for what it was.

"And he sent you to Grigori Dmitrovich," said Vasilli in a measuring tone but with a tinge of amusement. "Hardly releasing you, no matter what he promised your mother."

"Yes." Yuri could not conceal his resentment.

"And you still report to him?" Vasilli asked.

Yuri did not answer at once, and when he did there was anger in his face. "I go to him once a month and I tell him what has happened; oftener if it is worthy of his attention. When I was discovered at the house of the foreign alchemist, I was—"

"Rakoczy? You were at the exile's house?" Vasilli interrupted with interest.

"Grigori Dmitrovich sent me there. I did not remain there long. That devil of a manservant is always watching, spying on the staff, seeing everything we do, and he tells his master what he sees." Yuri stared at the grimy, parchment-paned window. "He—Rakoczy—sent me to the priests."

"Sent you to the priests? Why?" Vasilli wondered aloud. This foreigner perplexed him more than any of the others did. "What was his reason?"

"I don't know," said Yuri darkly. "He informed the priests of what I had done but said that my literacy made up for it."

"What a rash thing to do," Vasilli mused, fingering his beard. "And in spite of what he told them, the Poles took you on?"

In the yard of the cooperage there were shouts and the sound of a collision as barrels rolled and tumbled off the wagon-bed where they were being loaded. One man was screaming, for his leg was broken in two places.

"I don't think that Father Pogner believed him," said Yuri, laughing once. "That old man despises Rakoczy."

"Does he," said Vasilli, beginning to think that Yuri could be of use to him, after all. He regarded the young man with a deceptive expression of concern. "You want to serve me so that you can rid yourself of your family, do I have it right, Yuri?"

"Yes," said Yuri bluntly. "If you will not take me, I will search until I find someone who will. I will not continue to serve Nagoy, not without their name and their position to pay for all I have done."

"Ambitious servants are asps and traitors," Vasilli reminded him. "Men have been knouted for less, much less."

"That won't happen to me," said Yuri with such conviction that Vasilli believed him. "I would kill myself rather than face the knout. I know what it does. My father had a dozen peasants knouted for killing chickens in winter. All but two of the men died, and they are cripples now, sitting with begging bowls. Neither can walk and only one has his wits. Their families have been ordered not to aid them or risk the same thing for themselves."

"If you were seized before you could kill yourself, what then?" asked Vasilli, enjoying the determination Yuri displayed.

"There are always means to die. Some are not pleasant, but the knout is worse. I would find some way to end my life." He looked directly at Vasilli. "I would not do it to spare you, or anyone, but myself." Then his hard expression altered. "I will say this for Rakoczy. When he found me out, he did not order me punished." He grew more speculative. "I doubt he had the stomach for it."

"Foreigners are cowards and fools," Vasilli said, prepared to accept it as the explanation.

"Yes; but I think Rakoczy had other reasons." He studied the uneven tabletop as if the answer to the puzzle was written there. "I don't know what to make of him."

"He is foreign; there is nothing more to concern you," said Vasilli, although his interest was piqued by what Yuri said. He shook off the sensation and put his mind to the young servant sitting across from him. "How am I to know that you are truly willing to serve me, and will not make the same bargain with others as you offer me? You are proposing to betray your employers and your family. What is to keep you from turning against me if it should suit your purposes?"

At that Yuri's candid eyes grew crafty. "You must offer me an advantage I will not want to sacrifice." This was the part he had planned and he launched into his proposition with gusto. "Promise me a position on one of your estates when you are finished with me here. Assure me that the position will be protected, that I might marry and give something to my children that will advance my family in the world. Put my skills to use. And assure me that neither you nor your heirs will be able to displace me. You will endow me with lands or income that cannot be denied to me and to my children and their children, either by you or your children, and their children. I will swear you will have my faithful service through all my life, and the gratitude of my family. In return, I will do what you wish in the Polish household. I will give inaccurate reports to the Nagoys and I will perform whatever acts you instruct me to carry out. I will be your good right hand, or your left one, if you would rather." He met Vasilli's eyes boldly.

"My left hand?" asked Vasilli, surprised that Yuri would offer to be his assassin. "A dangerous offer to make, young man, if you are not prepared to do the deed."

"I am prepared," said Yuri, so readily that Vasilli was mildly taken aback. "I do not limit my loyalty once I swear it."

"But you swore it to your father, didn't you?" Vasilli inquired. "Surely a son must honor the wishes of his father."

"If his father grants his son a name and proper station, then he may expect his son to share his cause. But I remain unrecognized in law, and the bonds of family do not hold me." Yuri was sitting very straight, watching Vasilli's hands instead of his eyes.

"Yet you swore an oath to him," Vasilli pointed out.

"Upon conditions that have not been honored." Yuri's whole body tightened with hidden rage. "And so I abjure my oath to him, for his to me was not honored. He never intended that I should be free of him, or obligations to the family that will never grant me legitimization. For them, I am only a bastard and a serf, to be given shelter and food while I am working for their benefit, and turned away when no longer useful. My father can expect nothing from me now."

A group of carters came into the taproom, all of them dusty from their work, and ready to lose the rest of the day in drink. They jostled their way to two tables, calling out to the landlord to bring kvas and bread, holding up silver coins to prove they could pay.

"You might abjure your oath to me," Vasilli persisted.

"That is the risk you take if you do not honor what you promise to me," said Yuri, his confidence suddenly increasing as he watched Vasilli hesitate. "An oath broken on one side is broken on both."

"Strange, that you of all people should say this to me," Vasilli mused, his eyes cold. "I could leave here and denounce you. I could have you arrested at once and the Poles could do nothing. You would be imprisoned, at best." He waited to hear what Yuri would say in answer.

"I would say that you wanted to enlist my services against the Nagoys. I may be nothing more than a servant, but Grigori Dmitrovich might well come to assist me, and he would be believed. If he said that I was gathering information for him, there are many who would not be astonished to learn that you had attempted to suborn me." Yuri smiled now, proud of how well he had anticipated this meeting. He had been prepared for such a response and he had answered quickly, letting Vasilli know he was no naive youth from the country.

"And if Grigori Dmitrovich does not vouch for you, what then?" Vasilli's manner was pleasant, almost jovial. "You will be twice a criminal, for speaking against me without cause, and for implicating Grigori."

This was not part of Yuri's plan, and he hesitated, seeking the most practical response. "My father is a Naboy, and—"

"And you are his bastard with many reasons to seek vengeance on the family." Vasilli shook his head in false sympathy.

"You will have to manage better than that, my boy, if you are to prevail." He put his hands flat on the table, fingers spread and thumbs touching. "I have heard what you expect of me. Now you will hear what I expect of you." His voice was low and even; he might have been discussing the quality of flour in the markets. "You will give me reports, honest reports, of the activities of the Polish embassy, including all you can learn of Rakoczy. You will do this as long as I require it. You will provide your Nagoy relatives with information I will approve, and no other. You will give me information on all the correspondence coming into and going out of the Polish embassy—all of it, no matter how trivial it may appear. You will keep a record of all those who visit the embassy, from boyar to servant, Rus to foreigner, and you will provide it to me fortnightly. If there is any contact between the priests and Rakoczy you are to let me know of it at once. Do all this, and do it well, and follow all other orders I give you and in five years, I will consider placing you elsewhere. Fail to do my bidding and I will accuse you." He leaned back, watching Yuri's consternation with increasing satisfaction.

One of the carters had started to sing, his voice steady and strong as he launched into *The City in the Lake,* encouraging his comrades to join him in the chorus: *Kitezh! Kitezh! Heroic sunken city! Shining, shining, shining on Midsummer eve!*

"If I discover you have served me false, Yuri Piotrovich, you may be certain that you will regret bitterly that ever you were born." Vasilli gave Yuri a little time to consider what he said. "I will take your promise of faithful service, and if you are truly a faithful servant, you will be rewarded in time. Consider what I tell you. In time I will provide whatever you have earned for yourself."

This was no longer the bargain Yuri had assumed he could make; he looked at Vasilli suspiciously. "What is to keep you from accepting my service and then condemning me?"

"Why, nothing at all," said Vasilli. "You must rely on my word as Prince of Moscovy." He had to raise his voice in order to be heard over the energetic singing which had successfully drowned out the bells and the shouts from outside. "You came to me because you wanted to gain a better position for yourself than your family have given you. Very well, I accept your desire. But if you want my favor, you will earn it twice over or suffer the consequences."

Yuri stared at him. "I am prepared to help your cause now and—"

"You had better be prepared to do more than that." Vasilli leaned forward so that he could lower his voice and still be heard. "You had better be ready to carry out my orders promptly in all things. If I discover any laxity in you, that will end our bargain and I will denounce you, first to your Nagoy relatives so that they will not come to your aid. Do you understand me?"

Yuri nodded slowly, and began to wonder if he had made a poor bargain after all. "Yes," he said as he realized Vasilli was waiting for an answer. "Yes, I understand you."

"You will take your orders from me, and from me alone. You are *my* servant, mine; not the servant of Shuisky. You are to do *my* bidding. You will answer to none of the rest of my family: not to Grigori or Dmitri or Igor or Anastasi. Do I make myself clear?"

"Yes." Yuri ducked his head, loathing himself for such subordination.

"Again," ordered Vasilli.

This time Yuri rose and made a full reverence to Vasilli. "Yes, I understand your orders and I accept them."

Vasilli smiled. "Excellent."

The carters had reached the sixth verse describing the ferocity of the Mongols as they surrounded the city of Kitezh. The main singer was starting his second cup of kvas and was singing louder than before.

"And you, do you honor your bargain with me?" Yuri demanded, his eyes hot with emotion.

Vasilli did not answer the question. "How many languages do you know?"

Baffled and vexed, Yuri answered resentfully. "Russian, Polish, Latin, Greek, a little German."

Gratified, Vasilli rose to his feet and held out his hand for Yuri to press to his brow. "Then yes, I will honor our bargain, if you do your tasks to my satisfaction, and serve none but me." At last, he thought, at last he would not have to rely on Anastasi for the translations of those tongues. He regarded Yuri with gloating condescension. "Remember that: you serve none but me."

Yuri reverenced him a second time, then pressed the back of Vasilli's right hand to his forehead. "I serve none but you, Vasilli Andreivich."

The carters sang heartily, describing how the great city of

Kitezh sank miraculously into the depths of the lake, thwarting the pillaging Mongols.

Text of a letter from Atta Olivia Clemens to Sanct' Germain Franciscus, written in Latin; delivered on October 9th, 1584.

To my dearest, oldest friend, greetings from the harried shores of England;

But no more harried than matters are in Russia from what I have learned from Lovell. Elizabeth Rex may have had Sommerville and Throgmorton to contend with, yet they are small fare compared to what little I hear of Moscovy. For every noble family there would appear to be three plots laid, all to claim the power Czar Ivan wielded. Whatever will become of that poor innocent Feodor?

And while you consider that puzzle, consider this one as well: how does it happen that you are married? If I had heard it from Lovell alone, I would not have believed him. But now I have read your letter sent in early April—it made very good time, incidentally, arriving here in July—and you tell me the same thing. Who is this Xenya Evgeneivna Koshkin or Koshkinya? For what reason was she selected as your bride? You say that Czar Ivan ordered you to marry, and that he had in the past ordered other members of his Court to marry in just such a manner, at his whim. How does it happen you permitted this to occur? Surely you, of all men, would have it within your power to refuse such an order. I understand you had some influence with Czar Ivan, that he showed you favor. And I will not accept your assertion that the wedding was a show of favor: where is the benefit to you, if that is the case? Why did you not protest the marriage, or have the Polish embassy protest?

Sanct' Germain, think of the risk you are taking. You have warned me so many times about unwilling lovers. What can this woman be, if not your unwilling lover. Is she not an unwilling wife? It may be the custom in Russia to marry by arrangement, but you are not Russian. Those of our blood have hazard enough in our lives without increasing it through marriage of that sort, or any sort. You tell me you do not even visit her in sleep, but take your sustenance elsewhere from sleeping women who know of nothing but lovely dreams and a little lethargy. How long do you plan to continue this arrangement? And how long before this bride of yours begins to ask questions you will not want to answer?

You say this Xenya does not know your true nature. By all the gods of Rome, what does she think of your marriage? To say that she has been the pawn of her relatives is all very well as far as it goes, but it does not alter her dealings with you. She must be aware that your conduct is not what most brides receive from their husbands. In time she must come to question your behavior. Lovell tells me that those with what the English call the French vice are walled up in monastery cells. Is there not a chance she will decide you are one of those who take fleshly pleasure with men? If she makes such an accusation, how are you to refute it without damning yourself more completely. I know what it is to be walled up; I died walled up in my tomb. You yourself saved me from it, all those centuries ago in Rome. But how am I to rescue you if they immure you in Russia?

I am writing to Lovell as soon as I am finished with this letter. I am going to ask him to look after you, since you do not seem willing to tend to that yourself. Ever since the troubles in Florence, you have been careless of your safety, claiming that the world is grown contemptuous of its treasures. You have told me that there has been too much lost ground, that where there was hope there is now despondency. Perhaps so. But it does not follow that we must join with the rest in contempt, or misery. You taught me that, more than a thousand years ago, and I have been willing to be guided by it, little though I have garnered from it. In the past you have not let me give way to despair, and now, my dear friend, you see your old arguments come back to haunt you. If you will not protect yourself for yourself, then do it for me.

And so this letter will not be one long harangue, let me tell you of the New World plant I have recently started growing at Green-gages: it is called the patata, a root crop, very filling and useful. I have been told by my cooks—now that they are willing to deal with it at all—that it is a fine addition to the rest of our crops. I am told that it stores well in the winter, which will be useful. I have offered patata plants to some of the landholders around me and a few have accepted, most out of curiosity. On the other hand, I have tried to grow maize without great success; the plants do not thrive and the grains do not ripen. If I can discover the cause of this, I may be able to correct the fault. I have given myself three years to bring in a crop of maize, and if this is not possible, then I will turn the acres over to growing more patatas.

I have sent Niklos Aulirios back to Rome for the next year. Senza Pari is not being properly run and I wish some order restored there. I have also asked him to inspect Villa Ragoczy, to see what your administrators there have done, or have not done. I also want him to bring a few of my Italian horses here, to breed them to my English ones. When he returns, he will have the best of the lot with him, or so he has promised me. It is my hope that there will be time to establish good breeding stock before I leave here.

Already I am contemplating leaving, and I have not been here long. It always comes to that, does it not? Those of our blood cannot remain anywhere for very long, or there are unpleasant questions. That is another thing that must have occurred to you: how long you may remain in Moscovy before it becomes apparent to someone there that you do not age. You cannot excuse it as alchemical skills forever. And do not remind me that in the strictest sense it is alchemical, for the blood is the elixir of life. Such assertions would serve only to increase apprehension in those around you. How will you explain to your wife that you change too slowly for her to see it? Give me your word that you will not remain there more than a decade. I plead with you, my friend, do not stay there too long. Whenever you leave, know that I will always welcome you, wherever I am, should you decide to come to me. There is no place on this earth, no matter how vast Drake tells me it is, that I would not be willing to meet you. I would cross hundreds of leagues of open sea if you asked it of me—and very likely curse you when I arrived for making me endure such travel.

Incidentally, Drake has been knighted, and is now Sir Francis. Officially they say it is because he went around the world, but it is rumored that the real reason has been his privateering against Spanish ships. I am inclined to believe the whispers instead of the public reason.

Let me hear from you again before the onset of winter, so that the letter may be delivered in this year. It is absurd, the length of time it takes messages to get from place to place. When I was young, Caesar moved dispatches eighty miles per day. Now we are fortunate if they can cover so much distance in three. No, I will not fall to lamenting what is past. As you have warned me often enough, if it is gone it cannot be had again.

With all affectionate love, Sanct' Germain, with affectionate vexation as well.

By my own hand,
Olivia
July 11th, 1584 by the English calendar

8

For three days and nights rain had been falling on Moscovy. Grey streamers of it, like tattered lace, dropped from clouds as heavy and substantial as furniture. The noise from it was as persistent and omnipresent as the sound of bells, a steady drumming that offered no variety or relief.

Rakoczy had just come from the steamroom after spending two hours working with his Russian horses in the covered stable-yard. His damp hair hung in loose curls and his face, freshly shaven and massaged by Rothger, appeared younger than his years. He had wrapped himself in a dark-red scholar's cassock with a small white ruff at the neck above his black sapphire pectoral. He was sitting in his small library adjoining his laboratory, reading a copy of Torquato Tasso's *Aminta,* when he heard through the steady drumming of rain the sound of a wagon arriving. Glancing at his Dutch watch, he marked the page in his book and rose, wondering who would be arriving at this hour, when most Russians attended sunset Mass. He was not expecting anyone; it being a Wednesday, Moscovy fasted and there were no entertainments offered that night.

His new footman, a long-faced, lugubrious Russian named Alyoisha, was already at the door, disapproval in every aspect. He blessed the ikons by the door, then opened it, staring out into the downpour.

From his place at the top of the stairs, Rakoczy saw that the wagon was enclosed and curtained, and for the first time he felt alarm. Xenya had gone to the Convent of the Annunciation that morning and was not supposed to return until after sunset Mass, but the arrival of this wagon could mean . . . He started down the stairs as the driver of the wagon set a stool on the wooden paving so that the passenger could get out.

It was Xenya, drenched and shivering, a fur rug thrown loosely around her and reclaimed by the wagon-driver before he started his vehicle out of the small courtyard. She stood beyond the shelter of the eaves as if afraid to enter the house.

Paying no heed to the rain, Rakoczy went out to her, lifting her in his arms to carry her inside, calling out as he did, "Alyoisha, tell them to heat a bath for her at once. I will want hot spiced wine for her at once. And send Rothger to me. Have him knock on my wife's door." He took the stairs two at a time easily, unaware that Alyoisha was watching him agog.

"You must put me down," said Xenya distantly. Her face was mottled from tears; her sodden clothes dragged on her leaving a trail of water. "You'll get wet."

"It doesn't matter," said Rakoczy as he reached her room and knocked the door open with his foot. "You are cold, my dear, and something has distressed you." He spoke calmly, as he always tried to speak around her. Gently he set her on her feet. "You should get those clothes off."

"My maids are at Mass," she said in confusion, and started to reach for the fastenings, working at the knots with cold-stiffened fingers, making little progress. Her face was blank.

Rakoczy stopped her. "If you will permit, I will be your attendant."

She turned wide eyes on him. "But—"

"Surely a husband—even such a foreign husband as I am— may assist his wife to undress?" He made his tone light but felt an underlying urgency; if he had gained her trust, she would not refuse. "And you will tell me what has happened to upset you so badly." As he said this, he noticed that the small medallion she usually wore around her neck—an ikon of the Virgin of Tenderness—was missing.

In the last few months she had started to talk with him, and so this suggestion did not fluster her as it might have shortly after their marriage. "It isn't proper," she said; it was her only objection.

"You know that propriety does not trouble me." Rakoczy touched her arm. "You have to get warm, Xenya, and you can't do it in those."

She swallowed hard, then said, "Only you and I will know?" Tears welled in her honey-colored eyes.

"If that is what you wish," said Rakoczy carefully, aware of what a potent phrase that was to her.

"And who would I tell?" she asked a little wildly. "My maids? They would say that it is because you are foreign. It would make them laugh. They would be all that I could tell now——" Then she pressed her knuckles between her teeth, blocking words and sobs at once.

Rakoczy smoothed back the wayward tendrils of her hair, then took her face in his hands. "Xenya Evgeneivna, what is it?"

She started to bless herself, then whispered, "They brought me word today, one of Anastasi Sergeivich's servants brought me word that my mother is dying. God and His angels! She has been carried to the nuns at the Convent of the Mercy of God where the sick are taken for care and prayers, but there is no hope. I was told the side of her face sags and she cannot speak or eat."

Rakoczy knew there was more to it, and remained silent, his dark, compassionate eyes on hers.

"When they told me, I was with the nuns at the Annunciation. I asked the Superior to permit me to go to her. She agreed at once, and started the Sisters praying for her. The wagoner—the same one who brought me here—took me to the Convent of the Mercy of God. It was difficult getting there because of the mud." As she spoke she became eerily tranquil. "And when we arrived there, the nuns did not want to let me see her, and advised me to stay away. But I insisted." Her counterfeit serenity left her. *"I would not listen!* I made them take me to her. They showed me where she was, in the infirmary with the other dying women." She pulled away from him, unable to accept his gentleness or his strength. "I knelt beside her to pray for her. I said her name, I called her my beloved mother. She looked at me, one eye seeing me, the left eye." She crossed herself at this recollection of such an ill omen.

"Did she recognize you?" asked Rakoczy. He had seen apoplexy countless times and had learned that it was never quite the same twice. He had been able to help some of its victims when they had been accessible, but most of them were beyond his skills and his blood to mend.

"Yes." The enormity of that single word held his attention. "She knew who I was." Xenya crossed herself again, looking away from him. "She knew. She reached for my Virgin. With her left hand. And she grabbed it and flung it away." Her sobs were deeper, more wrenching than before.

"Oh, Xenya," said Rakoczy quietly, and looked around at the soft, double rap at the door.

Rothger held a large pottery mug filled with steaming wine redolent with cloves, cinnamon, and ginger. "Do you require anything more of me, my master?" he asked as he handed the mug to Rakoczy.

"The bath heated; I've already ordered it," said Rakoczy. "Let me know when it is ready."

"Certainly," said Rothger, then added, "I am afraid that Alyoi-sha is bragging of your strength to the rest of the staff. He watched you carry your wife upstairs 'as if she were no more than a fur cap', or so he says."

Rakoczy nodded. "I was not paying attention." His self-condemnation faded to a sardonic half-smile that was gone as quickly as it appeared. "Do what you can to minimize the damage, will you? Or they will be claiming I leaped the whole flight with anvils in my arms before the week is over."

"No one would believe that," said Rothger in a speculative tone.

"True enough," said Rakoczy with a second, more genuine smile. "I leave it to you."

Rothger bowed slightly and withdrew.

Xenya had dropped to her knees beside her bed, her hands locked together in anguished prayer as she wept. She broke off as Rakoczy approached her, and made herself stop crying. For the first time since she had seen her mother that afternoon she began to feel cold.

He held out his hand to lift her to her feet; once she had risen he gave her the mug. "It will help to warm you, Xenya."

She accepted the mug as if she had never seen one before, clinging to the handle in white-knuckled tenacity. "She cursed me," she said at last. "She cursed me. When she . . . she took the Virgin."

"She may have wanted it for herself," said Rakoczy, searching for some way to ease her pain.

"She cast it aside," Xenya insisted. "The nuns saw it all, and they understood." She started to cross herself but could not complete the gesture.

"She may not have known what she was doing, my dear," said Rakoczy, trying to soften this blow. "Those who suffer her illness do not often understand what has happened, or what they are doing."

"She saw me," said Xenya quietly. "She knew."

Rakoczy had no answer for that; he waited while Xenya drank a little of the hot spiced wine, then said, "What do you want to wear?"

She blinked, as if realizing where she was at last. "Something warm."

He had given her a silken night rail for her name day, and now he suggested it. "The silk is heavy enough."

"Yes," she said, dismissing the matter. "Whatever is best." She had another sip, then set the mug aside on the table beside her bed. She stood docilely while he worked to loosen the ties and fastenings of her sarafan and the long rubashkaya beneath it.

"How did you . . ." He was not sure how to ask her why she was so wet.

Xenya was half-naked now, and she seemed removed from herself. "You mean the clothes?"

"Yes," he said, continuing his task.

A shiver passed through her that might have been from cold. "The nuns saw her . . . saw my mother take my ikon and throw it away; I told you. They made me leave the convent. They could not let me remain after such a curse. And I could not find the wagoner at first. He had to remain outside the walls, and I had to search for him. I did not remember where he was."

He removed the last of her garments then gathered up all her clothing into a bundle. As soon as he had put this by the door, he took her night rail from the chest at the foot of the bed.

She had turned away from him, her hands crossed in front of her protectively. "Give it to me. I'll put it on," she said indistinctly, her face averted and rosy with compunction.

He handed her the night rail.

As she pulled the capacious garment over her head, Rakoczy saw the curve of her breasts—larger than he had guessed—the inward angle of her waist, and the swell of her hips. Although thin by Russian standards, she was ripe-bodied, with skin as rich and flawless as sweet cream. Then the night rail settled around her in deep folds.

For a short while there was only the sound of the relentless rain.

"Will you cast me out?" In the stillness her soft, hesitant words seemed loud. "Now that I have my mother's curse on me?"

"No," said Rakoczy. "You could have a hundred curses on you, or a thousand, it would make no difference to me." He looked at her through the twilight room. "I gave you my word, Xenya, to protect and provide for you as long as you live, and I will do so: believe this."

"Will you?" she challenged quietly. "Protect me and provide for me?"

"I have said so," Rakoczy reminded her, stung by her continuing doubt.

"But will you?" Her insistence was despondent instead of defiant, and it touched his heart.

"Yes, Xenya, I will," he said.

She could not look at him. "When I am nothing to you?"

"You are my wife," he said with simple conviction.

"Am I?" She could not face him yet, but she lifted her chin. "You do not show it. You have no . . . need of me."

His smile twitched and was gone. "No need?" Rakoczy sighed, knowing she deserved a candid answer. "When we married I told you I am not as other men." How many times in the past had he explained himself: it had never been more difficult than now. He paused before he added, "Nothing has changed."

"Your ways are foreign?" she said, as if hoping for a simple answer.

"More foreign than you realize," he told her with a slight, ironic smile she could not see; he felt her confusion and attempted to explain. "It is not simply that I am an exile in Russia. There is no place on this earth that my ways are not foreign." As always, when he admitted this he felt a pang of loneliness that never lessened. The room was nearly dark and the battering of the rain went on steadily, magnifying the silence between them. "There are those who would say *I* am cursed, not you. And all the forgotten gods know there have been times I would agree. But this is not one of those times." He came a step closer to her. "Those of my blood do not live as other men."

Her single spurt of laughter was as scornful as it was unexpected. She clapped her hands to her mouth in shame. Unbidden, her mother's reproaches rose in her mind and she crossed herself.

His low, palliative voice reached her almost as a physical presence. "Xenya, Xenya, can you never trust me?"

"I wish I could," she said, moving away from him.

Rakoczy remained where he was, sensing that she was balking because of her distress from the past. "Xenya, I will never do to you what you fear I will do." He wanted to give her what comfort he could, but guessed that she did not know how to accept it from him. It was troubling, being unable to break through her reserve, yet he did not give in to chagrin.

She was unfastening her damp braids, shaking out her hair in sharp, brittle movements, keeping him at bay. "You cannot promise that."

"But I can," he said, so openly and easily that he caught her attention as his sympathy had not. "Because I am impotent."

Turning abruptly, she fixed her gaze on him. "You are a *eunuch?*"

Three thousand, even two thousand years ago such a demand would have angered him, but now he answered with a wry chuckle. "No, not that."

"You were wounded?" Her curiosity increased but not enough to prompt her to get nearer to him.

"In a manner of speaking," he answered, for death by disemboweling was certainly a wound. "It happened long ago."

"When you were a boy?" The horror in her question was as much for her own blighted youth as for his.

"When I was younger," he said.

Her next question was interrupted before it began by a tap on the door and Rothger saying that the bathwater had been heated and turned into the large half-barrel next to the steamroom. "It will cool."

Rakoczy's dark eyes were not hampered by the gloom of the

bedchamber. He went directly to her standing chest and removed one of two heavy cloaks hung there. "Put this over your night rail," he recommended. "That way the servants will not stare."

She took it from him, her eyes lingering on his face. "My servants will not return for a while yet."

"Then I will serve you, if you will have me," said Rakoczy, opening the door for her, revealing his manservant waiting, an oil lamp in his hand. "And your women will take their supper before they come to you. Rothger, those clothes"—he indicated the bundle by the door—"take them. They will need to go to the laundress at once."

"No," said Xenya with repulsion. "No. I want to be rid of them. Give them away. Burn them."

Rothger glanced at Rakoczy for confirmation.

"By all means, if that is what my wife wishes, see it is done. And make sure that the clothes do not go to anyone in the household." He looked at Xenya, studying her face. "Am I correct to assume you would rather not have them around you again?"

She nodded emphatically. "I hate them." Her outburst ended as quickly as it came. "Thank you," she murmured to Rothger.

He bowed to her. "I will be pleased to carry out your wishes." He handed the oil lamp to Rakoczy.

As Rakoczy took it, he motioned to Xenya to accompany him, but was not surprised when she hung back. "Is something else troubling you? Tell me."

There was no trace of impatience in his question, but she winced as if reprimanded. "The servants will be shocked that you come with me; they will remark upon it," she said apologetically. "Men do not attend their wives in the bath, not in Moscovy."

"Tell them it is more of my foreign ways," he advised her as he bowed to her in the European manner, elegant in spite of his austere clothing. "Courage, little Xenya. You are safe with me."

Now that he carried the lamp she could read his features, and she was reassured enough to answer sharply. "You have many foreign ways, and no doubt the servants gossip about all of them."

"No doubt," he said, smiling his approval as he led the way

down the stairs and through the central part of the house, taking no heed of the inquisitive glances that followed them through the long corridors to the rear of the building, or the whispers that came after.

The room with the bath-barrel was steamy; the barrel itself blackened by water and smelling faintly of pine and rough soap sweetened with sandalwood.

"Give me your things," said Rakoczy as he swung the heavy door closed.

Now that she was alone with him again, Xenya wavered in her resolve. "You must not look at me."

He hung the lamp on a hook by the door. "But Xenya, you are beautiful."

She blushed furiously and shook her head with vehemence. "No. I am too thin; everyone says so." It was as much a plea for agreement as denial; she knew that beauty was dangerous.

"It must be my foreign eyes that see you beautiful, then," he said, adding gently, "I will do nothing you do not want, nothing you do not like. But Xenya, I will not lie to you; I find you beautiful."

"I do not want you to look at me," she said crossly, her fear increasing.

"All right," he said, and held his hand out for the cloak. "Let me put that aside. You may remove the night rail and enter the bath while my back is turned."

Her acceptance was terse, more gesture than word. She shrugged out of the cloak abruptly and shoved it toward him; she moved quickly and gracelessly toward the barrel. "You must not look," she reminded him as she tossed her night rail aside and scrambled into the large half-barrel. The water lapped over the sides and a new surge of steam filled the room.

Rakoczy hung up her clothing and selected one of the drying sheets from the chest by the door. He set this where it would not get wet, then turned his attention to Xenya, who huddled in the barrel as if seeking protection from marauders. He decided not to confront her and instead asked, "Is the water warm enough? If it isn't I will order more heated for you. Have you found the sitting wedge? Do you have soap? Do you need anything more?"

"No," she said at once, and sharply. "It is quite satisfactory." In fact, she thought, it was almost too hot, but she did her best to surrender to the heat of the water, wanting to convince herself that there was nothing more for her to do than lie back and let her sinews thaw. All she could think of was Rakoczy. She sank halfway to her knees so that the water lapped her collarbones.

"If you wish anything, tell me." Rakoczy sat on the bottom step of the short ladder leading into the barrel.

"Anything?" She laughed once, very sadly. She was almost floating in the water, and it filled her with a sense of dreamy other-worldliness. "If I could have anything, I would wish to be invisible."

"Invisible?" he whispered.

She did not hear him. "I would wish to banish . . . so much. Years and years . . . But foreign though you are, and alchemist too, you cannot do that, can you, my husband?" She leaned back so that her head rested against the worn wooden staves.

"Perhaps not," he granted her, torn with compassion for her he could not bring himself to express. And from that a sudden esurience redoubled within him, of such intensity that it left him shaken. "But there is solace I can give you, Xenya."

She had begun to spread out her hair around her, watching it fan through the water. "Solace?" she asked.

Rakoczy did not answer at once. "There could be solace. It is little enough to offer you." His voice grew deeper. "But Xenya, it is all I have."

"Solace?" she repeated. "How can you give me solace?"

Now he hesitated, aware that this tenuous intimacy between them could easily shatter. "For those of my blood, the pleasure we take is only the pleasure we give."

"Pleasure." She shifted her position in the barrel, her arms against the sides as if to gain strength from the wood itself, and to remind her of the barrier it provided between them. "How would you . . . what pleasure do you have that I would want?"

"You have *your* pleasure," he said quietly. "And what I have comes from you. There is no other."

"That is your solace? Your pleasure? And with it you banish grief." She made the last an accusation.

"Hardly that," said Rakoczy. "But pleasure can assuage grief, make it endurable, at least for a time." He stared down at the wet planks under his fine black boots; the soles were thick, lined with his native earth.

The rain grew louder, more intrusive in its steady beating as Moscovy settled into night. Two streets away the Church of Saint Pavel rang its bell for the end of Mass, and gradually the other churches joined in the brazen call, blending with one another and the rain.

"What pleasure do you find?" Xenya asked a short while later, when she had taken time to hear every distant echo of the end of sunset Mass. "How is it my pleasure?"

"In your fulfillment." He said this without preamble. "For those of my blood, it is the only pleasure we know."

Xenya scowled at the repeated word *pleasure,* but was unable to deny her fascination with what Rakoczy told her. "What do you mean? For women their fulfillment is children." She said this as the rote lesson it was.

He turned on the steps and looked upward through the drifting wraiths of steam at her face. The light from the lamp put half his features into stark shadow, and softened the rest. The glowing depths of his eyes were enigmatic. "I mean that if you can find pleasure, I can find it with you."

"But you are impotent," she said brusquely.

"That is why the pleasure must be yours." He moved a little nearer. "If you will have it."

She sank deeper into the tub so that only her head was out of the water; her hair provided a veil. "If I will have it?" she repeated, watching him.

"Yes." He was seated on the top step now, bending toward her. Inwardly he was shocked at his profound desire, his longing; he had been a dream for too many and for too long. He yearned for knowing response, for reciprocity.

"You are trying to persuade me to . . ." She wavered in her accusation. "What *are* you trying to persuade me to do?"

Her directness required the same of him. "I am trying to persuade you to let me love you."

She moved as far from him as she could in the barrel; the hazy light made her eyes seem enormous as she stared at him. "Love me?"

His calm, compelling gaze never left her face. "Yes. Will you trust me? Only a little? I will do nothing you do not like. There is no reason for me to, and no benefit." He held out one hand to her, the sleeve of the cassock trailing in the water; his dark eyes were so gentle that she could not look away from him. "Will you let me? I will not hurt you, or shame you. If anything I do is distasteful to you, you may tell me to stop; I will."

She continued to stare at him, half in apprehension, half in enthrallment. She thought he was unlike anyone she had ever known. "What . . . what would you do? What *can* you do?"

"I think, perhaps, I can give you pleasure," he said, his hand still extended to her. "Well? Will you let me try? Xenya?"

For an instant she recalled her mother Galina on the morning of her wedding: how adamantly she had urged Xenya to be a true wife to her husband, to shut the past away forever and strive to please the foreigner. Was it possible, she wondered, that her mother would not curse her if she became Rakoczy's true wife— as truly as he could have her? Very slowly she reached out and took his hand and attempted to compose herself for what was to come.

He slipped his fingers through hers and tightened his grip just enough to draw her toward him. "I want to touch your body. Will you let me?"

"How am I to stop you?" For all her intentions, her voice had a shrill note.

Rakoczy released her hand at once. "I will touch you if it is what *you* want, Xenya."

She reached out and grabbed his hand. "All right, you may touch me," she said, not certain it was true.

He was very still. "Is that what you want? What you *want*, Xenya. Or do you believe you must permit—"

"I don't know!" she snapped, but did not release his hand. "And I want. To know."

"Well enough," said Rakoczy softly, and reached for a soft bath brush with his free hand; his movements were slow and deliberate, never hidden or unexpected. He began to work the brush over the arm she had extended to him, keeping the pressure light and firm at once. From her arm, he went to her shoulders, and from there to her back.

"What are you doing?" she asked in bafflement as he continued to ply the brush.

"Do you like it?" he asked for an answer.

"Yes," she said, and was about to say more when he started on her other arm.

"Then I will continue," he said quietly. "Since it pleases you." A short while later he set the brush aside and began to massage her shoulders, his small hands restoring pliancy to her flesh as he tangled her hair. He said nothing, his whole attention fixed on what he was doing.

Xenya was astonished by him. Without realizing she was doing it, she began to lean into his hands, to move with them. Her eyes were half-closed as she drifted in the hot water. She heard Rakoczy's voice, low and sweet, by her ear.

"I want to touch your breasts."

She was jolted out of her reverie. "What?"

"I want to touch your breasts. Do you want me to?" he asked with the same serenity; he continued to knead the tension in her back.

"I . . . you may try," she said, and caught her lower lip between her teeth. She felt the curve of the barrel against her back.

He did not move his hands at first, and when he did, he worked down her sides, staying behind her as he gradually discovered what he sought. In gentle, sure movements he began to rouse her, his massage long since turned to caresses. His cassock was soaked.

For Xenya the sensations rocking her body were so new and unsuspected that she was not certain they were pleasant or shocking. She was increasingly awed by the depth of her response. She was terrified that Rakoczy would leave her, for she felt she was on the edge of a precipice.

"I want to touch inside you," he whispered to her.

She did not want to speak. The enormity of what he sought overwhelmed her. There was nothing she could say.

His hands stopped their delicious tantalization and moved away.

"No!" she cried out. "Go on."

Rakoczy put his hands on her waist. "I want to touch in—"

"—inside me. Yes. *Yes.* If . . . if it is necessary," she said, with no strong notion of what she meant. She hoped that whatever he did it would not take long or be too unpleasant, for she was loath to give up the rapture expanding through her, making her light-headed and luxuriously sensual.

But what he did with her was wholly enjoyable, a slow-gathering exploration that served only to increase her apolaustic fervor.

He did nothing in haste, giving her time to learn and savor the passion of his touch, so that when his lips were on her throat for that brief eternity while her spasms encompassed her, neither of them was alone.

Text of a letter from Father Krabbe to Archbishop Antonin Kutnel, opened and read by the houseman Yuri.

In the Name of the Trinity, may Our Lord bless and protect you, Excellency, and guide you in times of peril.

This will be the last letter I will be able to send this year, for winter is nearly upon us and soon the roads will no longer be passable. Therefore I wish to inform you that the conditions of the Court have worsened in the last two months, in large part because Czar Feodor is not capable of maintaining the tasks of his office, and has had to rely on Nikita Romanov, his uncle, and Boris Godunov, his brother-in-law, with the result that these two powerful nobles are often at cross-purposes, which leads to deceit and treachery. Since it is not within Czar Feodor's abilities to put an end to such conduct, it increases and has spread throughout the Court in greater abundance than before. All those with any link to the Throne, no matter how tenuous, are beginning to wish for supporters to advance their cause.

It is my task to tell you that I cannot agree with Father Pogner's belief that the Czar will be overthrown by rivals, or if it is to happen, it will not be soon. Father Pogner wishes to find a noble family with a reasonable claim to the Throne who will trade later advantage for Polish support at this time: I say that none of us can make such an offer without the direct order of King Istvan, and further, the king would be a fool to do it. There are those who are loyal to the memory of Czar Ivan and therefore will not act against his son until required to do so. It is not their devotion to Czar Ivan that inspires most of them, but fear of the consequences of failure. Those who challenge the Czar may expect their severed heads to be set up across the Square from the Savior Gate.

I have continued to meet with Ferenc Rakoczy in spite of Father Pogner's orders not to have any contact with the Transylvanian. I believe that it is part of the purpose of this mission to

*gather opinions of all its members, including those not in cur-
rent favor. I must tell you that Rakoczy shares my concerns in
regard to the situation at Court. He sees no immediate resolu-
tion to the weakness of the Czar for he does not think that any
of the powerful nobles are prepared for the destruction and
blood of an uprising. Therefore the plots will continue in secret
and the nobles will scheme among themselves to gain advancement without leading armies into the field.*

*I have spoken twice with Boris Godunov, who is the official
given the task of dealing with foreigners on the Czar's behalf. He
does not wish to break his few ties with Europe and England, for
he is convinced that for Russia the future is to the west, not the
east. His opinion is shared by few in the Court, who still fear the
day the Mongols come again to ravage Moscovy, and therefore
turn their faces toward Sarai. The last Mongol attack on the city
was roughly twelve years ago and many here are certain they
will return. Godunov has said now that Moscovy has reclaimed
much Russian lands from the Mongols that the city is safe. He
has given his support to Rakoczy because of the Transylvanian's
wide travels. There is also the matter of Rakoczy's alchemical
jewels, and while Czar Feodor does not have his father's preoc-
cupation with gems, Boris Godunov does not underestimate
their value, neither to the treasury nor in regard to aesthetic
worth; Godunov is a clever man and a capable one.*

*In my opinion, but not in the opinion of Father Pogner, it
would be wise to support Godunov and encourage his enterprises that bring Russia more into the European world; the time
is fast approaching when we will want their strength with us in
the field against the Turk. We will not have Russian support then
if we do not endorse Godunov now. To assume that because his
mother was a Tartar that he himself is not wholly dedicated to
the Czar and Russia is a great mistake that many of the Court
make. In time I am certain they will realize their folly. Godunov
is the most forward-looking of the nobles, and I have found him
to be reliable in ways many of the others are not. It is my
conviction that Europe will find a staunch friend in Godunov if
we will demonstrate our appreciation of him and his work.*

*Let me apologize for giving opinions contrary to those of
Father Pogner, but I would be failing in my duty if I did not
inform you of my doubts and conclusions in these matters. You*

charged me with the task of informing you, and I must do this with a clear conscience, though it challenges the position taken by the leader of the embassy. I ask you to forgive my disobedience to Father Pogner; it comes from my evaluation of the circumstances here, and is not meant to deride or discredit Father Pogner's opinions and leadership. My conclusions are not given to slight him, but to provide another perspective on what is taking place here in Moscovy; I pray you will regard everything I have said in this light and will respect that my dedication to this mission supersedes my deputy's position. Father Pogner has been at pains to provide as complete an assessment as he is able, and has done it in all stringent humility. What am I to do but emulate him, and present to Your Excellency the observations I have made?

For the sake of our Church and the Kingdom of Poland, let me implore you to consider what I have reported here. I know that Rakoczy would tell you much the same as I have. Before you take Father Pogner's part, I beg you will first reflect on what is in these pages, and include it in your deliberations.

With constant devotion to Your Excellency and the Church we both serve, and with honor to King Istvan, I sign this in the assurance that God knows all truth and gives the victory to His Son Jesus Christ and those who follow His Word.

> *Milan Krabbe, Society of Jesus*
> *November 14th, A. D. 1584, at Moscovy*
> *in the Goldsmiths' Quarter*

9

For the fourth time in a week, Father Pogner had been refused access to the Terem Palace; Czar Feodor Ivanovich did not wish to see him, or to speak with any of his priests. The old Jesuit fumed as he trod gingerly along the rutted, icy roads toward the Savior Gate, heaping abuse on his companion's head because he could not upbraid the boyars or the Czar for his embarrassment. It had snowed the night before, then the morning sun had warmed enough to melt the snow for a few hours, but now, as high streamers of clouds raced along the sky, what had been snow became ice, dark as mud, treacherous.

Father Kovnovski trudged along beside Father Pogner, the short wolf-fur cape of his kontush turned up to protect his head from the icy wind slicing through Moscovy. "Truly, Father Pogner," he said in his best mollifying manner, "these Russians are nothing more than barbarians. No proper ruler would treat the head of an embassy so disgracefully."

"That Godunov is despicable! Telling me that he would deal through Rakoczy! Rakoczy! The man is a Russian puppet now, if he ever was anything more. And Godunov supposes that we do not know this. He pretends concern for Poland at the same time he foists Rakoczy on us!" He lowered his voice when he realized he had been attracting unwelcome attention; as an added precaution he switched from Polish to Latin. "What arrogant fools they are!"

"Truly, Father, they do not know your mettle," said Father Kovnovski, his eyes lowered. He hated these times with Father Pogner but endured them, convinced that they would lead to favor and advancement when they returned to Poland.

"No, they do not," Father Pogner agreed grimly. "How dare they place Rakoczy above us. It is the greatest insult of all." He peered into the wind and gestured angry satisfaction. "In another week we will be trapped here for another winter."

"King Istvan has not recalled us, in any case," said Father Kovnovski, his manner more deprecating than before. "Until he does, we must strive to fulfill his mandate, for the victory of Poland and the glory of God."

Father Pogner squinted up at the gold and silver onion domes visible over the wooden roofs of the palace of Vasilli Shuisky. "Yes," he said, drawing out the word. "These Russians and their infernal Church! They call themselves the Third Rome. Hah!" He rounded on Father Kovnovski, his irritation exacerbated by Father Kovnovski's conciliating manner. "Do not try to defend them, Father; they are condemned already by God."

"It is their ignorance," said Father Kovnovski, not exactly apologizing, but softening the appearance of the insult.

They passed the gateway into the courtyard of the Shuisky palace; Father Pogner shook his head in condemnation. "They are deceitful and malign, all of them."

"They listen to their priests, who are misled," said Father Kovnovski. "They follow teachings that are in error."

"And their Princes," added Father Pogner as he glared back at the Shuisky palace. "Imperious, egregious miscreants, every one. May God send confusion to all of them."

"Amen," said Father Kovnovski devoutly. In this he was wholly in agreement with Father Pogner. "They are without grace and without honor, these Princes and boyars and the rest."

"And for that God will give them scorpions to eat, and disturb their nights with the visions of the damned," Father Pogner declared. "They will know want and shame 'til they repent." He slipped on a patch of ice and would have fallen were it not for Father Kovnovski catching his elbow.

They floundered together, then righted themselves, both breathing harder and with little clouds of steam coming from their mouths. They pretended not to hear the laughter around them.

"That was a near thing," said a voice from somewhere above them in acceptable Polish.

Father Kovnovski craned his neck and saw a blond, blocky man on a mincing strawberry roan, a Russian noble, judging by his beard and embroidered shuba. "It was," he said grudgingly.

"I saw one of the Guards go down in just this place not an hour ago. He was badly injured by the fall. You may count yourselves fortunate," the newcomer went on congenially. "I daresay you don't remember me: we met when you were first presented at Court? It was more than a year ago." He swung off his horse and approached the two Jesuits, making a slight reverence as he came. "I am Anastasi Sergeivich Shuisky."

Father Pogner stared hostilely at Anastasi, but Father Kovnovski nodded slowly. "Yes. I do recall you. It was before we were taken to Czar Ivan. You were at the Palace of Facets. In the anteroom. It is . . . an honor to renew our acquaintance, Prince Shui—"

"No, no," Anastasi corrected. "My cousin"—he indicated the palace on his right—"is a Prince. I am a Duke; the cadet branch of the family."

"Ah," said Father Pogner as if he understood. "Very interesting."

"It is often the fate of the junior branch to serve the senior one, and I am no exception," Anastasi said, not quite concealing the rancor he felt. "When the senior calls, juniors must obey." He offered the Jesuits an understanding smile. "Is it the same in Poland?"

"It is the same throughout the world," said Father Kovnovski with a philosophical lift to his shoulders. "It is kind of you to speak with us. I had begun to fear that no one in Moscovy—" He broke off at a warning glance from Father Pogner.

"You should not blame Moscovy for the actions of a few ambitious boyars," said Anastasi, sensing an opportunity he had not been aware of before. It was coming at precisely the right time, for not half an hour ago, Vasilli had told him that he was no longer in need of Anastasi's skills as a translator; Anastasi was still furious at the cavalier dismissal he had been given and avidly curious to discover whom Vasilli had found to provide translations in his place. His mercurial smile came and went.

"They told us that Czar Feodor had spoken with the British earlier today—Horsey and Lovell—and could not see other foreigners; he was too tired," said Father Pogner, deeply affronted. "And we have come every other day in the hope of being received."

Anastasi shook his head, exuding sympathy. "It is inexcusable that you should be given such treatment. Still, do not blame poor Feodor Ivanovich. He does not choose his company: that is done for him; he is given no opportunity to protest, or if he does he is ignored. Nikita Romanovich would remove the Czar from Court altogether, but Boris Feodorovich insists that he remain here, the better to control the Court." He saw the guarded fury in Father Pogner's face and determined to take advantage of it. "It is a reprehensible development, this arbitrary favor Godunov displays."

"Godunov," said Father Pogner icily, "admitted Rakoczy yesterday but would not admit us today. He claims that Poland has been given an audience with Czar Feodor, and that our presence is not required."

"There, you see," said Anastasi, feeding Father Pogner's indignation. "You know what these men are, ambitious creatures who seek to be Czar through Feodor Ivanovich, who cannot protect himself from them." He gave Father Pogner his most cherubic smile. "I share your dismay, good Pole. I have tasted the same bitter dish myself."

Father Pogner looked toward Anastasi in surprise. "You? You are a noble of high rank and excellent family. How could you be subjected to—"

"Ah, worthy Pole, you do not know what twisted purpose rules the Court." He crossed himself. "It is a dreadful time to be at Court. Everyone is aware that the current situation is dangerous. There are so few men to be trusted, and . . ." He let his words trail away as Father Pogner nodded emphatically. "I have prayed for an end to the rivalries, and for the Czar to claim what is his, but God has been deaf to me."

"God is not deaf," Father Pogner said severely. "He listens and He judges, and we must bow to His Will." He would have turned and walked away, but Father Kovnovski forestalled that.

"How have you fared at Court, then, good Duke?" he asked politely.

"I have hardly fared at all," said Anastasi, his anger unconcealed for once. "My greater cousin has usurped all other Shuiskys, including his own brothers. He has his eyes on the Cap of Kazan, I fear. Now he is risen so high, he does not soil his hands with lesser flesh, but attends only to those whose rank equals or exceeds his own." He folded his arms. "I fear he will act against the rest of the family to secure his own position, no matter what the cost to the rest of us. It is a dreadful thing to believe so terrible a motive in the man who leads my family; I realize my suspicions are sins if they are not true, yet I cannot be rid of them."

Father Kovnovski was truly shocked. "In this Court, what noble is so bold as that? Surely there are those who know what he has done—"

"But he does it to their advantage as well as his own," said Anastasi smoothly. He recognized the avidity in Father Pogner's eyes for what it was, and continued, catering to the ruthlessness of the Polish priest. "If there are those of lesser rank who see Vasilli Andreivich's treachery, they say nothing, fearing his influence and power. Doubtless I, too, should remain silent, but when my honor is compromised—"

"Yes. Yes," said Father Pogner passionately. "It is more than any man should have to bear."

"So you *do* understand," said Anastasi as if they were brothers in misfortune. "Then you will share my anxiety for Czar Feodor."

"We pray for him daily," said Father Kovnovski.

"As we pray for the salvation of Russia," said Father Pogner, meeting Anastasi's eyes directly.

Anastasi achieved an expression of great candor. "Such are my prayers also, good Poles, although I pray in Russian, not Latin. I am as troubled by the rule of Jerusalem as I am by the rule of Romanov and Godunov. Why must we accept the judgment of the Orthodox Church in Jerusalem in the governing of the Church in Russia? Why must the Czar accept the Metropolitan appointed by the Patriarch and not have his own priests advanced?"

"We of the Catholic Church accept the rule of the Pope," said Father Pogner at his most depressive.

"But the Pope has Cardinals around him, to advise him and advance men worthy of it, does he not? And the Cardinals themselves are not bound to Rome, but to their own countries and courts, isn't that so? The Pope has able lieutenants and captains to minister to him and do his bidding. The Patriarch in Jerusalem has no such advisers and yet demands that we bend to his will." He lifted one hand to indicate the cutting wind. "Good Poles, let me invite you to my house, where it is warm and we might speak more together more . . . openly. Will you do me the honor of calling on me? It would be a great honor to open my door to you, and to have the benefit of your understanding. In these chaotic times I am sure we share many of the same goals."

Father Pogner cleared his throat and spat. "We have been told that it is not wise to visit the houses of Russians."

"And who said that? Was it Godunov? Nagoy? Romanov? Kurbsky? Skuratov? Which one of the men who are clambering to greater power gave you such a warning?" Anastasi made a gesture that showed disregard for such advice. "They have imposed no such restrictions on your fellow-emissary, Rakoczy. I say that we can serve our rulers and our countries better if we work together than if we struggle alone." He reckoned the mention of Rakoczy's name would spur Father Pogner to accept his offer.

"You may be able to . . ." Father Pogner examined Anastasi through narrowed eyes. "There is no harm in conversation, I wager," he said with forced bonhomie. "Who knows? Perhaps we will discover something useful to both of us." His face was closed, revealing nothing, but his eyes were alight with eagerness. "You are most generous, Duke. We will certainly call on you."

"Will you come tomorrow?" Anastasi asked at his most solicitous, his cupid's-bow mouth curling into a charming smile. "I will tell my servants to prepare fancy breads for you, and roast kid."

Father Kovnovski, who was feeling nervous, said, "You offer us more than we deserve, Duke Shuisky."

"Nonsense," Father Pogner corrected him. "If this is what is appropriate for a Duke to serve, we will thank him for it humbly and be grateful to God for it for answering our prayers at last." He looked squarely at Anastasi in optimistic greed. "After so many months, it is most satisfactory to be asked to visit at someplace other than a palace in the Kremlin. You are restoring my hope that we might yet fulfill our mission. We will certainly be there at the hour you appoint."

"After mid-day Mass," said Anastasi at once, who would have preferred having the two Jesuits follow him home at once. "I will send a servant to you, with a wagon to carry you." Anastasi himself would find such blatant favor-mongering offensive but he could see that the Jesuits did not recognize this for what it was. "My servants will be at your disposal." He paused. "Oh. There is one thing. We cannot have musicians entertain you; the household is still in mourning for my cousin, Galina Alexandrevna, who died a month ago."

Both Father Pogner and Father Kovnovski crossed themselves. "God give her rest and keep her," said the younger priest.

Father Pogner glowered. "Is it right for us to visit at such a time?"

Anastasi gestured his unconcern. "She was my cousin, not my wife or my sister, or my daughter; she was a widow whose only daughter is married . . . to your Count Saint-Germain, the Transylvanian Rakoczy."

"That charlatan!" hissed Father Pogner. "May devils consume his entrails."

This response delighted Anastasi, though he strove to hide it from the Poles. "He is very cunning," he said measuringly.

"Cunning," repeated Father Pogner. "Yes, as a dangerous animal is cunning: a wolf or a hunting cat."

Father Kovnovski looked uneasy, but said nothing. He edged away from Anastasi as if there were illness clinging to him.

"Well, for that reason there can be no music while you visit," said Anastasi with a gesture of mild regret. "But as priests, perhaps you would not like to have music in any case."

Father Pogner did not actually smile, but there was an expression of satisfaction in his eyes. "A perceptive remark, Duke."

"Very kind," said Anastasi. He took a step back, taking care not to slip on the ice. "Very well, then. Tomorrow afternoon, good Poles, and my gratitude for your courtesy."

As Father Pogner blessed him, Anastasi went back to his horse and swung up into the high-pommeled saddle. He set his roan at a slow, delicate trot toward the Savior Gate, letting the horse choose the way as he was lost in thought.

By the time the Jesuits arrived the next afternoon, Anastasi had worked out his plans and was ready for their visit. Everything he knew about the Jesuits had been considered, including Father Pogner's obvious jealousy and distrust of Ferenc Rakoczy. The Polish embassy had much to tell him, he knew, and he intended to gain every advantage he could from the priests. He himself answered the door and ushered the priests in, pausing to bless the ikons in spite of the disapproving stare Father Pogner gave him.

"Welcome to my house, good Fathers. Enter freely, and know that your will rules here." He reverenced them both, and led them to the grander of his two reception rooms, which had been the last achievements of the carpenters who built the house. He indicated the cushioned chairs and bowed again. "I hope you will be comfortable here. My household has been alerted to your presence and the servants will answer your summonses if you call for them." He coughed once. "The priest who attends to this household, Father Illya, is not here at present. He informed me that after mid-day Mass he was going to offer prayers for the repose of Galina Alexandrevna's soul; he will not return until after sunset Mass."

"Most Orthodox priests do not wish to speak with us," said

Father Pogner, his modesty tinged with smugness. "Nevertheless we will pray for him, as he prays for the repose of your kins-woman's soul."

Father Kovnovski crossed himself at once, saying, "I was sorry to learn of your grief."

Anastasi was unprepared for this sympathy and did not answer as quickly as he might have. "Yes. She was stricken suddenly and died less than five days later, in the pious care of the nuns. She suffered much in her life, poor woman, but at least saw her daughter wed at last. They say her end was blessed." He crossed himself. "They pray for her morning and night." He did not add it was Rakoczy, not himself, who had paid for the prayers.

"A devoted gesture," said Father Pogner, choosing the hardest-looking chair and taking his place there, back pike-straight, hands in his lap. "I am curious about you and your remarks, Duke Shuisky," he said, getting down to business, his expression set and severe.

"And I about you," said Anastasi, clapping his hands to summon his servants. He refused to be hurried. "Bring refreshments. These good men of God should not have to beg their supper like pilgrims."

"It is our pleasure to do this," they said in good form. The two servants reverenced Anastasi and then Fathers Pogner and Kovnovski, hastening out of the reception room to carry out their master's orders and to inform the rest of the staff about these latest visitors to the house.

A few moments later the erect, searching figure of Piotr Grigoreivich Smolnikov appeared in the doorway, one hand clutching the frame. "You have visitors, Anastasi Sergeivich," he said, cocking his head to hear what he could not see. "I hear foreign voices. Not Greeks this time?"

"I certainly have visitors, most important ones. These men are from the Polish embassy: Father Pogner and Father Kovnovski." He said the names quickly, adding to the priests, "This is Piotr Grigoreivich Smolikov; he lives here. He is a great hero." He inclined his head in the direction of the blind old man. "He led the defense of the Armorers' Quarter twelve years ago, when the Mongols raided Moscovy. Before that, he rode in battle from Kazan to Bryansk. Czar Ivan himself honored Piotr Grigoreivich for his prowess in battle."

"An honor," said Father Pogner harshly.

Father Kovnovski was more kindly. "Your valor is inspiring."

"And a Mongol lance robbed me of my eyes," said Piotr quietly, making a hint of a reverence in the direction of the voices. "God spared my life, and Anastasi Sergeivich took pity upon me."

"Nonsense," said Anastasi heartily. "It is a credit to this house that you live within its walls." He let the Poles make note of this, then went on, "You may join us, if it pleases you. We are going to speak about religious concerns."

Piotr crossed himself at once. "I am not a religious man. I say my prayers and bless the ikons, but for the rest, I leave that to more learned men." He made another reverence in the direction of the Poles. Using his hand on the wall to feel his way, he left Anastasi and his guests to their conversation.

"I hope the intrusion did not distress you," said Anastasi. "You must understand that Piotr Grigoreivich was once used to the rigor and excitement of life in the saddle. Now he is confined to these walls and a few streets near this house, and it causes him much anguish."

"Your charity is commendable," said Father Pogner, tapping his fingertips together impatiently. "But I hope we may discuss other matters." He looked directly at Anastasi. "Unless you have changed your mind since yesterday."

"By no means," said Anastasi, coming toward the Poles. "Sit down, Father Kovnovski, and be comfortable." He indicated one of the other chairs and waited while Father Kovnovski complied. "You are certainly aware, are you not, that there are severe restrictions imposed on the Orthodox Church in Moscovy from outside? The Patriarch in Jerusalem chooses our Metropolitans and does so without regard to the requests and claims of the Czar or the Court. This is a disgraceful thing, for men who have devoted themselves to the Patriarch are promoted above those who are faithful to Moscovy and know the plight of her people. In these days, with the Orthodox Church as beleaguered as the Roman Church, such indulgence cannot continue without serious consequences to the souls of the Rus." He crossed himself. "You are Polish as much as you are priests, and you understand what it is to be far from the center of authority. You know the dangers we know. Surely you share the apprehension I have felt for the last dozen years, for the safety of Christian worship." He placed his square hand on his beard. "I am not the only noble-man who fears the time when Christ will be displaced by the green banners of Mohammed, and all our ikons destroyed to stamp out the Christian faith in all Russia."

"All of us are aware of the dangers presented by the Turk," said Father Pogner directly. "That is one of the reasons King Istvan ordered us to come here. Christian countries cannot be at war with one another when the forces of Mohammed are loose in the world."

"Yes. Precisely," said Anastasi. "You understand me com-pletely." He lowered his eyes. "And so many here are blind; because we have beaten back the Mongols and have reclaimed our lands for Rus, they suppose that the Turk will not touch us."

Father Kovnovski shifted awkwardly in his chair, glancing at Father Pogner before he spoke. "The Czar has said that the Turk does not want your forests and long winters, and that our battles against the Turk are not the battles of Russia. How are we to convince him otherwise?"

"But the battles against the Turk *are* the battles of the Ortho-dox Church, for the Turk captured Constantinople, and the patri-arch had to flee to Jerusalem, where he is surrounded on every side by the armies of Mohammed." Anastasi slammed his fist into his open palm. "That strikes at the heart of the Orthodox faith, and I say that we Rus cannot permit ourselves to become the servants of Jerusalem, for that would make us servants of the Turk!"

Father Pogner was struck by this argument and nodded in Anastasi's direction with the beginning of respect. "It could be a terrible blow," he said, anticipating the time when the Catholic Church would come to the rescue of Russia and convert them all.

"Yes, it would," said Anastasi, recognizing the blatant purpose in the old Jesuit. "You could provide a fortress against our ene-mies, who are also your enemies. You could save us." He held up his hand for silence as he heard the sound of his servants returning. "Your refreshments have arrived, worthy Poles," he declared as the door was opened. "Pray accept the hospitality I offer with a good heart and a strong appetite."

The servants carried a large tray laden with kulebyaki filled with roast kid, roast duck, and sweet cheeses surrounding a golden bowl of melon sections preserved in cherry wine. "Anastasi Sergeivich Shuisky offers this to you," he said correctly as the servants placed the tray on the largest table.

"It is a noble repast," said Father Kovnovski, once again fitting his response to Father Pogner's humor as best he could. "We are grateful to be received so courteously."

Anastasi bowed slightly and said to his servants, "Bring spoons and plates to my guests," for he knew that Poles did not carry their utensils with them and would not want to consume these rich stuffed breads with their fingers, as Rus would do.

The servants were aghast but went at once to obey.

"This is quite tempting," said Father Pogner, the corners of his thin mouth turned down. "We thank God for your generosity."

"Omeen," said Anastasi, crossing himself. He walked over to the stove as if to check its fuel, but in reality to provide the priests the illusion of privacy. As he bent down, he listened closely.

"It would be fitting to show King Istvan that Moscovy can be won to his cause against the Turk," said Father Kovnovski tentatively, just above a whisper in the mistaken assumption that he would not be overheard. "He would approve our dealings with the Orthodox faith if—"

"We cannot decide for King Istvan," said Father Pogner with habitual austerity. "But we will hear this man out. He has interested me, and I am willing to know more of his purpose. It may be that we can use his good opinion to our advantage, so that we will not have to depend on that Transylvanian traitor to gain our mission the ear of the Czar, or of Godunov."

"He will want more than our thanks," said Father Kovnovski with increasing apprehension. "We might compromise—"

"We are compromised already, because of Rakoczy," said Father Pogner. "He has smirched the whole of this mission with his presence, and I will not continue to tolerate his high-handedness. It is fitting that we avail ourselves of any opportunity that will end the tyranny of Rakoczy."

The servants returned with plates and utensils, which they offered at once to Father Pogner and Father Kovnovski, reverencing them deeply before they withdrew from the room.

Smiling, Anastasi strolled back toward the two priests, gratified that his endeavors had established such a promising beginning; it would not take much to turn this to an alliance that would be strong enough to shake the position of his high-ranking cousin Vasilli. And once Vasilli was put to rout, the downfall of Godunov was within his grasp. That marvelous prospect of advancement inspired Anastasi to make his most audacious suggestion of all.

"Since you do not want to continue in the patronage of Rakoczy, perhaps you would be willing to consider mine?" He managed another European bow.

"What do you mean?" demanded Father Pogner, looking up from his selection of food to glare at Anastasi.

Anastasi's blue eyes opened wide. "Why, only that it appears to me that you good Poles and I have similar goals and, in this corrupt world, might make better progress together than separately."

Father Pogner pursed his lips. "It may be as you say." he admitted after a judicious silence.

"If it is, we will serve our Church and our king while we assist you," said Father Kovnovski as if trying to convince himself of the wisdom of this alliance.

"Then we are in agreement," said Anastasi, and helped himself to one of the kulebyaki.

Excerpt from a report from the Captain of the English ship *Exeter* to Sir Jerome Horsey.

. . . We will leave Novo-Kholmogory in three days, bound for London with a full load of furs, amber, rope, whale oil, and silk. We have laid in stores for the voyage, including thirty live geese and two pigs, the which to butcher in our passage.

The crew numbers thirty-one, including the two cooks and one ship's barber. All men have been declared fit for the voyage, and all have been assured of increased shares for speedy arrival in London. All the sailors are English, but we have taken on a Norwegian sail-maker and a Dutch barber.

At the time Exeter *prepares to depart, a German ship has arrived in port. The Captain has announced his intention to remain in this port for the winter and to sail at the spring thaw. I have had some conversation with Captain Hengel, and I must state to you, Sir Jerome, that I suspect this man of ill-intentions.*

He has been cordial to me, but I have been informed that his men have been at pains to learn all that they may from my crew, including where we have secured our cargo and what prices we have paid. It is my fear that this Captain Hengel intends to attempt to secure our contracts from the merchants we have dealt with, increasing the prices we must pay in order to continue to trade. I do not wish to have to sacrifice all our profits to the German merchants, and therefore I pass this warning to you.

I will return to the White Sea in May or June, depending on the weather, and at that time the Exeter *will once again bring English cargo to Russia. During the winter, the English ship* Katherine Montmorency *will remain in this port, surrounded by rafts of cut logs, as is the Russian practice to keep the ships from being destroyed by winter's ice. I have charged her Captain, Henry Percival, to maintain a steady watch on Captain Hengel and report to you as soon as the roads are passable. If there is any attempt on the part of Captain Hengel to interfere with English trade, you will know of it as soon as may be.*

We urge you to arrange for a wider commerce for us, increasing the cargoes we carry. I am not the only Captain eager to enlarge our trade in the world. If we cannot purchase more of Russian goods, we must look elsewhere for our wealth: to China and India and Africa, and even the New World . . .

PART III

FERENC RAKOCZY
Hrabia Saint-Germain

*T*ext of a report from Yuri at the Polish embassy to Prince Vasilli Shuisky, written in Russian.

To the most powerful Prince, the devoted greetings of Yuri.

It is a curious thing and very much to your purpose that although these priests have employed me because I speak Polish and Latin, they often forget, and speak one of those languages, as they do in front of the rest of their staff in complete safety. I have been at pains to appear disinterested and only partially comprehending; they believe I am schooled in reading and writing, not in speaking, fools that they are. That is a mistake I would not have made at the Transylvanian's house, had I realized how observant he is.

From the Feast of Advent through the Mass of the Nativity these priests have kept almost wholly to themselves. There have been only two visitors in the last three weeks that I am aware of: Rakoczy, as a part of the embassy, and Nicholas Bower, the servant of the English Ambassador, Lord Horsey. These two have passed several hours in the company of the priests, and have received their attention and various written material from them. The priests here have not been included in any of the celebrations or feasts within the Kremlin, and therefore have had no occasion for formal banquets or entertainments.

I was able to see the letter intended for Lord Horsey before it was given to Nicholas Bower, which was written in Latin. In it, Father Stanislaw Brodski and Father Aniol Tymon have out-

*lined to Lord Horsey when they expect to receive dispatches from
Poland, and their planned schedule of dispatches to be sent in
the spring, for it is acknowledged that the roads to the west clear
more quickly than those to the north, and therefore it is possible
that dispatches intended for the Queen of England could travel
more quickly overland than by ship from the White Sea. Father
Brodski and Father Tymon have offered to send sealed documents for the English Queen. I have not seen any report from the
priests to tell whether or not Lord Horsey will act upon their offer.
Rest assured that I will take every opportunity to learn what the
English decision is, and to relay that information to you as
quickly and safely as is possible.*

*The problem of Rakoczy is different, for he is still officially part
of the mission, although only Father Milan Krabbe so regards
him now. The rest of the priests have stated that they believe
Rakoczy to have betrayed the trust of the Polish King because of
his friendship with Boris Feodorovich. He is not discussed when
the priests gather, except to be vilified by Father Pogner. Because
of Father Pogner's condemnation, all the others have declared
that they will permit him access to no part of the embassy without guards present and the approval of Father Pogner, which is
not forthcoming, which even Father Krabbe approves in order
to maintain peace within the embassy.*

*However, the last dispatch from King Istvan required the em-
bassy to continue to inform Rakoczy of all communication from
the King, and to include him in all decisions facing the mission.
These orders have not been welcomed by Father Pogner, who
has been as lax as he dares in executing them. He has done
everything ordered by the King, but with as little effort as he can
expend to accomplish it. Did not Rakoczy send his manservant,
Rothger, to this embassy once a week, I believe that Father
Pogner would hold all dispatches and letters from King Istvan in
this building; Rakoczy has not allowed that to happen.*

*There have been several occasions when the priests here have
left the embassy for reasons and tasks of their own. They have
gone to the Kremlin often, although not for the festivities of the
Nativity, as I have already stated; but there are other places they
visit. I know that Father Krabbe has called at the house of
Rakoczy on at least two occasions, but I do not know what
transpired there. He does not speak of those times, and I cannot
follow him, for fear of discovery.*

Father Pogner has been missing three times with Father Kovnovski. They have been gone for as long as half a day, and they do not discuss with the others where they have been, although it is supposed that they must have secret dealings with Godunov, for there is no other Rus they suppose would demand such activity from Father Pogner. The notes that Father Pogner keeps are in code and I have not been able to find the key to it. Father Kovnovski is very closed-mouthed about these absences, and Father Pogner never discusses any dealings he has with anyone at any time, although I have twice heard him forbid Father Lomza permission to go to the Kremlin alone.

Since the blizzard of two days ago, the priests here have not left this house for any reason. They are confined by the snow and by orders from the Czar that have instructed all foreigners save Rakoczy to remain in their houses until the streets are properly cleared and the activities of the foreigners can be watched. If the Czar permits, the Feast of Epiphany is to be celebrated here with what they call High Mass and a feast without red meat, which the Germans will share, but not the English, who have cut their ties to Rome. Every one of the priests here has spent most of these last days in prayer and reading holy books, most of them in Latin, although a few are in Greek; there is nothing in them that speaks against the Czar or addresses the purposes of King Istvan.

I swear on the soul of my mother that this is the truth and that everything I have said here is accurately reported. I vow to continue to try to learn the code used by Father Pogner. I will notify you as soon as I learn where it is that Father Pogner and Father Kovnovski go when they venture out on their own errands.

By my own hand,
Yuri
By the Polish calendar, January 4th, 1585.

1

Czar Feodor shoved the Cap of Kazan with one chubby hand and sent the fur-edged filigreed crown toppling from his head. All the Court stared, not one of the nobles willing to move or speak as the Cap came to rest near Feodor's mace of office. Feodor smiled benignly and motioned to Boris Godunov. "My little brother Boris," he called out in a pleasant, childishly high voice. "I've dropped the thing again. It itches."

Boris, resplendent in his heavy golden kaftan embroidered all in red, bent down awkwardly, one hand holding his tall hat in place, the other reaching out for the glorious Cap of Kazan. He knelt and reverenced Czar Feodor as he offered the Cap to him, not changing his position. "Do you want the Metropolitan to be summoned to replace it, Little Father?" That was what Czar Ivan would have done and all the court knew it.

"No," said Feodor, and put the Cap on his thigh, letting it balance there. "It's too heavy and I'm too hot." He motioned to Boris. "Get up from the floor, Boris Feodorovich, do. I don't like to see you all hunched over on your knees."

This Court, the first one after the Nativity, was becoming disastrous, thought Boris as he got to his feet.

"What are you going to offer me? You said there was entertainment?" The anticipation in Feodor's moon face was cheerful and demanding at once. One of his legs swung impatiently, his heel striking the ivory-and-jeweled tracery of the throne, leaving faint scuffs.

"Yes," said Boris unhappily. "Yes, there are those wishing to present themselves to you. Foreigners, Little Father, whom you have already commanded to appear before you." He reverenced Czar Feodor again, but not from his knees, then hurried out of the splendor of the enormous, golden Reception Hall.

Rakoczy was among the half-dozen dignitaries waiting for presentation to Czar Feodor, and Boris was relieved to see him. He approached the black-and-silver clad Transylvanian, saying in Greek, "A jewel will not hold his attention long, I fear, but he requires some distraction."

"I didn't bring a jewel this time," said Rakoczy, holding up a small leather chest. "You've made it clear that Czar Feodor's taste runs to other things." He looked over his shoulder at the German ambassador, noticing that the somber old man was trying to work the stiffness from his gnarled fingers. "As he is bringing a team of carved miniature horses with a miniature cart to hitch them to, I have also scaled my gift to the recipient." He patted the chest.

Boris found it disheartening to look at the German ambassador and his offering of toys. Worst of all, he had to admit that the German had reason to bring such a gift: it would probably be well-received. "All right. Then you will come first." He motioned to the Metropolitan. "Please let him, Most Worthy," he said, for the Metropolitan was entitled to the first presentation of the formal audience. "It would be for the best. The Czar likes him. It will make it easier for all the rest of you."

The Metropolitan stroked his beard and ran his hand down the pearl-studded front of his riza, his expression studied as he weighed his decision. "If it would quiet the Czar's mind, then it might be the wiser course."

"Thank you and God bless you; forever," said Boris with feeling. He gave his attention to Rakoczy, trying to appear patiently resigned instead of anxiety-laden. "We haven't actually finished the full presentation of all the nobles, but Feodor can't remember all their names in any case."

"And since his father did, it shows the son is not the equal of the father," said the Overlord of the Tartars, his black hair braided and hanging down his back.

Boris nodded once. "But he is Czar, and we have all given our oaths to obey him." He crossed himself, watching to be certain the Metropolitan had done the same. "Rakoczy, come."

At the far end of the room, Sir Jerome Horsey waited, rigged out in the highest fashion of Elizabeth of England's court. He stood beside Benedict Lovell, less resplendent in his academic robes. "Mark me," he said softly as Boris led Rakoczy away. "There is trouble coming."

"For Rakoczy?" asked Lovell in surprise.

"No; for Godunov. That poor dull-witted boy is turning Godunov into his creature; the Court will not accept it, having Godunov ruling them. It is the same for him as it is for us. We are all foreigners, and that is—" He made a gesture indicating calamity.

"Does he know?" Lovell wondered aloud, for he was the one who had warned Sir Jerome about this at the beginning. "Does Godunov realize what is happening?"

"How can he not?" Sir Jerome countered; he would have shaken his head but his high, wired ruff prevented it, so he swung his upper body as he did when dancing the galliard. "Let us be last today, in any case."

Once they left the antechamber Rakoczy obediently fell in the required four steps behind Boris, his leather case carried in front of him so that the Guard could see it clearly. He said to Boris as they entered the cavernous room, "Will he be content to remain at Court through the morning, do you think?"

"No; he is already fidgeting." This was only a whisper, but it was enough to prepare Rakoczy for his presentation to Feodor.

The young man on the throne was studying the turquoises in the Cap of Kazan, one of them caught between his forefinger and thumb as if he wanted to pull it out. He looked up as Boris approached, the Cap forgotten for the moment. "Boris Feodorovich, it is boring. No one is talking to me but you," he complained as Boris reverenced him again.

Rakoczy went down on one knee, in the European fashion. "God give you happy days and pleasant nights, O Czar," he said.

"You haven't lowered your head," said Czar Feodor.

Boris stepped between them. "Rakoczy is from the King of Poland, Feodor Ivanovich." It was in these fits of mulish obstinacy that Boris recognized a distant echo of Ivan Grosny's implacable determination. "This is how the men of Poland reverence their King. It is fitting that he should show the same distinction to you, Feodor Ivanovich, to avoid offense to you or King Istvan."

A distant echo of his imperious father Ivan showed in Feodor's mild features. "I want him to lower his head. I want him to make a reverence. He is not to defy me."

"But Little Father—" Boris began.

"If the Czar asks it," Rakoczy cut him short; he executed a perfect reverence from his knees and was rewarded with a delighted grin. "It is true that Russia is the Czar's country, and the people are his people. I am a foreigner in Russia," he said, speaking directly to Feodor. "If you tell me to learn new ways, I must perforce do so."

Boris watched as Rakoczy prostrated himself in proper form, shaking his head. He could not imagine what would happen if Czar Feodor made the same demands of the British ambassador, or the German.

Czar Feodor clapped his hands in delight. "You do that very prettily. I like the way you bend over." He regarded his brother-in-law. "Boris Feodorovich, you forget how much I like seeing the foreigners in their strange clothes. Black and silver." He gestured to Rakoczy. "Russia is a country red and gold. We do not see black and silver."

"The Czar is gracious to mention this," said Rakoczy with commendable seriousness, with an understanding glance in Boris' direction. "Oftentimes we foreigners feel our foreignness the more because we are required not to wear Russian dress. It makes the law less troubling if we foreigners know that our clothes are welcome in your eyes."

"How prettily you speak. Better than Uncle Nikita." Czar Ivan motioned to Rakoczy, who finally got up from his knees, his leather case beside him. "You bring me a gift, don't you? People are always bringing me gifts. I like them."

"Gifts are pleasant things," said Rakoczy. He picked up the leather case.

"I hope it isn't another jewel," said Czar Feodor suddenly. "You gave my father many jewels, and I have seen them. But they are just stones."

"Very true, O Czar," said Rakoczy. "And very wise."

Of all the compliments Rakoczy had given him, being called wise was by far the best. Czar Feodor giggled. "The courtiers have to say that, not you."

"All the more reason to believe me, then, O Czar," said Rakoczy with such candor that Boris was shocked. "This is not a gift for your father, however. It is a gift for you."

The young man's wide, bland face blossomed into smiles. "What would you bring for me? What do you want to give me."

Rakoczy picked up the leather case. "If you will permit me, O Czar, I will open this." He looked at the four Guard officers who stood at the corners of the dais. "If any of you want to watch me open this box, to assure yourselves it contains nothing to harm Czar Feodor?"

"I am here," said Boris, forestalling any activity on the part of the Guard. "I will vouch for whatever you have there." He moved a little nearer to Rakoczy, saying in an undervoice in Greek, "I trust it is safe."

"Eminently," said Rakoczy, folding back two hinged panels to reveal a set of miniature bells, fifteen in all, shining gold and topped by little jewels. "For the pitch; the amethysts are the same note, so are the diamonds and the emeralds and the topazes, the aquamarines, the sapphires, the tourmalines. The top, middle, and bottom notes have pearls to distinguish them from the rest," Rakoczy explained as he held up the bells in their metal frame. "They are bronze, carefully tuned—Europeans would call their tones the Dorian mode—and their bronze is plated in gold, to honor the Church as well as the Czar."

Feodor had got down from the throne, setting the Cap of Kazan on the empty ivory chair as he came to stare at the gift. "This is wonderful," he whispered, his voice so soft that hardly any of the courtiers heard it. "You say their tone is true?"

"Try it for yourself, O Czar," Rakoczy recommended.

His hands shaking a little, Czar Feodor reached out for the frame with the bells. He tugged one of the silken cords—all matched in color to the jewel atop the bells—which served in place of the rough hemp ropes that controlled the larger versions. The sound of the bell was perfect, so masterfully made that the note pulsed as if the metal possessed a beating heart. He cocked his head and rang the next: another flawless tone.

"It is an honor to please you, O Czar," said Rakoczy, stepping back from the young man with the wispy, fine beard of a thirteen-year-old. "I will convey your gracious remarks to King Istvan."

"May King Istvan reward your service," said Boris very deliberately with a single, pointed look. "What do you think, Little Father?" he went on, to keep Czar Feodor from abandoning his Court at once for the pleasure of ringing these golden bells. "Is this not a splendid gift?"

"Splendid," said Czar Feodor, entranced by what he saw and heard. "Splendid. Splendid," as he proceeded to ring every one of the sixteen bells, listening with an intensity that was remarkable in so childlike a man.

"I am gratified you are pleased, O Czar," said Rakoczy when Feodor had satisfied himself that each and every bell was true. "It is ever my wish to do those things that will be welcome to you."

"This is welcome. It is very fitting. Tell him it is fitting, Boris Feodorovich." He rang the first morning cadence, beaming happily. "How the Metropolitan will envy me, for I do not have to climb into a cold and windy bell tower if I have these beside me." He looked sharply at Rakoczy. "I want you to make more, many more, much bigger."

Rakoczy opened his hands in resignation. "Alas, O Czar, that is not possible. I do not operate a foundry, and I have no means to make bells much larger than these. Foreigners are not permitted to have so much bronze." While it was honest enough, he was relieved that he could offer such an excuse to Feodor, for he sensed the Czar's demands might suddenly escalate beyond his abilities to fulfill them. He did not like considering that possibility although he could not escape it entirely. "O Czar, you have fine bell-makers here in Moscovy, far better than I am at making those bells with deep, strong voices."

"These bells are more true," said Czar Feodor suspiciously.

"Because they are very small," said Rakoczy, bowing to Czar Feodor. "It is easier to make perfect bronze for something the size of a cup than something the size of a horse. The bronze can be made very uniform, more than in a huge bell." He did not add that in order to get sixteen perfect bells he had cast more than eighty of them and selected the best of the lot.

"I am proud of our Russian bells," said Boris, taking up Rakoczy's stance. "This Transylvanian is right, Feodor Ivanovich. There are no bell-makers in the world to compare with Russian bell-makers."

"That is the truth, O Czar," Rakoczy said at once.

"None in the world," agreed Czar Feodor with pride.

"Therefore Rakoczy is to be thanked, for showing respect to you and to those men who make our bells. He is a foreigner who knows that Moscovy is the bastion of Russia." Boris crossed himself. "The air of Moscovy trembles with the song of bells."

The Czar's smile was so fixed that it appeared to be carved into his face. "I want you to thank the foreigner. Let him have whatever he wants for these wonderful gifts, if it is in accord with the Metropolitan," said Czar Feodor, waving both men away from him. "I want to ring these. Tell the Court we will resume later, after Mass."

"After Mass," Boris echoed, for that instant hating Feodor for being such a benign simpleton. "You called Court, Little Father. You were the one who commanded these nobles, these boyars to appear and listen."

"Well, now I command them to go away until after Mass," said Czar Feodor, picking up the metal frame of bells when he had scrambled to his feet. "After Mass I will see the other foreigners, and I will listen to everything the nobles have to tell me. Everything."

Boris put one hand to his beard, the only outward sign of his agitation. "But it would be better, Little Father, if you would tend to the Court now. That way you will not have to interrupt your enjoyment later; Court will be behind you and you may ring these bells for as late as you wish."

"That is so: I cannot— Tomorrow I will have Court again," said Czar Feodor, settling the matter. "Tell everyone they are to leave the Palace. I don't want to see anyone remaining behind, for men who do that are plotters: my father told me that before he died."

"Many of them will be insulted, Little Father." Boris' protest was desperate and useless. "They do not want to be deprived of your attention and—"

"Tomorrow they will have it, after morning Mass. We will all assemble here, as we did today," said Czar Feodor, pointing to one of his Guard. "Come with me. I will use the Beautiful Staircase, so that everyone will be able to see these bells." He shook the metal frame and all sixteen bells jangled in gorgeous dissonance. "This is better than jewels, Rakoczy. You have found a sublime gift for me: you will discover my gratitude."

"You are gracious beyond my worth, O Czar," said Rakoczy at once, then dropped to his knee as Czar Feodor, his treasure clasped in his arms, swept out of the Reception Hall, his Guard in pursuit.

"This could become difficult," said Boris when Feodor was gone.

"It has already," Rakoczy told him as he got to his feet. He made a quick, sweeping glance around the huge golden room, watching the dismay and anger in the faces of the assembled nobles and boyars. "They were discontented before this. And if

Feodor intends to delay Court for every gift, it will be the worse for everyone. Look at them. They know Feodor Ivanovich cannot hold the reins of Russia. With the Mongols only recently pushed back in the east and the Poles and Swedes prepared for war in the west, their gains could be losses in a matter of months. It was not so long ago that the Mongols sacked Moscovy, and could still do it again if Romanov forbids Feodor to resist, as the rumor suggests he will."

"How do you come to know these rumors, Rakoczy?" Boris marveled. "I have spies and I do not discover as much."

"Because the boyars know you are important. I am only an exile, so they say things when I am about they would never reveal to you. They are more worried than they are affronted. They are worried that their Czar will fall prey to dangerous foolishness. They would rather have tyranny than weakness."

"Not without cause," said Boris slowly. "And I cannot blame them; I share their fears. That is why I want to strengthen our alliances in Europe, so that we will not be without friends. Nikita Romanovich claims that to deal with foreigners is to invite invaders, but I cannot agree with him, not if the treaties are reasonable ones, made by reasonable men." He cocked his head in the direction of Vasilli Shuisky and his brother Dmitri. "And there are those who will take any advantage offered them. They have claims of birth, and rank. For all that I try to keep—" He interrupted himself. "Maxim Sevastyanovich Khorsky," he called to one of the lesser boyars who was about to leave the Reception Hall. "There is food prepared for all of you. No one has to leave, no one will go hungry."

Khorsky ducked his head appreciatively. "I will be certain everyone understands," he said, and started down the long line of brilliantly clad boyars, pausing to speak to them every dozen paces or so.

"You will join us?" Boris suggested.

"Sadly, no," said Rakoczy. "I fear I would not be welcome."

"And besides, you do not dine in company," said Boris bluntly. "Or did you suppose I had not noticed." He saw hesitation in Rakoczy's manner. "I was not sure at first, for it appeared that circumstances worked against you, while Ivan Vasillievich lived. But I have watched, Rakoczy, and never have I seen you eat, or drink."

Rakoczy made a show of mock-surrender. "Very well. I admit

it. You are right. I . . . prefer to eat privately. For those of my blood, dining is . . . much too personal to perform where others can see. We are very private in our habits." He stared down at his ruby signet ring. "I do not intend to give offense."

"Nor have you, not to me," said Boris.

There was a softening in Rakoczy's face, something at the corner of the eyes that was eloquent. "Thank you, my friend."

Boris smiled; it was a weary smile. "That does not offend me either."

Text of a letter from Benedict Lovell to Ferenc Rakoczy, written in English.

To that most excellent representative of the Exalted King of Poland, my greetings on this day of the Feast of the Holy Deaconesses Tatiana and Prisca, as the Rus call it, or the Feast of Saint Ita as they keep it in Ireland.

I think you are correct, and English is almost certainly as safe as any coded message, for few outside this embassy and countrymen can read it, and it will put no one on the alert. What a very clever suggestion. I have taken the liberty to tell Sir Jerome of this ploy, and he approves it highly.

Recently I learned an interesting thing from Father Symeon, who has come to explain the rites of the Orthodox Church to us: the feasts of the saints are counted in numbers of days from Christmas, not unlike the Roman calculations from Christmas to Easter. For the Russians, all the feasts save Christmas are movable feasts. And yet most of their clergy neither read nor write and few can calculate beyond ten. I have been told that there are many disputed feast days, and this does not astonish me, for surely such methods must result in many disagreements.

In regard to English ships, we have one in Novo-Kholmogory waiting out the winter, the Katherine Montmorency, *under the command of Captain Henry Percival. Other ships are expected back in the spring, once the ice has broken up in the White Sea. If it serves your purposes I will certainly send word to Captain Percival and tell him to expect to carry cargo for you, both to England and upon his return, from there.*

It is not proper that I ask this, yet I cannot help but be curious what it is you seek to exchange with Lady Olivia. She told me before I came here that you have shared such enterprises before, and this is quite interesting to know of. I suspect that whatever she wants has to do with the horses she raises. Are you planning to send a few of those silver mares? If you are, you will have to notify Captain Percival to prepare a stall or two below decks so that there will be appropriate places to carry the animals. He will not take them aboard otherwise.

It might also be prudent to inform him what you expect him to carry on the return voyage, so that you will have space reserved in the hold. Captain Percival is a wise seaman, I have been told, cautious and canny. It would count in your favor if you were willing to let him know what you required of him, and perhaps paid him a portion of his profit as surety.

Let me take this opportunity to thank you for lending me those four books. They have been most useful to me, although where you found the manuscript of Huon de Bordeaux I cannot guess, nor the Latin comedy which I cannot believe came from the pen of a German nun. Who is this Roswitha of Gandersheim? Surely the name was used in jest. The Latin, as you warned me, is worse than most, and some of the lyrics appear to be in a dialect of German, that is true. I believe you have uncovered a very clever conceit, and when I have leisure, I will do what I can to discover more about the comedy.

I am sorry to say that I have not been able to discover if there is any truth in the tale that the Metropolitan of Moscovy has within his possession a Testament of Saint Luke in the Greek language that—according to what has been hinted—was written during the life of Saint Paul. I have asked Father Symeon on several occasions, and all he will reveal is that such a manuscript was entrusted to the Metropolitan shortly before Constantinople was conquered by the Turks. He said that such a treasure would be in the Czar's chapel in the Cathedral of the Annunciation, if it actually exists at all. Since no one enters there but the Czar, perhaps you could persuade Feodor to tell you, because of the bells you made for him. I was told that he takes your bells with him when he enters that chapel to pray, so perhaps he will provide an answer on behalf of your gift.

The donations Sir Jerome has offered the Czar have not been welcomed as your has been. I had occasion to send eight glass goblets on behalf of the Norwich Weaver's Guild, to encourage trading wool for cloth. I have been told that the Czar presently dropped one of the goblets, whereupon it broke; one of the pieces cut Feodor's hand. Since then he has refused to touch them and has ordered that they be kept locked in a chest so that they cannot break again.

According to what reports have come from Germany, the winter has been especially fierce in the south of Bohemia and Hungary. The snows have been deeper and it is expected that it will take longer for roads into Europe to be passable. Therefore it may be that we will sail from Novo-Kholmogory as soon as wagons break through from Praha, for the winter north of Moscovy, although it is severe, is no worse than it is in most years, or so we have been led to understand by our English sailors and the Russian traders with whom we deal.

Sir Jerome bids me extend his thanks for the maps you have provided. We have done as you suggested and hidden them: the Court would condemn us if they knew we had them, as they would you, for the same reason. For these Rus, to possess a map is to declare yourself a spy.

Sadly, I have not been able to speak with Father Krabbe. It seems that Father Pogner has ordered him to remain within the embassy. His distrust of you continues to increase, does it not? It annoys me that he will listen to none of the foreign mission in this regard. Sir Jerome taxed him with his behavior not long ago, describing the new limitations recently imposed upon foreigners as the result of Father Pogner's overt actions against you. Father Pogner is convinced the restrictions are the order of Nikita Romanov and have nothing to do with him.

On the excuse to return these books and to borrow more, I will give myself the pleasure of calling upon you in four days' time, at mid-afternoon. With the many assurances of my friendship and the appreciation of the ambassador, Sir Jerome Horsey, I am

> *Your servant to command,*
> *Benedict Lovell*
> *of the English Embassy at Moscovy*
> *by my own hand*

2

Those who waited in line had red, chapped faces from the sleety snow pelting across the Beautiful Market Square: the moat around the Kremlin was so deeply frozen that twenty mounted men could not break through it; the sky overhead was the same color and appearance as the ice. On this, the Feast of Saint Porphyry of Gaza, several hundred worshippers waited to pray at the tomb of Vasilli the Holy Fool in the Saint's honor. After a week of blizzards, the weather had calmed somewhat, bringing the people of Moscovy out of their houses.

"Are you certain that the Metropolitan will not be offended?" asked Rakoczy as he strode along beside Boris Feodorovich Godunov. "I am not of your faith."

"Well," Boris said very deliberately, his shuba held tightly across his chest, his gloves lined with ermine. He breathed out a cloud of steam. "You are a Christian—"

"Of a sort," Rakoczy murmured. He wore a black Polish wilczura with the wolf-fur hood up.

"You have suffered at the hands of the Turks, and you are here with the embassy of a Christian king. It is senseless to abide by the rantings of one Roman priest. You are known to the people of Moscovy as a worthy foreigner, an exile for your religion." Boris acknowledged the greeting of a wealthy merchant with a conspicuous wallet slung over his shuba. "That man, Nikolai Sobrimovich Donetskoy, he vouches for your reputation, and not just in Russia but throughout the world. He would not refuse you entrance to the Virgin's Cathedral any more than the priests would."

"For my blood," Rakoczy observed with a faint, ironic light in his dark eyes. "And my reputation."

"Certainly. Every man in Moscovy who fought the Tartars twelve years ago respects both. This is Moscovy. The disapproval of that Polish Jesuit has no currency here. You have been favored by Czar Ivan and Czar Feodor. Therefore I can see no reason for the Metropolitan to deprive you of the comforts of Mass. You are respectful; you were married in a Kremlin cathedral in the company of the Czar. You honor the ikons. Your wife is known for her charities, and you have made donations in her name to the honor of the saints. Besides, no one has protested before. There is no reason to protest now." He said it loudly enough to be easily overheard, which was his intention.

"Except for Father Pogner," Rakoczy corrected him. "He has attempted to bar me from Mass again."

"So we have been informed." Boris nodded, his heavy boots so crusted with snow that he had to stop and kick at them several times. "From Catholic Mass. We are Orthodox." When he resumed trudging toward the gigantic Cathedral of the Virgin of the Intercession with its cluster of dissimilar cupolas, he made certain that Rakoczy was right beside him, clearly in his company. He paid no attention to the four Guardsmen trailing behind him, preferring Rakoczy's escort to theirs. "If the weather remains clear we will set men to work removing the snow here."

Rakoczy accepted this shift of subject, knowing that if this ploy of Boris' did not force Father Pogner to make certain concessions, he would find another tactic. "I have been told that the signs are for more storms." They were nearing the Cathedral—a tremendous Virgin's star of eight points, with the chapel for Vasilli the Holy Fool making the number of stellations nine— when a slow-moving sleigh drew up to them, the horses steaming as they strained at their bowed yokes. As Rakoczy heard his name called, he turned. "Father Krabbe," he said, bowing a little to the passenger riding behind the coachman. "I trust I see you well."

Father Krabbe looked deeply worried, and it took him a short while to frame an answer. "I have been to your house, Rakoczy. I wanted to speak with you."

Boris stopped walking and gave Father Krabbe his attention, as well.

"Is something the matter?" asked Rakoczy with some concern, as much for the public place as any message the priest might have for him. "There is no bad news from King Istvan, is there?"

"No." Father Krabbe looked around the square. "That is, there may be, but I know nothing of it. No. It is . . . nearer to Moscovy." He once again gave the square an uneasy, quick glance.

"Something to do with the embassy?" Rakoczy suggested.

"Yes," said Father Krabbe at once. "Yes, that's it." He stared at Boris, faltering a third time. "But I should not . . . I should not burden you with these concerns now." He signaled to the coachman. "I will call later."

"Tomorrow? Tonight? When?" Rakoczy inquired, doing his best to appear interested but unconcerned.

"Tomorrow," said Father Krabbe at once. "We celebrate Mass at six and ten. I will come before mid-day. Unless," he added as an afterthought, "there is a storm. In that case I will come as soon as the weather clears. I'll send someone to tell you . . . when it is possible. Not Yuri, of course."

"No, not Yuri," Rakoczy agreed.

"But someone. Soon. It is . . . not urgent, but . . ."

"Needing attention?" Rakoczy suggested. "I am grateful for this . . . information. I'll expect you at your convenience." He watched as the coachman signaled his three-horse team to move off again.

Boris shaded his eyes, looking into the sleet as the sleigh turned at the squat, drum-shaped Chapel of Athanazius the Athonite. "It will not end, you know, until one of you is gone from Moscovy."

"Father Krabbe or I?" Rakoczy inquired with amusement, deliberately misunderstanding him.

"Father Pogner or you, as well you know," said Boris dauntingly. "He is your enemy, Rakoczy, as surely as the Turks are. You should never forget that: you may be certain he never does."

"You make too much of it," said Rakoczy with more indifference than he actually felt; long experience had taught him to avoid entangling his friends in his strife if he could. "He may despise me, but he has a duty to King and Church, and he will not let his petty dislike endanger their trust." He knew as he said it that Boris was not convinced.

"I pray you are right," said Boris as he reached the entrance to the cathedral and paused to bless himself before stepping inside.

Rakoczy crossed himself as well. "Do you ever wonder," he said softly, "why God wishes signs like these made? Is it to remind Him, or to remind us, do you suppose?"

"Us," said Boris at once. "And it is typical that the Romans put form before worship. Had you grown up in the Eastern Rite you would never need to ask such a question." He stood back, indicating the tremendous, ancient ikon of Christ in Glory raising up His mother in Heaven; Christ, in red-and-gold robes with red hair and beard looked more like a beneficent Shuisky Prince than a carpenter from Galilee, and Marya, with her narrow, sloe-eyed face resembled the ancient Russian ruler Vladimir Monomakh's favorite wife far more than a peasant woman from the Dead Sea. Boris blessed himself and the ikon, and while Rakoczy did the same thing, he said, "We have not lost the way in useless ceremony as the Romans have. We place our trust in the Prophets and the Gospels. Our faith remains true to the teachings of Christ."

"It is a remarkable Cathedral," said Rakoczy sincerely.

"There is nothing else like it in the world," Boris declared with satisfaction. "Not even the temples of China are more beautiful than this." He had heard only the most exaggerated accounts of the temples in the south of China, but the accounts of tremendous palace-temples of gold with thousands of golden statues of Buddha shining so brightly that it hurt to look at them could not help but impress him.

Rakoczy nodded and let Boris think what he wished: if he had discovered one thing in his three thousand five hundred years, it was the futility of religious debate. He kept to the side of the entrance away from the pilgrims going to Vasilli's tomb. The Holy Fool had begged his bread and spoken of his visions in the Beautiful Market Square, and had been buried in the old Church of the Trinity where this Cathedral of the Virgin of the Intercession now stood. Some of the older peasants and artisans in the line vociferously recounted hearing Vasilli speak.

"I was barely old enough to handle my father's grain sacks: hardly more than ten," one of these men declared. "Yet even I could tell that he was more than one of those who have lost their wits, or never had any in the first place. This man was consumed with the Sight. Devout monks would think a lifetime of prayer were well-spent for that Sight. He cared nothing for power or position or honor, but only for the Sight." He crossed himself.

"It was more than thirty years ago," said a man not far from him in the line, encouraging the others around him to share his skepticism. "You cannot remember such things."

"If you had seen Holy Fool Vasilli, you would never have forgotten him. Never," the first insisted.

Boris led Rakoczy further into the Cathedral, toward the magnificent ikonostasis. "Czar Ivan thought this his greatest achievement in all Moscovy."

Rakoczy nodded. "Not without reason." He glanced around at the ikons on the whitewashed walls, and asked in a lowered voice, "Is it true he put out the eyes of the architect so that he could never do anything more beautiful?"

For a moment Boris said nothing; he hardly breathed. Then he touched his beard, smoothing it as if stroking a nervous cat. "Yes. I have heard that rumor; everyone has, and everyone repeats it, in the Kremlin, in the markets, and in church. But blind a man for something so resplendent?—I never saw it happen." He looked around the echoing interior. "He was capable of it, of course."

Again Rakoczy nodded. He paused as the choir suddenly burst out in unaccompanied sixteen-part harmony, extolling the endless compassion of Marya, their supplication to her as vast and relentless as an avalanche.

Boris took his place with the other worshippers, insisting on no position of privilege, telling the young priest who approached him, "If we were within the Kremlin walls it would be another matter. There it is fitting that rank be maintained, for it is the Czar's as well as God's. But here, we are all Rus, and all of us come naked and sinful before Judgment."

The young priest gave the two men a blessing, hesitating at the sight of Rakoczy's Polish clothing. Then he repeated a short prayer and hurried away.

"Also here we are more invisible than in other places," Boris added a short while later as the metropolitan intoned the opening phrases of the Mass.

As the liturgy was celebrated inside the Kremlin, this one, outside the walls, was relatively short, lasting little more than an hour and a half. The Metropolitan and his priests led the worshippers in blessing the ikons as they made for the doors, once again passing those waiting to pray at the tomb of Yurodivyi Vasilli.

Boris once again stared up at Christ in Glory and crossed himself. "Some of the pilgrims have said that because of the Turks, Christ must come again soon to save His Church, and to bring faithful Christians to Heaven. But I do not think it will be so." He looked out into the gathering mist that glared beyond the door. "I think it will be many long years before He comes again, and it will not be the Turk who brings Him. What do you think, Rakoczy."

"I know that whatever I think, it will change nothing," he answered gently. "These things are mysteries. If the pilgrims feel safer or more certain of their purpose, what is the harm in their belief that God is waiting for them when they get where they are going?" So many memories crowded his thoughts, from the unseen god in the sacred grove at the dark of the night and the year, to the masked faces in Babylon, to the thousands at the Temple of Imhotep, to the Greek acolyte up to his elbows in the blood of goats, to hermits made famous by their austerity and piety, to the Turkish dancers whirling for endless hours, to the Dominicans following Savonarola down the Via del Battistero toward the Piazza della Signoria, each carrying paintings to be burned . . . "Their faith is admirable, if it is not used against—" As he stepped out into the light-riddled haze he heard his name called sharply.

Standing a short distance away in a muddy depression between two high drifts of snow, Father Pogner stood with Father Kovnovski and Father Felikeno to support him. He was wrapped in his pluvial over his cassock and he carried a tall crucifix, the corpus in silver, the cross in gold. He glistened in the shiny fog as he advanced on Rakoczy. "You are not worthy to take Communion. You are unworthy to be Catholic, but I have not the authority to excommunicate you—not yet. Rest assured that when the roads are clear, I will address the Archbishop, and he will deal with King Istvan. Your days of impunity are drawing to a close, traitor." He held up the crucifix.

The worshippers leaving the cathedral took a ragged step back, and most of them blessed themselves. The pilgrims turned away, most of them scandalized by the intrusion of Polish Catholics on the sacred grounds of the cathedral.

"Bring a dozen of your fellows," Boris said to his Guard in an undervoice. "Do these men no harm, treat them with respect, but get them out of this place or we will have a riot."

The Guard officer nodded. "At once," he said.

"At the walk," Boris cautioned him. "No need to attract attention before you want it." He motioned them off and then walked over to Rakoczy's side.

"If I had been granted that right, I would pronounce the anathema right now. As it is, I have instructed the embassy that you are to be regarded as excommunicated already. They are to have no contact with you, send you no messages, deal with you—on those rare occasions when it should be necessary—through messengers who cannot be contaminated by the lack of faith and the evil of your intent." He was screaming in order to be heard over the bells which rang from all over Moscovy as mid-day Mass came to an end. The discordant wobbling tone of the bell at the badly damaged church of Saint Varvarka the Martyr was a jarring addition to the rest, but no Moscovite complained.

"You have disgraced the Church!" Father Pogner shouted. "You have disgraced all Poland!"

"It is a pity he does not speak in Russian," said Boris in a low tone, his mouth narrowed in disapproval. "No more than a dozen people here speak Polish, I'll wager. As it is, there will be many who claim to have understood him, and there will be rumors about this, not all of them welcome to you—or to me."

Father Pogner continued his denunciation, his face growing rosy with cold and choler. He pointed at Rakoczy. "You deserved to lose your lands in Transylvania. You have abused the trust of King Istvan! You deserve to be an exile and a vagabond!"

Rakoczy touched his hands to his ears and shook his head, as if he could not make out what Father Pogner was saying.

"You are a disgrace to Transylvania and your blood!" Father Pogner declared so loudly that his voice broke.

Something changed at the back of Rakoczy's penetrating eyes; a darkness unrelated to the color came into them. Very slowly and carefully, he started forward, his stride deceptively easy.

"Rakoczy," said Boris behind him. "Let the Guard handle it."

Rakoczy nodded and kept on walking, directly to Father Pogner, ignoring Fathers Kovnovski and Felikeno. He had not raised his hood when he left the cathedral and now snowflakes and shards of sleet clung to his dark, loose curls. He dropped to his knee and kissed the hem of Father Pogner's pluvial; next he rose so that he could kiss the feet of the crucifix as well. If the cold metal burned his lips he gave no sign of it. Then he turned to the badger-haired priest and said very softly and distinctly, "Remember that you are the one who forced this meeting: I will say this to you once, Father Pogner. I do not disgrace my blood. I do not abjure my vows—to anyone." He dropped to his knee once more and again kissed the hem of the pluvial. He looked up. "Not even to you."

Boris stood with his arms folded, hands once again gloved. He considered the outrage he saw in Father Pogner's prominent eyes. "A pity you do not often kill priests in the West. That one would be better off."

"That one is the leader of the embassy I am sworn to serve," Rakoczy said evenly as he rejoined his friend. "In the name of King Istvan."

"The embassy," said Boris thoughtfully. "Not the man." He saw his guard returning and made three quick signals: the soldiers veered off and formed a line near the three Polish priests.

"And I cannot desert the embassy, for it would compromise more than my word," Rakoczy said. "As you cannot set aside your duty to Czar Feodor because Nikita Romanov is unpleasant."

"An apt comparison, up to a point," said Boris, and flapped his arm in the direction of the priests. "Move them out of here. See that they return to their embassy without incident."

Father Pogner swung his tall crucifix like a pike as the guard approached. "You will all keep back. *Back!*" He faced Boris across the expanse of grubby snow. "It pleases you to use Rakoczy. You think he is your creature. He is a *cur*. And he will turn on you as he has turned on the Church and Poland."

Father Felikeno broke and ran, wanting only to get away from the gathering crowd in the Beautiful Market Square.

"Let him go," Boris advised his guard without emotion. "He will manage."

"You are the servant to the Devil!" Father Pogner shouted; he might have meant Boris instead of Rakoczy. "You are a tool of evil."

Rakoczy deliberately directed his attention away from Father Pogner. "Father Kovnovski," he said to the younger man, his voice very calm and level, "tell me: do you think you can return Father Pogner without incident to the embassy if the Guard escort you?"

Father Pogner started to scream a protest, but Boris held up his hand and sharply ordered silence. For once the haughty old priest was held wholly in check by the strong arm and large gloved hand of a Cossack Guard. He shoved against the soldier to no effect; he could not speak or move, and his crucifix was kept upright by another Guard, serving to deepen the insult Father Pogner felt: not only was he being treated like a barbarian interloper, but his God was being mocked by these idolaters.

With a strained laugh Father Kovnovski made a deprecating motion. "There's no reason to send the Guard along. Once away from here he will not lose his composure. He'll be reasonable. It isn't necessary to . . . have the soldiers lead us."

"I'm afraid it is," said Boris in excellent Polish. "The pilgrims are very offended by what you have done, and I cannot permit you to walk the streets without protection while they are so affronted."

Father Kovnovski looked deeply miserable; he was embarrassed, frightened, and cold. Much as he admired Father Pogner, at this instant he wanted nothing more than to abandon the old priest to his fate. When the ambassador had requested his company, there had been no mention of this confrontation. He squared his shoulders and regretted again that he had not worn the long rabbit-skin cloak he had purchased just three weeks before; he was shivering from cold, not fear. "If that is what you advise . . ." He spat, then looked at Rakoczy, his eyes doing the begging his voice could not.

Rakoczy shrugged. "Accept the offer. Under the circumstances, Boris Feodorvich is being very magnanimous. You might tell Father Pogner that. Not that he will believe it," he added sardonically, glancing once at the ambassador.

"Father Pogner will not regard this . . . kindly." His manner was as ingratiating as he could make it and the opinion he offered was still bound to be unwelcome. He stared at Rakoczy. "If you could apologize to him?"

"I?" Rakoczy inquired cordially, shaking his head gently once. "For what cause? I have done nothing to offend him. If he believes otherwise, I am grieved that his mistaken apprehension has brought us to such a pass as this." He drew on his black Florentine gloves. He bowed slightly to Father Kovnovski. "Let me know if there are any incidents against you—any of you—or the embassy."

Boris clapped his hands and shouted brisk orders to the guard;

he marched forward a short way and looked around the Square. "I do not want anything to happen to these foreigners. Those who harm them bring shame to the Little Father, and his honor will be avenged." His big, gloved hands were on his hips and he was already muffled in his shuba so that he looked like a large, bronze-and-black bear.

There was jostling in the long line of pilgrims as the various men who had been watching turned away, demonstrating their indifference to what they had seen.

The Guard closed around the priests, the leader presenting himself to Father Kovnovski with a flourish. The Guard holding Father Pogner frog-marched the old man to Father Kovnovski's side.

"You come with me," said Father Kovnovski in awkward Russian; he turned back to look at Rakoczy. "You are not free of this, I do fear."

"No more do I," said Rakoczy, and watched as the small party of priests and Guards disappeared into the thickening snow. He raised his hood at last, then folded his arms. "Boris Feodorovich," he said speculatively, staring at the place where the Poles had vanished, "do you think it would be permissible for me to hire a Guard or two? Your men, of course."

"You mean because of the Polish priests?" Boris asked, very conversational now that the moment had passed.

"I mean because my wife could be in danger," said Rakoczy bluntly. "She has been dragged into this through no fault of hers. The least I can do is provide for her protection."

"And you?" Boris began the laborious task of walking back to the Kremlin. After the first few steps he motioned to Rakoczy to follow him, remarking, "Had we gone to Mass at the Dormition this would not have happened."

"Possibly not here, possibly not today," said Rakoczy softly, "but eventually it would come to—"

"It could be dealt with," said Boris, leaning into the wind as he walked. "There are ways these things are done." He jerked his chin in the direction of the Polish embassy.

"But—" Rakoczy was alarmed at the implication.

"Oh, not now, not today," Boris said with a shake of his head. "Not after such an event as . . . this." He flung his hand back toward the snow-shrouded Beautiful Market Square. "But there would be a time, a quiet time, when the worst was over and the gossips wagged their tongues in other breezes. Then a man such as Father Pogner, if he were wise, would retire to the country and surround his estate with faithful retainers or he would face the consequences of his acts—the invisible dagger or the sweet poison or . . . any number of things."

Rakoczy opened his gloved hands. "My task here is clear to me: I am sworn to the King of Poland, and Father Pogner's distress does not change that."

"Not for you, perhaps, but for Father Pogner it does, and you should not forget your position," said Boris heavily. He was beginning to pant from the effort of walking through the drifts against the wind. "Father Pogner is in Moscovy, and King Istvan is in Poland." He stopped and turned to speak to Rakoczy directly. "Your wife is not the only one who requires protection."

"Ah, but I have Rothger, and he is worth a company of fighting men, I promise you," said Rakoczy, his dark eyes meeting Boris' black ones. "Without him, I would have been very truly dead fifty times and more."

Boris gave a grudging nod, his expression growing less harsh. "He is a good start, then; a good start." Slowly he resumed his trek toward the Savior Gate. "But he cannot be with you every hour. He must sleep and eat and tend to the needs of men. Anyone sent to work against you would know to disable your servant before facing you."

Rakoczy chuckled as he trod along beside him. "Boris Feodorovich, I am not entirely a novice at fighting. And any man who seeks to harm Rothger answers to me."

"As many have learned to their cost?" countered Boris, and added the aphorism he had learned long ago from his Tartar mother. "You have yet to meet the man who will slay you."

This time Rakoczy's smile was inward, ironic. "Do you think so?" He paused with Boris and blessed the ikon of Jesus.

As they entered the Kremlin, Boris abruptly changed the subject, preferring now to speak of celebrations and the anticipated state arrival of a noble messenger from the King of Sweden, far safer topics than enmity and assassination.

* * *

Text of a letter from Vasilli Shuisky to his cousin Anastasi Shuisky, written in Russian.

To my most honorable and esteemed cousin, Duke Anastasi Sergeivich, my most respectful greetings and my apologies for being remiss in my attentions as a blood relation.

It has been some months now since we have spoken together, which has increasingly troubled me, and I fear that through some misunderstanding we have become estranged. It is my utmost hope that our purpose and bonds hold us more firmly than the lapses of my duty to you. My conduct has been inexcusable, and for that I am most heartily sorry. It is not my wish, good cousin, to see any separation plague our family, and I pray it is not yours. In order for any of our family to advance, we must all work to that end, and not waste our strength vying against each other for the advantage that is by right that of Shuisky, and Shuisky above any other seeking high advantage.

Perhaps you assumed that I no longer needed your advice now that I have found a servant who can provide the translations you were used to give me. This is absurd, Anastasi Sergeivich. I would never trust a servant with the secrets that must be kept between members of our House. It would be imprudent. Both of us know to our bitter sorrow how foolish such conduct is, and what consequences come from misplaced trust. It was never my intention to supplant you with a servant. Why should I do so reprehensible a thing? Why would I place the entire family in the hands of a servant? You cannot think I am so despicable as that.

Certainly we have differences. It is the nature of men of vision to disagree on what is seen. We have had occasion to be at cross-purposes in the past. You are aware of them, as am I. It may be that we have allowed our goals to be forgotten because of our differences, but I trust this is not so. You and I both seek glory for Shuisky, and both of us have done many things to achieve that end. It may be that success is finally at hand. That would please me, as I trust it would please you, for if one of us is exalted, all of us are. Shuisky is our great cause, and the triumph of Christ. It is our task to see that we make every effort to bring our family to the prominence it has earned and deserves. Any other decision must be treason to our blood. You know as well as I that there is no way for us to proceed without the support of the other. Not my brothers, nor any of the rest, are as crucial to the great prize we seek as you are, Anastasi Sergeivich.

Therefore, let me propose that we meet soon, as privately as we may without bringing attention to our privacy. Together we will surely arrive at the means to end the many obstacles that appear to mitigate against our success. You are wise in Court-craft and you have allies among the boyars who may be seeking a stronger Czar than the pitiable Feodor; those are the men we must convince of our righteousness, and for that I utterly depend upon you.

The servant bringing this is a deaf-mute and cannot read. Anything you say to him, any message you give to him, is as safe as if it were sealed in limestone. He is faithful as a hound, as well, and will carry this to me though I were in the farthest pit of Hell.

May God and the Czar show you favor and distinction, and may you be a figure of pride for the House of Shuisky, from this day to the Last Judgment.

Vasilli Andreivich

3

April arrived timidly, uncertain of its welcome, and throughout Moscovy the buds on the trees showed less promise than usual. Most of the people within the city's walls shrugged and went about their work.

At Rakoczy's house, its owner converted part of his stable to an alchemical center, with oiled sheets of parchment set in the ceiling that let in heat and light during the day. In the manger and around the walls, plants sprouted in tubs and long troughs of rich red or black earth, rising up toward the veiled light. At night the oiled parchment was covered over from the outside with huge, square, hinged shingles, a task the servants performed grudgingly in spite of the extra silver coins such duties gained them.

Four of the staff had just completed battening the shingles for the night, clambered down from the roof, and were headed off to supper when Xenya came into the center, her head held up in defiance, her eyes filled with fright.

Rakoczy paused in his lighting of oil lamps; he looked at her through the loamy twilight. Although she had never visited this part of the house before, he was not surprised. "Come in, Xenya Evgeneivna," he said, resuming his work. "If you will permit me a little time, it will be brighter."

She stood just inside the doorway, looking around in bafflement, her posture changing as she became curious about the plants her husband tended. "But these—"

"As I explained," said Rakoczy. "I have not finished everything, but this is about half of it."

"They said—" Xenya began, then stopped herself.

Those two damning words were expected but they shook him anyway. "They?" he inquired gently.

Color flamed in her cheeks. "Unkind . . . people." Now that there were two dozen lamps burning, the plants were much more easily seen. "This isn't a—"

"Graveyard?" He was able to keep the bitterness from his tone but not the irony.

She was eloquently silent as she came farther into the room. She reached out and touched new-furled leaves of a thyme seedling, and bent nearer to savor its delicate scent. "You are making a garden."

He smiled slightly. "You might call it that." He did not add that the red and black earth in which the plants grew was his native earth: with his own servants becoming more suspicious of him and his embassy protection all but gone, he had thought it prudent to conceal it not in leather trunks but with living things: what better place to hide earth than in flowerpots?

"It isn't a garden?" she questioned, leaning over a tub where a young birch grew.

"The Queen of England or the Pope in Rome certainly would not think so. I am an alchemist, and these plants are part of my studies," he said, cordial enough but curious what tale she had been told, and by whom, that had brought her to this cobbled-together room in the first place. "That willow, for example, when it is a little taller, will provide an anodyne remedy from its bark, for the ease of aching sinews and fever."

She nodded, more to show that she was listening than that she understood. She made her way between two rows of tubs of blue-green bulbous sprouts, frowning at them. "What are these? I have seen them before, in the country when I was a child."

"China poppies, fairly young," said Rakoczy. "When they are grown they provide a syrup, very powerful, to soothe the pain of serious injuries. I used the last in my stores when I set Nemmin's broken leg."

"He was in great pain," she said, her voice sounding remote. "But he slept for more than a day and a night."

"It was the best remedy for him," Rakoczy said calmly, permitting her to approach him in her own time; he had realized sometime before that she was not as quickly frightened of him if she decided how far away from him she was. He watched her closely, continuing as if her visit were an ordinary occasion. "I will have pansy, too, shortly; it is another anodyne. One not so severe as the syrup of poppies but stronger than willow bark."

Now that she was almost up to him, Xenya took a deep breath. "Ferenc Nemovich," she said after a hesitation, "I have to talk to you. Please. Listen to me. I've decided I must. I am uneasy in my mind."

"Ah?" Rakoczy pinched out his long taper and set it aside near the drum of lamp oil. His dark eyes warmed as she stood before him.

Now that she had his full attention, she faltered. "I have wanted to speak to you of this for . . . some weeks." She swung around so quickly that the skirt of her sarafan almost knocked over a potted low-growing juniper. "Mercy of God! My husband, I'm sorry—"

"There is no harm; it's nothing," he said, calming her with his voice. "Tell me what you want to say to me."

"I've tried before, but you . . . you were busy or there were other things . . . between us, and I . . . I didn't want . . ." She lifted her hands once. "It was not right that I . . ."

He reached out and trailed the backs of his fingers over her shoulder. "You don't have to run from me, Xenya. I won't hurt you."

Immediately she turned back to face him, but kept the distance between them. "No; you have not. And I have been ungrateful. I'm sorry. I don't know why you do not beat me. But I thank God and the Virgin that you do not."

This time he turned away. "I know what it is to be beaten, little wife. I promise you are safe from me."

"You may change your mind," she said, anxiety making her voice shake. She took a deep breath. "I might, if I were a man, married to such a woman."

As great as his sympathy was for her, he wanted to know what she had done. "If my word that I will not beat you is not enough, I'll loan you my poignard. It's tucked in the back of my belt in a leather scabbard. I'll hand it to you." He saw the confusion and doubt in her eyes as her countenance went deep red. "I beg your pardon, Xenya. That was uncalled for."

This admission reassured her, and she did her best to face him directly. She folded her hands but had some trouble meeting his eyes, for fear of his compassion. "I have done a thing . . . I thought it was correct to do. I supposed that I would not have been given the task if it were wrong . . . Perhaps that was foolish of me. For now that I have done it, I believe I was in error, and I have sinned against you, which I would never want to do. It was not my intention to do you any wrong. I was told it would not work against you. I may not be a very good wife but I would never work against you, Ferenc Nemovich. Never. Not for the world and the joys of Paradise." It came out quickly, this confession of hers, and when she finished she took half a dozen steps away from him.

The deep alarm Rakoczy felt was not reflected in his expression. His voice was gentle as before, his manner as unruffled. "What is it you have done, Xenya Evgeneivna?"

She opened her hands and folded them again. "I . . . I was asked by my cousin to . . . to tell him about Yuri, the servant you sent to the—"

"I know which Yuri you mean," he interrupted her quietly.

"Yes." She took a long, deep breath. "Yes. Anastasi Sergeivich wanted to know why he was sent to the Jesuits. He suspected you wanted to gain favor with Father Pogner, or so he informed me." She began to pace, walking past the poppies to a tub of wolfsbane; she circled this twice, then came back toward Rakoczy, passing a large leather chest with the lid open, half its earthen contents still in it, along with a large trowel. "He said that the Polish embassy has turned against you: Father Pogner has denounced you as a heretic, at least Anastasi Sergeivich says he has. Is it true?"

Rakoczy shrugged. "Yes. It is. I'm barred from Catholic Mass."

"And Yuri is to plead on your behalf? He is to show your good-will?" she guessed, looking eager.

"I should hope not," said Rakoczy wryly. "Doubtless Yuri would describe me as one of the servants of Satan; Father Pogner would welcome that."

Xenya crossed herself, as pale now as she had been rosy before. "One of the servants of Satan."

This time Rakoczy laughed, the sound of it unspeakably sad. "Little wife, in time you will realize that when most men call another a servant of Satan, it means that the other disagrees with him or is disobliging." His dark eyes grew distant. "And they call a man brave when they mean he is expendable; wise men praise that valor. They say a man is devout when they mean he is condemning, or honorable when he is avaricious, or faithful—" He broke off.

"When he is what?" she asked when he neither went on nor changed the subject.

He shook his head once. "It's nothing, Xenya Evgeneivna." He watched her, noticing how she had caught up a part of the skirt of her silken sarafan and was pleating and unpleating the soft red fabric as she stood, more like a recalcitrant child than a mistaken wife. He held out his hand to her. "Is that all your cousin Anastasi wanted to know? Why Yuri was sent to Father Pogner?"

She did not answer at once. "There was something else. He wanted me to tell him when I become pregnant. As soon as my courses stop, he wants to have word of it."

"Did he indeed." His hand remained offered to her. "And what did you tell him?"

"I said that I was not with child that I knew of," she answered at once, pleased that she could offer him that much display of her loyalty to him.

Rakoczy knew better than to assume that was the end of it. "And what was his response?"

"He said . . ." This time her breath was more unsteady, as if she was about to cry. "He said that he . . . wants to protect me.

Because you will leave me here, with nothing. You will be ordered to return to Poland in disgrace and will be forced to refute our marriage."

"I have received no such orders, Xenya Evgeneivna, and you could come with me if it is your desire." He saw that she was not reassured. "If you would prefer to remain here, I have already given funds to Boris Feodorovich to care for you." There were other protections as well, arranged through the English, in case Boris could not fulfill his agreed duties.

Xenya continued with less distress. "My cousin said he would try to provide for me when that time comes. He said you were making preparations. He said that if Yuri was your spy in Father Pogner's—"

"Whoever spy Yuri is, he is not mine," said Rakoczy softly.

Xenya stared at Rakoczy, dawning shock banishing her apprehension at last. "Yuri? Spied on you?"

"Yes." Rakoczy smiled easily and again extended his hand. "He is not the first or the last."

"So you sent him away? To priests?" She crossed herself.

"At least I know where he is," said Rakoczy, finally lowering his hand. "He reads and writes." He did not add that Yuri knew more than Russian.

Xenya shook her head in amazement. "But my cousin said . . ." She hesitated, then came nearer. "My cousin said that Yuri was to gather information for you, to be your eyes and ears in the Polish camp."

"I have Father Krabbe for that," he reminded Xenya, thinking that Anastasi's inquiry revealed he knew more of Yuri than he had admitted to Xenya. "Neither he nor I make a secret of it, as I am still a member of the embassy, no matter what Father Pogner would like." He watched the tiny, denying shake of her head. "Yuri was a spy in this household. I assume he is a spy in the Polish one. I do not know to whom he answers."

"Yes." Xenya nodded several times as she answered, her apprehension giving way to understanding. "Yes. There are those who might try such a ploy. Anastasi Sergeivich always claims that we are in a nest of spies. I see how that is possible." She put her hand down on an improvised table where a confusion of leaves and bare roots lay; she withdrew it at once, sucking the side of her hand. "What is that?"

"Nothing that will harm you," said Rakoczy, taking two steps toward her and hoping it would not trouble her that he did. "It is the roots I want, not the brambles. I'm sorry you—"

She took a step back and almost fell over a small pot of dragon's-beard. She shrieked.

Rakoczy stopped at once. "I am not going to hurt you, Xenya. I want to see how badly your hand is injured, in case it requires—"

"It's nothing," she said quickly, making sure he was not between her and the door.

Rakoczy saw her concern and moved back another step, very slow and deliberate in his actions. He watched her while her panic faded. "Xenya Eveneivna, may I ask you a question."

She watched him warily. "Of course. You are my husband."

"No, no, not as your husband, little wife, as your . . . friend. Will you answer a question for me?" He stood, waiting for her answer, no suggestion of impatience about him.

Finally she nodded as she licked the side of her hand once more. "All right. What is it?"

Rakoczy's steady, compelling gaze rested on her. "Since we were married I have come to you three times, twice to your bed, once in your bath; three separate times."

"Yes?" she asked, tension back in her voice and her face slightly averted.

He made his voice light and precise. "Each time, where have I been, in relation to you? Where were you? Where was I?"

"Where?" She glared at him. "You were with me—in your manner." She laid her hand on her neck; the fine punctures on the side of her palm left a faint smear of blood behind as she dropped her hand.

"No; where was I—in front of you or behind you?" His smile was little more than a curve at the corners of his mouth, but it gave her the determination to reply.

"You were behind me," she said. "Is that what you mean?"

He waited for two slow heartbeats. "Why do you think I did that?"

She answered very carefully, as if she suspected a trap. "So that I would not see . . . your impotence."

Rakoczy chuckled, and shaking his head in amusement offered, "Look for yourself." He unfastened his belt and opened the front of his dolman; he paid no heed to the sound of his sheathed poignard dropping to the floor. The camisa beneath, of fine Italian linen, was untied at neck and waist and opened as well. His codpiece, nothing more than what a prudent man would wear for a day in the saddle, followed the rest, and the underbelt holding his leggings was loosened. "There."

Xenya had never seen scars like the ones that made a ridged white swath across the front of his body from just below the joining of his ribs to just above his penis. She crossed herself twice. "God in mercy!" she whispered.

"I have remained behind you," said Rakoczy in the same steady, easy voice, "so that you could escape me, if you wished. I have never pinioned you with my arms. I have always made it possible for you to break free of me, if you wished. If I had not done so, you would have been filled with terror no matter how compliant you wanted to be, which benefits neither of us. There is nothing you can do to gratify my senses if you are not gratified; you cannot counterfeit fulfillment. I have said from the first that I want to do what will bring you the most pleasure." He secured his underbelt and then his codpiece, but he pulled the dolman off and dropped it into an empty tub. His camisa remained open.

"Ferenc Nemovich," she said, her anxiety increasing with each breath she drew. "It . . . isn't right."

"Would you rather face me, now that you understand my reasons?" he asked as if he were inquiring about a length of cloth or her preference in gloves. "You know what you would see— which is more than most of those I have loved ever knew."

"And there have been many?" She stood straighter, her hands tightening at her side.

"Yes," he answered quietly.

"And were they all whores, that you have not married until now?" Her audacity astonished her and she was about to apologize for it, and the quick stab of jealousy she had not thought it possible for her to have, but he answered her candidly, without indignation.

"Almost none were whores. They were women who"—their faces, their voices filled his mind—"who could not love as they wished and accepted me instead." There was no regret in him, and no rancor: certainly no self-pity. Strongest in his thoughts was Demetrice, who gave herself the true death less than a century before; she had not been able to live as those of his blood must. "I loved them. Love them." He regarded her steadily. "There is a bond, little wife; with the blood there is a bond; it cannot be broken."

"Bonds are always broken," she whispered.

"Not this one," Rakoczy said quietly and with such certainty that she stared at him.

"And you have this bond with me?" She held her breath for his answer.

"I've already said so." He observed her closely, his dark eyes tranquil, his body still while she considered what he had told her.

"It would be fitting, to have such a bond, if it were possible," she said somberly. What followed was more difficult to voice. "You should have the . . . You have shown me . . . those." She indicated the scars. Her next question was out before she could stop it. "The scars . . . are they the reason for your impotence?" And though she clapped her hands over her mouth, it was too late.

"They're not unrelated," he said with great composure.

She heard this out, concentrating, listening to more than the words. "Then I suppose I ought to try. To face you."

"As a painful duty?" Rakoczy asked, aware of the effort this required, and added, softening his tone, "No, Xenya. It will be as you wish, if you wish it." He waited as she made herself walk toward him.

How much she prayed that her fears were groundless! She was a grown woman, not a cowering child. This inward chastisement increased the nearer she came to him. He was a good man, foreigner or no. He would not harm her: he had given her his word he would not. Her feet felt weighted with lead. The eight steps it took to reach him were like climbing a mountain of ice, and every instant she dreaded falling back. When she was close enough to reach out and touch the scars she could see above his underbelt, she stopped, unable to bring herself to look any higher than his chin, level with her eyes. "I am here."

"Not quite," he admonished kindly.

She lowered her eyes and nodded. "Well . . . you can . . . put your arms a-around . . . around me." Her heart beat faster as she spoke.

"Yes, I can. But I will not." Instead he leaned back, his shoulders supported by a rough-hewn pillar that had once anchored two stall walls. "I meant what I told you, Xenya Evgenievna: I want only your pleasure, for without it I have none of my own."

"But you can embrace me," she said, feeling suddenly petulant.

"And you would loathe it," said Rakoczy. "I would disgust you and myself. What is the sense in that?" Without abandoning his relaxed posture he turned his suddenly intent dark eyes on her, and she was reminded of the black sapphire in his pectoral. "I seek your desire, Xenya. I seek your joy. You may be willing to accept mere acquiesence and security, but I am not; there is no fulfillment for either of us in such fare. For you and for me I seek your release. If you wish this, I will have nothing less."

She was precariously close to fleeing, but now her pride had been stung, and though principle could not keep her where she was, umbrage could. Her determination increased; she fixed her stance and directed her gaze at him. "Why?" she demanded.

"Because it is my life," he said simply.

"And the blood?" she persisted.

"The blood is you." He waited, expecting her to challenge him again. When she did not, he went on. "It is the very core of you, your life, your blood; it is all your passion."

Very slowly she reached out her hand and laid it against the center of his chest, just above the highest scar; his camisa brushed her hand as he drew a long breath. Her fingers were cold and not quite steady, but she would not move away. "How did it happen?"

He shook his head, about to refuse, then considered all she had been through and said, "You know what ferocity there is in men. My father's enemies had already killed him sometime before, and now they were supposed to kill his son, who had won a battle." He indicated himself with one hand, which he laid over Xenya's on his chest. "They began by flaying me here, starting at the base of my abdomen, intending to pull out . . . everything." Which, he added to himself, they had. "Those of my blood are not killed easily; we must be . . . destroyed—burned or broken or beheaded—before we are truly dead. But they did not know this and did not finish their task correc—"

"Did you avenge your wounds?" she asked, not wanting to imagine his suffering.

"Oh, yes," he said distantly, and for that one flicker of time he was glad she was not looking at him and could not see what was in his eyes. The echo of that distant rage appalled him now, and he sought the anodyne of her presence.

She gave a single, small nod. "Good." Tentatively she laid her other hand on his chest. "Would it hurt if I touch the scars?"

"No," he assured her.

They did not seem like skin at all; hard and white and stretched, falsely taut with faint striations through the tissue like fine silk. There was not much give to them, and Xenya thought they were colder than the rest of him. Slowly she ran her hands down to his abdomen. She trembled and stepped back to the length of her arm. "They left . . . you weren't castrated."

"I am a King's son," he said, "and our conquerors feared our god."

Immediately she crossed herself. "For Christ will come in victory over all who oppose Him," she said with fervor.

Rakoczy did not tell her that his god had died in battle two thousand years before her Christ was born. He released her hand. "Tell me when you decide what you would like me to do."

"I don't know what I would like," she said. "How can I?"

He did not attempt to answer her question. "Imagine what would please you the most. Tell me, and I will try to do that thing. If it turns out not to be to your liking, then think of something else, and we will do that, until we discover what you treasure."

"But you?" She watched for him to betray eagerness or insistence.

"Ah, Xenya, what must I do to convince you?" he asked with a single, desolate laugh.

She stepped away from him, and after the greater part of a minute while neither of them moved, said, "I want you to hold me. In a short while I want you to hold me." Her courage faltered. "Start behind me."

"All right," he said, remaining where he was while she paced restlessly at the edge of the lamplight, looking at the barren, unfinished side of the new room. "In another month there will be shelves and tables for all the plants."

"Doubtless," said Xenya bluntly, coming to a halt at last. She steeled herself. "All right. Come."

Rakoczy could move soundlessly as a cat, but he made sure his thick-soled boots rapped sharply on the flagging, the steps not too quick, for he did not want her to feel pursued. As he reached her, he held out one hand, and slipping it around her waist, drew her slowly back against him, taking care to stop when he encountered resistance. He enjoyed the gradual change that came over her as she leaned back on his chest. "There are a dozen sheepskins in the last stall. The saddler wants them for pads. They are soft and warm."

She hesitated. "If you wish," she said uncertainly, her dawning pleasure fading. She wanted to encourage him because she thought he expected it, and because she was afraid to refuse, but all she felt was the need to break away from him, to run out of the room.

"No," he reminded her, his hold lightening. "As *you* wish." He bent to kiss her neck at the place where her jaw and ear met. His swift kisses barely brushed her skin, yet she shivered from something other than cold.

Why did it have to be so confusing? she asked herself. Why could she not will herself to take the satisfaction he offered her? Why could she not trust him? He was her husband. They were properly married. The priests and Metropolitan had blessed them. He had treated her far better than many women were treated by their husbands, and for less reason. He had never done the intolerable thing to her. He had been kind and patient and considerate. Then why did she not desire him? Or why did she desire him and cringe from her feeling at the same moment? Why did she dread the rapturous things he had done to her, offered her now? Why could she only find pleasure when he was behind her and she had a clear path to the door? She shook herself mentally and attempted to pay attention to those light, playful kisses he gave her, now at the edge of her brow, now along the nape of her neck as he moved her long plaits aside. She felt his deep chest through the back of her sarafan and rubashkaya, his steady breathing and the heat of his body. Mercy of God, what was she to do? "I . . . don't know," she whispered.

His kisses slowed, became more sensual and lingering. Then he stepped away from her, saying, "I am going to hold my hands out to the side. If you turn and face me, you can put your hands on mine. You will move them where you wish them to be."

Her voice was a few notes higher than usual, but otherwise she sounded undisturbed by this suggestion. "What . . . what an interesting idea," she said, and feeling as if she were falling from the top of a mountain, she made herself swing around to confront him.

His hands were at his side, just as he had promised her they would be. He gestured his approval, waiting for her to put her hands on his. "The door is behind you, Xenya," he reminded her. "I will not move between you and it."

What embarrassed her the most was how accurately he had spoken her thoughts, for she had feared he would maneuver to block her escape. Not that she intended to run from him, she insisted silently, but without the chance to be free . . . She wanted to tell him he was wrong, but the lie would not come. Instead she reluctantly put her hands on his, laying them palm to palm, fingers to fingers. She noticed that his were somewhat wider but no longer than her own; his thumbs were unusually long and well-formed. Strange, she thought, that she assumed his hands were huge when they were small and beautiful.

As she moved their hands together, experimenting, he watched her face closely. She had so much anguish hidden within her, and it had been there for so long. What more could he do to free her from it, he wondered, than what he had done already? He had been able to share her fulfillment three times, but each time he realized afresh the monumental inward battle she had waged to achieve those few moments of exultation. "If I could erase the past, I would," he said suddenly.

She was startled. "Your father's death? And the scars?"

"Not my past; yours." He leaned forward and very gently kissed her mouth.

Puzzled, she neither responded nor resisted. Their hands were extended to the side, about waist height, their bodies less than a handsbreath apart. Only when he started to move back did she realize their nearness. She pushed hard against his hands, and for an instant felt the immensity of his strength; then he acquiesced, and she realized her authority as she had never known it before, sensed it in the fiber of her being. Amazed, she looked directly at him for the first time, her honey-colored eyes meeting his dark ones without hesitation. "It's true," she murmured. "You mean what you say."

"Yes."

Her eyes remained fixed on his, but carefully she brought her hands down and behind her so that his arms encircled her waist. In spite of her determination she was trembling. "Leave them," she said as she let go of his hands.

"Are you certain it is what you want?" he asked, with new hope beginning within him.

She nodded, willing herself to try to hold him. "We should be closer?" The doubt had come back into her manner.

"If you wish it," he said quietly, "come nearer."

Once more she hesitated; if he had pulled her close or tightened his arms, she would have been frightened, but not as wary as she was now of his abiding tenderness. As much as she wanted to deny it, she yearned for his nearness, for the succor of his hands and his body, for the deliverance he offered her. Gracelessly she leaned against him. "There."

"No," he said very gently. "I won't be your ravisher or your seducer. I am your lover, and I will do nothing if you are not willing—"

She stepped back, testing him, feeling his hands release her with a relief that quickly turned to regret. She glanced toward the door, then made herself give him all her attention, saying with difficulty, "Do you want to take off my clothes?"

"No," he answered; his face was well-lit and without guile. "But it would make me very happy if you wanted to remove them."

She nodded, feeling numb. "What do you mean?" she asked, although she knew the answer, stiffening in anticipation of his demand.

His answer was not what she anticipated. "If you want them off, you will have to take them off yourself." He gave her a moment to protest; when she said nothing, he went on, his voice deep and musical, unhurried. "It would delight me to touch you, Xenya, if you want my touch. I want the scent and the weight and the taste of you. I love your flesh, Xenya, the texture of it, the warmth. I love it because it is yours, because it houses your soul. If you would like—"

She put her hand to his lips. "All right. All right. Don't bully me." She reached to unfasten her sarafan, letting the lovely damask red-and-gold silk drop into a puddle at her feet as she shrugged out of it. Now she was in her rubashkaya, and she shivered and told herself she was cold.

He indicated the alcove that had been a stall, and the pile of sheepskins there. "You would be warmer, and more comfortable," he suggested, but made no move toward it.

"If I wish it?" she ventured, an edge in her tone. "Or do you intend we should lie there?"

He would not be provoked. "If it is what you wish, Xenya Evgeneivna."

She was trembling at the enormity of her fright and her longing; her need of him was more shocking than the impact of her hideous memories, which she tried futilely to banish. Laggardly she stepped free of her discarded sarafan and dawdled her way to the alcove. "I suppose you're right," she allowed, remaining standing. "They look more comfortable than the stones."

Rakoczy followed her, coming to her side, away from the door. "And now? What now, Xenya?"

Her answer was so soft that he almost did not hear it. "Love me."

"If you wish it," he said, all but closing the distance between them though he did not reach out to her.

"I wish you to love me," she said less doubtfully.

"Tell me how," he persisted.

"I don't know," she said, her tone a little wild. "I don't know. Show me how." She turned; her eyes met his. "It is what I want."

He studied her face, and was convinced at last. "All right. Yet if anything I do displeases you, stop me at once, for both our sakes."

Her breath caught in her throat. "I will," she promised him, preparing for what he would do next, for an onslaught of demands.

They never came. He reached out and unfastened the top of her rubashkaya, letting the fabric fall open of its own gossamer weight; he leaned forward and kissed the arch of her collarbone, his hand moving lightly to her breast, cupping it lightly. The distance between them narrowed still more. His left hand joined the right, the touch as gentle, the sensations awakened tantalizing without urgency. In a single gesture her rubashkaya was slipped off her shoulders, leaving her naked but for short leggings and felt indoor shoes. "How lovely you are, Xenya," he whispered.

She wanted to shove him away, to run for the door, but had no desire to end the warm lethargy that had come over her. His hands were too persuasive and too evocative for her to leave with their promise unrealized. As long as I am standing, she told herself as she quivered at the discoveries his hands were making, as long as I am standing, I can break free and run.

Slowly, gently he drew her toward him until his arms enfolded her and she was pressed close to him. He opened her lips with his own in a kiss that left them both breathless. The second kiss lasted longer.

His hands were reverent, and the gifts they offered were revelations to Xenya, who had thought she had discovered all that her senses could encompass already. Gilded by lamplight in the green and loamy chamber, she learned with growing amazement that she had been mistaken, that what she had assumed was the end of her journey was the merest beginning. Her body responded to Rakoczy's touch as the fiddle responds to the expert bow; the harmony was sweeter and more resonant, striking chords within her she had never known were there to be sounded—or if she had suspected they existed, she supposed they had been silenced thirteen years ago.

He traced his way over her breasts and belly with myriad kisses; kneeling before her, he explored the sea-scented petals between her thighs, luxuriating in her emerging rapture as she caught her hands in his hair. He held her up as her first delirious spasms radiated through her.

As she sank to the pile of sheepskins, she stared at him, dazed. "How did you know?" she said when she was able to speak. Tears glazed her face.

"Because I know you." He stretched beside her, cradling her.

"But . . ." She touched the corner of his mouth. "There was no . . . you didn't . . ."

"Not yet," he said, his smile coming from deep inside him.

Her eyes were startled but without fear. "Is it possible?"

"If it is what you wish," he whispered as his slow, glorious caresses began again, drawing her inexorably to such consummate passion that she cried aloud in triumph as his lips grazed her neck. Only then, when she was wholly subsumed in fulfillment, did Rakoczy relent and soothe her into untroubled, opulent sleep in the haven of his arms.

Text of a letter from Benedict Lovell to Ferenc Rakoczy, written in English.

To the most excellent Ferenc Rakoczy, Count Saint-Germain, of the Polish embassy in Moscovy, greetings;

At the request of the English ambassador, Sir Jerome Horsey, I write to you to inform you that your presence is always welcome aboard English ships, as your cargoes have been in times past. The trading we have carried on in your behalf has been profitable to our mariners, to our embassy in Moscovy, and to the Queen's Grace. Because of this we wish to inform you that we recognize the value of continuing what has been such a worthwhile association, and if access to English ships will ensure that association, then we ask that you accept our hospitality at any time convenient to your purposes.

Sir Jerome has also requested that I warn you of certain events that have transpired in the last week. We at the English embassy have discovered that Nikita Romanov and Vasilli Shuisky have both placed spies in this household; from them we have learned that there are spies in the Polish embassy and the German embassy as well. These spies are not there to benefit Caesar Theodore but to add to the power being amassed by these ruthless princes who vie for the right to control their ruler.

We know that you have enjoyed a long friendship with Boris Godunov, and it would appear that he is in great danger from the machinations of the nobles we have mentioned. Between that friendship and the increasing condemnation of you by your own ambassador, it would appear that you are likely to be at risk, and the possible target of malign comment. It may be that you will be set upon by the enemies of Godunov. Such things have happened before.

Circumspection is always wise, and never more so than when servants and guests are not always trustworthy. In this regard, I am loath to entrust certain questions to the page and will wait until a more favorable time to put them to you.

We of the English embassy do not wish to see you so endan-

gered, not only out of consideration for your position, but in respect to our situation as well. Once the nobles decide to involve foreigners in their intrigues, then our days of safety here are limited. Let us assist you in any way we can in order to prevent being compelled to participate in the titanic clashes of these powerful lords.

I will call upon you myself for the purpose of hearing your response to the offer Sir Jerome has extended, and to discuss in what manner you wish to avail yourself of the hospitality we are pleased to present to you. Expect me in two days, at mid-afternoon. If this is not convenient, send your manservant to inform me of an alternate time and site.

I look forward to speaking with you, and pray God will hold you safe in these uncertain times.

> *Benedict Lovell*
> *The English embassy in Moscovy*
> *April 22, in the Year of Grace 1585*

4

"You have been meddling again," Vasilli said to his cousin Anastasi as soon as the two were alone in his private study. "What must I do to keep you from interfering?" He fingered his beard, letting the curls encircle his fingers as he watched his blockier relative falter before the ikons.

Anastasi's smile was masterful—cordial and cold at once. "What makes you believe this of me, Vasilli Andreivich?"

"You have been too blatant in your activities, I fear," said Vasilli.

This accusation caused no change in Anastasi's gelidly affable manner. "Why do you say this, sweet cousin?"

"There was a letter. You entrusted it to a Greek courier. He said he had performed such work for you in the past." Vasilli selected his most comfortable chair and sank down in it. "He has met with greater misfortune than serving you: the poor man will have to become a beggar, I fear, if he is to keep from starving."

"Who is the hapless man you describe?" Anastasi inquired, not waiting for Vasilli to offer him a seat; he chose the upholstered bench.

"The Greek. His name is Stavros Nikodemios." Vasilli achieved an expression of saintly patience. "His feet were beaten on the soles with iron-studded clubs, as if he were a Mongol spy. There was much suffering for the poor man, due to his resistance. I fear he will not walk again. Yet he told us a great deal before all the bones shattered, much of it not to your credit, little cousin." He indicated the ikon to Saint Vladimir of Perm, with his severed feet incorporated into his halo. "You may wish to pray to him on Nikodemios' behalf."

"Beaten on his feet with studded clubs—a very painful torture. No doubt he was in unreasoning agony when he answered your questions. And you believed him, after so much had been done? Surely he was raving, giving you what he thought you wanted to make you stop." His expression was pleasant; he spoke as easily as if they were talking about crops.

Vasilli was not distracted by Anastasi's demeanor; he remained adamant. "The man is a spy. Do you think the Patriarch of Jerusalem will give him charity, if he can drag himself so far?"

Anastasi made himself shrug. "It is sad to learn of his affliction, of course, but I haven't seen the Greek in more than two years, and then I received him but once; when I learned his purpose, I did not allow him admittance again. My household will tell you that, if you have not asked them already. If you bother to inquire, you will discover the truth. At that time I was not able to aid him; he must have said so. I do not know what he has done since then."

"Father Illya has already informed me that he—Nikodemios— visited you while Czar Ivan was still alive. He claims he over- heard your conversation." He folded his arms and regarded Anastasi distantly.

"How could he have done that? He keeps to his prayers and his holy books, and shuns strangers. What do the others say, those in my house? Have you spoken to all of them?" Anastasi achieved an easy, pleasant tone of voice but the effort it cost him was formidable. "With my cousin Galina Alexandrevna dead there is only Piotr Grigoreivich or Father Illya to speak for me. Who else has knowledge?"

"And your cousin Xenya Evgeneivna, what of her? What could she tell us? Surely she knows what you have done, living with you as she did," Vasilli reminded him pointedly.

"Her husband might not permit her to come forward in a matter of this sort, even if it were possible for women to give testimony. But I doubt he would consider any request to expose her to public scrutiny, especially now that he is under suspicion himself." It satisfied Anastasi that he had such a reasonable objection to make. He stared at Vasilli, verging on impertinence. "She is a woman, Vasilli, and her report would have to be unofficial. And with that husband, who would believe anything she said, no matter what it was."

"And Boris Feodorovich would prohibit it, in any case," said Vasilli, reluctantly accepting Anastasi's protest. "Very well, there is Blind Piotr and there is Father Illya. Perhaps they are not good witnesses; they are grateful to you for giving them a living and will support your claims. What they say because of their position might not be sufficient to direct suspicion away from you, and therefore from all the House of Shuisky. You are still taking risks that place our whole family in grave danger, Anastasi Sergeivich, at a time when only a fool would indulge in religious intrigue."

"Why does that bother you, dear cousin?" asked Anastasi with false concern. "You have brothers who share your position at Court, and they are as dedicated to you, the leader of our House, as I am." He smiled, his cupid's-bow mouth curving delicately. "Or is that the trouble? Are they unwilling to endorse your claim when theirs are as valid as your own? You are the head of Shuisky, but do your brothers do your bidding willingly, or because they are mandated by law to obey you? Do you come to me because I cannot seek to climb as high as you might?"

Vasilli's face was like stone. "Your implication is reprehensible. As a cadet member of this House, you are unwise to speak to me in that way."

"You are not Czar yet, revered cousin, only a Prince. You are nothing more than a man with ambitions—ambitions that may not be realized, and for that reason if no other you are dangerous to know. I cannot embrace your hopes, not as your brothers ought to, for your gain leads only to hazard for me and my family whether or not you succeed in your plans. Your brothers would advance before your cousins, or have you forgotten that? If you were to gain your prize I would have to leave Moscovy and retire to my estates with my wife and children, or be forever watching behind my back."

"You indulge in fantasies, Anastasi Sergeivich," Vasilli informed him.

"And what do you indulge in, sweet cousin?" asked Anastasi with exaggerated courtesy. "You are aching to be Czar; it is a fever in you; you are delirious with it, and you would dare anything if it brought you to the throne and the fur-trimmed gold. What I have done—if I have done something—is nothing compared to your actions. Or have you convinced yourself that you will succeed where I must fail?"

"You are reckless, Anastasi Sergeivich. And by that you endanger more than your own worthless neck." Vasilli tapped his long fingers together, deliberately refusing to look at Anastasi as he went on. "You are in no position to press for your advantage, not now. You would do better to agree to assist me, and to wait for the opportunity to advance your cause with mine."

"Truly?" Anastasi rocked back on his heels and looked squarely at his handsome cousin as if unaffronted by Vasilli's conduct. "How generous you are, Vasilli Andreivich. To think you would permit me to serve in your cause, and for no other purpose than to move you toward the throne." He chuckled. "I will say this: you are clever, and you are single-minded, and your ambitions are far higher than mine. But yours is not the only claim that might lead to glory."

"You have no chance to rise," said Vasilli, all pretense of good-will abandoned. "You are doing nothing but bringing misfortune to Shuisky by allowing suspicions to fall upon it. I will not allow you to do that. I have it in my power to banish you from this city, and I tell you now, I will exercise that power if you continue in your current activities. If you supported my claim and my actions, you could still achieve a higher place for yourself than you have any prayer of achieving on your own."

"Until you decided I had risen too high, and did away with me, to the advantage of Dmitri or Ivan." Anastasi smiled broadly. "How foolish you must think I am, dear cousin."

"I am coming to believe you *are* foolish," said Vasilli, his eyes steely with hidden anger. "Your actions are not those of a wise man."

"You mean that my actions are not contrived to gain what you seek for yourself. You seek to make me your creature, dependent on you for my position and rank, therefore always at your service." He bowed in the European manner. "You are eager to rule. Very well, that is your desire; I have other goals to pursue."

"What would they be, will you tell me?" Vasilli rose from his chair and walked toward Anastasi. "You will tell me."

"For what reason? So that you can work to thwart me?" He laughed easily. "Vasilli Andreivich, let us agree that you have need of my help, or you would not bother to summon me in this fashion. Certainly your brothers are of no use to you if you seek the throne, for they, too, hanker to be Czar and would climb to the highest station over your corpse. You care nothing for my aspirations, and therefore I suppose that you would require some service from me. I gather that as you no longer trust your brothers, you must appeal to me for what Ivan and Dmitri are unwilling to provide without more recompense than you are willing to give. My title grants you protection from me, is that it, Prince? Or do you worry that Dmitri's wife is sister to Boris Feodorovich's wife, and therefore untrustworthy? A pity you did not make so convenient a match."

"You presume too much," said Vasilli, his eyes hard and his mouth now compressed to a straight line. "My success will not depend upon your assistance; I thought merely that it would benefit the family if you were part of my supporters. If you are not, then I will have nothing more to do with you."

"For that I thank God. You think to rule from the throne, without the endorsement of the Church," said Anastasi bluntly. "But the rule of the Church is greater than the Czar. Do not forget that, Vasilli Andreivich. More than the Czar, the Church is the heart of Russia, and the center of her power. If the Church opposes you, it matters little what position you attain."

"And you assume the Church will support you?" Vasilli asked with obvious disbelief. "What senseless pride you possess, Anastasi Sergeivich, and how dangerous your game is."

"It is no game," said Anastasi affably. "It is your first mistake to suppose that my devotion is a game." He laced his fingers together and pressed them down on his beard. "I strive to save

my soul and preserve the soul of Russia from the terrible heresies
of the Mongols and the Catholics. You care little whether we are
guided by Moscovy or Jerusalem, and bow to the cross, thinking
it is enough." His tone darkened. "It is a pity you do not grieve
for our faith, august cousin. We are besieged by those without
God, from the highest to the lowest. Only our faith and our
unwavering purpose will bring us salvation."

"And yet you permitted Xenya Evgeneivna to marry one of the
Polish embassy," Vasilli pointed out, no longer making a pretense of amicability.

"Xenya Evgeneivna is fortunate to marry at all," said Anastasi,
dismissing the matter. "Since she had no wisdom to become a
nun, she has had to find a husband where she could."

"Yet you expect the Church to reward your support, when you
permit such men as Rakoczy to enter the family." Vasilli was
openly contemptuous now and he glowered at Anastasi. "But
doubtless you have reached satisfaction for all this in your mind
and you do not suppose that anyone could question your motives."

Anastasi heard his cousin out. "It saddens me that we are at
such cross-purposes." He got to his feet, and kissed Vasilli in
good form as if there were no rancor between them. "It was
good of you to ask me here, as it was kind of you to inquire after
my fortunes, and offer me so great an advancement. It is lamen-
table that we cannot come to terms that would benefit both of
us, but such is the case in families when one branch seeks to
advance over the other. There is no argument you can put forth
to convince me to lend you my support. If I shared your vision,
I might abandon my purpose, but since I do not, I see no point
in lingering to cause you distress. You must have others you seek
to draw to your cause. I shall bid you good fortune and leave you
to your quest."

As much as Vasilli wanted to detain Anastasi, he could not
reveal such weakness to his cousin, for Anastasi would certainly
use such dependency against him. So he offered a proper Russian bow and indicated the ikons by the door. "Another time,
perhaps, you will favor me with your company, when we might
discuss our hopes with greater enterprise."

"Perhaps," Anastasi allowed as he crossed himself before the
ikons. Then he repeated the ritual farewell and left Vasilli alone

in his study, taking care to head directly for his own house when he left the Kremlin, so that anyone following him could report to Vasilli that he had made no detour on his way home. This was not the time for him to reveal the depths of his plans, or expose his allies to Vasilli's wrath.

Vasilli remained alone in his study for most of an hour, deep in thought. He was very annoyed at Anastasi, for his plans had required the cooperation of his cousin. His brothers could not be persuaded to set aside their own ambitions in favor of his, and now his cousin had scorned the advancement he proposed. All the devils in Hell, Anastasi was more bothersome than a persistent flea. With his cousin's aid no longer available to him, Vasilli determined to find another way to come to power. More than that, he would decide upon the means to punish Anastasi for the insolence he had shown: it would be gratifying to number Anastasi with his enemies and to include him in his vengeance when the time came for him to ascend to power. The notion was entrancing, and Vasilli indulged himself in his dreams.

This did not seem as impossible as it once had. When his brothers had declined his request for their help, he had feared he could not carry through his visions of rule. His despondency had given way to renewed purpose and careful undertakings. After several months of planning and the suborning of officers and servants, Vasilli was now far more hopeful of success. Given another year he could strengthen his position so that it would be unassailable, so powerful that even his brothers would not dare to move against him. There were a few obstacles to overcome: he would have to discredit Boris Feodorovich Godunov, a task that was not impossible given Boris' Tartar mother. There were many boyars who would never trust Boris. Nikita Romanovich Romanov was a more difficult opponent, having noble position comparable to his own. Czar Ivan's beloved first wife had been Romanova, strengthening Nikita's credentials to rule now that he shared the burden of caring for Czar Feodor Ivanovich, a position the boyars would continue to approve until such time as Vasilli planted the malign seeds of doubt in the court.

It would have been so much easier with Anastasi to act for him, taking on those awkward tasks that increased the risk of discovery. If suspicions fell upon Anastasi he could be sacrificed without giving up all he had gained. Vasilli rose and paced his study, glowering at the ikons as he moved. He did not want to confront the Church, for he would require the approval of the Metropolitan if he were to be Czar, and if the Church would not recognize him, he would not live to reign. Anastasi was worse than a fool to go his own way at such a time, Vasilli decided as he completed his third circuit of the room. Anastasi could have secured himself advancement and power if he had agreed to assist his cousin. Vasilli cursed Anastasi, calling him worse than his enemy. He decided that if Anastasi would not serve him voluntarily, then it would be by compulsion. His contemplation of how he would bring Anastasi to ruin was interrupted by a servant who told him that a servant from the Polish embassy had arrived some time ago and was waiting in the servants' common room to see him.

Vasilli heard this with satisfaction, convinced now that his cause was favored. "Show the messenger here to me," he ordered his servant, and sat down, anticipating the report Yuri would give.

The Poles had insisted that Yuri dress in Polish clothes, and so he arrived in Vasilli's study wearing a wilczura, the hood thrown back and the upper lacing open. He reverenced his host as soon as he had blessed the ikons.

"I had not expected you for another five days," said Vasilli without any of the polite phrases he ordinarily offered visitors; Yuri was a tool and deserved nothing more than his attention. He indicated one of the wooden chairs near the wall. "Sit down and tell me what has happened to bring you to me earlier than usual."

Yuri tugged at his unfamiliar clothes and tried to look affable. "It is a minor thing, great Prince."

The use of his title alarmed Vasilli, but he concealed the reaction with a formidable glower. "If it is a minor thing, then why have you come? Why should I want to know of a minor thing?"

This challenge made Yuri draw back. "I . . . I thought I should inform you."

"No doubt, no doubt," said Vasilli quietly, enforcing his authority with unapproachability. "Tell me what you wish me to know."

"There was a message delivered yesterday, brought from Poland, the first of the spring." He cleared his throat and went on steadily. "It appears that Father Krabbe has been advanced, and will become a Bishop when he returns to Poland. He has been requested to leave Moscovy at the end of the summer. King Istvan has ordered another priest to come in Father Krabbe's place, and this new member of the embassy ought to arrive here in August, or so the King assumes." He was not quite able to meet Vasilli's icy gaze. "They don't know I've seen the dispatch, let alone read it."

"A wise precaution," said Vasilli, already pondering how this information could be turned to advantage. "Is there to be any other change in the embassy?"

"Not that was mentioned in the dispatch. However, I should tell you that Father Pogner has recently refused to send Rakoczy's reports with embassy documents. Father Krabbe has sent them with his own reports to his Archbishop." He coughed once. "Father Pogner cannot forbid him to do it, but he is displeased, and has criticized him."

"That is nothing new," said Vasilli accusingly.

Yuri looked around the room as if seeking salvation. "Father Pogner has never been so adamant as he is now. He is determined to have Rakoczy excluded from the embassy completely. With Father Krabbe leaving, he might be able to achieve his ends. It has been his ambition for some time, but he has now taken steps to bring his wishes to fruition." He shifted in the uncompromising embrace of the chair. "The animosity Father Pogner entertains for Rakoczy is of long standing. I have heard Father Brodski and Father Kornel discuss Father Pogner's determination to be rid of the exile more than once."

"And what have the two priests said?" asked Vasilli, no geniality whatever in his tone. "I do not want to hear gossip."

"They have said that Father Pogner intends to exclude Rakoczy from the embassy; he is to be barred from entrance and then he is to be forbidden the use of embassy functions. If Father Krabbe leaves, none of the rest will aid Rakoczy and it is likely that Father Pogner will have his way." Yuri folded and unfolded his hands. "The embassy will turn against Rakoczy. To some degree the process has already begun among the mission. They are starting to claim Rakoczy has given his soul to Satan."

"They are Catholic priests," said Vasilli, dismissing the matter.

Now Yuri hesitated. "He is not like the Poles," he said at last.

"It is not simply that he is an exile. He keeps to himself, in his study where he has built an oven for smelting, or so he claims."

"Where he told Czar Ivan he made jewels? Is that the oven you mean?" asked Vasilli.

"I suppose so," said Yuri, growing disheartened. "Father Pogner has said that it is wrong to have such an oven. He says that all alchemy is the work of Satan's angels. He has also denounced Rakoczy because he will never take a meal with us, or with anyone. I know that is true, for when I was in his house, the servants all remarked on it, as they praised him for his humility."

"Why did they praise him?" asked Vasilli, knowing that he was supposed to, which irked him, but at the same time too curious not to want to have the answer.

"They said that unlike most Catholics, he was content to keep his quarters without mirrors, showing he had no vanity. They said he was chaste as a monk before he married, and without vice." Yuri realized that for the first time he had Vasilli's full attention, and made the most of it. "His manservant tends to his appearance, like any proper Moscovite, and the servants thought this admirable. They spoke of his clothing as correct for his rank—whatever that may be—and his conduct as without fault. But Father Pogner does not approve. He says that this is proof of Rakoczy's diabolism. He claims that it is not humility but darkest pride that keeps Rakoczy from hanging mirrors in his house. He says that Rakoczy is afraid to see his soul, and therefore will permit no mirrors; he has complained of this to King Istvan." He paused. "Father Krabbe agrees with the Rus, that Rakoczy has become humble in his exile and has turned away from vanity."

"Yet he dresses in magnificent garments and wears precious jewels." Vasilli pulled at his beard. "What do the servants say about that?"

"They admire him," said Yuri with remembered anger. "They say he is showing honor to his exiled House."

"But you do not agree," Vasilli said to encourage Yuri.

Yuri nodded emphatically. "I do not trust Rakoczy. As much as I think Father Pogner is a jealous old man whose claims are those of wrath, I believe that Rakoczy is more than an exiled Count who has learned alchemy. I am certain that he is different in nature than he appears to be. It may be that he has some influence over King Istvan that protects him, or it may be that as a Transylvanian he has obtained the King's approval without deserving it. But whatever it is about Ferenc Rakoczy, I cannot accept that he is only an exiled nobleman striving to make his way in an unfriendly world."

"There are those who would claim you have reason to despise him, and as a servant you are seeking to strike at a master who dismissed you with favor, which casts a poor light on your assertions." Vasilli's eyes were speculative and his manner was less daunting. "What is your reply?"

"I know what I saw," said Yuri stubbornly. "He is not like other men; he has declared the same himself. His servants would tell you his ways are unfamiliar. He is . . . foreign."

"He is Transylvanian," said Vasilli, growing disgusted with Yuri. "So is King Istvan of Poland. Is there nothing else?"

Yuri realized he had lost Vasilli's interest, and strove to recapture it. "Yes, but I hardly know a way to put it into words."

"You are unfamiliar with his ways," said Vasilli, dismissing the subject; the hope that Yuri might have stumbled upon something of interest had faded.

But Yuri shook his head vigorously. "No. There is more, and whatever it is, Father Pogner fears it as well as hates it. He has contempt for Rakoczy's wealth, but his fear is another matter. Anyone who has worked for Rakoczy must have felt it at least once. I don't think Father Pogner knows how great his fear is; it is the dread of one in the presence of great evil." He clasped his hands together, hoping that Vasilli would be persuaded to bring Rakoczy down; he knew how sweet revenge would be. "Father Krabbe says that Rakoczy saved his life when he was struck with putrid lungs, that without him, he would have died long before he reached Moscovy; but Father Pogner refuses to believe it, and says that it was God's will in the hands of a corrupt tool that saved him."

"Father Pogner is a fanatic Catholic," said Vasilli, but once again was listening to what Yuri told him.

"He is, and he is as arrogant as a boyar with a purse of gold and two hundred serfs," Yuri said. "But he dreads Rakoczy, for all he would deny it. I can see it in his eyes."

Vasilli stroked his beard. "And what does this suggest to you?"

"It suggests to me that Rakoczy is dispensable for the embassy." Yuri stood straighter and patted the front of his wilczura as if to assure himself that the Polish garment was still in place.

"If anything happened to Father Krabbe, Rakoczy would surely lose his link with the Polish embassy, and it is possible that Father Pogner would blame him for Father Krabbe's misfortune." It was the only way he had hit upon that could ruin Rakoczy. Now he hoped that Vasilli Shuisky's ambitions would lead him to be Yuri's tool as he was Vasilli's.

"But Father Krabbe is being recalled. Why should anything be done to him when he will shortly be gone?" Vasilli asked, once again feeling a quickening of interest.

"Because he is known to be Rakoczy's advocate in the embassy. A blow struck at him would be recognized as a blow struck at Rakoczy as well." He beamed at Vasilli. "And if it appeared that it was Rakoczy who had done the deed, then he would be condemned by the act itself."

Now Vasilli was truly curious. "But why would that be?"

Yuri was glad that he had thought the matter out so carefully. "If there seemed to be a falling out, if it were assumed that Father Krabbe no longer defended Rakoczy but now shared the condemnation of the rest, then his . . . injuries might be credited to Rakoczy."

Vasilli nodded slowly, his striking features showing true vitality for the first time since Yuri had entered his study. "And what would Rakoczy's disgrace gain that would benefit me?"

This was the part that made Yuri sweat; if his gamble succeeded, he would triumph beyond his hopes. "Could the circumstances of Father Krabbe's trouble be handled correctly, they may be made to embarrass Boris Godunov."

There was silence in the study. Then Vasilli asked, "And how is that possible?" the words drawn out as if he were bored, though his eyes were alert and acquisitive.

The first hurdle was behind him: Yuri took a deep breath and continued with greater confidence. "I have hit upon a way," he said. "It will seem that Father Krabbe was about to reveal something damning about Rakoczy, and that with the help of Boris Feodorovich, he was prevented from speaking."

"He will have to be silent, this Father Krabbe, if the plan is to succeed," Vasilli pointed out. Perhaps there was a way to salvage his ambitions without needing years to accomplish his self-created goal. It shocked him that Yuri would do so much to aid him when Anastasi had done so little.

"Very true." Yuri swallowed nervously.

"You speak of killing a priest," said Vasilli with unaccustomed bluntness.

"A Catholic, great Prince," said Yuri with a shrug.

Vasilli smiled, eyes frigid. "Yes. A Catholic."

Text of a letter from Father Illya to Xenya Evgeneivna, sent to her through her husband.

To the gracious noble lady, Xenya Evgeneivna, my blessings.

It distresses me to have to send you word in this way, but I have been warned by Anastasi Sergeivich to have no dealings with you until certain questions in regard to the Polish embassy have been answered. In recent days there have been rumors which have caused Anastasi Sergeivich much concern, the more so because he has been unable to trace them to their source.

It would seem that your husband has been wholly condemned by King Istvan's mission, and that he may soon have to answer official inquiries on the subject of his actions here. There are those who have spoken out against Rakoczy as a dangerous person, working against the good of Russia. For the sake of your soul and for the piety you have shown, I have gone against the orders of your kinsman in order to warn you that you stand in danger while you live within the foreigner's house. Let me urge you to leave Moscovy at once and take refuge with your mother's relatives, so that the fate of your husband may not be visited upon you, as well. It is May; a visit would not be thought odd, and would spare you much unhappiness.

I will ask God and the Virgin to lend you wisdom in this perilous time, and I will beg the Angels to keep watch over you. God permits us to suffer because of the suffering of His Son, so that we may better come to know His mercy. I admonish you to remember the devotion of your father and the honor of his death so that you will be able to understand God's purpose in the trials visited upon you, and bow humbly to God for what He has demanded of you; more was required of Our Savior.

In the Name of God, His Son, and Holy Spirit
Father Illya
The Feast of the Great Doctor Saint Grigori of Nazianzus

5

They were less than twenty paces from the Beautiful Market Square, but the narrow street shadowed them as the night alone could not do.

"Hurry," Father Krabbe admonished his escort, as he had done since they left Rakoczy's house a quarter of an hour ago. "It is very late, and we will have to answer for our tardiness; it is bad enough that the carriage was damaged."

"That is why we're taking this street instead of the wider one," Yuri reminded him, fingering the ring in his pocket; he had purloined it from Rakoczy's house while Father Krabbe had sat with Rakoczy, conversing and drinking the wine his host offered him. "I know this district well," he assured the priest honestly, and went on less truthfully, "This will bring us to the embassy more quickly."

"It will not be quickly enough, I fear," said Father Krabbe with a sour laugh. "Father Pogner expected me some three hours since. He will be very displeased." He kept up a steady, rapid pace, staying to the middle of the road in order to take advantage of what little light was afforded by the gibbous moon and the special brightness of the June night.

"Father Pogner will understand the delay, when you explain it to him," said Yuri as he hurried after Father Krabbe, doing his best to soothe him. "Embassy carriages have been damaged before. He knows what these streets are like. I will describe the condition of the wheel and the axle, and he will be sympathetic to your predicament. He must understand that your delay could not be helped."

But Father Krabbe was not so sanguine. As he extended his pace as much as he dared in the night he complained, "I can't imagine how the wheel came to break. The uneven paving did not seem enough to cause the spokes to collapse as they did. It doesn't make sense. The carriage has been over far worse roads before and the spokes did not—"

"You know what it is," said Yuri, all but running to keep up with Father Krabbe. "A carriage will endure one rough journey after another and appear to be none the worse for it, and then, without warning, it will come apart at the slightest jarring. This is another such occasion, that is all." He was almost abreast of Father Krabbe now, breathing quickly. He could see that he had not succeeded in mollifying the Jesuit.

"I have been ordered—we have all been ordered—not to venture out at night without a carriage. If it would not have meant a longer delay, I would have accepted Rakoczy's offer of his carriage, but it would take another half hour to have the horses put-to to ready it." He waved away the mosquitoes that hummed around him. "I would prefer to obey Father Pogner when I can."

Yuri was well-aware of the meaning behind the words, but he said, "It must be your visit to Rakoczy that will cause Father Pogner greater annoyance than the damage to the carriage. He will not like it that Rakoczy is planning to tend to the repairs himself." Whether Father Pogner approved of this or not, Yuri could not like it, for he feared that the Transylvanian would not accept the explanation he had been given: that the carriage had struck a hidden rock in one of the deep ruts, and that had broken the wheel, falling over as a result, not five doors away from Rakoczy's house. He had not anticipated that: to Yuri's consternation, Rakoczy's servants had hurried to lend their assistance, and to claim the obligation to repair the carriage. A close inspection of the spokes and axle might reveal where the woodworker's saw had weakened six of them, and he was fairly certain that Rakoczy would not be content until he had looked at the vehicle for himself. He knew his work would not escape those dark, knowing eyes.

"Which street is that?" asked Father Krabbe as he straggled to a halt, intruding on Yuri's apprehension with this nervous inquiry. "I don't recognize it. Shouldn't we be at Bread-seller's Street?"

"It's just beyond," said Yuri at once. "There's another turn, and then the little square, you know the one, with the yellow-fronted bakery? We've come from a different direction, that's all." He glanced around, hoping that the priest had not noticed the ancient church they had passed twenty strides back, for then he would realize that they were going the opposite direction to the one Father Krabbe supposed. His pulse grew faster at the thought of the risk he was taking—if he succeeded, Vasilli Shuisky would give him gold for a reward and would make him his servant and confidant; from that position Yuri knew he would be able to advance in station and wealth. With the protection of the formidable Shuiskys, Yuri would never again have to be ashamed at his heritage. For the first time since he had come to Moscovy, Yuri was persuaded he would come far enough in life to spite his father.

"These small streets twist so," said Father Krabbe, a little breathless with his determined walk. "I can see how apprentices become lost."

"Moscovy has many secrets," said Yuri, grateful that Father Krabbe could not see his smile.

"Truly," said Father Krabbe, faltering a bit from the pace and from his own growing disorientation. "But I am sure that we ought to have turned right before now. We are going east—look at the moon, and you can see that."

"You must be mistaken," said Yuri, hearing stealthy sounds behind them. He kept moving, his confidence returning.

Father Krabbe heard them, too. "What was that?" he demanded. "Did you hear anything?"

"Dogs? Rats, perhaps," Yuri suggested. "Better they should be dogs. In these streets the rats are as hungry as wolves."

"Rats!" Father Krabbe shook his head. "Why should there be rats here? Or dogs, for that matter?"

"As you have said," Yuri reminded him at once, "the streets twist. Near a bakery there are always rats, foraging. Shortly we will once again bear to the south, to come into the square. If we could climb through walls, we would be inside that yellow-fronted bakery. You need not be troubled." His tone was so blandishing that it caught Father Krabbe's attention.

"You have no reason to humor me, Yuri," he said with severity. "It is fitting that you show the way. This is, as you say, your city. But you cannot blame me if I am concerned."

"Of course not," said Yuri, moving a few steps ahead of Father Krabbe as they continued along the old, uneven stones. "I would be bothered if you were as easily misdirected as Father Brodski."

Since Father Brodski was recognized as having almost no

sense of direction, Father Krabbe did his best to chuckle through his panting and his increasing unease. "Yes, I would like to think I have found my way in more places than he; I hope I am more attentive than he is, certainly." He crossed himself. "And may God forgive me for my pride."

"It is no pride to know what abilities God has given you, it is gratitude," said Yuri, repeating what Father Igor had told him all through his childhood. Never had he believed it more than now, but not because of Father Krabbe's sense of direction. He felt the welling glow of achievement and decided that it was not possible for him to fail after all had gone so well.

"Possibly not," said Father Krabbe, who had received other instruction in his youth. He stumbled and caught himself, and this time he was not distracted by Yuri's manner. "This *is* the wrong direction."

"It will be right soon enough," said Yuri testily.

"We ought to return to the Beautiful Market Square and take the main street. It may be longer, but I am sure of it. This does not appear—" Father Krabbe was about to turn around when Yuri seized him by the shoulder.

"Not quite yet, good Jesuit Father," he said, the subservience gone from his demeanor and his voice hard. He came nearer to Father Krabbe, and for the first time menace was in his stance. "There is something I require of you first."

Father Krabbe stared at him in shock, his vitals turning cold in the warm night. "I am a priest. I have nothing worth taking, you Russian fool. Even my crucifix is only silver," he declared.

"Ah, there you are wrong," Yuri corrected him mildly, then whistled, the sound low and sinuous. "You have something I want very much, and I will have it from you or die myself." He had drawn his long coachman's knife from its scabbard and now he held it in front of him. "You will have to forgive me for my sin, Father Krabbe." His soft laughter was the most terrifying sound Father Krabbe had ever heard.

There were two men in the street behind them now, big men stinking of sweat and strong drink, one older, one younger, both capably brutal. They approached confidently, one of them offering the suggestion of a salute to Yuri.

"I'm not alone here, Father, and you are," said Yuri with satisfaction. "You will not escape."

"Yuri . . ." Father Krabbe was about to step back when he realized that the two big men were closing in on them. His voice grew sharper. "What is it you want? Tell me. What?" He made himself speak more calmly as his fear grew sharper. "You need only tell me, Yuri, and I will do whatever is in my power to aid you. You have my sworn—"

"You're doing that already," said Yuri, covering the distance between them once again. "You will help me very much."

"But how?" Father Krabbe glanced over his shoulder, fright making his eyes wide and his hands wet. "What can you hope to accomplish—" He screamed as Yuri's knife sank through his habit into his abdomen. He staggered, trying to reach the knife, to undo what it had done. "Yuri!" he gasped.

"Die, you godless Jesuit," whispered Yuri, all the anger and wretchedness of his early years fueling his deed. "Die, and make my fortune."

Father Krabbe tottered, crying out as Yuri withdrew the knife and used it once more, again striking deep into his abdomen, ripping. The weight of the blow was enough to drive him to his knees, but the knife in Yuri's hand gave him mock support. The priest sagged forward into Yuri's arms as the full impact of pain possessed him.

"Pull him off me," Yuri ordered the two men breathlessly. "We have to drag his vitals out. I want his intestines pulled across the street so that the rats will eat them tonight and apprentices stumble over them in the morning." Now that he had actually given the orders, Yuri felt a surge of engulfing joy. To have such power! he had known it would be sweet, this power, for life was so bitter without it. But the gratification was much greater than he had hoped. "Hurry, take him."

The two hired ruffians moved to comply, one of them taking Father Krabbe under his arms, the other methodically cutting his clothes open. "It's a shame all this is Polish priest's wear. It's a waste. We could sell it if it were Russian," he observed to Yuri.

"No!" Yuri said. "You will take nothing from him. Nothing. He must be found dead, not robbed." He fingered the ring once more, smirking as he thought of the use he would make of it. It pleased him to contemplate how much a little ring could do, properly used.

"Still, it is a shame such goods will be wasted," the older man said.

"They won't be wasted," said the younger in disgust. "The first man who finds the corpse will strip it."

"That's not important," Yuri rebuked him. "You're being paid to help me kill him. You won't suffer because of this. You lose no value leaving his clothes on him, and his property. I want nothing here that will cause anyone to suppose that I had anything to do with his death."

"Yes, little boyar," said the second sarcastically.

Father Krabbe had barely heard this. There was a rushing in his ears and his senses swam in an effort to carry him away from the enormity of the pain in his vitals. The cold that had invaded him was increasing, sinking into the very marrow of his bones. He tried to cross himself, but his arms were held in a restraining grip and nothing he did could break free of it.

"There," said the younger man as he stood back from Father Krabbe, the front of his body exposed, his two wounds bleeding heavily, the deeper one pumping out heavy gouts with every heartbeat. "Gut wounds," he said contemptuously. "He won't last long, bleeding like that."

Yuri came close to his victim. "I'll start. Be ready to pull when I tell you to."

The two men nodded, and the older took a stronger grip on Father Krabbe. "He's going to fight when you start to work on him. They always do when you go for their guts."

The second added, "And they stink, guts do. Especially when you cut into them, like you did."

Yuri did not hear this as criticism. "No matter. At this hour there's no one to notice."

"Except the rats," said the older, steadying himself.

"Of course," said Yuri, and prepared to slice into Father Krabbe as he had done with pigs at home.

The priest knew the knife as heat more than pain, a heat that did not warm him but made the cold greater, and for a little time it robbed him of his breath and the holy words he wanted so desperately to say in order to show God his devotion. The weight increased, comprehensive, enveloping, and he felt the splattering of his blood like a hot rain. He choked on half-uttered prayers. It was inconceivable to him that he was being murdered.

Then the pain was gone and he no longer bothered with breathing, or trying to pray, or life.

"He's going," said the first man, sounding disappointed. "No fight."

"It doesn't matter," Yuri told him, breathless with effort and excitement. Too late he thought about the blood on his clothes and boots, and realized he would have to account for it in some way. He reached into his pocket and drew out the ring which he pressed into Father Krabbe's right hand, hoping that it would not fall or be stolen.

"Slit him open," ordered Yuri, stepping back from Father Krabbe's corpse.

The older of the two men sighed and tugged his knife out of his belt. "As you wish," he said. He exchanged glances with the other, and then they bent over the body, ignoring the stench as they cut into the flesh.

"Good," said Yuri softly. "Very good." He had paid these men in gold, and had feared it was a useless extravagance, but now he decided he had done the right thing, the wise thing. Father Krabbe's death would point to Rakoczy, and Vasilli Shuisky would be as pleased as Father Pogner.

As the younger man straightened up, he turned in Yuri's direction. "What else, little boyar?"

"Cut him, oh, mercy of God, cut him," said Yuri, excitement rushing his words. "Slice him. Make him look as if Mongols had been here."

The older man laughed unpleasantly. "Mongols? But you want to cast guilt on the foreign exile. Don't you?"

Yuri nodded once. "Yes. Yes, I want to do that," he agreed. It was hard to remember his purpose now that the priest was actually dead. He wanted to shout his victory to the world, to let everyone know what he had done; it was an effort to remain silent.

"Yes," seconded the older man. "So we will break his bones instead. That way you can say it was the exile who did him, for Poles are always riding horses over their foes, aren't they? Mongols cut the corpses to pieces, Poles break them."

"Yes," whispered Yuri. "You're right. Yes, it must seem that Poles did this. You must make it appear . . . you know how to make it appear." He folded his arms to keep from shaking. His

face was pale with an excitement he could not name. His throat
tightened against a scream.

"Yes, little boyar," said the younger man, and brought his heel
down on Father Krabbe's chest; the ribs broke audibly.

"It will not take long," said the older man.

"No; not long," the younger agreed as he smashed Father
Krabbe's hand with a length of wood he had picked up; it was
the hand into which Yuri had put Rakoczy's ring.

The older man kicked Father Krabbe in the side of the head;
there was a soft, pulpy crack as the skull gave way.

"Good," said Yuri. "Very good."

"Priests are soft," the younger man complained as he drubbed
Father Krabbe's thigh. "There is no strength in them."

Yuri watched the beating, his pulse hard in his temples. As the
priest's body was distorted and battered, Yuri could no longer
quell his elation. He grinned with ferocious pride, and droned a
hum to himself. Father Krabbe was nothing more than discarded
offal, and all because of him. He bounced on his heels. How
marvelous it was to have the might of death at his command!

At last the older man straightened up, his face expressionless.
"Is there anything else?"

"I don't think so," said Yuri, disappointment robbing him of
his relish. "No, I suppose this is enough."

"The little boyar likes what he sees," said the younger, and his
mouth twitched. "What does it feel like, little boyar?"

"It is necessary," said Yuri brusquely. He could not take his
eyes off Father Krabbe's corpse, the gaping wound where the
blood was already starting to congeal, black in the wan summer
night.

"For you, yes, it is necessary," said the younger man with
contempt. He hefted the length of wood. "Do you like what this
does? Does it please you?"

"It is necessary," Yuri repeated, too caught up in what had
happened to realize the danger of his position. He knew that the
two men were taunting him, but he refused to be intimidated. "It
was ordered by highly placed men. I have carried out my orders,
with your help."

"And you enjoy your work," said the younger. He was less
than two steps away from Yuri now, so that when he swung the
length of wood, it caught Yuri hard on the side of his head,

striking with such force that his arm shuddered with the shock.

He had just seen the movement of the younger man's arm when he felt the blow, enormous, as if a cannon had exploded in his ear. He dropped at once into a lifeless heap.

"We can take his clothes," said the older with satisfaction. "And the money he carries. Make sure you get his boots as well."

"They're bloody," said the younger as he wrestled with Yuri's body.

"So are his clothes. No one will notice, and if they do, we will say that he had been to the swine market; one always gets bloody there." The older set about his work methodically, pulling Yuri out straight before taking off his Polish garments. When he reached the pleated camisa, he remarked, "The linen's very good. It will fetch a high price."

"What about the priest?" asked the younger as he tugged on the boots.

"It's bad luck to rob a priest. Leave him be." He had the long Polish doublet off him now, and paused in the act of rolling it up. "It's bad luck to rob a priest."

"He's Catholic," said the younger. "It means nothing."

The older glared. "I said leave him be. Including the crucifix. No one wants it, anyway."

"It's silver. We could melt it down. Evgeni would do it for half the value, and he would say nothing." The younger man reached out and lifted the crucifix from beside Father Krabbe's ruined head. "If we don't take it, someone else will."

"Bad cess to them," said the older. "I will not have it said that we defile godly men, even Catholics." He paused in his task to cross himself. "God knows what we are, but He will not pardon us for robbing Him."

The younger man shrugged. "It would buy food for a month, for what Evgeni would pay," he pointed out.

"Leave it," the older insisted.

"All right," the younger conceded. "But it bothers me."

They finished their work in silence, bundling up their spoils with practiced haste, and as soon as they were done, they fled silently into the warren of alleyways of that quarter of Moscovy, leaving Father Krabbe's mutilated body beside the nude Yuri.

By the time the first church bells sounded in the predawn of a summer morning, rats had helped themselves to bits of the two corpses. They were still gnawing at Yuri's fingers when two early-rising bakers' apprentices found the bodies and gave the alarm with their screams.

First the local priests rushed from their little church dedicated to Saint Tatiana the Martyr, and upon seeing the body of the Catholic priest, refused to bless or pray for the two dead men. They reluctantly agreed to stand guard over the bodies until one of the Czar's Guards could be sent for to attend to the men.

"Best send word to the Catholics, too; they will want to claim their priest," said the baker, who had been summoned by the apprentices. "They will not want to have him lie here in the street."

"Yes," said one of the three Orthodox priests guarding the bodies, and he started off at once for the Kremlin, grateful to be away from the presence of death. He did not know more of the fallen priest but that he was Catholic, and therefore he decided to go to the greatest concentration of Catholic priests in Moscovy, the Polish embassy; he reasoned that surely they would know if a Catholic priest was missing. It took him more than half an hour to find the house where the Jesuits were, and by that time the streets bustled with merchants and farmers bound for market with goods and produce and stock of every kind.

The servant who answered the door of the Poles' house had clearly been awake for some time; there were circles around his eyes and his embroidered rubashka was stained with food. He regarded the Orthodox priest with a combination of apprehension and curiosity, for Orthodox clergy rarely came here. "Yes, Father? What do you want here?"

"Are the Jesuits available?" asked the priest, adding, "I am Father Jascha, of Saint Tatiana the Martyr's."

"They are at Mass," said the servant.

"I fear this may be urgent," said Father Jascha, and faltered. He crossed himself before he went on. "We may have found one of the . . . Catholic priests. At least the man is dressed like a priest—"

"Found?" the servant asked.

"In the street, near my church. There are two—"

The servant saved Father Jascha from more floundering. "One of the Polish embassy did not return to this house last night. There has been much concern for his safety. We have sent a messenger to the . . . the place he was visiting. I thought you were bringing an answer to the—" He broke off as he heard someone behind him.

Father Brodski was pale and his thinning hair uncombed, but he greeted Father Jascha in good form, asking God to extend his blessing to the Orthodox priest as well as to all Christians. "I heard you talking," he said to his servant. "I had hoped it was Father Krabbe."

"It may be," said Father Jascha quietly, and stared at the Jesuit for a short time, then began his explanation again. "We have found two men . . . one of them is in a Jesuit habit."

"And where is he? And who is the other? Father Krabbe was in the company of our servant Yuri." Father Brodski pulled at his lower lip, reading Father Jascha's expression more expertly than he wanted to. "The men you have found—what is the matter?"

Father Jascha hesitated, disliking his duty. "They were attacked."

"Attacked. Killed?" said Father Brodski, wanting an answer other than the one he knew he would receive.

Another priest appeared at his shoulder. Father Kovnovski was ready to upbraid Father Brodski for leaving Mass, but one look at Father Jascha stopped the rebuke. "Christ and His Angels, what's the matter?"

"I am sorry to tell you," said Father Jascha. "But it may be that this is not your priest. I do not know the man. He may have stolen your priest's clothes, or have come by the habit in some other way." He said this quickly, trying to soften the blow.

Father Kovnovski looked dismayed. "What are you saying?" he demanded of the Orthodox priest.

But it was Father Brodski who answered the question. "He says he has found two men who were attacked. It may be that they are Father Krabbe and Yuri." He crossed himself again as he said this.

Father Kovnovski echoed the gesture. "Poor Christians, whoever they are."

"So it would seem," said Father Jascha, and turned as a black-clad man on a grey horse rode up to the Polish house, the hooves of the horse clattering on the cobblestones of the courtyard.

"Good morning, Hrabia," said Father Brodski.

Rakoczy swung out of the saddle and strode to the open door, leading his horse by the rein. "I regret this intrusion, but from what I've been told, Father Krabbe did not return to the embassy last night. That was the gist of the information I received. Since Father Krabbe left my house not long before midnight, I share your concern for him. Your messenger this morning was so distraught, I thought it best if I came myself to lend you whatever assistance I can," he said directly to the two Poles, and then turned to Father Jascha. "Mercy and grace of God on you for this day, Father." If he was surprised at seeing an Orthodox priest in the Polish embassy courtyard, he did not mention it.

The Orthodox priest acknowledged the greeting formally, finding some consolation in the traditional phrases. "And may He guide and comfort you through all your life, my son."

"Father Jascha has just arrived," Father Brodski said for Rakoczy's benefit. "He may know something of Father Krabbe."

"I pray I am mistaken," said Father Jascha softly.

"I trust he does," said Rakoczy at the same time. "I have been overseeing the repair of your carriage, and I believe he may have come to some trouble." He fell silent as a third Jesuit approached: Father Pogner was glaring at the gathering in the doorway.

"I hope," said the senior member of the embassy, "that there is some good reason for your presence?" He directed his gaze at Rakoczy and made no excuse for his abrupt manner.

Rakoczy was unperturbed; he regarded all three Jesuits, singling out no one. "I fear there may be," he said, "for it seems that the accident that disabled your carriage was no accident at all, but a deliberate act. I have discovered places in the spokes of two wheels and on the axle where the wood is sawn almost in half."

"Impossible!" exclaimed Father Pogner.

"Sadly, no," said Rakoczy. "The carriage would not have gone very far; the first real jolt . . ." He made a gesture to finish his thoughts. "I must conclude someone wanted Father Krabbe on foot."

Father Pogner was about to question this, but was silenced by Father Jascha. "There are two men in the street. They were killed by robbers, for one of them has been stripped. The other wears a Jesuit habit and was used cruelly." He crossed himself once more at the memory of Father Krabbe's body.

As the Catholics also blessed themselves in the left-shoulder-right-shoulder Roman manner, Rakoczy spoke for them all. "Then I suppose we had better go and see."

Father Pogner drew himself up, unwilling to follow any suggestion of Rakoczy's, no matter how reasonable. "Why should we dignify this insult? It is impossible that such a thing would happen to one of this mission."

Rakoczy was about to ask Father Jascha to lead the way, but he paused, his dark eyes resting on Father Pogner for a long while before he said, "Is it. I trust you may be right." And all the while he knew in his sinews that the arrogant priest was wrong.

Text of an anonymous letter from Anastasi Sergeivich Shuisky to Istvan Bathory of Poland.

To the honorable and revered Transylvanian, King of Poland, most genuine greetings from your true friend in Moscovy.

I do not like the necessity of informing you that one of your embassy has met with misfortune, but such has come to pass: Father Milan Krabbe was found murdered in the streets of Moscovy ten days ago. His Russian servant Yuri died with him. Father Pogner and the alchemist Rakoczy identified the two men, although both said that the priest was almost unrecognizable. It is Rakoczy's contention that most of the treatment meted out to the priest occurred after he was dead, and for Father Krabbe's sake, I pray that Rakoczy is correct.

Perhaps members of your embassy have already informed you, and provided what few details we know of the crime: the servant was naked, and killed by a blow to the head that broke his skull. The priest was beaten and slaughtered like an animal, though he was still in his clothes when he was found. These deaths have caused a scandal at Court, for it is rumored that the killing of these men was brought about at the instigation of those opposed to the Polish presence in this city. Already there have been veiled accusations made at various nobles and the Metropolitan. There are also those who say it is a clever ploy to make it appear that they were the victims of Your Majesty's enemies and that instead they were killed at the orders of one of the members of the embassy. This is the more controversial theory, but it is gaining followers, for the court would prefer to think ill of Poles than Rus.

At the promptings of certain high-ranking nobles, blame is being cast on your countryman, Ferenc Rakoczy. It is said that he was the last to see the two men alive, that they were deprived of the protection of their carriage while at his house, and that his claim that the carriage was damaged deliberately was actually the result of his own nefarious deeds, which put Father Krabbe at the mercy of the desperate men who roam the streets at night.

The strongest proponent of this accusation is Prince Vasilli Shuisky, one of the most powerful and ambitious nobles of the Court. He has reason to want to see all Poles discredited, and it would serve his purpose to have the exile or the Jesuits answer for the crimes than any of his adherents at Court. He is hungry to rise in position, and he is prepared to undertake crimes and mendacity if it will improve his chances to replace Czar Feodor on the throne. For make no doubt about it, Your Majesty, this Vasilli Shuisky will stop at nothing to be Czar. To accomplish his ends, he must discredit both Godunov and Romanov, and as Godunov is the friend and Court patron of your Rakoczy, he undoubtedly plans to use this opportunity to show that Godunov's judgment is poor and his motives untrustworthy. Once Godunov is fallen, he will confront Romanov, who is not powerful enough to stop him.

Be warned that your countryman Rakoczy is in grave danger. He will be made the scapegoat for all of Shuisky's actions. Only if Vasilli Shuisky is stopped can Rakoczy be spared the vengeance Shuisky seeks to visit on all your embassy, starting with Rakoczy but intended to eventually account for all the Jesuits who have come here to serve your interests in Moscovy. To that end, I offer to do all that I can, for although I am not placed as highly at Court as the mighty ones, there are yet things I can do to prevent the worst from happening. All I ask is your consideration when the moment is right. At that time, I will reveal myself to you, and be proud of your friendship and the honor of the Polish crown. It would be the satisfaction of a lifetime for me to aid you in bringing down the treacherous Vasilli Shuisky, and made greater by vindicating the Polish mission to this Court.

Let me encourage you to take action now if you wish to help

Rakoczy. If it were not for his friendship with Godunov, he would be imprisoned by now. As it is, Godunov cannot long afford to protect the Transylvanian. Therefore any action you may wish to undertake on his behalf must be done soon or I fear it will no longer be possible to spare him from the demands of the laws of Moscovy. I would name myself your champion, but without support I am helpless against such puissant nobles as Vasilli Shuisky. If you have men here to defend your embassy, authorize them to come to Rakoczy's defense immediately or be prepared to condemn your alchemist to torture and an un-marked grave. Already there are petitions to Czar Feodor de-manding that Rakoczy answer for his transgressions before the Court and before God.

From one who seeks to benefit you

6

After he had blessed the ikons and recited the proper phrases of greeting, Boris Godunov came at once to the point of his visit. "I wish I did not have to tell you this, my friend: I don't know how much longer I can keep the Court from turning against you, not without your help. Between Vasilli Shuisky and the Metropoli-tan, there are many who have decided that you are no longer acceptable to them." His Asiatic features were creased with con-cern and he gestured apologetically. "They are dissatisfied with the foreigners at Court, in any case, except for the English. You are not the only one to feel their suspicions."

"But I receive more of them than most," said Rakoczy as he bowed to his guest and closed the door against the day; the summer sun was glarey and the air heavy and close.

"You have been more noticeable than most, and now that notice is not to your advantage," Boris allowed.

"Do they want more jewels, or bells, do you think?" Rakoczy asked with light irony. Then he added, "I do not mean to slight your friendship, Boris Feodorovich, for you have defended me most . . . diligently. You are not bargaining with our friendship. In my experience, that is rare." His experience was much longer than he would ever admit to the Czar's governmental adviser and guardian, and the compromises he had seen were too many to number.

Boris made a gesture of dismissal. "I do as I think is wisest. My wife says I am a fool to speak with you, for there are those who would think that suspicious."

"Your wife is a prudent woman, and she knows the court from her powerful family," said Rakoczy to his guest. He stood in his reception room, his silken black dolman edged in silver embroidery. Midsummer sun shining in the windows made sharp patterns of light on the floor; Boris paced around him, passing from brightness to shadow to brightness again. The light striking his kaftan made the golden fabric glisten. "For the sake of our friendship, I should endorse her advice. But to speak truly, I am pleased you are here."

"I am, as well," said Boris uneasily. "But I am not certain that I can do anything more to help you."

Rakoczy touched his hands together; aside from a slight frown his manner was calm. "That is worrisome. I had hoped there might be one or two things you would still be willing to do. They aren't trivial, or tests of your loyalty."

"Oh, it is not a question of willingness, my exiled friend, it is whether I am able to. And loyalty is not the issue. The Court is not likely to permit me to act on your behalf." Boris paused, gesturing toward the open window. "There are rumors all over the city about the death of Father Krabbe. The wind is alive with them, and they grow louder every day. Even among those who despise Poles and Catholics, and they are many, there is a belief that we must act to avenge his murder. Some claim that Father Krabbe will curse them in Heaven if his murderer is not brought to answer for his crime."

"But the Court is always rife with rumors," said his host reasonably. "You yourself said, when I was making jewels for Czar Ivan, that I must not be drawn into the constant speculation. What makes these developments any different than the usual whispers and scandal?"

Boris paused and nodded his head twice in a measured way.

"They *are* different. This is no mere indulgence of spite or envy or ambition. These rumors are to the point, and they serve little purpose to advance those spreading them. They are more specific and thus more damaging. The Court is affronted. And sadly the Poles have taken up the same theme, all but accusing you of murdering Father Krabbe and his escort."

"Yuri," Rakoczy supplied.

"Yes. There are those who claim it is significant that he came from your household, and that you made him your spy in the Polish mission, and you killed him because of what he knew about you." It was not easy for Boris to admit so much; his voice cracked as if his throat were dry. "That is the most prevalent accusation, in any case."

"But there are other accusations, more serious ones, aren't there," said Rakoczy with certainty, his face revealing little more than polite interest. "What are they saying: will you tell me?"

Boris hesitated. "In friendship I would prefer not."

"It is in friendship I ask it. If I do not know what is being said, I cannot refute it." Rakoczy's smile was fleeting. "It is a kindness to tell me, Boris Feodorovich."

Clearly, Boris was not entirely convinced of this. He stared at the floor, and at last made up his mind. "Very well, but I do not like it. They are saying that you had a falling out with Father Krabbe, that you required him to act for you against his vows, and for that he turned on you in order to save his soul and do penance for the sin of apostasy. It is said that because you are an alchemist, you are a servant of the devil, and Father Krabbe was not able to forgive you for your sins any longer. When you found this out, you placed Yuri in the embassy to act as your spy, and in time arranged that Father Krabbe should die and Yuri as well, to protect you and increase your power. They were sacrifices, or so it is reckoned, which is why Father Krabbe was so badly beaten as well as disemboweled, and why they were found—"

"Of all the ways I might kill someone," said Rakoczy in a low, inward voice, "the one I would never use is disemboweling." He touched his belt and felt the scars beneath it; even now he could recall the agony of his death three and a half thousand years before.

Boris heard something in Rakoczy's voice that made him hurry on. "—why they were found in such a poor part of the city. Some claim that you have gathered a gang of desperate men to serve you, men who will maim and kill at your command, and that you will order the deaths of others who have earned your enmity. Poor people are always willing to sell their souls for a few pieces of gold and a week of chicken soup."

"If that is what I did and why I did it, the act was ill-conceived," said Rakoczy, his manner remote as his eyes. "Why would I do something so foolish and obvious, supposing for the moment that the suspicions were true? Or does anyone venture to guess that?"

"They say you worship Satan, and there need be no reason in anything you do if it serves the cause of Satan," Boris answered, his words a bit muffled.

"So they are willing to think me a dupe as well as a fool," said Rakoczy in a resigned tone. "Is that because I am foreign, or because Father Pogner speaks against me?"

"They do not wish to listen to foreign priests, but Father Pogner tells them what they want to hear, and so they praise him for his learning and wisdom, and hail him as a foreigner who understands the ways of the Rus." Boris was disgusted; he turned hard on his heel and began to pace in the opposite direction. "Nikita Romanovich has visited him twice, both times in the company of Vasilli Andreivich. They come away claiming they share Father Pogner's indignation. Whether this is a pose or their sentiments, I cannot decide."

At the mention of Romanov and Shuisky, Rakoczy stiffened. "Have those two become allies?" he inquired with deceptive nonchalance.

"In this regard, apparently they have, and I like it less than you do," said Boris, and now he was worried. "At first I paid no heed to them, for both of them thrive on the workings of the Court. But now they appear to be more ambitious, and I fear that if Shuisky puts his power with Romanov's, then I will be fortunate to live to be forty."

Rakoczy agreed more than he wanted to. "If they are in accord, then—" He broke off, disliking the sense of foreboding that came over him. Deliberately he shifted the subject. "Boris Feodorovich, tell me: if anything . . . untoward were to happen to me, would you be willing to see that my wife is protected and my manservant returns to Poland? He is a native of Spain, from

Cadiz, and it would be no kindness to require him to remain here."

"He is Spanish?" Boris said, as if Spain were as remote as the moon.

"Yes," said Rakoczy, and did not add that when Rothger was born, Spain was a Roman colony, and his city was known as Gades. "I would not like to think that either my manservant or my wife had to suffer on my account."

"Well, I already have the money you have provided for Xenya Evgeneivna, and there may be some additional protection I can extend to her. I will do everything that I can on her behalf. I don't think Vasilli Andreivich will mind if I take some measures to protect her—they are distantly related."

"If he or his cousin seek to bring her once again into their households," Rakoczy said, his voice very soft and level, "I want you to give your assurances that you will not allow it, not now or ever. Keep her with you, or find another noble who is not allied with the Shuiskys. Do not let the Shuiskys reach her, I beseech you. She may have family connections with them, but that is not sufficient claim to make her their drudge. And you may be sure that is the least of what they would require of her."

"If you think so poorly of them . . ." Boris wanted to know the reason for this unexpected caveat, but there was something in Rakoczy's manner that did not encourage further questioning. He cleared his throat. "Very well; I will see that Xenya Evgeneivna does not live with Shuiskys. Your manservant may be more difficult, but if it is possible I will see that he is not hindered if he decides to leave Moscovy; but it might not be . . ." The words trailed off again, and he forced a heartiness into his tone that convinced neither Rakoczy nor himself. "Besides, these precautions are hardly necessary. There will be no trouble, I am sure of it."

"Nevertheless," said Rakoczy gently and persistently, "indulge me, my friend. So that neither of us will have cause for recriminations later."

Boris swung around again. "What do you think of me, Rakoczy! I would never permit—" He stopped, and when he spoke again his voice was softer. "Yes. I understand what you mean, little as I wish to. Very well. I will do what I can for Xenya Evgeneivna, and for your manservant Rothger. You have my sworn assurance that if I am able to guard them, I will. If the Court removes me from my position, I will try to find someone who will look after your wife, someone away from the influence of the Shuiskys. But I doubt anything I would do then would help your manservant, as he is a foreigner. At best I could arrange for him to be expelled from Moscovy."

"He has survived worse," said Rakoczy evenly.

"Fighting the Turk, yes, of course," said Boris, and Rakoczy did not correct him. "I can take him into my household for a time if I remain in Moscovy; he can read and write, and I will give him work to do making translations. No one will think it strange that I employ him for such skills. But if Nikita Romanovich and Vasilli Andreivich continue as they are, I may not be able to stay in the city, and if I must flee, your manservant would be safer crossing to Sweden on foot at midwinter than in my company." He had stopped walking; he stared down at his feet, noticing how the light struck them, and the hem of his red-and-gold kaftan.

"I trust it will not come to that, Boris Feodorovich," said Rakoczy evenly. "Czar Feodor would not allow it."

Boris shrugged. "Who can tell what that poor young man will tolerate?"

"You are his trusted adviser and his wife's brother," said Rakoczy.

"And as my mother was a Tartar, the rest counts for nought." Boris folded his arms. "Of late, that is all any of them talk about, my Tartar mother." He shook his head once, twice. He glared at the window as if the light hurt his eyes. "My father-in-law wants to take up my cause; if he does there will be war here, and it will be between Rus. Everything we have gained and regained, and at so high price, will be in danger. I don't think I can accept such developments." He coughed. "I do not want any more divisiveness than we have seen already."

"It may not be your decision to make," said Rakoczy kindly. "If Vasilli Shuisky and Nikita Romanov are determined to oppose you, you must stand against them or leave Moscovy and Czar Feodor to their forces."

Boris' sigh was eloquent. "Yes. That is precisely the difficulty, isn't it? If I do not defend Czar Feodor, he will be in the hands of those who wish him ill. He does not know how to deal with men of such guile. He is puppet enough already."

"Your puppet?" suggested Rakoczy.

"When it comes to foreigners, yes," said Boris directly. "He has allowed me to guide him." There was no trace of cynicism in his demeanor.

"And does he listen to you? Does he heed your advice?" Rakoczy asked, and turned as Rothger approached from the direction of the kitchen with a large brass tray laden with stuffed eggs, fish roe, and mincemeat-and-honey-filled breads. One golden cup stood beside an opened bottle.

"There is hot tea as well, good boyar, if you wish a samovar brought, and we have French spirits the English have kindly provided to us," said the manservant with the slightest inclination of his head. He put the tray down on the low table and regarded Rakoczy. "Is there anything else you wish me to attend to?"

"Not just at the moment," said Rakoczy distantly, aware that Rothger wanted very much to convey some message to him. "Not in regard to my guest, that is. But I would appreciate it if you would review the accounts on my worktable. They are in the black leather case—you know the one."

Rothger was alarmed by the request but did not do more than raise his sandy brows. "Certainly."

This exchange embarrassed Boris, who was never comfortable with Rakoczy's informal manner with servants; to him it was another foreign affectation that only served to confuse the Moscovites. He busied himself selecting the best from the delicacies on the tray.

"And if you will send word to the English while you are about it?" Rakoczy went on in the same half-attentive way. "I want to have word with Lovell at his earliest convenience. I'll want a missive carried to his embassy before sunset, the meeting no later than mid-day tomorrow. Would you be good enough to arrange that for me?"

Now Rothger realized that there was something very wrong, and it was an effort not to ask for some explication. He inclined his head once more. "I'll do what I can, my master."

"Thank you," said Rakoczy gently. "You are always dependable." He made a gesture of dismissal and returned his attention to Boris. "If my wife were here, I would ask her to join us, but she has gone to the—"

Boris cut him short, speaking around a mouthful of stuffed egg. "More of your foreign ways, having your wife present at your entertainments, and that is the sort of thing that brings disapproval upon you. We Rus see you treating your wife like a Polish woman, and—"

"More Italian than Polish," Rakoczy corrected him with kindly irony.

"You see? This is precisely what I mean." His black eyes glittered with frustration. "You flaunt your alien manners and you set yourself against Russian ways. There is very little I can do for you if you insist on flouting Russian customs in this way. Everyone will think your motives are . . . foreign. This is Moscovy. I wish you to understand that there are good reasons for everything we do, and that our actions are not arbitrary."

In the last three thousand five hundred years Rakoczy had heard similar protests in many countries, many languages. He had long since stopped debating with the earnest men who expressed their feelings so sincerely. "Boris Feodorovich," he said very politely, "I do not wish to give offense to anyone by my words or actions. But even if I were to become as Russian as I could force myself to be, I would still not be able to make any Rus think I was one of them, and instead of being the target of their umbrage, I would become the object of their contempt."

Boris shook his head, having no argument to offer. He waited while he considered what Rakoczy had said. "I don't know what to tell you."

Rakoczy smiled. "Tell me that you will guard Xenya and my manservant and I will be content."

"You have that already," said Boris, relenting.

"Then I am satisfied," said Rakoczy, and made a sweeping gesture toward the brass tray. "Take what you want, Boris Feodorovich, and tell me how soon I should prepare to leave this city."

Boris all but choked on the bread in his mouth. "God's mercy! Why should you leave?"

"There is no reason for you to ask, after what you have told me. I will have to make arrangements quickly; with your help I can be away before the end of July," said Rakoczy, standing with his back to the largest window so that his shadow blocked out half the light.

"But if you leave, they will say the rumors about you are true," Boris objected after swallowing hard.

"Let them. Let them have their rumors and their myths and their superstitions. Let them believe I am a servant of Satan and a leader of assassins. I have had worse accusations; believe this," Rakoczy said with a weariness of soul that astonished Boris.

"Holy angels, what can be worse?" Boris asked, pouring himself a cup of the French spirits as he stared at his host. "Or do you mean the Turks? It is said that they claim that all who oppose them are inspired by their Satan."

"Shaitan," Rakoczy said quietly.

Boris ignored the interjection. "Does it not worry you to be cursed by Christians? God hears our prayers, Rakoczy. It is an honor to have the Turks inveigh against you, but to have God's Hand against you, that is another matter."

Rakoczy's dark eyes flickered with amusement, then he moved away from the window. "I am no devil and I am no martyr, Boris Feodorovich. But an exile is always subject to . . . misfortune."

"This is no misfortune, Rakoczy," Boris insisted. "You must be shown to be innocent, or disaster will befall you and yours."

"And you as well?" Rakoczy suggested gently as he watched Boris drain his cup of spirits.

Boris waved this away. "It is a minor thing for me. My mother is my greatest hazard. If it were necessary, I could always claim that you had cast a spell upon me, and that my friendship was sham, nothing more than the machinations of a clever, wicked man." He poured another generous tot into his cup. "But I will not do that if you will defend yourself to the Court. It could be arranged quickly. The Court could hear your explanations in a month—I doubt anyone could move quickly enough to interfere with you before then. Won't you permit me to arrange this?"

Rakoczy shook his head once. "If you like," he replied after a short silence.

Now Boris looked relieved. "Excellent! *Excellent!*" he enthused. "That Polish Jesuit will be dealt with, and you will not have to worry about what might happen to your wife and manservant." He drank again. "And I will have another means to combat the malice of the Shuiskys."

"In fact," said Rakoczy, a sardonic note in his voice, "it would benefit both of us tremendously."

"Yes," Boris said seriously. "And it is foolish for us to overlook such an opportunity." He pulled his spoon from his belt and scooped out a generous portion of fish roe, all black and smelling of salt. "Fine quality," he said, and downed the caviar in two bites.

A clatter of hooves in the narrow courtyard caught Rakoczy's attention. He glanced toward the window but could not make out the number of horses or any identification.

Boris had heard them too. "Your wife is coming back?"

"I didn't expect her yet," said Rakoczy, and did not add that she would have been driven directly into the stableyard.

"Perhaps you have a friend on an errand similar to mine," said Boris as he had more fish roe. "I am not the only noble at Court who would prefer to support you than Father Pogner."

"That's comforting," said Rakoczy, trying to listen to what was going on outside without offending Boris.

"And there are those who are willing to align themselves with anyone prepared to work against Shuisky," Boris went on expansively, pausing to lick his spoon. "Czar Feodor does not grasp how difficult the situation is, but he is aware that to advance Shuisky just now would cause a great schism at Court that would weaken us in the face of our enemies."

There came a series of sharp raps at the door, and in answer to it, Rothger descended from the floor above.

Boris looked around as Rothger opened the door, and stepped outside as the arrivals held out a rolled parchment with the double-headed Byzantine eagle of the Czar sealing it as their introduction; they said nothing as they waited to be invited into the house.

"Who is it, Rothger?" Rakoczy called out, anticipating his answer.

"I do not know their names, but they are in the uniform of the Czar's Guard," Rothger answered coolly, coming into the house again.

"The Czar's Guard," Rakoczy repeated in a musing tone, and saw the look of consternation on Boris' face. "Have them in."

Three Guard officers stood in the covered porch, all armed. As they crossed the threshold they made a perfunctory blessing of the ikons before advancing on the reception room.

"I am Guard Captain Kurbsky," announced the tallest of the three as he lowered the parchment. His form was the best Court standard and he did not stare at the contents of the exile's house, much as he wanted to. "I have been sent on the mandate of Czar Feodor to detain the foreign exile Ferenc Rakoczy, Hrabia Saint-Germain, of the Polish embassy in Moscovy."

Before Rakoczy could speak, Boris recovered himself and surged forward, going directly toward the young officer who had spoken. He kept a proper, respectful distance between the Captain and himself. "Rurich Valentinovich," he said, rebuking Guard Captain Kurbsky as if he were a ten-year-old child, "what nonsense is this? Why have you come here?"

Captain Kurbsky stood straighter, his back rigid; he did not so much as glance at Boris but directed his remarks to the opposite wall. "We have been given the orders of the Czar, Boris Feodorovich, and we are bound to execute them."

Rakoczy had come up behind Boris in the archway to the reception room, and now he signaled to Rothger, a gesture that had meaning only to his manservant. As Rothger bowed and slipped away, Rakoczy stepped forward to confront these soldiers. "I am Ferenc Rakoczy, Captain Kurbsky. What do you good officers and Czar Feodor want of me?" His voice was level and his manner as genial and correct as if he were serving them a banquet.

"We have orders to bring you with us," said Captain Kurbsky, more woodenly than before. "You can bring nothing with you but the clothes you wear."

This last angered Boris, who strode directly to Captain Kurbsky, coming much closer than convention permitted. "How dare you treat this man as if he were a common outlaw. You haven't the right. He is part of the Polish mission. He is Hrabia Saint-Germain. He has lost his lands through battling the Turks. And you will show him the respect he deserves or you will answer to me and to—"

"It is in the Czar's order," Captain Kurbsky said miserably, and it was apparent that he was dismayed at the terms of the orders as well.

Boris sighed. "And who gave you these orders, Rurich Valentinovich?" he asked with a touch of impatience.

"The Little Father," said Captain Kurbsky.

"At whose instigation? Who was with him when the orders

were issued?" Boris persisted, making a motion to Rakoczy to stay where he was. "I am certain Czar Feodor was not alone."

Rakoczy strolled up to Boris, his manner deliberately deferential. "It may not be proper for the good Captain to reveal that, my friend."

"Proper or not," said Boris emphatically, "you will tell me, Rurich Valentinovich, and you will withhold nothing unless you wish your sister Zenevieva to remain unmarried." He flung the golden cup away and folded his arms. "Well? Who was with Czar Feodor?

Captain Kurbsky rubbed his upper lip with his lower teeth, setting his impressive mustaches bouncing. "He was with Prince Shuisky."

"I *knew* it," Boris whispered, his black eyes kindling with ire. He would have said more but felt Rakoczy's restraining hand on his shoulder.

"Never mind," said Rakoczy. "It is not your fault." He did want to be caught in a long discussion, so he turned to Captain Kurbsky. "All right. What do you require of me." He chided himself for his predicament, for trusting to his position to serve as a modicum of protection. There had been signs for months, but he had supposed that between Boris Feodorovich Godunov and King Istvan he would be proof against danger.

"You must accompany us, at once," said Captain Kurbsky, growing more distressed with every word. He blinked once, then stared at Rakoczy. "If it were for me to decide, Hrabia Saint-Germain, this would not be happening."

Rakoczy heard Boris' muffled expletive, but said with composure, "I am grateful to you for telling me." He paused. "Should I take one of my own horses, or would you——"

"We will provide a horse," said Captain Kurbsky, breathing a bit more quickly. "We are supposed to shackle you, but I will not put the irons on you."

"Will you tell me why I am being . . . detained?" Rakoczy asked, his voice still light and faintly ironic.

"It is not permitted," said Captain Kurbsky.

"Then tell me," said Boris, and with such authority that Captain Kurbsky took refuge in speaking to the wall again.

"He is accused of being a Satanic magician and a murderer," said the Captain as if reciting the order of march. "Because he is

noble he cannot be executed except for treason. Because he is
foreign, he must be punished. Therefore the Court magistrates
will decide what is to be done. You will have to learn from them
what they determine, Boris Feodorovich."

"And that I will," said Boris with energy, starting toward the
door. "You may be certain of it."

Rakoczy paused before blessing the ikons. "I would appreciate that," he said and added, "After you see to the safety of my
wife and my servant."

Text of a letter to the Court magistrates of Czar Feodor from
Father Pogner on behalf of the Polish embassy in Moscovy.

*To the most learned and potent boyars, the magistrates of the
Court of the Czar of Russia, this carries the most humble greetings from the leader of the Polish embassy, in answer to the
inquiries sent yesterday:*

*You say you wish to know of any extenuating circumstances
that would account for the activities of Ferenc Rakoczy of Transylvania other than those of the charges made against him: that
he is a witch and magician in the legions of Satan, and that he
slew or caused to have slain the noble and too-trusting Father
Milan Krabbe; that he exercised his magical arts upon your late
Czar Ivan, leading Czar Ivan into greater madness through the
demonic jewels he made and further corrupting him in pander-
ing to his lusts for riches and the acquisition of treasure, which
is the sin of avarice.*

*I can offer no defense for this despicable man, for I am one
who has believed from the first that the purposes of this Rakoczy
were malign and that his arts sprang from no holy source. At the
beginning of this mission I urged King Istvan not to send this
man with us, but my protestations were not sufficient to persuade a Transylvanian that a countryman of his was a nefarious wizard, one who would bring calamity and disgrace on
himself and Poland. My warnings went unheeded and my arguments were dismissed as folly, so great was Rakoczy's influence with King Istvan.*

*In that regard, you inform me that you have considered
knouting Rakoczy, but fear that it might be interpreted as an*

insult by the Polish king. Istvan Bathory is a virtuous man, and as such he will not countenance malfeasance and mayhem in one of his mission. Were he here himself, I am convinced that he would not deem that severe lashing inappropriate to the many injuries Rakoczy has inflicted, for we have learned that should a Rus noble commit such reprehensible acts, he would most surely be decapitated.

If a sentence of knouting is your decision, then I implore you to order a great number of blows, not a mere five or ten administered by a Kremlin Guard, but twenty or thirty, with the knout in the hands of a Don Cossack. This Rakoczy is no ordinary miscreant, and his deeds demand suffering commensurate with the suffering he has caused. He must not be permitted to trade on the good-will of the people of Moscovy, nor on the favors he had extended to the nobility. If there is any justice in the world, then it requires that Ferenc Rakoczy be made to answer for his many transgressions.

I pray God will send you wisdom and His Angels to guide you in your decision, and I beg you to recall that those who excuse crime participate in it as surely as if they were the ones who wielded the knives.

> *In respect and reverence, in the Name of the*
> *Father, Son and Holy Spirit,*
> *Casimir Pogner, Society of Jesus*
> *Embassy of Istvan Bathory of Poland*
> *to the Court of Czar Feodor*
> *July 9, by the new calendar, in the Year of Grace 1585*

7

The beating had stopped sometime before but the pain of it was unrelenting; Rakoczy, chained over an ancient brewer's barrel in the barracks' courtyard behind the Cathedral of the Virgin of the Intercession, faded in and out of consciousness as night came on.

Vermin of every description had sought out the feast of his

mauled flesh; insects and rats competed for every torn scrap of skin and muscle, and for every drop of blood. Ravens lingered around the courtyard, one occasionally swooping low over him to snatch some prize morsel from the rest. Rakoczy could feel the passage of their flight in agonizing licks of air over the ruin of his back. He had bled very little, given the damage the knout had inflicted. In two places his ribs showed through the lacerations, and his shoulders were so torn that it appeared he had been held in the talons of a gigantic bird of prey. What little was left of his clothes hung in tatters. He despised his helplessness and he could not move.

There was a smell of death in this courtyard, a deeper stench than the spilled blood and bowels. He knew it well; he had come to recognize it in Babylon and Thebes, and since that time had encountered it in more places than he cared to recall. The sullen summer heat carried it like distant thunder.

In the blur of pain he thought of Tamasrajasi. Of those he had been remembering, only she would be drawn to this, would seek to embrace it and sup on it, this heat and misery and death. She had drowned more than three hundred years ago, but Rakoczy could still wince at the thought of her, and find her echo in the corruption around him.

The weight of his body pulled relentlessly against the manacles, and now the iron dug into his wrists; although he could not see them, he knew his small hands were swollen and dark for he could no longer move his fingers but he could feel them press into each other, and the knuckles ached from stretching. Shackles held his legs far enough apart that his knees were aching from strained ligaments. Even if he could free himself, he thought distantly, it would likely be impossible for him to escape, for his legs would not be able to support him. The soldiers had taken his boots, and each foot had been given a single blow of the knout; his feet were as bruised and swollen as his hands.

He was supposed to die. The thirty blows with the knout that had been ordered were more than sufficient to kill living men. That heavy cable lash could strip skin off the bone without the iron ring at the end, let alone the weights that were attached to it. They had used the second-largest weight on him, an iron bauble nearly the size of a hen's egg. He had come close to biting through his lower lip when the weight broke his rib.

In the Cathedral of the Virgin of the Intercession the priests were singing the praises of God's mercy, their rich harmonies vying with the flies and mosquitoes and rats for his attention. The ravens were gone, and the rosy glow in the western sky. He realized that it was growing late, that sunset Mass was long over, and this must be the Slumber Mass, as the people called it, sung at the time most Moscovites were preparing to go to bed. He had lost another two or three hours since day's end.

They would be expecting to find a corpse in the morning, he told himself, trying to concentrate against the torment of his wounds. If they did not find one, there would be greater trouble for him, and suspicions that would bring him more anguish than the knouting had. And that would lead to far greater difficulties than the ones he endured now. So often in stories those who were not properly dead gained magical abilities; they could change into wolves or birds or bats and escape from their pursuers. They could command the elements and those around them to assist them. It was a fable of power he wished were true, though he suspected that even a new shape could not travel far with the injuries he had received. All his death had given him was durability and strength far beyond that of the truly living, a degree of control over animals, superior night vision, and one specific thirst. The rest—the skills, the learning, the music, the compassion—he had acquired for himself in many long and painful lessons.

He realized that the priests were no longer singing, and that the torches outside the barracks fronting the courtyard had been extinguished. How long ago had that been? One hour? Two? What time was it? He wished for his Dutch watch, knowing he would be unable to hold it or read it. He squinted up at the sky, but thin, ruched clouds obscured the stars and he could not reckon the time accurately; the effort to hold his head up was too painful for him to continue it for long. Splinters from the old barrel dug into his cheek as he lowered his head.

Not far off dogs growled and whimpered, whining as they strained at their iron-studded collars. Whether they sought the rats or Rakoczy himself, he did not know. Outside the courtyard walls a few tradesmen shouted and called as they hurried for the protection of their homes.

The next thing Rakoczy was aware of—he had lost another unknown amount of time—there were soldiers coming back to the barracks, well after hours, all drunk. A few of them were singing, finding it hard to get the words out and straying from the tune. They came from the stables, footsteps unsteady and direction uncertain; they boasted of their prowess at whoring, swore they were the greatest cocksmen in the world, and blundered away to their beds, accompanied by the complaining shouts of their less adventurous comrades.

Rakoczy listened intently: the poignance of the brevity of their lives struck him as his own hurt had not, and wrung his soul. He could offer himself the equivocal anodyne of his long centuries of living. But those soldiers were all no older than thirty, and most of them would never see fifty. By the time Rakoczy had been on the earth for fifty years, he had been dead for seventeen.

The soldiers were gone and now some of the rats were fighting. The battle raged around him, chittering and slashing in the dark. Occasionally a furry body would brush against his legs, and once he felt claws sink into the mangled flesh of his shoulder, and he screamed, though the sound was no louder than the shrieks of the rats, which he loathed.

And then, from the wall near the cathedral, there was a noise, a soft, stealthy noise, a noise that was not supposed to be heard.

At once Rakoczy was alert, forcing himself out of the lethargy that had enveloped him. He battled the pain as he raised his head, staring into the darkness and seeing only the curve of the barrel and the movement of fleeing rats. He could feel the abrasions on his face start to bleed once more.

Now there was a footfall, and another.

Two men approached him, walking gingerly, not speaking. Rakoczy listened intently and cursed his chains that immobilized him. He wondered if they had come to help him or to give him the true death at last.

Then someone knelt by his feet and unfastened the shackles.

Rakoczy cried out as his legs gave way and his arms were more cruelly pulled. Only his damaged feet were numb.

"Not yet," hissed Boris Feodorovich Godunov, as he went to unfasten the manacles. "Hold him."

"His back's—" protested Benedict Lovell, hesitating to touch Rakoczy now that he was somewhat aware of the hideous damage that had been done.

"It won't be better if he falls," muttered Boris, and undid the left manacle.

Rakoczy moaned as his battered muscles were wrenched

afresh. He feared he was being racked again, and his long memories ran together for an instant, so that he was not only here in Moscovy, but in a dungeon in Toledo, in a secret chamber in Trebizond, under the Flavian Circus in Rome, in the bear pit in Chotin. He choked back a scream as Lovell grabbed him to hold him up; his vision clouded and he drifted into unconsciousness.

"Just as well; it's less difficult for all of us," said Boris as he struggled with Lovell to support Rakoczy upright between them. "It's a wonder he's alive at all."

Lovell did not answer at first, and when he did, he spoke very softly. "I've seen men beaten before, but not like this. If this is half as drastic as I fear—" He indicated the darkness. "I am afraid of what I will see."

"The knout is intended to punish," said Boris, dismissing the observation as they started back toward the narrow side door. He was testy, fearing discovery in spite of the late hour. "Don't let his feet drag."

"Of course not," said Lovell, and hitched his shoulder more firmly under Rakoczy's side.

Rakoczy groaned and his head lolled as he came out of his faint. The pain of his release melded with the agony of his beating, consuming him. Supported between the two men, he had the continual sensation of falling, which left him dizzy and apprehensive as consciousness faded and sharpened.

"Almost there," whispered Boris as they neared the door. "I hope he hasn't left a trail of blood."

"I think most of it has clotted," said Lovell. "It appears it has." He fingered the shredded remains of Rakoczy's dolman. "It's tacky, not wet."

"Well enough," said Boris heavily. "We don't want them following us."

"No," agreed Lovell.

Slung between them Rakoczy swallowed hard to contain the nausea their movement caused. How strange it was, he thought in a still and distant part of his mind, that he of all men should feel nausea. His senses lurched with every move his rescuers made, and he could not hold his attention on anything for more than a few seconds because of the dark current washing through him borne on pain. Suddenly he shuddered and would have fallen had not Lovell seized his hair to hold him upright. Gradually the spasm passed and his senses grew less disordered. He turned his will to keeping silent; he was remotely aware of the great risk of discovery they ran.

They reached the door and paused while Boris edged near enough to glance out into the deserted street. He signaled to Lovell to move forward, and between them they managed to get Rakoczy out of the courtyard. As Boris turned to close the door and secure it again, he whispered, "If anyone should come upon us, brandish your dagger, and swear like a boyar. Say that this servant will not steal from you again. No one will dare to interfere with us."

"Except perhaps another boyar?" suggested Lovell dryly.

"You would do well to pray that no boyar finds us, for if he does, we will have to kill him." Boris glanced at Lovell once, to measure his reaction. In his short riding kaftan of dark leather he looked more like a seasoned officer than a guardian of the Czar. "No one can know of this, not if we are to save him, and ourselves."

Lovell nodded once. "Then I will pray," he assured Boris.

Feeling was returning to Rakoczy's hands and feet, and with it came greater pain, as if knives were being shoved under the tendons of each finger. It had been centuries since he had been so severely damaged; he would need long rest to recover and heal. He tried to move his fingers and only achieved more anguish for his efforts.

"Be still," Lovell whispered to Rakoczy in English as they started along the street. "Make no sound."

Rakoczy wanted to assure Lovell of his silence, but could not trust himself to speak without giving voice to his hurt. In order to distract himself he wondered where they were taking him. Where in Moscovy would he be safe?

"I don't like having to touch his back," Lovell said to Boris in Russian. "It sickens me."

"And it sickens him, I'd wager," said Boris brusquely. "Watch. Be quiet." He was apprehensive as they reached the edge of the Beautiful Market Square, standing eerily empty at the ebb of night. "We must hurry now," he warned Lovell, and began to walk faster.

Slung between them, his useless arms draped over their shoulders, Rakoczy clamped his jaw tight. He was riddled with agony that increased steadily.

Lovell was panting by the time they reached the wide street angling away toward the north. He gasped out "Stop," as they turned away from the Beautiful Market Square and the mass of the Kremlin. "I need time to recover my breath." Reluctantly he shifted his grip on Rakoczy, flinching as he heard the soft moan his burden made. Anxiety as much as effort had taken its toll of him and he fought now to regain not only his strength but his nerve. He was determined to master both before they set out again.

"Do not take long," warned Boris, looking from one end of the street to the other. He stifled a nervous, incomplete yawn and then got a more secure grip on Rakoczy. "We should not linger. We must reach the warehouse before the apprentices are in the streets."

"I know, I know," said Lovell, preparing himself for the second and more crucial stage of their rescue, and went on, "Do you think he will live?"

It took a short while for Boris to form his answer. "I think it is a miracle he is not dead now," he admitted and went on unhappily, "And if fever doesn't kill him, I don't know if his sinews or bones will knit again. He may yet curse us for what we are doing."

Rakoczy wanted to tell them both that he would recover, that he would be whole, that there would be no lasting impairment, no cicatrices from the lash. But he could not hold the thoughts together and resist his excruciation. His vision wavered and faded.

"But we could not leave him there," protested Lovell. "Not in that courtyard. The rats alone would—"

"No, we could not," said Boris, and glanced down the street again. "We had better move quickly. There will be pilgrims stirring soon, to be at dawn Mass." He was growing more nervous as he spoke, his inactivity sapping his reserves as much as it restored Lovell's. "Neither you nor I can afford to be seen with him."

"No one would know him, the way he is," said Lovell. "And how many pilgrims would recognize me, or you?"

"It would only require that one knew me, or you, and we

would be discovered. We must not let anyone observe us, not if we are to remain unknown. We Rus are persevering, and the Guard are tenacious. One accurate description and our fate would be sealed." He indicated an old beggar sleeping in the shadows. "With enough incentive, the Guard will question all those poor wretches who sleep in doorways, and if any of them——" He broke off. "And we cannot kill them all to silence them. That would be worse still."

"It is night," said Lovell. "What could they say? You are not dressed according to your rank, and I am not. And Rakoczy is hardly dressed at all. Who would suppose that an English scholar and a Russian noble were harboring a foreign criminal? Even if they saw us, what could they say, those beggars?"

"They could say they saw three strange men," whispered Boris fiercely. "And that they might have been well-born, because of our accents."

"Three well-born men on the street at night—it could be any three of hundreds," said Lovell, thinking more of London than Moscovy. "Surely—"

"Perhaps you and I would not be noticed. If it were just the two of us, it would be little hazard. But how many men are like him? If they see him, they will remember, won't they? especially if they see his back?" asked Boris, and wiped his forehead with his free hand. "Who else would they suspect of helping him but me? And I must not be suspected. Are you ready?"

"All right," said Lovell, readying himself for the long walk.

Rakoczy steeled himself for the jolting that was coming, but was not prepared for the disorientation the night would add to his torment. Movement made him dizzy. His breath hissed through his teeth as Boris and Lovell set off at a brisk pace, holding him with what little care they could; Rakoczy sought for a focus that would keep him from succumbing to vertigo. He attempted to count the steps his bearers took but after half a dozen lost track as his mind reeled under the assault of his deliverance.

By the time they reached the warehouse, Rakoczy was semi-conscious, hanging limp in the grasp of the two men who had saved him. Rothger admitted them through a stout wooden door, an oil lamp held up to guide them through the greater darkness of the building.

"I have to rest," muttered Lovell as Rothger opened a second door, this one much smaller than the first.

"Let me take him from you," said Rothger, and moved swiftly into position before Lovell could object.

The room where he had brought them was not very large. The walls were lined with shelves filled with locked leather boxes of spices and herbs; their odor was penetrating, ginger and pepper predominating. In the center of the room there was a long table where the spice merchant's clerks measured out their orders, but tonight the scales had been removed and a simple linen quilt spread out upon it where Rakoczy was laid down prone.

"He's badly hurt," said Boris in a steady way. "I don't think he will be fit to travel for weeks, not with such wounds." He looked away. "If he recovers at all," he added.

Lovell rubbed at his shoulder, swinging his arm to ease the ache in it. "He will have to until we make arrangements to get away," he said, then paled as he had his first look at Rakoczy's back in the lamplight.

Livid, torn, swollen muscles were revealed the length of his back where the skin had been ripped away by the knout. His small hands, hard as sausages, were mottled purple and black; his feet were bruised and the arches broken, large scabs forming where the knout had struck. His face was starkly pale, his eyes shadowed and sunken. His ears, his fingers, and the edges of his most severe wounds showed the vicious serrations of rat bites.

Boris crossed himself as Rothger brought a second lamp.

"Jesus Lord and Christ's Fish," whispered Lovell, appalled. "They've mutilated him."

Boris was not as distressed as the Englishman. He studied Rakoczy, his head to one side. "He's very strong," he said at last, speaking to Rothger.

"Yes, he is," said Rothger, his expression revealing nothing as he began to strip away the tatters of his master's clothes. He was efficient and gentle, doing as little damage as possible as he worked.

Lovell found it difficult to watch. He half-turned away, saying over his shoulder, "Is it possible he will be able to travel in two days? The arrangements for travel were already made and we cannot change them now. The English train will have to start in two days. No one warned me that he might be so . . . We have to leave then, you know, with or without him."

"I know," said Rothger. "He will travel," he added, thinking of the three chests of Rakoczy's native earth that had been installed as his bed in the wagon that would carry them north.

"Pray God he will," said Boris. "I have arranged to send the Guard after him toward Poland, but they will not continue for many days if there are no reports of your passage. And once they return, they may well seek him in the north, and I will not be able to stop them." He clapped his hands once. "Those Jesuits will howl for him more loudly than Nikita Romanovich and Vasilli Andreivich combined."

"I fear you are right," said Lovell. There was a sour taste at the back of his tongue; he hated the smell of blood.

Rothger regarded Boris levelly. "He will be ready to travel. The wagons are being prepared, just as my master instructed. They will be leaving with the English wagons, bound for Novo-Kholmogory, as Doctor Lovell has arranged. No one will pay attention. We will not be discovered."

Boris nodded several times as if trying to convince himself; then he said, "Look at him. How can he go anywhere in such condition? You cannot save him."

"He will travel," Rothger repeated with calm certainty: once resting on the annealing bed of his native earth, Rakoczy would begin to recover. Rothger had seen him restored in that way four times in the past, although he had to admit that he had never seen Rakoczy injured so severely.

Although he could not believe Rakoczy would live much longer, Boris was willing to dissemble in order to get the foreigner beyond the grasp of the Romanovs and Shuiskys. "Very well, he will travel," he said, gesturing his resignation. "May God be merciful." He looked around the room once more. "Does anyone know you are here? Is there someone who might report your presence?"

"The owner of the warehouse is here," said Rothger truthfully, indicating Rakoczy. "No one thinks anything of his coming, for he had been here often before, and the Russian merchants who serve him know he is frequently here at night, to tend to his own projects. My master is an alchemist who deals in herbs and spices as well as gold and jewels. Who is to remark on his presence in his own warehouse?"

To Rakoczy, lying face-down on the table, the voices of Boris and Lovell sounded a very long way off. He could make out the words but not the sense of what they were saying; he yearned for the revalescent presence of his native earth, and the remedy of sleep. He wished he did not have to breathe, for his broken rib marked every inhalation with a pang deeper and sharper than the rest of his tortured body. He could feel Rothger's ministrations but dimly through the enormity of his pain.

Boris accepted this unhappily. He could not refute the claims Rothger made, but he took no consolation from them, either. He crossed himself again. "This man is in great danger every hour he remains in Moscovy, and will be in danger for as long as he is in Russia."

"We're doing what we can to protect him," said Lovell bluntly. "Boris Feodorovich, I know you are taking a very great chance, aiding Rakoczy this way, and I know that it would go hard for you if it were ever learned that you aided his escape. But I do not intend to tell anyone, and Rothger will not, so you have no reason to fear us." He gestured to Rakoczy, flinching at what he saw in spite of his determination to remain composed. "You could not have left him where he was, could you?"

"No," said Boris quietly. "Not after he had done so much." He stared at the labels on the leather boxes, reading one after another very carefully. "And there is little I can do for him in return. I cannot stop the damage to his reputation, not now. Later, if I am free to act, I might be able to salvage his name. But I have arranged for Xenya Evgeneivna to leave for the country estate of Nikolai Grigoreivich Danilov, near Vladimir. That's little enough but better than nothing. They are distantly related and he is not interested in politics, mine or Romanov's or Shuisky's. His wife has agreed to have Xenya Evgeneivna live there, in a separate house with servants. She will not be troubled there. That, at least, I can do for Rakoczy: protect his wife. Her position will be secure. She will never want for money; that is certain."

Rothger heard him out. "My master would thank you."

Boris shrugged. "It isn't necessary," he said, with such genuine feeling that Lovell was surprised. "I regret only that I cannot discharge all my obligation now to him and remove the stigma from his name at this instant." He studied Lovell's face. "It is not Rakoczy's struggle, the battle that is fought constantly between Russian nobles. Yet he was dragged into it and made to answer for it, some of it on my behalf. And that is an affront to me."

Lovell motioned agreement. "Yes; a question of honor."

Rakoczy tried to speak but the effort hurt him and he made only a soft mewing sound. When he tried to move his arms great agony welled in him; his consciousness faded into a twilight state where both pain and sense were banished.

Rothger tossed away the last rags of Rakoczy's dolman and paused to decide on how to remove the codpiece and leggings. It was obvious to him that he must not draw them over his master's wounded feet. That meant they would have to be cut off. He looked around the room for the place where the shears were kept.

"If ever I discover certain proof who has acted against Rakoczy, I will do all that I can to see he pays for it," Boris was saying to Lovell, as if he expected the scholar to record his vow. "I do not want to go to God with this against me." He was increasingly restless, taking short, urgent turns about the small room, his brow darkening. "The bells will be ringing soon, and I must return to my palace before that hour." He tapped Lovell's arms. "And so must you, English. You must not let any questions be asked about you or you could endanger him." He turned his hand in Rakoczy's direction. "And yourself."

"I will be careful," said Lovell.

"Then I will wish you God's blessings and leave you. Do not contact me again unless I send a messenger to you—a messenger carrying my little ikon of Saint Mamas of Cappadocia. If the messenger does not carry the ikon, keep away. And do not send anything to me, no matter how urgent. Is that understood?" Boris fidgeted with the bloodied end of his sash.

"It is understood," said Lovell.

"Mercy and grace be on you, and on him," said Boris with a last nod toward Rakoczy before he hurried from the room. His footsteps were soft as he crossed the larger part of the warehouse; then the heavy outer door swung open, closed, and Boris was gone.

Rothger watched Lovell, a degree of speculation in his steady blue eyes. "He gave you excellent advice, Doctor Lovell," he said to the Englishman in Latin. "It is less dangerous for my master as well as for you if you leave before you can be seen."

Lovell accepted this. "I know. It would be a bad thing if he were discovered, and I realize it is a mistake to wait any longer.

Dawn is no more than an hour away. But I am afraid that—" He stopped himself before he made the unthinkable admission.

"You are afraid that he is going to die," said Rothger with unflustered sympathy. "He will not."

"I wish I could be as certain as you are," said Lovell quietly as he made himself look at Rakoczy one last time. "His back is wreckage. He has been so badly beaten . . . how can he live."

"He will," Rothger promised. "He has survived worse than this. But you might not if you are apprehended. So leave us. I will tend to him."

Slowly Lovell capitulated, bowing a little before going to the door. "It is still quite dark. That's something in our favor," he said to Rothger.

"Yes it is," said Rothger.

"Tomorrow I am supposed to bring my chests to be stowed. I will speak with you then. As soon as the wagons are ready, I will . . ." He ran out of words; with a short, impatient sigh he pulled the door closed behind him, leaving Rakoczy to his man-servant's care.

Rothger worked swiftly and competently, setting about the unpleasant task of cleaning Rakoczy's hideous injuries with dispatch. He was not distracted by the occasional groans that shuddered through the Transylvanian exile, though his austere features hardened when he assessed the extent of the damage; Rakoczy drifted in and out of consciousness, finally succumbing to the lure of sleep as Rothger wrapped him in soft clean linen to cover his wounds and his nakedness.

The first of the morning chimes had rung from the Kremlin bell towers when Rothger finished his task. Very shortly the apprentices and merchants would arrive, and before then he had to put Rakoczy into the larger of the two wagons being readied for the journey north, atop the chests that contained his native earth. With care he slung Rakoczy over his shoulder, and walked carefully out into the warehouse, moving steadily toward the two wagons.

A noise in the dark corner near the thick outer doors halted his steps. He listened intently, inhaling through open lips so as not to be distracted by the sound of his own breathing. Taking a firmer hold of Rakoczy's legs with his left hand, Rothger reached for his short-sword with his right, calling out as he did, "All right, whoever-you-are, show yourself."

The warehouse was silent. Then a soft, stifled cough came from the same corner as before.

"I said, show yourself." For emphasis he slapped the flat of the sword's blade against his leg. "I will come after you if—"

"No." Xenya Evgeneivna stepped out of the darkness into the predawn gloom. "You need not come after me, Rothger," she said in a small voice.

Of all the many persons he might have expected to find, Rothger had not anticipated confronting his master's wife. He stood quite still before sheathing his sword. "How do you come to be here?" he asked without preamble.

"I followed you," she admitted, keeping to the edge of the shadow where the muted light of the lamps could barely reach. "I said I was going to the Convent of the Mercy of the Virgin, to offer charity. No one stopped me. They were afraid to."

"It wasn't very wise to come here," Rothger chided her.

"It wouldn't be wise to be sequestered in the country, as invisible as the dead. I am where a wife should be, with her husband." She took another step forward, determination showing in every line of her. As she came nearer she faltered, staring at the muffled burden over Rothger's shoulder. "Ferenc Nemovich?" She crossed herself.

"Yes," said Rothger, and added, "He's alive."

She came the rest of the way to Rothger's side. "Will he live?"

Rothger met her eyes directly. "Yes, he will," he said. "He is very badly hurt but he will recover. Do not worry for him, give your thoughts to yourself and your own safety. Rest assured he will survive; you are still in danger. Little as you may want it, invisibility can be an asset. My master would tell you the same thing, if he could. You must leave Moscovy." He did his best to reassure her with a tight smile as he continued on toward the larger wagon.

"I must," she agreed, and her eyes became bright as she followed him. "But not to go to Nikolai Grigoreivich Danilov, running for cover like some cur. Oh, most surely I know the plans are well-intended, but I want none of them. I will not leave him to the depredations of his enemies." Her attitude was defiant as she faced Rothger. "I will not leave him."

"What?" Rothger halted again.

"I will not leave him," she repeated; her defiance became dignity. "I know what it means to be left in danger, and how grave the consequences are because I myself have suffered them and I know their cost in my soul. I will not abandon him. Do not ask it of me, Rothger."

Rothger had been about to try to persuade her to change her mind, but there was something in the way she stood, in the timbre of her voice and the resolute purpose that filled her that convinced him utterly. "Very well," he acquiesced. "I will not."

Text of a letter from Piotr Grigoreivich Smolnikov to Czar Feodor, dictated in secret to Father Illya at the Chapel of Saints Hipparchus and Philotheus.

To the most gracious and high-born Czar Feodor Ivanovich, with the devotion and dedication of your servant Piotr Grigoreivich Smolnikov, in the sincere belief that he must reveal that which he has learned:

Your servant was once an accomplished officer and has stood in the defense of this city four times until Mongol arrows robbed him of his sight, and for that reason is still determined to act to protect Moscovy and the Little Father.

Duke Anastasi Sergeivich Shuisky has provided me a living since the loss of my sight, and he has shown generosity and charity to me in age. I owe him my gratitude, and were it not required that I serve the Czar first and foremost, I would have to continue in my loyalty to the noble who has so ably demonstrated Christian virtue and Russian purpose. But the duty I have sworn to the Czar is greater than any but the duty I have to God, and therefore I must set aside the demands of gratitude in order to serve those of fealty. Most reluctantly, I must inform you, great Czar of Holy Russia, that my benefactor, the noble Duke Anastasi Sergeivich Shuisky, has foresworn his oaths to you and to Russia in order to strive for his own advancement even at the price of your sacred life, Little Father.

It is true that I can no longer use my eyes, but my ears are still acute, and God has not sent me a double affliction. I have put my ears to use, giving my attention to everything that has taken place in Anastasi Sergeivich's house, and from this I have come to learn that my gracious host has become embroiled in a number of nefarious schemes contrived to diminish your power, Little Father, to the advantage of Shuisky.

In the last year I have heard bitter arguments between Anastasi Sergeivich and his cousin Vasilli Andreivich, for each man seeks to place himself on the throne for the glory of Russia and Shuisky. Both men have employed spies and other despicable creatures to undermine their rivals for power. They have often worked against each other in the hope that the family would lend full support to one or the other of them.

There have been many nights when I have awakened to the sound of hushed conversations when Anastasi Sergeivich has received his hirelings when he thought that no member of the household would know of the visit. I have overheard Anastasi Sergeivich suggest mayhem and slaughter to some of these men, in the hope that the Court of Nikita Romanov and Boris Godunov might be overthrown and other men given the task of guiding you, men who share the purpose of Shuisky instead of being dedicated to the good of all Russia. At such times I have prayed to God to show me the error of what I had discovered, to reveal the farce I longed to know was being played.

There has been no such revelation. I have come to realize that Anastasi Sergeivich, with or without the cooperation of his cousin Vasilli Andreivich, has deliberately striven to seize your throne for himself. I cannot keep such knowledge to myself, but in all faith as your sworn officer, I come to you, Little Father, to give you my warning and to beseech you to put strict watch on all the Shuiskys, to prevent any greater mischief they might otherwise bring upon our poor, bleeding country. They seek to plunder Russia as the wolf plunders the fold or as the Mongols have plundered Mother Russia in the past, and will brave any opposition if it appears they will prevail.

With every prayer of the day, I ask God's mercy for you, Feodor Ivanovich, and for the Rus, who have endured so much for so long. I swear as a soldier that what I tell you is the truth and that the danger I have described is real. Do not ignore this humble warning if you seek to remain on your throne.

> *Sworn as truth at the ikonostasis,*
> *Piotr Grigoreivich Smolnikov*
> *The Feast of Saint Symphrosa and her Seven Sons*
> *by the hand of Father Illya*

8

Father Pogner's face darkened as he stared across the writing table at Boris Feodorvich Godunov. "How can you be so willfully blind, you heathenish Russian!" he burst out, no longer guarding his words.

"We are more true to Christian teaching than you Romans," Boris countered sharply. "But none of that matters in this instance. We are not here to debate theology but to discover treason."

"That is no burden of mine," said Father Pogner, mastering his temper enough to respond coolly. He glanced once at the two Guards flanking the door of the large reception room in Boris' Kremlin palace. "I am in this Godforsaken country at the behest of King Istvan of Poland, not to serve your Czar."

"Nevertheless," said Boris, paying little heed to the epithet Father Pogner had used to refer to Russia, "there is treason here, and you are tainted with it, Jesuit." He spread out the papers that littered his table; he was sitting with his back to the open window so it was not easy to see his expression. "These are the reports to prove you are part of it," he went on, holding up three of them. "They are sworn as truth, and when they are presented to the Czar, he will decide how you are to be dealt with." He paid no attention to Father Pogner's cynical laughter. "In the meantime, I am informing you that a messenger has been sent to Istvan of Poland, alerting him to the developments of the last month. I hope that I have acted in time."

"And did the messenger ride with the soldiers chasing Rakoczy?" asked Father Pogner at his most snide. "It would be more efficient that way, would it not, but would he be fast enough?" He made his face bland. "Has there been any word from them? Have they caught the charlatan yet?"

Boris decided not to respond to the barb. "I have no information on Rakoczy's present whereabouts, and it would not matter if I had. His unjust condemnation was due in large part to you, and you will answer for it. You have aided those who worked against Rakoczy because of your envy of him. You have taken every opportunity to cast his efforts into the most damning light. In doing this, you have compromised your mission and traduced the rule of the Czar." He rose from his chair, facing Father Pogner directly. "That cannot be excused, though you are a servant of the King of Poland and an avowed priest. Be grateful that you are, or your beating would be more extreme than Rakoczy's was."

Father Pogner cleared his throat, glaring at Boris and hating the Asiatic cast of his features, his dark, slanted brows and black eyes. "This is a country of savages and superstition," he declared. "You pretend to Christian virtue and civilized conduct, only pretend. Your Czar Ivan was nothing more than a heathen war-lord, pillaging for treasure and calling the conquered cities his kingdom. Your Church is corrupt, proven false by the fall of Constantinople. God has sent His Angels for the protection of the Pope and Rome, but your Patriarch was cast out of his city, and rules on sufferance in Jerusalem. The message is clear for any with the mind to read it. And your Czar Feodor has no more wits than a child of ten, and is as much use."

In the time it had taken Father Pogner to speak, Boris had passed from rage to disbelieving curiosity, for surely Father Pogner was mad to say what he did. "And why have you come here, if you have such contempt for us?" he marveled.

"God demands it of me. As a priest called of God, I have given myself up to the holy cause of Christ's Church and the triumph of faith. Each of us is given our burden by God, and we are judged by our ability to bear it. The Church and King Istvan have ordered me here, and for the glory of God, I have come." Zeal shone in Father Pogner's eyes. He crossed himself Roman style, his severe countenance now a mask of self-satisfaction. "To those God intends the greatest honor He sends the greatest trials. It has been my privilege to serve God here, in this most difficult place, to bring true salvation to Russia and her people."

"True salvation," Boris repeated, musing on the words. "Is that what you think?" He placed his fingertips together, letting his breath out slowly between nearly closed lips. "What am I to do with you, Father Pogner? You think God sent you here as a test of your dedication. Your embassy has vowed to protect the interests of King Istvan. And Nikita Romanov wants you out of the country, with all your embassy. Vasilli Shuisky wants you condemned and imprisoned. Whatever becomes of you, as the Czar's guardian for dealing with foreigners, it is my decision to make." He rose and walked toward the window, gazing out into the avenue of grand wooden palaces which clustered in that quarter of the Kremlin. He could just see the corner of the Terem Palace beyond the red-painted cupola of the Kurbsky palace next to his.

It was a hot, clear day, the July sun bright as a golden platter in the sky, and all the colors of the Kremlin and the Beautiful Market Square seemed more brilliant than usual; the central spire of the Cathedral of the Virgin of the Intercession looked glossy as lacquerwork. There were festival sounds on the air, and the heavy smell of sheep and pigs from the marketplace.

Father Pogner was not inclined to answer Boris' question at first, and then he pursed his lips. "I have been given a task by my Church, my King and my God. I have sworn to do as I am required to the very limit of my strength. It is not for the likes of you to keep me from it."

Had the Jesuit not spoken so arrogantly, Boris might have postponed his decision, but the high-handed answer stung him. He swung around and strode back toward his writing table. "There are questions you will have to answer, questions about your activities and associates. I must and will have answers before you are once again at liberty. You will remain here until I am satisfied that we have the truth from you. We will speak with your other priests, as well, in private, in order to confirm your answers. If there is any discrepancy it will go badly for you."

"You have no right to demand anything of me, Godunov," said Father Pogner. "On what authority do you issue your orders? You cannot command an ambassador of the Polish King."

"Perhaps not," said Boris. His smile was thin and false. "Yet the only member of your embassy who might have convinced me not to question you has become a hunted fugitive, largely due to your efforts. If Rakoczy were here, and if he asked it of me, I might be persuaded to grant you more latitude. As it is . . ." He made a sign and the two Guards came forward. "Take this Polish priest to the Yellow Chamber and keep him there. See that he has something to eat."

The senior Guard bowed before securing Father Pogner's upper arm. "Please to come with us," he said in a voice wholly without emotion.

For once Father Pogner remained silent as he was led away.

Left alone, Boris wandered to the other windows in the room. He stood for a time, staring northward, wondering how far the English party had traveled in the thirteen days since it left Moscovy. So far there had been no word from them: he had told Father Pogner the truth when he said he did not know where Rakoczy was at present. And fortunately he had not yet had to order the search extended to the north as well as the west, though Romanov and Shuisky both wanted it. A small company of mounted soldiers covered three to four times the distance the British wagons could in a day, which meant they could still be overtaken before reaching Novo-Kholmogory. The reports brought to the capital had indicated that the roads were open and passable all the way to Novo-Kholmogory, and that aside from the ferry across the Sukhona River beyond Vologda, there were few delays. Rakoczy should be aboard a ship bound for England in August if there were no delays. Often in the last several days Boris had wondered if he had been mistaken in his decision to remain in Moscovy instead of leaving with Rakoczy and the English merchants.

There was a rap on the door and one of the two Guards stepped inside. "He ordered me to tell you that you have no right to detain him. He would like to have parchment and ink so that he may write to the King and the Roman Pope. He demands that he be allowed a courier to deliver the complaint, as well."

"A complaint? Well, it is his privilege." Boris waved his hand to dismiss the matter. "Tomorrow. We will deal with that tomorrow. Let Father Pogner have a night to consider his situation." He left the window and went back to his table, sitting down once more and stacking the papers in a single neat pile. "It is in here."

"What is in there?" asked the Guard, who regarded the written word with a combination of hatred and awe because he could not read.

"Whoever it is who has been maneuvering me, and the Court." He leaned back against the high, hard chair. "I feel as if I had the snout and tail-tip of an animal in the dark of night, but only enough to know it is large and has long teeth. Wolf or bear or tiger?" He set his elbows on either side of the pile of paper. "Who is being hunted? Is it me? Is it Nikita Romanovich? Is it Czar Feodor? Who?"

The Guard began to retreat toward the door. "Shall I stand inside or out, Boris Feodorovich?"

Boris glanced up at him. "Outside, I think, would be better." He started with the top page and read through, searching for some information he had not noticed before. When he was done, he put the paper down and placed his next one directly beneath it, simplifying the process of comparison. He made himself think clearly, doing his best to shut away his own wrenching emotions for the cool-running clarity of reason. "I will want tea, very sweet and strong," he called after the Guard as the door began to close.

"I will inform your servants," said the Guard, thinking he had made a fortunate escape.

Four cups of tea and two hours later, Boris at last found what he had been looking for. There were two reports—and neither on its own was particularly damning—that when read together revealed nefarious intent. It was a puzzle, made up of many disparate parts, but there was enough to piece the whole together. At last he had the answer. He rose to his feet, the sheets gathered in his hands, and shouted his victory.

The Guard stuck his head around the door, apprehensive of Boris' wrath. "Is something the matter?"

"Shuisky!" thundered Boris, a world of condemnation in that name.

"Boris Feodorovich—" the Guard began cautiously, seeing the rage in Boris' black eyes.

"Bring them to me. Every one. The Shuiskys—Vasilli, Dmitri, Ivan, their uncle Mikhail, their cousins Anastasi and Igor. All of them. Now." He swung around, his arm extended. "Do you hear me? I said bring them."

"Shuisky?" the Guard asked, not anxious to move against so powerful a family. "All of them? But only Vasilli, Dmitri, and Anastasi are in Moscovy," the Guard reminded him, hoping that this would alter Boris' purpose. "Mikhail is in Novgorod and Ivan is in the country. Who knows where Igor is; you know what he is like with his whoring and drinking."

"Bring all you can find. Start with Vasilli Andreivich—his palace is within Kremlin walls. Do it quickly, before they are warned. Go. *Go!"* He thudded his fists into the table.

The Guard retreated with alacrity, and called to his fellows as he left Boris' reception room. He was going to need more than two officers to accompany him if he had to bring the Shuiskys. It would not be easy to find men who would carry out Boris' orders against the great Shuiskys; he would have to be careful in his choice of companions. If he selected the wrong soldiers, he might as well hand his weapons over to the Shuiskys at once and spare himself the farce of pursuing them. He crossed himself hurriedly before the ikons, then rushed out the door toward the Guard barracks.

Boris was pacing now, taking long strides that carried him the length of the room in less than a dozen steps. He was holding the two reports in his hands, reading from one to the other. "I should have seen it," he told himself indignantly, offended with himself for what was now an obvious oversight. "God forgive me, I ought to have seen it." Over the tolling bells of mid-afternoon Mass he cursed Shuisky, and consigned the whole family to everlasting darkness, Hell seeming much too lenient a sentence for them.

A Guard Captain rapped on the door, asking to be admitted. "Come in," said Boris, anticipating the arrival of Vasilli.

The Captain was alone. "We have been to the palace of Vasilli Andreivich," he said, apology in his demeanor. "Four Guards are posted there, awaiting his return. We are told that he and his escort are at the horse market."

"Outside the south gate?" Boris did not trust the information, for he feared that Vasilli might well choose to run from him. "He is not inside Moscovy's walls?"

"He is with Nikita Romanovich and Czar Feodor, and a dozen Guards. They are under close escort, for the honor of the Czar: four soldiers for each of them." The Captain coughed once. "It would not be wise to try to take him there, with the Czar, and—"

Boris nodded his agreement, knowing better than to press for advantage when there was none to be had. "Of course. You are wise. When he returns it is time enough to bring him to me. But see that it is done, for the safety of the Czar and yourself, Captain." He looked toward the far window. "Bring me the others, then. Bring me Dmitri Andreivich and Anastasi Sergeivich."

The Captain bowed and hastened away, leaving Boris to read over the reports he had gathered again. Now that he was aware of what he sought, every phrase in the reports accused Shuisky.

From direct descriptions of what Anastasi Sergeivich had done to the implication and innuendo about Vasilli Andreivich, there was a catalog of wrongdoing and a host of reasons once the stakes were recognized. As he read, Boris grew impatient with waiting, and to keep from fuming he paced his reception room as if it were a cage. The time went by slowly except when Boris worried that Romanov and Shuisky might act against him before he could protect himself; then the time rushed on the wind.

At last the door slammed open and four Guards brought Anastasi Sergeivich Shuisky into the room, not quite dragging him, but all of them holding his arms forcefully with both hands.

Anastasi shook himself, his features indignant as an owl's, as if he found his predicament both ludicrous and absurd. He tugged the wide sleeves of his loose summer kaftan away from the Guards, smoothed his blond beard, and bore down on Boris, his face flushed with effort and choler. Blocky and massive, he seemed intent on smashing Boris into the floor. "By what right do you send Guards to my house, Boris Feodorovich?"

"By the right of the guardian of Czar Feodor Ivanovich," said Boris, determined not to be dragged into an argument with Anastasi. He kept his writing table between them. "I speak to you now on the Little Father's behalf. There are very important questions you must answer, Anastasi Sergeivich, as you would answer to the Czar himself. I thought you would prefer to do it here than in the secret rooms of the Terem Palace, or prison." He pulled out his chair and sat down, his hands folded on top of the reports. "These reports on your endeavors have provided some peculiar information about you, Duke Shuisky. You have been very busy, have you not?"

"Of course I have been busy. Every noble at Court is busy," snapped Anastasi, flicking imaginary dust from the wide collar of his kaftan. "Where is the error in that? A man with my responsibilities is always busy."

"And what are those responsibilities?" asked Boris with interest.

"I have property and estates and my family in the country, and my position requires my presence here at Court." He said it as if Boris were as slow-witted as Czar Feodor. "Or did you mean something else?"

Boris would not be goaded into an unwise rejoinder. "If these reports are to be believed, you have devoted your time and your fortune to removing Czar Feodor from the throne in your cousin's favor." He tapped the papers. "It appears that you have taken on the task of deposing the Little Father, among your other tasks. That is treason, Duke Shuisky."

The smile froze on Anastasi's cupid-bow mouth. "I am no traitor," he said.

"No?" Boris lifted his brows. "Strange, how one may be misled by reports and vows; don't you think so? If it were not for the information gathered here I might never have come to suspect that you had anything to answer for but the pride of your family. Yet now that I have seen these reports, I realize that there has been much more to gain than I assumed. How do you explain your activities of the last four years, then?" He held up a report that ran for two pages. "I am most curious about the messengers you have used, sending them into Poland and to Kursk, to the upstart priest Yuri Kostroma. He is a connection of yours, isn't he? Illegitimate, but a cousin, nonetheless."

"A second cousin," said Anastasi.

"Yes," said Boris. "And you have used him, when it has suited your purpose, and required him to serve you." He held up another report. "A servant at the Polish embassy says that you twice visited Father Wojciech Kovnovski, to request that he assist you in your misdeeds. You sent dispatches with his messages, this servant—"

"Spy," corrected Anastasi.

"—servant claims; you convinced the priest that it would further his career to be on good terms with the great Shuisky family. According to what the servant has said, you spoke with Father Kovnovski for several hours when you visited him, and afterward you sent dispatches to those I assume are your associates." Boris peered up from the pages. "Is that a lie, Anastasi Sergeivich?"

"It is not the truth," said Anastasi without inflection.

"Isn't it?" Boris pulled out another paper and shook his head with assumed sadness. "I wish I could think so, Anastasi Sergeivich. But you see, there are others who report the same thing."

"They are nothing," said Anastasi, now far more composed than when he arrived. "Discontented mutterings and gossip."

"To your disadvantage because of your title and high position: it would appear so," said Boris in false commiseration. "Taken singly, you have nothing against you but ill-feeling and rumors, hardly worthy more than the most cursory attention. But taken all together, something else emerges. The reports reveal the scope of your schemes, and from them it becomes apparent that you have been engaged in the quest for advancement, a very dangerous quest for you, but glorious for your family if you succeed. You are a diligent and ruthless opponent to the Czar, and you seek to bring down Czar Feodor in order to raise your family and yourself."

"Oh, not I," said Anastasi, his smile reviving and his eyes fixed on the ikon of Saint Barlaam of Antioch. "I am the lesser branch of the family, and nothing I could do would advance me or my sons to the throne. It is my cousin Vasilli Andreivich who is born well enough to aspire to the throne. He has reason to hope for advancement, not I. Had you forgot that, Boris Feodorovich?"

"No more than you have," Boris replied with his own ugly smile. "Which is why I have given orders to bring all your family here, not just you." He was pleased to see that Anastasi was startled, and then something more than that, much closer to fear, flared in his blue eyes, and Boris decided to press his advantage. "He made you do his bidding, didn't he?"

Anastasi recovered himself in an instant. "Who?"

"Vasilli Andreivich," said Boris impatiently. "You have been working for him, doing what he has needed you to do. you have accepted Vasilli's ambitions as your own. Haven't you?"

"There is no reason why I should," said Anastasi darkly, and then his manner changed suddenly, becoming slippery and expansive. "What a terrible thing to ask of you, Boris Feodorovich, that you spend your time looking for enemies who do not exist for the Czar. It is the only way to control Romanov, is that it?"

"But there is reason for you to be led by your cousin at this time," Boris said, ignoring Anastasi's mercurial shift of mood, and rubbed his mustache. "There are excellent reasons for you to help your cousin rise in the world. You seek to place Vasilli on the throne by bringing about the fall of Czar Feodor and all his Court. And while it is true that you would not be able to claim the throne for yourself, not while Vasilli and Dmitri and Ivan all live, you are willing to gamble on the years to come, knowing that the nobles of the Court of high blood will war for position.

You long for that war. Not for yourself, of course, nor even for your cousin. But you have how many sons?" He let the question hang between them, all but visible in the warm, still air.

"God has given my wife and me six sons, and five of them are living," he said, annoyed and proud at once. "There are also four daughters, for I visit my wife one month of every year, and I seek to guard them, my wife and children. They do not live in Moscovy."

"Very wise," said Boris with a feeling that was almost approval. "It keeps them safe and most of the Court forgets about them. I am familiar with the ploy myself." He met Anastasi's eyes directly. "So your cousin becomes Czar, and you his close adviser, the one serving the Czar and the Court. In time this will bring you honor and the recognition you have sought so diligently, and one day your sons rule. In order to achieve such a goal the sacrifice of your own advancement is of little importance." He regarded Anastasi with an amiable smile. "Isn't that your vision, Anastasi Sergeivich? the vision of your sons ruling Russia in a way you never can achieve? You can bear to see Vasilli Andreivich reign if it brings your sons to the throne as well, in years to come. It is not impossible, once Vasilli mounts the throne. After all, Vasilli's only surviving children are girls, and direct blood is better than marriage. And if one of your sons marries one of Vasilli's daughters, so much the better."

"You are ridiculous," said Anastasi, but there was a wildness in this denial that was more eloquent than his words. The sweat on his face was not entirely due to the heat of the afternoon.

Boris regarded him. "How much is your dream, and how much is Vasilli's tyranny, I wonder?"

"What is that intended to mean?" asked Anastasi bluntly.

"It is a reminder that you may have put yourself at a disadvantage for no purpose," said Boris even more bluntly. "It may be that Vasilli Andreivich is well-aware of what you plan, and is using your aspirations to aid his own cause without any benefit to you. He may have already arranged marriages for his daughters with Nikita Romanovich, who has sons, too. You may have done his bidding to the detriment of your children, not their advancement." He enjoyed the discomfort he saw on Anastasi's features. "Why should Vasilli aid you when he can have your devotion to his cause without it?"

"Vasilli Andreivich is not so cynical," said Anastasi with a laugh that almost came off. "He is not about to advance Romanov when he can advance Shuisky."

"Possibly not," Boris conceded immediately. "But suppose that you were his goat, Anastasi Sergeivich?" He indicated the papers on his writing table. "Read them for yourself, if you like. There are indications that Vasilli has gained certain advantages from your deeds, but nothing here indicates that you have acted in any way but at your own instigation." He put his hands on the table, leaning forward. "If the Metropolitan does not speak out in your behalf, then I must assume that you are responsible for all the acts recorded here."

"You do not suppose that either my cousin or I would be so reckless and stupid as to leave clear blame for more than one of us, do you?" Anastasi cocked his head as if waiting to hear a child answer. "Do you think we are so unable to guard ourselves, Boris Feodorovich?"

"I think it would be possible for a Shuisky to betray more than the Czar," said Boris. "If you have to answer for what your cousin has done, you will be more than a fool, you will be twice the traitor, and betray yourself."

"Twice, because Vasilli Andreivich—assuming he has done anything—would still be free to plot the overthrow of the Czar? Have I taken your meaning correctly?" Anastasi waved the whole idea away with a quick, fussy gesture. "Why do you try to force me to speak against my own family? I am ambitious, and I would rather that Shuisky ruled here than Czar Feodor, but I am no tool of my cousin's will."

"And all you have done has been for your benefit and the advancement of your sons?" Boris inquired, his voice rising with incredulity. "The Church and the Court will condemn you for all you have done."

Anastasi fingered his beard. "Do they tell you I am very bad?" he asked sarcastically. "Am I a demon's servant?"

"You are without doubt a criminal," said Boris deliberately, "and you will answer for your crimes. But who will answer with you, and spare you the plight of a hard, long death?"

This time Anastasi's laughter was rich and loud. "What an obvious trap you lay, Boris Feodorovich. I thought you more subtle than that." He took a step back from the writing table. "Oh, yes, I have sought to remove Czar Feodor from the throne, that I freely acknowledge. I will say so again if you demand I confess to the Court as well. I will also confess to blasting Czar Ivan's wits—"

"His grief did that," Boris interrupted.

"Do you know that beyond cavil?" Anastasi challenged, beginning to enjoy himself. "I will confess that I blasted Czar Ivan's wits, and that I summoned the tailed star to increase his madness, that I influenced the Lappish witches to predict the day when I would kill him, so that no one would realize that I murdered him." He rubbed his hands together. "And then we will see what the Court will say. They might order me killed, if I maintain my silence and my dignity as the Europeans would have us do. They dare not order me imprisoned, in case Shuisky ever rises to Czar, for then they would have reason to fear my vengeance. If they are wise it would be death." He beamed seraphically. "Or they might send me to one of the distant monasteries to pray for the restoration of my wits by the mercy of God. They would leave my wife and children alone, except to pity them because of me. Think of it: Anastasi Sergeivich Shuisky as a humble monk, penitent and striving to expiate his pride. Do you reckon it would take long for everyone to forget what I have done? In time I may become a Holy Fool, and speak words of wisdom. The Metropolitan would like that, wouldn't he, having a noble wandering the streets in rags preaching his madness. Guilt and tribulation and a reward of visions. How the Court would envy me then, getting to say precisely what I like and to be venerated for it. What do you think?" He laughed again, letting all his dread and all his hope go with it.

Boris regarded him narrowly. "What am I to say to you?" He hated the sound of Anastasi's laughing. "It is very clever."

Anastasi was silent at once, then said, "Madmen are often clever."

"Yes; they are," said Boris, wondering how true it was now.

Text of a dispatch from Czar Feodor to the Guard station at Spaso-Kamenny, countersigned by Nikita Romanovich Romanov and Vasilli Andreivich Shuisky, carried by Czar's messenger and delivered on August 2.

As Czar of all the Russias, it is my wish that you seek out and detain a foreigner, one Ferenc Rakoczy, late of the embassy of

King Istvan of Poland, believed to be in the company of English merchants bound for Novo-Kholmogory. This foreigner has been given thirty lashes with the knout and it may be that his injuries have brought him to answer before God instead of permitting him to answer to me.

You may proceed in the full confidence of my approval and reward of your actions, even if they must be taken against the subjects of my ally, Elizabeth of England, who has been my staunch friend as she was the friend of my glorious father before me.

If there is resistance to this detainment, you are authorized to take whatever actions are necessary to bring Rakoczy back to Moscovy to answer questions of vital importance to me and to those of my Court who have been maligned and otherwise slandered by this foreign exile.

You are also ordered not to kill this Rakoczy. As part of the Polish mission, he is to be respected, but as an enemy of the Czar, he is to be arrested so that he may answer all claims brought against him, and reveal those Rus who have joined with his nefarious plans to murder the Czar. If Rakoczy is killed, he will not be able to inform us who his associates are. Should Rakoczy die in your care, you will answer for it.

However it is done, Rakoczy must be returned to Moscovy, to the protection of Prince Vasilli Sergeivich Shuisky, who will undertake the task of questioning the foreigner. He will give a full report to the Czar, and that report will include his opinion of how well you have discharged your orders. His good review will bring you favor; his condemnation will disgrace you for the rest of your lives.

You are warned that this Rakoczy is a magician, of great power and influence. He has already caused Prince Shuisky's cousin to go mad, and he presented cursed jewels to Czar Ivan, to disorder his addled senses so that God's mercy could not restore his sanity in spite of the prayers and devotions of all Rus. Beware that this alchemist does not work his spells on you. Do not think you can conquer his magic. Others have tried and paid a high price for their assumptions. Therefore guard against his might with your faith and your weapons. Never let him have access to one of you alone, but be diligent: two of you must always be present with him, otherwise you expose yourselves to his influence.

Give thanks to God that Czar Feodor has escaped the sly
efforts of this Transylvanian devil. May He send you good horses
and a swift arrest.

Under the double eagle of Russia
at the mandate of Czar Feodor Ivanovich,
last of the Danilov dynasty
Vasilli Andreivich Shuisky
Nikita Romanovich Romanov

9

Nineteen days out from Moscovy the English wagons met their
first delay: a bridge over one of the small rivers cutting through
the vast northern forestlands had collapsed during a thunder-
storm when an ancient pine had fallen on it. Peasants from the
local village were attempting to rebuild it without interrupting
their summer farming, and so the reconstruction was not rapid.
Ordinarily they would have welcomed the assistance offered by
the travelers, but they looked askance on the English volunteers.

"You are not Rus," the local priest Father Sevastyan explained
to the head of the company, a tall young man with pale hair and
a sea-weathered face named William Flemming. "It would be a
bad omen, to have the bridge built by those who are not Rus. It
would fall again when the first Rus merchants crossed over it."
He crossed himself and waited to hear what else the English
would say.

"We have over three dozen men," Flemming said, using Benedict Lovell to translate for him. "They're all willing."

"It is not right, having them build the bridge," said Father
Sevastyan with a sigh. "If you were Rus we would gladly accept
the offer, but——" He gestured. "There is a cleared field, not too
far off this path. You may spend the night there. And if you
cannot wait for the bridge, there is a place some way upstream."

"Some way?" said Flemming suspiciously; in Russia distances
were vast, and they could go many days out of their way looking
for the ford.

"Seven, perhaps eight versts," said the priest as he thought about it. "There is a village there, with a cattle market."

"And they probably call it Oxford," said Lovell to Flemming at the end of his translation. "The place you can get cattle across the river."

Father Sevastyan scowled at their laughter, and held up an admonitory finger. "It is a serious business, traveling here. If you are light-minded, you will not survive."

Lovell translated the warning and regarded Father Sevastyan with sympathy. "We meant no disrespect. We were recalling a town in England where the same thing has happened." He patted his chest. "It is my home."

Some of Father Sevastyan's caution diminished. "Ah? Well, it may be so." He did not allow the foreigners to draw him into talk about England; he pointed in the direction of the field. "You may stay there for the night. Our women will cook for you, at the charge of three golden coins for all."

"We will pay it gladly, and one more for your church," said Lovell, who had become familiar with the expected social forms in Russia. "We have traveled a long way, and one grows tired of stews. There are eleven wagons; two drivers and two out-riders per wagon. All but the last belong to Mister Flemming here, and are laden with Russian goods bound for markets in England. It is his men we want to have food prepared for. The eleventh is the property of a foreign nobleman." He indicated the last wagon in the line. "He has been injured and we do not want to disturb him while he mends." He could not quite keep the surprise from his voice, for he had never supposed that Rakoczy would recover from the knouting.

Flemming glanced uneasily toward that last wagon. "He is traveling with his wife and his servant. His driver is hired by him for this journey and therefore not one of mine." He looked at the villagers who had gathered around them. "I am certain that they will want food along with the rest of us."

Lovell was not as convinced as Flemming was. "The driver will, certainly, but the others with Rakoczy might not." He stared at Flemming. "I will speak with them, and find out what they want."

"If you think that best," said Flemming, dismissing the matter, and looking annoyed while Lovell translated it for the benefit of

Father Sevastyan. "Don't you think this is unnecessary?" he asked when the scholar was silent.

"I think we need the goodwill of these people, and travelers like Rakoczy occasion remarks; it's best to anticipate them." He shaded his eyes and peered up at the sun. "It's getting late. Unless you want to be on the road at sunset we might as well stop here, though it is early. We either stay here for the night or try to find our way to the cattle ford, and as we don't know the road between here and there—"

"Yes, yes," said Flemming impatiently. "It makes more sense to stay here even if we go to the cattle ford tomorrow. We will have all day for the journey, and on these narrow tracks we will not make much progress." He sighed. "Tell the priest we will have our camp set in an hour. Invite him to visit us, if you think it wise."

Lovell translated some of what Flemming had said, and embroidered the invitation so that he sounded more eager to have the peasants visit them. He assured Father Sevastyan that the English wanted to have a last taste of Russian hospitality before they went aboard their own ships and settled in to the long, arduous days at sea. "There must be good singers in this village. Perhaps you would favor us with a few songs. We will not hear good Russian songs for a long time, once we are gone."

"It is a great honor," said Father Sevastyan, beaming in anticipation. "There are fine singers here. Fine, fine singers."

"What did you tell him?" asked Flemming as they made their way back to the wagons. "It turned him up sweet, whatever it was."

"I asked him to arrange for us to be entertained tonight," said Lovell, and reading the sudden greed in Flemming's eyes, he added, "Not women—no one should touch the women—but singing."

"Loaves and fishes!" swore Flemming. "They'll be at it half the night."

"And they will cook for the occasion," added Lovell, smiling a little as the significance of what he said sank in. "Better than having to buy old bread, as we had to last night in Nizhkovo."

Flemming gestured his approval. "Yes. I see your point. Very canny." He clapped Lovell on the back. "Not bad for an Oxford scholar. You're not one of those muttering everything in Latin hexameters and trying to decide what Pliny meant about the shape of the cloud over the volcano."

"No," agreed Lovell. "I'm not that kind of scholar." He felt a shiver of regret as he spoke, for now that he was going home, he began to feel his life closing in. It was true enough that he was no longer young, that he was past the age when most men thought about leaving the rigors of life to the next generation. Yet he had come to realize that he did not want to give up his adventuring in favor of reading about what others had done. He was still turning over these disquieting thoughts as he approached Rakoczy's wagon at the end of the line.

The three-horse hitch had by far the finest animals in the line, and the six trailing after were as splendid as the three yoked to the wagon. All the horses glistened the color of old silver. The driver was part Hungarian and came from a family of horse trainers going back five generations; since Rakoczy had hired him four months earlier he refused to let anyone touch the reins but himself. His name was Geza and he clung proudly to his Hungarian accent, though he had long since forgotten the language.

"We're staying here tonight," called out Lovell, and quickly explained the reason for this decision. "This is the first time we have faced any delay. One afternoon isn't much of a sacrifice." He recalled the reason for his visit. "If you want to eat with the rest of the train, let me know."

"I'll want to eat. As for the rest, that's for the master to hear," said the driver when Lovell was through. "It's as well with me that we stop early. The horses could use the rest." He folded his arms in his tooled-leather shuba.

From behind the wagon Rothger rode up, leading the six relief horses. He listened to what Lovell had to say, then got out of the saddle, securing the lead to the wagon and looping his mount's reins over the edge of the driver's box. He motioned for Lovell to follow him, then went to rap on the door to the wagon interior. "My master, Doctor Lovell would like to speak to you."

Xenya opened the door. "He is awake, but he still isn't very strong. Don't be deceived by his manner." She moved aside, making as much room as she could in the cramped interior.

Rakoczy lay on a large pile of cushions set atop four massive chests which contained his native earth. He was dressed in a loose Burgundian houppelande of black sculptured Italian vel-

vet, the standing collar edged in red piping. He lifted one hand
in greeting; there was no swelling left in his fingers but the fading
bruises turned the skin an acid green patched with brown. When
he spoke his voice was soft and sounded unused. "Good afternoon, gentlemen. I thought you might come by. I take it there is
some reason why we are stopping?"

"The bridge is out," said Lovell in English. "The repairs are
about half-done. We're told there's a ford upstream, but—"

"But you don't want to leave the known road," Rakoczy finished for him. "Very sensible." He took a long, deep breath as if
to cover pain, then went on with unruffled calm. "We will stay
the night here, then, and in the morning decide what is best to
be done?"

"That's it," said Lovell, and glanced over at Xenya, continuing
in Russian, "I'm afraid you'll have to stay in the wagon again,
Madame, though I can arrange for you to have food," he told her.
"I don't think the peasants here would take well to a woman of
your station venturing out among them."

Xenya sighed. "I have veils," she said wistfully, all the while
keeping an anxious eye on her husband. "But I suppose you're
right. It's wiser not to be seen. If I leave the wagon and the
peasants aren't offended, the drivers would be, and you would
have to calm them down again. One disruption was sufficient."
She shook her head at the recollection of the difficulty an evening walk had brought her when they reached Vologda. "But I
long to stroll beside the river, watching the light fade."

"There'll be time enough for that aboard ship," said Lovell. "It
is only another—"

"Another thirty days," said Rothger sternly, with a flicker of
concern in his eyes as he looked up at Rakoczy. "If there are no
more delays." He had crouched down by the chests on which
Rakoczy and the cushions lay.

"It could be less," said Lovell hopefully. "Henry Percival of the
Katherine Montmorency came to Moscovy from Novo-Kholmogory in thirty-nine days."

"He was very fortunate," said Rothger.

"That's true, but it is also correct to say that we could be
fortunate as well," Lovell insisted. "The *Phoenix* will be waiting
for us, whenever we arrive. It cannot sail without Mister Flemming, can it?"

"I suppose not," said Rakoczy. It was becoming an effort for him to speak, and moving caused an ache so deep he could not conceal a grimace. "Your pardon."

Xenya and Rothger exchanged a single, swift glance, and Rothger spoke. "The broken rib is still unhealed," he said to Lovell, as if this were the extent of the damage remaining. He moved toward the door and slid it open. "Come. We can speak outside."

They were four strides away from the wagon when Lovell said, "Is he getting better? Truly?"

Rothger smiled once. "Yes. In time you will never know it happened. But now he is in . . . unimaginable pain."

"But surely he . . ." Lovell faltered, then began again. "He has preparations he had given others, syrups and tinctures I have been told take pain away. I had heard he cured one of the Polish priests of putrid lungs."

"Sadly, he cannot avail himself of those nostrums." There was something in his eyes that warned Lovell not to pursue the matter.

Ahead of them William Flemming was ordering the wagons into a U-shaped formation, the open end toward the village. He called out to Lovell, "I want that wagon on the east side of the camp, behind my first wagon. All right?" That would put Rakoczy's wagon behind the bottom of the U, not quite excluded from the rest, but oddly apart from them. "All right?"

"If that is what is wanted," agreed Rothger. "Tell Geza where the wagon is to be." He went a little further, Lovell trailing behind him. Only when he was satisfied they would not be overheard, he spoke again, in Latin, "My master fears we may still be followed."

"For what reason?" Lovell answered in that language, his accent—to Rothger's inward amusement—like none that was ever heard in Imperial Rome. "They must suppose he is dead by now."

"Possibly," said Rothger. "But he has remained alive a long time, in large part because he has not denied danger." He paused. "He is in no condition to fight. He can barely hold a quill to write with. His muscles have just begun to knit, and he cannot yet walk without assistance."

"Are you telling me you need more protection?" Lovell asked, his concern increasing.

"I am saying we *may* need protection." Rothger frowned slightly. "There are times I sense it, myself, something behind us."

Lovell laced his fingers and pressed his palms downward. "I'll speak to Flemming in the morning. But I don't think he'll like it. He doesn't want to compromise himself with the Rus. If he decides you will bring him trouble, he could order you to travel behind us, rather than with us."

"That is not acceptable," said Rothger directly. "Our passage is paid and half this cargo comes through my master. We travel with the cargo as well as the company."

"Still, Flemming is a cautious man," warned Lovell.

"We'll sweeten the proposition with gold. Nine golden angels for his trouble. Tell him. There is more if necessary." Rothger turned as Geza slapped the reins, directing the wagon to the place Flemming wanted it. "We'll put the horses on a grazing line tonight," he called to the driver.

"And have someone watch for bear," Lovell added. "With so many horses, we could attract them."

"Truly," said Rothger, bowed once to Lovell in the Italian manner, and turned toward where the wagons had grouped.

In the long dusk of northern summer the English camp rang with Russian songs and excited laughter. Fragrant steam rose from several cooking fires where piglets broiled on spits and onions soaked in raw berry wines burst their cracking skins. Even those men assigned to patrol the outer camp whistled as they went about their rounds, notched and quarreled crossbows held negligently; they drank the cups of yeasty dark beer they were regularly offered.

In their wagon, Xenya hummed along with the songs she knew, and fought the impulse to burst into tears. How long would it be before she heard these songs again? England was a distant, strange country: who knew what they sang there? She sat facing away from Rakoczy, afraid that even now his keen eyes would detect her distress. Earlier she had urged him to sleep, for it was apparent his pain was worse; but he had said he wanted to listen to the music.

"One day—it will take more time, but one day—I would like to play something for you, Xenya Evgeneivna. One of Lauro's songs, perhaps." He had touched her bronze-colored braids, his dark eyes on her honey-colored ones; it took him some time to speak. "I am sorry I brought you to this, Xenya."

"Never say that," she had answered him at once. "I am not sorry at all." But sitting and listening to the music now, she could not avoid a pang of regret. She tried to work up her courage, to ask him about England, but could not.

His voice in the dark was very low. "You could have been safe, Xenya; that is what troubles me."

She took a chance; she turned and looked at him. "Safe? I would be safe if they forgot about me, and what safety is that?"

One of the village women had a low, sinuous voice, and the song she sang was plaintive and insidious, coiling its sad little melody around and around until it fixed in the listeners' thoughts, stirring memories and awakening ghosts of forsaken loves. *"His kisses were the staff of life for me; I dined on them better than a boyarina on her pheasant and dumplings."* As she lamented the death of her faithful lover at the hands of a jealous enchantress, everyone who could hear her was caught up in it, captured by the sweet, mournful dirge.

The singer was in the middle of the last, most heart-wrenching verse when the company of eleven Guards rode into the village, their lances held at the ready, bows strung for use.

As the melody trailed away, the villagers were the first to be alarmed. Most of them drew back, away from the cooking fires, many of them crossing themselves and reciting prayers when they saw the mounted soldiers. They not so much panicked as vanished. Father Sevastyan hastened toward his church, calling for the villagers to follow him to sanctuary; quite a few of them did.

In the silence they had created the leader of the Guards called out, "Where is the foreigner Rakoczy? We are mandated by Czar Feodor Ivanovich to return him to Moscovy at once."

At first no one spoke, and then there was a sudden babble as many of the English reached for their weapons; they had not understood the Guard, but they knew a threat when they heard it, and they responded to it.

"Wait, wait!" called out Lovell in English, walking toward the Russian troops. "We are foreigners," he said in Russian. "Bound for Novo-Kholmogory with cargo to be shipped to England. We are English." He turned slightly so that he could address Flemming in English. "Tell them to put their weapons down, will you? These men will attack if they think you've provoked them."

"I don't think so," said Flemming in a genial tone. "Not for that lot."

"I thought you disliked the idea of defending our foreign friend," said Lovell, surprised at Flemming's attitude.

"Oh, I do," said Flemming. "But the man is injured and these caitiffs are too high-handed. If they want him, they'll have to walk through us to get him, but not until we're ready for them." He folded his arms, waiting for Lovell to translate.

When Lovell had done this, with some softening of Flemming's remarks, he listened to the Guard's commands, and relayed them back to Flemming. "He wants you to put down your weapons. All of them."

Flemming scowled, but said, "All right, you men where the Rus can see you, put your weapons down. The rest of you, stay ready. I don't like this." He motioned toward Lovell as he put down his dirk. "Tell them we're laying down our weapons, and only that."

Lovell did as he was told, adding, "These are merchants, not soldiers. You can see that for yourself."

"We have no interest in merchants," said the Guard leader. "We only want the foreigner. We have this"—he held out the dispatch from Czar Feodor—"as our authority against foreigners."

In his wagon, Rakoczy was attempting to sit up, but collapsed with the effort. "Never mind," he panted as dark threads wavered through his sight. "Give me the sword, Xenya. The short one. There. Beside the chest." He lifted his hand but could not master his trembling. "Bring it to me. Now." He closed his hand around the hilt but he could not hold it for more than a few heartbeats. "And hide. You must hide. I don't want them to find you." He glanced around the wagon. "In the front, under the driver's box. If you huddle in there, they won't find you."

Xenya had turned back to the leather case beside the chests, and she pulled out a Byzantine longsword, hefting it uncertainly. "I am not a mouse, my husband, to hide from such as those."

"We are English," said Flemming to the Guards once more, standing beside his translator. "We are carrying goods to my ship, the *Phoenix*. We aren't doing anything against the Czar. We have a document signed by him and by Boris Godunov giving us the right to trade in Russia. Tell them that, Lovell. And take as long as you can about it. I want to give my men time to notch their crossbows and ready their quarrels where the Rus can't see."

Lovell was sweating, but he hoped that the Guards would think it was because of the heat and all the food and drink of the evening. He did as Flemming ordered, adding, "We cannot help you, Guards. If we could—"

"They told us in Vologda and in Nizhkovo that you had a foreigner with you. Let us take him, and you will be left alone. Our dispatch is for him alone, but it tells us to detain him at any cost. If you stand against us, then we must fight you in order to capture the man." The leader rose in his stirrups. "I will order my men to bring you down."

"Our Queen will protest this," said Flemming when Lovell relayed it to him.

"Your Queen will never know. You will vanish. Many people vanish in this wilderness." He turned to his men and spat out sharp orders.

"What did he say?" asked Flemming, edging toward a large wooden table where trays of abandoned food lay.

"He said to search the wagons and shoot or lance anyone who tries to stop them," Lovell replied. "They mean to do it."

"And I mean to stop them," said Flemming, his voice loud enough to carry to his men. "If the English are prepared to take cover? Then, Lovell, tell them they are outnumbered and we will not allow the wagons to be searched."

"If that is what you want," said Lovell with a sigh, and translated this for the Guards. He could see them preparing to make a rush, the tips of their lances rising, their hands tightening on the reins of their rugged Don horses. He had already decided he was going to dive under the nearest wagon.

"So be it," said the Guard, and signaled his men.

The charge was short but furious, the horses spurred to a bounding gallop down the middle of the wagon U. They succeeded in wounding one man, lancing his shoulder.

From the grazing line where Rakoczy had sent him, Rothger watched the charge begin, and strove with Geza to keep all the horses from bolting. They had two others to assist them, but with more than fifty horses, it was taxing and dangerous work.

Lovell had barely rolled into the protective cover of the wagon when he heard the wounded man scream, but then there were other screams, startled screams that came from the Guards as the first of the crossbow quarrels found their marks. One of the horses went down with thrashing hooves that overset a cooking pot; her rider was pinned beneath her, shouting in fear. Another one of the Guards dropped from the saddle, blood welling from his mouth and ears. A third Guard had taken a quarrel high on his leg where it joined the hip. He howled and grabbed the quarrel, howling more loudly as he touched it. The leader of the Guard shouted for them to turn.

But now four of Flemming's men were at the open end of the U, firing another round of quarrels.

The leader's horse went down, the quarrel deep in his neck. The leader shouted to his men to scatter and use their shashkas instead of their lances. "Cut! Them! Down!"

Six men were still mounted, and their leader had abandoned his stricken horse, bringing only his long, curved shashka to defend himself. The Guards wheeled about and broke through the wagons, scattering to the outside of the U, intending to drive the English into the center.

Two of the crossbowmen broke and ran for the trees, unwilling to fight mounted men with swords. The other two fired at the most opportune targets, one taking a Guard high in the chest and flinging him from the saddle.

"This is terrible," whispered Flemming to Lovell as he crawled under the wagon with him. "We'll have to kill all of them, or Heaven knows what these devils will do to the villagers." He clicked his tongue. "We surely cannot permit them to take Rakoczy. No telling what they'd do to him, and he's been through enough."

"I suspect you're right," said Lovell, his love of adventure suddenly deserting him; at that moment he longed for the quiet and solitude of Brasenose College so desperately that he bit his lip. "Do you think the villagers will help us, after this?"

"They're savages, these Rus," Flemming announced. "They're worse than those painted, feathered folk in the New World, or those dervishes in Turkey." He wriggled to draw a long dagger with a fishhook tip from its scabbard. "In case," he explained.

"I see," said Lovell, aghast at the thought that Flemming might use it on him, or himself.

"I wish I had my pistols, but they're in the wagon. God's Teeth, I could use them now." Flemming pointed out to the nearest of the mounted Guards and mimed firing at him.

The leader of the Guards ran along the outside of the wagons, his shashka up and ready. He heard another of his men fall and he cursed. As he passed each wagon, he cut through the heavy canvas rear flap and glanced inside. Only once was he offered any resistance and that man he killed in a single thrust of his Russian saber.

By the time he reached the wagon at the end of the U, he knew that he was down to three men, and impossible as it seemed, he realized he might lose the encounter. His outrage increased as he thought of himself defeated by a handful of English sailors and a group of merchants! It was unthinkable. It was unbearable. He ran to the rear wagon, and noticed that instead of heavy canvas at the back there was wood, like the rest of the wagon, and a small door. He rushed forward and pounded on the door with the hilt of his shashka, demanding the door be opened. When there was no response, he kicked it in, calling on the saints to aid him. His face was flushed, for he sensed that triumph was finally at hand. He cried out as the wood gave way.

He faced a woman holding a long, straight Byzantine sword; behind her a black-clad man lay on a makeshift couch of chests and cushions. He was certain he had found his man. "Rakoczy," he said, satisfaction coming over him at last.

"You will not," said the woman, her strange, light-blue sarafan gathered and tied so that she could move freely. She swung the sword toward him. "Out! You will get out or I will kill you."

"Xenya," the man in black protested weakly.

She ignored him, advancing toward the Guard, the sword held unsteadily but with clear determination. "Leave," she said purposefully, without a trace of fear; there was no hesitation in her.

The Guard chuckled once, and swung his shashka; she batted at it with the flat of the longsword, as he hoped she would. It was what anyone would do who knew nothing of swordplay. He brought his blade around in an arc and swung it up so that it caught her under the left arm, slicing deep up into her chest. He shouted victory as her blood erupted in huge, steady pulsations, spraying the Guard, the walls, everything.

"NO." Rakoczy had seen it about to happen, and strove to

gather what little strength he had to protect her or fight back. He forced his hand to close on the hilt of the short sword, and with a will that overrode the relentless pain that clawed and tore his wounds, he levered himself onto one elbow, and with the other arm he flung the short sword like a dagger with the very limits of his fragile energy an instant before Xenya toppled and fell across him.

The short sword took the Guard straight and true at the base of the ribs, cleaving through his body to his spine. He stood for a moment, an expression of surprise on his face, and then he tottered, falling out the door, to land splayed, the short sword still quivering.

As Rakoczy fell back, he pulled Xenya more closely to him, as if he could stanch her blood and bring life back to her. The last thought Rakoczy had, before he surrendered to agony and darkness, was that that wound would have been as fatal to him as it was to the Guard.

The last of the soldiers were out of the saddle and their horses were turned loose by the time Lovell found the carnage in Rakoczy's wagon. He called at once for Rothger, and the two of them stood together in mute horror.

Finally Rothger spoke. "You make the arrangements for the Guard. I will tend to my master and his wife. If I need assistance, Geza will help me."

Lovell swallowed hard and offered no protest. He bent to pull the short sword from the Guard's body, tasting bile as he did. Then he took the body by the feet and dragged him away.

As the English finished burying the Guards with their own dead, Rothger offered a small ruby to Father Sevastyan. "To ornament your ikon of the Virgin, in her memory. Say the Masses for her, and see that no one despoils her grave," he ordered as he watched Geza carry Xenya's body through the church door and toward the ikonostasis.

"But surely . . . surely it would be better if she were buried with her husband's family, or with her own," the old priest protested, wary of having such a grave at his church. "As his wife——"

"My master is an exile, and her father and mother are dead," said Rothger simply. "There is no place he can bring her. Be merciful, Father." He made one last attempt. "Let her lie in Russian earth, Father Sevastyan, for she is Rus."

His eyes were troubled but Father Sevastyan took the ruby. "All right. We will bury her with the others of the village, and mark the place with a cross. We will pray for her soul." He crossed himself. "And for his."

"That's a kindness," said Rothger, who had seen the blood matting Rakoczy's black houppelande and realized how much of it was his master's; he was grateful that Rakoczy was unconscious and would not learn of this until later, when it would not rend his heart as it would now.

Father Sevastyan glanced toward his ikonostasis; Geza had laid Xenya's body down before it, and was kneeling now to pray for her. He nodded once. "You had better go."

"Yes." said Rothger, and signaled to Geza before he walked away toward the English wagons.

Text of a letter from Boris Feodorovich Godunov to Istvan Bathory, King of Poland, written in Polish, sent with the escort of the returning Polish mission to Moscovy.

To the august and puissant leader of the Poles, the most exalted Transylvanian Istvan Bathory, the respectful greetings of Boris Feodorovich Godunov, guardian of foreign concerns for Czar Feodor Ivanovich, Grand Prince and Czar of all the Russias.

This accompanies your Jesuits, and brings you my greetings as well as my good-will. Because of the high regard in which I hold Your Majesty, I will take this opportunity to inform you of certain events you may not otherwise learn of, events that are in your best interests to know.

As you must be aware, Father Pogner has been requested to remain in Moscovy to answer questions regarding his activities in association with certain traitorous nobles. Once he has given satisfactory information, he will be permitted to leave Moscovy, and you have my assurance that he will travel with appropriate escort so that any attempts against him by the remaining forces of the perfidious nobles may be thwarted. It would be unfortunate if he were made the object of their vengeance.

The apparent leader of the traitors has sought the mercy of the Church, and the Metropolitan has declared that the penitence of this noble is sincere, which removes him from the judgment of the Court to the judgment of the Metropolitan. The noble has renounced the world and declared his abhorrence for what he has done. I wish I could inform you that the man will answer for all he has wrought in this world; he and all of us will answer at the throne of God.

It has been learned that all implications of illegal and immoral acts that were made against your countryman Ferenc Rakoczy, Hrabia Saint-Germain, are false, as I have always known they were. His reputation has been cleared and his name will be honored in the Russian Court. Any stigma that may linger will be punished by branding. The severe punishment Rakoczy suffered was wholly the result of the schemes of the traitors, and the Court will issue a formal apology for his injuries as soon as we locate him. However, I must report that I cannot inform you where Rakoczy is at this time. He left Moscovy with a company of English merchants bound for Novo-Kholmogory and the English ship Phoenix, *which sails for London. I have not received word that the ship has departed, nor do I know if he left with it. I have learned that an illegal order sent Guards after Rakoczy to arrest him as part of the plot of the traitors, but the Guards have not returned to their station at Spaso-Kamenny and remain unaccounted for. If they detained Rakoczy, there is no record of it, for guards and Rakoczy have vanished. I regret deeply that I cannot tell you what has become of Rakoczy. His wife, as well, has disappeared, which causes me deep personal distress, for I agreed to guarantee her safety and fortune and this would appear not to be possible as long as her whereabouts is unknown. I pray that when we find Rakoczy, we find Xenya Evgeneivna as well.*

I urge you to reconsider your plan to press the Polish borders eastward at this time. You have claims in the region, but we have them as well, and it would mean long battles and much ruin of cities and crops. With the Ottomites coming into Europe, would not your armies be better employed against the forces of Islam than against fellow Christians? Is it not more reasonable to have the land in question in the hands of the Rus than the Ottomites? Let me ask you to think of this before you take up the sword against us again.

The selection of wines from France and Hungary you have

been gracious enough to send to us through the good offices of the merchant Zygmunt Dzerny are greatly appreciated by Czar Feodor and all those who are privileged to dine with him. We have long enjoyed tokay in the Court, but many of us had never tasted the Bull's Blood. It is strong, as you warned, but hearty, and many of the nobles who were permitted to drink it spoke highly of it. I would be grateful if you could tell me how the Polish wine merchants so often contrive to have the best drink.

The Court of the Czar will always welcome the embassy of the King of Poland. You need not fear to send your representatives to us at any time. I believe it is wisest to have such ministers at hand, for in difficult times these officers make it possible for rulers to understand one another. Send your new embassy, I urge you, and I will select four men of education and integrity to come to you, as well, in the interests of the Czar and the Rus.

May God send you good counsel, prosperity, and wisdom, King Istvan, and may he show us all the way of brotherhood and charity. May you increase in virtue and prudence as Poland increases in strength. May God spare you from famine and plague and war. And may your good angel ever guide your thoughts and the destiny of your kingdom.

By the hand of
Boris Feodorovich Godunov
Guardian to Czar Feodor Ivanovich
September 11, in the Roman Year 1585,
at the Kremlin in Moscovy

Epilogue

Text of a letter from Atta Olivia Clemens at Greengages in England, written in Latin to Sanct' Germain at Ghent.

To my dearest and oldest and most treasured friend, Ragoczy Sanct' Germain Franciscus, my fondest greetings;

You did not have to leave, you know. I would have been delighted to have you remain here for years. I can understand why this bucolic life might bore you after a time, but I had no reason to assume you were filled with ennui; I would rather call it melancholy. If traveling to the Lowlands will end that, then I wish you good fortune and the speed of one of your forgotten gods. But if you are seeking only a place to hide, then I warn you there is a good chance I will come after you.

Your Russian horses are thriving, but I must tell you that they are not much admired by the English, who prefer heavier, bigger-shouldered horses than these. I may cross them with some of my Italian horses if that meets with your approval. If I can keep the color, I think the Italians might have a taste for them. I still find it hard to believe that you used these magnificent animals as cart horses.

Benedict Lovell is coming to visit me next month. Yes, I know he is in danger to become one of our blood, but I have told him of the risks and he is willing to take his chances. I am not certain he believes me, or truly understands what could become of him, but if it is his decision, I will not cavil for I know he is aware that those of our blood are not as other persons are, and about that he is convinced. He has said that he knew there was something beyond ordinary human strength in your recovery from the knouting you received. His description of your condition still makes me shudder. To have had your muscles tattered by the knout, and to tear them afresh. What on earth possessed you.

No, do not tell me. I know what possessed you. And much as I might castigate you for the injury you did yourself, I can never have anything but the most profound compassion for your loss of Xenya. You say you regret that there was no time to make her one of your blood, yet you told me she loved you for what you are, not for what you are. And I know how you long for someone who will knowingly love you. But, Sanct' Germain, you loved her for what she was, and it is your grief that troubles me, not her understanding. It may be that she found greater deliverance in standing against that soldier than she would have in coming to your life, for you were not of her choosing.

And so your back is healed as if the beating had never happened and only your soul carries the scars. As you taught me yourself, those are the only lasting wounds a vampire knows. But what wounds are worse than those to the soul, and what scars are deeper?

Do not be offended, dear, dear friend. I say this in concern, not to reprimand you. If I reprimand you, it will be for living in Ghent, not for your courage in love. So, speaking of Ghent, you will have to let me know how long you plan to be there, and where you intend to go next. I myself will not remain in England much longer, though I am quite fond of the place; it is a pleasant change to be in a country where a woman rules. I must return to Italy in the next two or three years. Why not join me there? We can visit all the places we knew when I was still alive. Give me your word you will not say no out of hand. And I will give you my word that I will not hector you about it.

By my hand with my enduring love
Olivia
April 14, 1586, by English reckoning,
at Greengages, near Harrow